AF478134

Books Without Borders, Volume 2

Also by Robert Fraser

BOOK HISTORY THROUGH POSTCOLONIAL EYES: Re-writing the Script

PROUST AND THE VICTORIANS: The Lamp of Memory

THE MAKING OF THE GOLDEN BOUGH: The Origins and Growth of an Argument

LIFTING THE SENTENCE: A Poetics of Postcolonial Fiction

VICTORIAN QUEST ROMANCE: Stevenson, Haggard, Kipling and Conan Doyle

WEST AFRICAN POETRY: A Critical History

Also by Mary Hammond

READING, PUBLISHING AND THE FORMATION OF LITERARY TASTE IN ENGLAND, 1880–1914

PUBLISHING IN THE FIRST WORLD WAR: Essays in Book History (*co-editor with Shafquat Towheed*)

Books Without Borders, Volume 2

Perspectives from South Asia

Edited by

Robert Fraser
Open University, UK

and

Mary Hammond
University of Southampton, UK

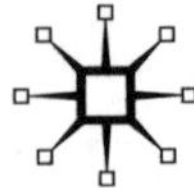

First published 2008 by
PALGRAVE MACMILLAN
Houndmills, Basingstoke, Hampshire RG21 6XS and
175 Fifth Avenue, New York, N.Y. 10010
Companies and representatives throughout the world

PALGRAVE MACMILLAN is the global academic imprint of the Palgrave
Macmillan division of St. Martin's Press, LLC and of Palgrave Macmillan Ltd.
Macmillan® is a registered trademark in the United States, United Kingdom
and other countries. Palgrave is a registered trademark in the European
Union and other countries.

ISBN-13: 978-0-230-21033-2   hardback
ISBN-10: 0-230-21033-3   hardback

This book is printed on paper suitable for recycling and made from fully
managed and sustained forest sources. Logging, pulping and manufacturing
processes are expected to conform to the environmental regulations of the
country of origin.

A catalogue record for this book is available from the British Library.

Library of Congress Cataloging-in-Publication Data

Books without borders / edited by Robert Fraser and Mary Hammond.
        p. cm.
    Includes bibliographical references and index.
    ISBN-13: 978-0-230-21033-2 (v. 2 : alk. paper)
    ISBN-10: 0-230-21033-3 (v. 2 : alk. paper)
    [etc.]
    1. Books—History. 2. Book industries and trade—History. 3. Books and
        reading—History. 4. Literature and globalization. 5. Globalization.
        6. Civilization, Modern. I. Fraser, Robert, 1947– II. Hammond, Mary,
        1960–

    Z4.B648 2008
    002.09—dc22   2008016739

10   9   8   7   6   5   4   3   2   1
17 16 15 14 13 12 11 10 09 08

Printed and bound in Great Britain by
CPI Antony Rowe, Chippenham and Eastbourne

for Benjo, Alex and Sarah

Contents

Figures

Tables

Notes on Contributors

Sarah Brouillette is Assistant Professor at the Massachusetts Institute of Technology. After completing her doctorate in the Collaborative Program in Book History and Print Culture at the University of Toronto, she was an Emerson Fellow at Syracuse University. She has published work in *Book History* and the *Journal of Commonwealth Literature*. Her monograph *Postcolonial Writers in the Global Literary Marketplace* appeared with Palgrave Macmillan in 2007.

Victoria Condie originally trained as a medievalist and has taught Middle English Literature and History of Art for Oxford University's Department of Continuing Education and at Greyfriars Hall. She is currently researching the history of Thacker, Spink and Co.

Kitty Scoular Datta gained her Ph.D. from Oxford University in the 1950s and was Professor of English at Jadavpur University, Kolkata from 1974–1990. She is now an associate lecturer with the Open University. Her research interests include Renaissance literature, the poet Hafez and British Orientalist collectors to 1835. She is the author of *Natural Magic* (Oxford: Clarendon, 1965), and more recently *A Map of Manuscripts* (forthcoming) and an essay on the figure of Alexander the Great in Persian literature.

David Finkelstein is Research Professor of Media and Print Culture at Queen Margaret University College in Edinburgh. His publications include *The House of Blackwood: Author-Publisher Relations in the Victorian Era* (Penn State University Press, 2002), *An Index to Blackwood's Magazine, 1901–1980* (Scolar Press, 1995) and most recently, as co-author, *An Introduction to Book History* (Routledge, 2005). He has also co-edited several works on nineteenth-century media, and is the co-editor of *The Book History Reader* (Routledge, 2001), and of the *Edinburgh History of the Book in Scotland, vol. 4: 1880–2000* (Edinburgh University Press, 2007).

Robert Fraser, FRSL, is the author of *Book History through Postcolonial Eyes* (2008), *The Making of the Golden Bough* (1990), *Proust and the Victorians* (1994) and books on Ayi Kwei Armah (1980), Ben Okri (2002), West African Poetry (1986), Victorian Quest Romance (1998) and the poetics of postcolonial fiction (2000). He edited *Sir James Frazer and the Literary Imagination* (1990), and his biography *The Chameleon Poet: A Life of George Barker* was Spectator Book of the Year for 2002. He is Professor of English at the Open University, and a Fellow of both the Royal Asiatic Society and of the Royal Society of Literature.

Anindita Ghosh is Lecturer in Modern History at the University of Manchester. Her academic journal articles and contributions to edited volumes have focused so far on the vernacular book market in Bengal and discuss the shaping of literary tastes and linguistic identities, and the social and cultural history of print and reading in colonial India. Her monograph based on these themes is *Power in Print: Popular Publishing and the Politics of Language and Culture in a Colonial Society, 1778–1905* (New Delhi: Oxford University Press, 2006). She has also edited a volume reconceptualising power networks and resistance, *Behind the Veil: Resistance, Women and the Everyday in Colonial South Asia* (London/New Delhi: Palgrave Macmillan/Permanent Black, 2007).

Mary Hammond is Senior Lecturer in Nineteenth-Century Literature and Culture at the University of Southampton. She is the author of *Reading, Publishing and the Formation of Literary Taste in England, 1880–1914* (2006), co-editor of *Publishing in the First World War: Essays in Book History* (2007) and has published a number of articles on the readers, writers and print culture of the Victorian and Edwardian periods, including entries for *The Cambridge Companion to Literature 1830–1914* and the forthcoming *History of Oxford University Press*, Vol. II.

Priya Joshi is Associate Professor of English at Temple University in Philadelphia. She is the author of *In Another Country: Colonialism, Culture, and the English Novel in India* (New York: Columbia University Press, 2002; New Delhi: Oxford University Press, 2003), a cultural history of the consumption and production of the English novel in nineteenth- and twentieth-century India. The book has won numerous awards including the Modern Language Association's Prize for an Outstanding First Book; the Sonya Rudikoff Prize for best first book in Victorian studies by the Northeast Victorian Studies Association; a Choice Magazine Outstanding Academic Title award; and honorable mention for the SHARP Book History Prize. Professor Joshi is currently at work on another book-length project entitled *Crime and Punishment: Nationalism and Public Fantasy in Bollywood Cinema* in which she studies popular Hindi film and the fabrication of national identities in postcolonial India. Prior to joining Temple University, Joshi was associate professor of English at the University of California, Berkeley, where she taught since 1995.

Hemjyoti Medhi graduated with Honours in English from Miranda House, University of Delhi in 1997. She pursued research in the Department of English and was awarded an M.Phil. degree by the

University of Delhi in 2001. She currently teaches postgraduate students in the Department of English and Foreign Languages at Tezpur University. Her research interests include Postcolonial Literature, Women's studies and Translation Studies.

Susheila Nasta is Professor in Modern Literature at the Open University and an Associate Fellow of the Institute of English Studies, where she founded the M.A. in National and International Literatures in English (NILE). She has published widely in the field of contemporary twentieth-century literatures, particularly on the Caribbean, postcolonial women's writing and the fictions of the black and South Asian diasporas. As founding editor of the international literary magazine, *Wasafiri*, she has produced over 45 issues of the magazine since 1984. Her most recent monograph *Home Truths: Fictions of the South Asian Diaspora in Britain*, appeared in 2002. Her volume of interviews *Writing Across Worlds: Contemporary Writers Talk*, containing conversations with over thirty contemporary writers, was published by Routledge in 2004. A monograph on Jamaica Kincaid, *Writing a Life* is forthcoming.

Ruvani Ranasinha is Senior Lecturer in English at King's College London. She is author of *Hanif Kureishi* (Writers and their Works, Northcote House, 2002) and *South Asian Writers in Twentieth Century Britain: Culture in Translation* (Oxford University Press, 2007), and is one of the joint editors of *Interventions: International Journal of Postcolonial Studies*.

Shafquat Towheed is Lecturer in Literature and Book History at the Open University. Educated at University College London and at Corpus Christi College, Cambridge, he also teaches on the History of the Book MA at the Institute of English Studies, University of London. He is the editor of *The Correspondence of Edith Wharton and Macmillan, 1901–1930* (Palgrave Macmillan, 2007), of *New Readings in the Literature of British India, c. 1780–1947* (Ibidem Verlag, 2007), of the forthcoming Broadview edition of Arthur Conan Doyle's *The Sign of Four*, and with Mary Hammond, co-editor of *Publishing in the First World War: Essays in Book History* (Palgrave Macmillan, 2007). He is currently editing a collection of essays on Edith Wharton and the material cultures of the book, and writing a monograph on Vernon Lee.

Harish Trivedi is Professor of English at the University of Delhi and has been Visiting Professor at the University of Chicago and the University of London. He is the author of *Colonial Transactions: English Literature and India* (1993; 1995) and co-editor of *Interrogating Postcolonialism* (1996), *Postcolonial Translation* (1999) and *Literature and Nation: Britain and India 1800–1990* (2000).

Acknowledgements

The editors would like to thank the Institute of English Studies (IES), University of London, for their support during the 2005 conference from which these volumes emerged, together with an accompanying exhibition, 'The Colonial and Postcolonial History of the Book, 1765–2005: Reaching the Margins', for which the Oxford University Press and the School of Oriental and African Studies in the University of London generously loaned materials. We are especially grateful to the IES's director, Warwick Gould, for his role in smoothing the path through to publication. Our thanks are also due to the British Academy for sponsoring our keynote speakers at the conference, and the Arts and Humanities Research Council for funding the Open University's Colonial/ Postcolonial History of the Book project of which the conference and this two-volume collection were long-anticipated outcomes. Research for Chapter 4 was funded by grants from the National Endowment for the Humanities, the American Institute for Indian Studies, the University of California at Berkeley, and Temple University in Philadelphia. An earlier version of Chapter 9 appeared in *Script & Print: Bulletin of the Bibliographical Society of Australia & New Zealand* 29: 1–4, the editors of which have kindly allowed us to reproduce it. Thanks are further due to the Bodleian Library in Oxford for permission to reproduce Figure 3.1, and to the BBC picture archive for the photograph that appears as Figure 10.1. We acknowledge Shakuntala Tambimuttu and the BBC Written Archives Centre for their gracious permission to quote words by Meary James Thurairajah Tambimuttu from the relevant radio talks files. For assistance with archival research, the contributors are indebted to Martin Maw of the Oxford University Press, the staff of Edinburgh University Library, the librarian and staff of the Connemara Public Library in Madras (now Chennai) and the staff of the Bodleian for their great courtesies. For advice on Chapter 5, the author would like to thank Professor M. M. Sarma, Dr P. K. Das, Chandan Sharma and Apratim Barua. Every effort has been made to trace all copyright holders, but if any have been inadvertently overlooked, the publisher will be pleased to make the necessary arrangements at the first opportunity.

Introduction
From Palmyra to Print: The Book in South Asia

Robert Fraser and Mary Hammond

I

Zadie Smith famously begins *On Beauty*, her novel of 2005, with a parody of – or at least an act of homage towards – an opening passage by E. M. Forster. To be exact, she echoes the first sentence of *Howard's End*, referring not however to 'Helen's letters to her sister' but to 'Jerome's e-mails to his father'. When introducing the long history of textual transmission in South Asia, one is tempted to pull off an equivalent trick. Predictably enough perhaps, the Forsterian preamble one longs to rework is that to *A Passage to India*. Here is what one might write:

> Even apart from the city of Bhubaneswar – and that is forty miles inland – the state of Orissa presents much that is extraordinary. Edged and washed by the Bay of Bengal, it spreads out like some ample sari in sun, and the satin scintillates as it glides. Its streets are colourful and democratic. Its ancient temples are legion. At Puri the bee-hive-shaped towers of the Temple of Jagannath soar irresistibly into the sky whilst, fifty miles distant, the sculptured figures round the chariot-shaped Temple of the Sun at Koranak instruct as they cavort. The chariot wheels turn in their stasis. The stonework glows like honey. The guides are as informative as they are obliging.

In a more sober vein, one might continue thus. Eight miles from the sea, along the well-worn road from Cuttack to Puri, a hillock rises above the coastal plain. On its crest are some inscriptions in the rock face, protected by wire. Written in the Brahmi script and the Prakrit tongue, they were caused to be set up there in 261 BCE by the Emperor Aśoka, ruler of much of Northern India, whose conversion to Buddhism they announce.

This is the oldest known writing in the sub-continent, and its sentiments are humane. Aśoka had recently put down the local hereditary rulers of the region, the Kalingas, and the scale of the slaughter had appalled him. His change of heart, his revulsion from bloodshed, are evident from these, and from texts inscribed on other rock faces, or pillars he ordered to be erected across what are now India, Nepal and Afghanistan. All are idealistic in tone, and all enjoin universal tolerance.

> All men are my children. What I desire for my own children, and I desire their welfare and happiness both in this world and the next, that I desire for all men. You do not understand to what extent I desire this, and if some of you do understand, you do not understand the full extent of my desire.
>
> You must attend to this matter. While being completely law-abiding, some people are imprisoned, treated harshly and even killed without cause so that many people suffer. Therefore your aim should be to act with impartiality. It is because of these things – envy, anger, cruelty, hate, indifference, laziness or tiredness – that such a thing does not happen. Therefore your aim should be: 'May these things not be in me.' And the root of this is non-anger and patience.

These texts are in many variants and they survive at several far-flung locations. One of Aśoka's pillars now stands on the ridge a kilometre from the Mutiny Monument above Old Delhi, whither it was brought overland from Meerut. The writing is high up, and difficult to make out from the ground. Another inscription on granite is on display in the museum of the Asiatic Society in Kolkata. James Prinsep (1799–1840), Secretary to the Society from 1832, was the first to translate it into English, and to identify Aśoka – or 'Piyadasi' (beloved of the gods) as he calls himself in all these proclamations – as its author.

Prinsep's translation and accurate attribution were, true to form in those imperial decades, heralded as discoveries. They represented, and still represent, a colonial unveiling and appropriation of a pre-colonial past. From our own perspective, the implications are challenging, though from a rather different angle. For, not simply are the sentiments of Aśoka texts such as in the early twenty-first century would put the United Nations to shame, but the ratios of period involved are such as to dwarf several of our most cherished and modish conceptions of cultural history. Consider these facts. Aśoka's victory over the Kalingas, and his inscriptions near Puri, date from 261 years before the Common Era. The age of British colonialism in India (taking the activities of the

East India Company as colonial) is usually dated from the annexation of Bengal in 1765 CE. The Independence of India and Pakistan took place in August 1947. Dividing this entire cultural time span into relevant dispensations, one arrives at the following unsurprising statistics. The precolonial phase lasted 1,926 years, the colonial 182. The postcolonial age has so far gone on for 60. Salman Rushdie's novel *Midnight's Children*, from the publication of which in 1981 some contemporary pundits (including sometimes Rushdie himself) date the inception of modern Indian literature, is now mere 27 years old. To what extent is Indian literature therefore pre-colonial? The unavoidable answer is overwhelmingly. To what extent is it colonial? The true answer is, transitionally. To what extent is it postcolonial? The proper answer is, to a very modest degree.

One could of course, if so minded, perform an equivalent arithmetic on successive technologies of textual transmission. Regarding Aśoka's inscriptions as the first surviving examples of writing in India – a conclusion to which scholars now seem wedded – and estimating the inception of print from an absconded though bibliographically listed edition of Francis Xavier's *Doctrina Christiana* issued by Portuguese Jesuits in Goa in 1556, the epoch of script in the subcontinent could thus be said to have lasted for 1,817 years, and the era of print for 451, a little under a quarter of that period. These are games, of course, albeit enjoyable and instructive games. They concentrate our attention on the salutary disproportions of cultural history, but they are founded on a conceptual flaw that has vitiated a great deal of global book and communication history to this very day. For all such perspectives and calculations rely on a notion of succession, even when they are not based on an even more spurious premise of evolution. *Pace* the once-fashionable school of Marshall McLuhan and Walter J. Ong, communicative technologies just do not follow or supersede one another in this formulaic kind of a way. History, and more especially communication history, is a mesh.

II

To understand the deeper history of textual transmission in South Asia, it is therefore necessary to supplement diachronic exercises of the sort sketched out above with a more synchronic, and ultimately a more realistic, view. How, to take one magisterial instance, has the *Rgveda* lived on? It is recited daily in Kerala by Namboodiri Brahmins, it exists in a welter of manuscripts, the earliest of which dates from the eleventh century CE, and it has been printed in numerous editions and redactions, in abridgement and in translation. The epic *Ramayana* likewise is hawked across the length of India by itinerant folk artists who supplement their narratives with painted scrolls; manuscript redactions exist in many of the languages of India, and it has been printed dozens of times in different versions, with commentary and without. Episodes from the *Mahabharata*, the other great epic of the subcontinent, are performed in puppet shows and in local mystery plays; its diversification is attested by a bewildering number of vulgates in the separate regional tongues, each one of which flavours it with distinctive episodes of its own; it has been standardized, with some difficulty, by an editorial team in Pune, and currently a professor and poet in Kolkata is rendering the whole thing into English, regional variants and all. It has been performed in a variety of dramatic realizations; it has been televised. The classical literature of India is thus an ongoing multi-media performance staged in every city, town and village in the land. No succession here. And emphatically no 'evolution'.

Or examine the street life of Kolkata, in any period you care to mention since the construction of the Kali Ghat. For the mid-nineteenth century that office has been performed by Sumanta Banerjee in his indispensable *The Parlour and the Streets: Elite and Popular Culture in Nineteenth-Century Calcutta* (1989). You do not have to share Banerjee's Marxist viewpoint to recognize that here is a model for the way in which book history in its broadest sense can and should be tackled. Here is culture flourishing in every medium, and at every social level: from satirical doggerels aimed at the *bhadralok* middle class, to *panchlali* (rhymed devotional songs), to *malashi* (bootmen's songs), to *biyaya* (songs to the goddess Durga on the last day of her festival) to *jatra* (dramatic performances set to music). Add to these the circulation of cheap religious prints from the northern district of Battala (described by a snooty British resident at the time as the 'Grub Street' of Bengal); the picture scrolls employed by itinerant storytellers; the *pukker* performances at the elite theatres – such as the Chowringhee on what is now Shakespeare Sarani, or its successor the Sans Souci – the growing network of libraries, the polyglossic editorial efforts of the Asiatic Society, the swotting *babus* of the academies with their attendant suppliers of cribs, the book stalls around College Street, the Hellenistic hobbies of the *sahibs*, the triple-decker novel reading of the *mem-sahibs*, and you have a totalizing scene that confounds any attempt at straight jacketing or allocation to simple phases of production. Everything and anything was going on for much of the time.

The essays in this volume, the second of a set simultaneously issued by their publishers under the joint title *Books Without Borders*, are mostly concerned with the interpenetration of communicative norms through the thickets of South Asian culture. In a survey both methodological and polemical, Harish Trivedi sets the scene with an evocation of three historically placed reading moments. He reopens a debate about the centrality of orality to the cultural life of South Asia, and examines the legacy of *granthas* or palm leaf manuscripts, over three million of which, many uncatalogued and unstudied, are known to languish neglected in the libraries and archives of the subcontinent. The existence of this Himalayan shelf of thought and expression is enough to place in proportion our more historically parochial concerns; it also raises the problem of how we account for the phenomenon of print in our writing up of textual histories from this prolific part of the world. Is and was print, as it is sometimes taken to be elsewhere, the decisive event that altered communicative possibilities forever? Did it represent a fundamental refashioning of art, science and society, or simply a change of medium? Anindita Ghosh takes up this thread by examining the persistence in the popular culture of urban Bengal, whether in India or in Bangladesh, of oral and scripted forms infusing memory, performance and the book. Among the most talented and farsighted of her generation of historians, her work may be viewed as part of a current assault on the hegemony of print; it is more realistically seen as an attempt to place print culture in an authentic continuum, to understand what it has transformed and what it has not.

Turning our attention to that northwest corridor along which so much of worth has spread out across the peninsular, Kitty Scoular Datta stresses the cross-cultural versatility of the *ghazal* poetic form, Persian in origin, adopted in courtly performances throughout northern India, and in translation through the emerging hybrid of Urdu and in the English of the certain eighteenth-century orientalists. The written history of the form embraces the Persian of Hafez and the sorrowful nineteenth-century masterpieces of Bahadur Shah Zafar II, last of the Mughal emperors, calligrapher and poet. Even today ghazals are a staple of North Indian Sufi worship, and flourish simultaneously in bazaars and discos as a much-loved pop vogue. Ghazals transcend divides between oral, scripted and printed. They run across strata of society, technology and taste, from the scholar's bookshelf to the piped background music of local eateries. It is difficult to think of another tradition that amplifies quite so impressively Ghosh's case for the intermingling of artistic forms, both across national boundaries and across generic types.

One possible way of describing the role of print in South Asian culture is that it has supplemented the presence of script; another is that it has reinforced both the presence of alternative writing systems and the ways in which they occasionally impinge on one another. Hemjyoti Medhi offers us a shrewd case in point. Until the early nineteenth century, Assamese literature was written down in the Assamiya script; following the intervention of American missionaries in Upper Assam, however, two developments occurred. First Assamese texts were printed in some numbers; second to facilitate this exercise Assamiya characters were forsaken in favour of the neighbouring Bangla system, a shift exacerbated by the influx of educated Bengalis into the local government service. The ascendancy of Bengali characters for writing has continued to this day; it amounts, to adopt Sudipta Kaviraj's term, to a form of 'subimperialism' that has only recently been challenged. Polemically, therefore, Medhi's contribution might seem to swim against the tide of the volume as a whole. She is evidently and passionately an Assamese cultural patriot, keen that her overlooked region of India should assert its semiotic independence. Analytically, nonetheless, her essay illustrates more poignantly than most the interaction of codes in an industrializing world, its consequences, the dilemmas in which it places peoples and languages.

From 'subimperialism' we pass on to imperialism proper, to the heyday of print and to the activities of those who may be considered Lord Macaulay's proverbial children and grandchildren, or at least his successful agents. There follows a quartet of essays concerned with the role of overseas publishing firms during the Raj. Academically this is proving something of a growth area. In the wake of Rimi B. Chatterjee's recently published research into Macmillan and the Oxford University Press, we have here a couple of essays by David Finkelstein and Victoria Condie that look at the thriving Calcutta firm of Thacker and Spink. Thackers were leaders in their day; they produced books on most subjects, carrying both fiction and non-fiction lists. They were a recognized conduit for certain official publications; they took out, or rather were sold, the copyright on Kipling's apprentice work. In an incisive archive-based piece Shaf Towheed peers into that particular authorial relationship, the fracture that it led to, the permanent distrust of publishers in general it stirred in Kipling's mind, and the alternative arrangements he then made with the railway list of W. H. Wheeler of Allahabad, before leaving for London and a lasting, if guarded, understanding with Macmillan. Railway editions of course were far from unique to India. They had started with Routledge's Railway series in the steam-randy Britain of 1848; by the 1890s Thomas Nelson and Sons in Edinburgh were issuing their fivepenny classics in a format convenient for this mode of travel. To this very day the extensive Indian railway system has served as a valuable stimulus to literary production. But to linger over the work of now extinct firms such as Thackers and Wheelers is to enter the literary atmosphere of Victorian India: its packed stores, its heaving book marts, its enterprising street vendors. Nowadays one can glean a transient impression of this vitality by walking up Kolkata's College Street from Presidency College northwards. But one can also sense the latter day ripples of such activity around Rajiv Chowk in Delhi, a city that since the early 1970s has usurped the place in the South Asian book trade once occupied by Bombay. Robert Fraser's essay takes us back to the decades of Bombay's ascendancy by examining, through archival files on which Chatterjee was unable to draw, the fortunes of the Oxford University Press's India Branch during the dark but energizing days of World War II. His lesson is one both of interdependence and autonomy, as the starvation of resources caused by that widespread distribution of trade encouraged the boys in Bombay to take the publishing initiative into their own hands.

The literary generation that emerged in the 1930s, and which used to take up such a large slice in courses on 'Commonwealth Literature', was in very many ways a transitional one. They were national and international, local yet Anglophone in expression. They wrote, they published, and also like Mulk Raj Anand, the publication of whose first novel *Untouchable* is the subject of Susheila Nasta's essay here, they involved themselves in broadcasting and journalism. Nasta and Ruvani Ranasinha examine the position of such writers, who found themselves talking both to and for India. The double angle is perhaps especially obvious in the work of Nirad C. Chaudhuri, ardently Bengali yet always seeming to address an audience at the other end of what he was to call the *Passage to England*. An awareness of addressing different arenas can be heard too in the inflections of Meary James Thurairajah Tambimuttu, Sri Lankan and founder of *Poetry London*, who for a few years before, during and after the Second World War was the darling and gadfly of the Soho pubs. Espousing yet scourging tradition, these writers were part of an international literary cosmopolis; yet they aspired via their work to a version of modernity all their own. Some of them were well on the way to becoming media stars; certainly they grew conscious of addressing a late imperial world arena, and in so doing transformed the views that outsiders took of India, as well as influencing in oblique ways the imminent approach of independence.

The apotheosis of that movement in its lurid ambiguity is the globalized and celebrity-studded school of South Asian fiction that has taken the international world by storm since 1981, year of the publication of Salman Rushdie's *Midnight's Children*. Who or what is speaking from this floodlit stage: the medium or the message, the publisher or the writer, the book jacket or the word? In a culminating tour de force, Sarah Broulliette argues through the alternatives and reaches a heartening, if to some it may seem a counterintuitive, conclusion. At the very end of the day the centripetal pressures of worldwide presentation – all that would pre-dispose or condition self-expression and imaginative ingestion – possess less potency than individual vision and choice. Even amid the madding crowd of global marketing – that unreal airport of a location which publishing cartels address and inhabit – the individual writer, like the folktale teller and the scribe, enunciates a will that is personal and elective, elusive, and, in the long run, free.

III

The evident challenge posed by such a survey and sharing of views to historians of the book is this: how do you begin to encapsulate all of this wealth? It is a dilemma that has so far elicited varying responses from diverse quarters. Specialists in South Asian languages have given us copiously annotated editions of the classics. Social historians have supplied us with a frame (to be frank, they have actually supplied us with several frames, not all of them compatible with one another). Critics have criticized. The theorists have done what they are best at: theorizing. What is lacking is a total and holistic view, one that draws on all of these areas of expertise to shed light on the almost inconceivable long epic of textual transmission in South Asia.

In January 2005 in Wellington, New Zealand, and again in February 2006 on her home turf of Kolkata, Rimi Chatterjee outlined an awe-inspiring scheme to involve scholars the length and breadth of the sub-continent charting two and a half thousand years of written and printed literature. The campaign is bold, and it resolves itself at first sight less into a campaign than a series of questions. How does one organize this programme of work, seeing that there is so much and so far to cover? Who should be involved? What approaches, theoretical and practical, should be entertained? How, to begin with, do you divide up a subject so vast?

The contributions to the present symposium perhaps have a tendency to suggest that geography, that most obvious of recourses, is not necessarily our best guide to such questions. A set of regional histories is unlikely to amount to a national history, and, even were such a project possible, what avails a national history of the book in India when attention is fast turning elsewhere? There is also, and perhaps has always been, an implicit contradiction between an approach governed by successive pages of a political atlas and the driving, centrifugal force of the discipline itself. Characteristically book historians examine cultural objects rather than places: they pore over paper, ink, print, binding, book jackets, all of which may come from anywhere and everywhere. Book history is not the Olympic games, and flags look very out of place there. In the introduction to volume one of this set we suggested that paying attention to the modes of transportation that govern and facilitate the spread of books might yield some interesting insights. In South Asia especially, more enlightenment may be found by fastening of the materialities of production across the board than splitting the subject up into zones.

One matter is clear: attempts up to the present have sometimes been bedevilled by misconceptions we would be better rid of. To return to a topic already raised: what in this particular context has been the role of print? The inception of this technique – or rather range of techniques, since too little notice has been taken of the effects of different methods of printing – has been described as an 'arrival' or an 'inception'. In either case its significance has frequently been both exaggerated and transplanted in place and time. Wood block printing or xylography was invented in China in the tenth century of the Common Era, movable type in Korea in the twelfth. Xylography was known in Tibet long before the Jesuits introduced hand presses to South India in the late Renaissance. Despite Marshall McLuhan, the astronomy of print does not describe an outwardly expanding galaxy, but a universe with multiple points of origin. Asia is one of its cradles.

The nineteenth century, on which a number of our essays fasten, was characterised by impetus and diversity. Beginning in Bengal – an initiative distinct from earlier and localized developments in southerly milieus such as Tranquebar – moving in a broad swathe across upper India, then down the Deccan and both coasts, print drove onwards, adapting itself as it went to varying scripts, conditions and needs. In the south it joined up with an existing industry founded by the Catholic missions to produce a vigorous regional offshoot. Meanwhile lithography – which had originated in Central Europe in the 1820s to meet the practical requirements of music publishing and book illustration – entered India, migrating thence to Central Asia where Persian printers were quick to recognize its potential for the rapid and faithful reproduction of cursive scripts. The new technology dispensed with the need for typesetting, and the cumbersome manufacture of fonts. It enabled printers at minimal cost to write text on stone: albeit mirror-style and in wax.

The significance of the resulting revolution has by and large been lost on book historians, concerned as they have been with unilinear tracks of advance. Lithography was both an innovation and a rebirth; it empowered printers to reproduce texts in multiple copies while drawing on the age-old manual dexterity of the scribe. Within a few years it facilitated a burgeoning print industry in Lucknow and Benares; almost single-handedly it inspired a surge in Urdu literature, both of reprints and of original works. The social, educational and even political repercussions of this movement are incalculable. Concentrating exclusively on lithographed reproduction, one single enterprise, the Nawal Kishore Press of Lucknow, produced many hundreds of titles in dozens of genres. Its archives have been purchased by the University of Chicago and will absorb book historians of Urdu literature in particular for years to come.

The British, who had India in their wavering grasp, surveyed this advance with a mixture of fascination and misgiving. Very little of it had been sponsored or organized by government. Private enterprise had been the engine, local capital the fuel, but beginning with the celebrated Act XXV of 1867 – the so-called Press and Books Registration Act – some official attention was now applied to the steering. On the question as to whether this legislative measure represented a delayed reflex reaction to the Sepoy Rising, there has been some disagreement. Robert Darnton feels on the whole that it did, Priya Joshi that it did not. A realistic middle view may be reached by extending the theory put forward by Benedict Anderson in a chapter added in 1991 to his influential study *Imagined Communities* on 'Census, Map, Museum', where he remarks of such late imperial provisions that 'taking together, these powerfully shaped the ways in which the colonial state imagined its dominion – the notion of the human beings it ruled, the geography of its domain, and the legitimacy of its ancestry.' If to Anderson's trinity you add a further trio – Book Registration, Gagging Order and Copyright – you begin to get a sense of the broad front along which the newly christened Raj after 1858 consolidated its growing control. Homosexuality, for example, was outlawed in India during the very same decade, two decades before legislation in Britain. There has been a tendency of late years to play down the consequences of the 1867 Registration act and to sideline its motives and effect. It is, however, far easier to discount it in this way than to undertake painstaking research into the contents of the massively informative registers and reports to which it gave rise. The annual centrally prepared reports, for example, afford us invaluable information over many decades as to the balance maintained in different locales between different genres and languages. The more detailed registers maintained in every Presidency on a quarterly basis yield in addition insights into the identities of publishers, and into print-runs, formats, price and methods of reproduction. The quarterly digests of the contents of the vernacular press are another largely unexplored mine. On this mass of data, out of which an empirically honest survey of print culture in India through the late imperial period could with necessary effort be built, work on a sufficiently extensive scale has hardly yet begun.

For better or for worse, South Asian literature is now international news. Bangalore, where this very book and its companion volume were typeset, Kolkata's Salt Lake City and the sprouting New Delhi suburb of Gurgaon are currently centres of communication rivalling any in the world. Indian literature has made the headlines: it features spectacularly on Booker Prize short lists; its practitioners, whether out of notoriety or fame, have become household names, even in a blasé Europe. What connections if any do these recent developments possess to the deeper history and meaning of book culture in South Asia? In the essays contained in this volume we have, we are bold to claim, traced the outlines of certain continuities that will need to be taken into account as we grope towards an answer. To cut so broad a sweep across the face of one of the most productive regions of textual reproduction in the world may seem so courageous as to amount to mere foolhardiness. Never fear. To view the whole picture in one staggered aerial view may help us to make out the peaks and troughs. We require a broad vision of South Asian communications history to enable us to find our bearings once on the ground. As Piyadasi himself might have put it, 'You must attend to this matter.'

1
The 'Book' in India:
Orality, Manu-Script,
Print (Post)Colonialism

Harish Trivedi

I. The 'Book' and the colonial

Any treatment of the history of the book in South Asia undertaken in the early twenty-first century is likely to feel the need to engage with what has come to be known as postcolonial discourse. It thus behoves us to enquire at the outset just how fitting a backdrop to the subject this discourse provides. This is all the more pressing a requirement since, despite being self-consciously and even apologetically informed by the best liberal-guilty will in the world, certain strands in postcolonial discourse continue to betray some of the fondest vanities of the colonial enterprise itself in its confident heyday. One of these abiding pieties is that imperial rule offered the colonies, for example, the book. On the other hand, some of the more radically deconstructive strands of postcolonial discourse appear to institute a kind of ex post facto discursive parity between the colonizer and the colonized, the ruler and the ruled, the centre and the periphery, and indeed between any similar 'binary', purportedly because of the inherent ambivalence of all experience, representation and meaning-making. Is this easy assumption of equality, resting as it does on indeterminacy, perhaps more blithe and feckless than politically engaged or sincerely egalitarian?

Inequality, however, has been a constant fact of human history, and of colonial history in particular, and no amount of ready political correctness can, or should be allowed to, erase it or write it off the record. It is no use denying that, in a colony such as India, the printing press and the technology to produce books were imports from the West. Despite evidence of sporadic printing activity since the late sixteenth century, it was in the last quarter of the eighteenth century, a little after 1765, that book production in India got going in a sustained and substantial manner.

Indeed, the Indian incunabula can be said to comprise books published before the year 1800 and thus to lag a full 300 years behind the European incunabula. The introduction of the book in India, whether locally produced or imported from the West, may not have been an innocent or beneficent 'gift', nor perhaps was it a conscious instrument of 'civilizing' the natives, but with all the mixed motives that lay behind it, it was undeniably sponsored and facilitated by Western personnel and technology, and it was a novelty and an innovation which soon took root and flourished and went on to have all kinds of incalculable consequences.

A major difficulty that remains in the treating of such a vital historical phenomenon is how to construct a narrative that would not be patently overdetermined by an ideological bias of one kind or the other. For example, how does one say that the book began to be produced in India only in the 1770s without implying that, therefore, India must be thought to be, in this respect and perhaps in general, seriously deprived and far less advanced (or 'civilized') than the West? How credible can this sound, especially in a discourse conducted in English, the language of the colonizer, infected by all kinds of value judgements favouring – however obliquely – the Western way of doing things, to assert that the tradition of knowledge and learning in India relied on oral transmission and cultivation of human memory in ways that were not basic and primitive but instead highly sophisticated in both capability and performance? And how does it nuance and complicate our understanding not only of colonial history but even of contemporary reality to seek to demonstrate that – notwithstanding 150 years of British rule and exposure to Western values – these alternative, 'other' traditions of producing, storing and transmitting knowledge organically, so to say, rather than through mechanical reproduction, are still prevalent and indeed valued in India in ways that constitute and illustrate aspects of civilizational diversity, which should be recognized on their own terms and honoured in their own right rather than thought to be simply inferior and obsolete?

In this chapter I seek to outline and highlight three aspects and stages of the history of the book in India. Firstly, I attempt to sketch out a pre-colonial history, namely a pre-print history, of knowledge transmission in India with reference to the role played not only by human memory and oral transmission, but equally by script and writing which existed alongside – as embodied in the indigenous kinds of 'books', in Sanskrit called the *grantha*: that is the tied-together leaves (palmyra or other) of a manuscript. Secondly, I seek to identify three different moments in the evolution of the idea of the book in India between the seventeenth and the early nineteenth centuries, illustrating them each with one book of a of a distinctive origin, genre or kind. Finally I wish to offer some general reflections on the history or what may be called the career of the 'book', whether in an oral form or in manuscript or in print, juxtaposing Indian trajectories with those from the West. It is hoped that such an impossibly ambitious and sweeping survey, with all its inevitable inadequacies, will still help provide an alternative and complementary perspective to the history of the book in the Occident. In so doing it may serve to suggest what the 'book' may be, do and stand for in other cultures: how the book-function, if one may call it that, may be conceptualized and fulfilled differently in different times and different places. To locate the 'book' in India as a colonial as well as a pre-colonial and postcolonial phenomenon may on the one hand be to register the great transformative impact of the book as a cultural commodity of the highest significance. It may also be to put both the book and colonial rule in their relative places, by viewing them in a long extra-colonial perspective.

II. *Granthas* and scripts

Lucien Febvre and Henri-Jean Martin, who as authors of *L'apparition du livre* (1958) may be said to stand at or very near the beginning of the new sub-discipline of Book History, saw the printed book as 'one of the most effective means of mastery over the whole world'.[1] And yet this claim to the effect that Print is Power seems as difficult to substantiate in the colonial context as the cognate but wider and more familiar Foucauldian-Saidian claim that Knowledge is Power. In India, for example, it was not the British who brought in the printing press – any more than it was William Caxton who invented printing. 'Interestingly enough', as David Finkelstein and Alistair McCleery point out,

> the British were among the last of the European powers active in India to introduce the printing press into their enclaves. It was not until 1761 that the British in India acquired a press, and even then it was a press that had been taken from the French.[2]

Even before the French, the Portuguese (who like the French went on ruling their little enclaves in India well beyond 1947 when the British quit) had been printing in India in an Indian language and script, Tamil, since 1578, and their rule in Goa, which lasted for twice as long as British rule over any part of India, had an administrative and ecclesiastical machinery in which from early on print played a wide role. Bartholomaeus Ziegenbalg (1683–1719), the first Protestant missionary in India, began operating a prolifically productive press in Tranquebar in South India in 1712, printing in Portuguese, German and Tamil;[3] he was, incidentally, a native of Germany working in India under the patronage of the King of Denmark, two countries not exactly famous for their colonial domination of India.

When the British did finally begin to publish books in India in the 1770s, their first productions were not classics of Western literature through which they hoped to disseminate the values of Western civilization or to assert their power/knowledge superiority; they were, instead, translations into English from Sanskrit of foundational works of Indian law, scripture and literature. These did not appear to promote or strengthen British rule in India in any obvious manner, but led on the contrary to an exciting discovery of the greatness of Indian culture and civilization dating from a period when Britain had not had so much to show for itself. The first flush of what came to be known as Orientalism enjoyed an impact in Europe so startling and enormous that one scholar has described the phenomenon as an 'Oriental renaissance'.[4] Until the 'Anglicists' among the British in India vanquished the 'Orientalists' over half a century later, with Lord Macaulay's decisive intervention in 1835, British presses in India printed and propagated mainly Indian books either in English translation or in the original Indian languages. The traffic in books and knowledge was nearly all one-way, from the margin to the centre.

Though they had not been printed before, these Indian works had for long existed not in inchoate or fluid oral versions but as written down, finalized texts, sometimes in varying recensions and regional variants, the form in which the British found them. For example, the first text that Sir William Jones (aka 'Oriental Jones') translated, the play *Sacontala* by Kalidasa (fourth century CE), had for long existed in two recensions to which Jones in Calcutta had access in the so-called Bengali recension. This play shows, incidentally, the eponymous heroine in her hermitage writing a love letter to her royal suitor, probably one of the early examples in world literature of the act of writing being staged. In any case, these Indian works already existed as fully formed texts before the printing press turned them into 'books', and serve to underline the primacy of the text over the book (in a sense quite different of course from that current in 'postmodernism').

Such texts also affirm the long tradition of writing in India, in a larger variety of languages and scripts than the Western world has perhaps ever known. The oldest instances of writing preserved in India are conventionally dated back to the middle of the third century BCE, when Emperor Aśoka converted to Buddhism in recoil from his excessively bloody conquest of the kingdom of Kalinga, and proceeded to set up tall, round, polished stone pillars all over his far-flung kingdom, inscribed with his new message of non-violent coexistence, mutual harmony and a benevolent humanist social order. The script in which these messages or edicts were inscribed, Brahmi (or Aśoka Brahmi, as it came to be called to distinguish it from later variants such as Tamil Brahmi), with the passage of time became unintelligible. The Muslim king of Delhi, Feroze Shah Tughlaq (r. 1351–1388) is believed to have spent sleepless nights after discovering that none of his subjects could read or interpret the message on an Aśokan pillar he had grandly carried off from its original location in the north to his capital, the undeciphered words of which he dimly feared to be some kind of supernatural warning to him from God, no less. When an early Orientalist, James Prinsep, was able to (re-)read the Aśokan inscriptions, it led to a recovery of the ancient Indian past that was perhaps as substantial and significant as that facilitated by the deciphering of Linear B in the case of Western history.

But there is an even older Indian script that lies undeciphered even in our age of immense computational and permutational capability, and whenever that yields its Rosetta Stone or some other kind of key, new discoveries about the origins of Indian civilization will be made which may augment and modify our notions of older civilizations. This, the script of the Indus Valley civilization, has in recent decades been discovered as having extended far beyond its eponymous location, now in Pakistan, to large areas of North and even Central India ('it was', some scholars have asserted, 'greater in extent than Egypt and Mesopotamia combined'[5]), sustaining commercial and cultural transactions with areas beyond India to the west. The Indus Valley civilization and script is dated, by Finkelstein and McCleery in their survey of book history, as extending 'from about 3000 to 2400 BC', with only the Mesopotamian and the Egyptian scripts thought to be of comparable antiquity, and the Aegean script (c. 1650–1200 BCE), the Chinese script (c. 1500 BCE), the Greek alphabet (c. 800–700 BCE) and the Mayan script (c. 50 CE) all being of distinctly more recent invention.[6] With all the talk of the ancient oral tradition of India, the Indian tradition of scripted texts also needs to be acknowledged as no less ancient and perhaps even more significant potentially for our understanding of Indian civilization as well as of book history. The printed book may have come to India only yesterday, but writing in India is as old as almost anywhere else in the world.

III. The claims of the oral

This is, of course, not to underestimate the astounding oral tradition of India and the unique civilizational uses to which it has been put. Most famously, it was the four Vedas, commonly dated from c. 1500 BCE and thus probably the oldest extant scriptures in the world, which were orally transmitted from generation to brahminical generation until the coming of print, and indeed continue to be so transmitted in some small priestly communities even today. The fact that a text of such length and complexity – and the first of the Vedas, the *Rgveda*, alone contains 1028 hymns in over 10,000 verses of four lines each – has been orally preserved for three and a half millennia with phenomenal accuracy is remarkable enough in itself. No less remarkable is the mode of its transmission. In the case of these scriptures, not only do the words need to be repeated exactly, but there is a particular rhythm, cadence and sonority that need to be replicated if the verses are to carry their spiritual charge. This is based on the belief central to Hinduism that the sounds of words signify just as much as the words themselves. In fact, in some kinds of recitative or incantatory verbal formulations such as the *mantras* used at fire-offerings, sacrifices and other oblations, the sound matters even more than the words, while the primal sound 'Om' is believed to have accompanied if not caused the very creation of the universe. It was this *Om* in the valedictory mantra from the *Brihadaranyaka Upanishad, Om Shantih Shantih Shantih*, that T. S. Eliot in 1922 significantly left out when incorporating it into the closing lines of *The Waste Land* – even four years before his reception into the Anglican Church in 1926, it was perhaps a little too arcanely unchristian for him.

Be that as it may, such ritualistic punctiliousness with regard to sound, probably as much as any other factor, has helped ensure that the Vedas have come down the centuries with, so to say, not a single misprint, for the misplacing of a single syllable in that unique metrical frame would disrupt the ordained rhythm and instantly be detected. As a further guarantee of accuracy, the recitation of each vedic line is traditionally accompanied by a set pattern of hand movements, so that the verbal language and the body language move in tandem in an integrated enunciative harmony.[7]

But oral transmission, whether so elaborate or not, was not confined to sacred texts. Sanskrit treatises on all manner of secular subjects were often written in verse (though unrhymed, since traditionally Sanskrit used no rhyme), and anyone who claimed any expertise in a given subject would be expected to know the relevant treatise(s) by heart. These included the most authoritative thesaurus in Sanskrit, the *Amarakosha* (c. 400 CE), and the aphoristic rules of grammar composed in prose by Panini in the fifth century BCE. Awesome portions of both these texts used to come rolling off the tongues of some (though fortunately not too many) of my classmates when I studied Sanskrit for my B.A. degree at the University of Allahabad in the mid-1960s. These friends of mine had come through the traditional schools of Sanskrit, the *pathashalas*, or at least had old-style pandits as their teachers, and it was quite clear that while the rest of us who came from 'regular' schools might learn as much Sanskrit as we liked, it was they who really *knew* the language.

There is, of course, and there was even then in our grudging young minds, an air of anthropological quaintness about such practices, and they are in any case even sparser on the ground now than they were some decades back. At the beginning of his scholarly 'compilation' of sources titled *The Book in India*, B. S. Kesavan, distinguished bibliographer and librarian, cited a verse from the *Mahabharata* (itself a marvel of textual transmission, being the longest epic in the world, extending to over 200,000 lines of verse):

> *Vedavikrayinashchaiva vedanamchaiva dushakah*
> *Vedanam lekhakahashchaiva tevai nirayagaminah.*[8]

[He who makes money out of the Vedas, or pollutes the Vedas (by mispronouncing them), or writes down the Vedas, will surely go to hell.]

Such dire punishment may seem a matter more of faith than reason, but another Sanskrit verse of a more didactic nature seems based solidly on this-worldly pragmatism:

> *Pustakastha tu ya vidya parahastagatam dhanam*
> *Karyakale samutpanne na sa vidya na taddhanam.*[9]

[Knowledge that exists in a book and money that one has lent to someone else is not knowledge and is not money because when you need it, it is not there.]

This statement too may, of course, seem woefully dated in the present age of instant laptop googleability, but it enshrines an attitude still held in respect in India. It is obviously not true that Indians remember more than persons from other nations, or even any longer try to condition themselves culturally to do so, but it is probably true that recourse to a printed or written text in social or public discourse is less well-thought of in India than in the West. It is still common for (many of the older and in their own way revered) university teachers to walk into classrooms without a scrap of paper on them, and for eminent scholars and public figures to deliver keynote addresses and named and endowed lectures from scant notes, or none at all. But what may from a Western point of view seem to take the cake is that the Prime Minister of the day climbs up on to the ramparts of the Red Fort in Delhi on Independence Day every year, unfurls the national flag, and then proceeds to divest herself/himself of a speech without any notes and at his or her own sweet length – with full live TV coverage, of course.

The said tradition was inaugurated by Jawaharlal Nehru, prime minister of India for the first 16 years after independence, no demagogue but rather a slow, reflective and even rambling speaker. Educated at Harrow, Cambridge (Natural Sciences at Trinity) and the Middle Temple, he had delivered, 'at the stroke of the midnight hour' on 14/15 August 1947 when India attained freedom, one of the most memorable and oft-cited speeches of the twentieth century, and he had done so from a fully written-out text. Nehru was by his own admission as Westernized an Indian as one could find, until he threw himself into the deeply indigenous Gandhian nationalist movement, and he knew, better even than Gandhi, how to arbitrate between the claims of the Western and the Indian traditions and practices. Thus it may seem as if his scripted 'midnight' speech was his farewell gesture to the Western mode of public discourse, while his first Red Fort speech, delivered within a few hours the following morning, represented an instinctive and apt switch-over to a mode of speaking to his free nation in the nation's own heart-to-heart oral medium. The fact that one cannot even begin to imagine the Queen delivering an unscripted address to the British parliament, or the US President an unscripted State of the Union address, merely underlines the abiding validity of the oral tradition in India. Unscripted communication is still seen as an index of one's innate ability as well as one's unrehearsed sincerity; it is also an affirmation of the belief that while what is written can always be read, what is meant to be heard must be spoken with a live, situationally adaptable and at least implicitly dialogic charge, and not just read out from cold print/ script pre-composed at another time and place.

IV. The 'Book' as guru

Of course, it is not as if the scripted finality of a finished text, with many of the implications of what Mikhail Bakhtin has called (at least in English translation) 'finalizability', has been absent in the Indian tradition. The old painstakingly scripted *granthas* lie stored ceiling-high in numerous libraries in India, especially those located in the capital cities of the Indian states ruled semi-autonomously by enlightened Indian maharajas and princes throughout the period of British rule, such as Mysore and even remote Darbhanga, or in temple towns such as Banaras and Tanjaur. In such places as well as in some of the larger Indological libraries in Britain, Europe and the USA, the sheer quantity of the *granthas* preserved (though a far greater quantity must naturally have been lost) is so daunting that a large proportion of these manuscripts has not yet been catalogued, let alone edited and printed. But occasionally, a cluster of manuscripts heaves into view with spectacular consequences. Such are the 13 plays discovered in Kerala in the 1910s, thereby confirming the status of their author Bhasa (first century BCE) – until then known only by reputation and by some meagre extracts in anthologies – as one of the greatest playwrights in Sanskrit.

In modern times, however, the advent of a book, or more accurately the material circumstances of its production and reception, can be documented and historicized in ways less haphazard and fortuitous. Of the three books that I wish to examine as case histories in this respect, the first two stand on a cusp constituted by the seemingly capricious presence in the roman script – and the absence in most other scripts of the world including all the Indian scripts – of both capital and lower case letters. The most flagrant example of the arbitrary discrimination between, as well as the conflation of, the capital and the lower case letter in the roman script one can think of is that between the 'book' and the 'Book' (with 'god' and 'God' as close runners up).

It remains an unsolved mystery to many English-language learners that a particular 'Book' should be placed in a category by itself and above all the other 'books' on the strength of a distinction merely typographical, and not in the least oral and audible. It does not help that in Hinduism there exists no such scripturally designated 'Book' but rather any number of 'books', both original and translated/retold in many languages, out of which a Hindu may choose any, just as s/he may choose any one or more of the innumerable Hindu gods (never in roman spelt as 'Gods' as they rightly should be) to whom to offer his or her personal allegiance.[10]

As the British Library newsletter of 2007, announcing a major exhibition devoted to the three Abrahamic religions, put it simply enough, 'Jews, Christians and Muslims all believe that their Scriptures preserve God's words to humanity, and that those words were spoken uniquely to them.'[11] By contrast, Hinduism, along with two other ancient religions born on Indian soil – Buddhism and Jainism – made no such claims of divine authorship; indeed, some strands of Hinduism as well as Buddhism and Jainism held that there was no God at all. It is in this context that one approaches what is probably the only Indian book that approximates to the condition of the 'Book', all the more remarkable for being distinctly pre-colonial in origin.

This is the one and only scripture of the Sikhs, called the *Guru Granth Sahib*. The Sikhs arose initially as a militant sect of Hinduism in opposition and resistance to Muslim and especially Mughal rule and its discriminatory and oppressive policies and practices. It was only in the twentieth century that they legally and formally separated from Hinduism to constitute a distinct religion followed by about 1 per cent of the current population of India (also comprising around 13% Muslims and about 82% Hindus).

The *Guru Granth Sahib* is probably the most remarkable single specimen in the history of the book in India, for several reasons. Though the undisputed one and only scripture of the Sikhs and thus their 'Book', it does not claim to be the Book in the sense of being the voice of God, who remains an abstraction. It is instead an anthology of the works of many poets who existed before Sikhism constituted itself into a separate sect, poets who include not only Hindus but also several Muslims, albeit of a non-orthodox Sufi variety.[12] In the absence of an anthropomorphic God, the Sikhs have a pantheon of ten Gurus or prophet-like teachers, while the word *sikh* itself, derived from the Sanskrit *shishya*, means disciple. The *Guru Granth Sahib* contains devotional verses composed not only by the early gurus, but also by numerous non-Gurus, simply Hindu or Muslim bhakti/sufi (devotional) poets whose works are coincidentally taught on university syllabi in Hindi and Panjabi as secular texts representing some of the best poetry in these tongues.

This eclectic poetic anthology, which has come down as the great scripture or the 'Book' of the Sikhs, is a compilation that was finalized by the fifth of the ten Sikh gurus, Arjun Dev, 'on the first day of the bright [fortnight of] Bhadon [July–August] in 1604', or as another more punctiliously confident scholar has put it, 'on August 16, 1604',[13] when it was duly installed in the Golden Temple at Amritsar, the holiest shrine of the Sikhs. It continues to be worshipped at the sanctum sanctorum there as if it were not only the Book but the great God itself. It is wrapped up in several layers of red silk, and priests continuously sing verses from it while waving a flywhisk over it, as is done over statues of human-looking gods in Hindu temples. The tradition of one guru succeeding another came to an end with the death, in 1708, of the tenth guru, Gobind Singh, and thereafter the book itself has served as the one and only guru. This accounts for its name: the *Granth* (or the Book), regarded as the *Guru* (Teacher), and therefore addressed honorifically and in human terms as *Saheb/Sahib* (or Master). The words *Guru* and *Granth* are both from Sanskrit, while *Sahib* is derived from Arabic. The latter is a title by which the British rulers of India were later happy to be called, as in the verbal forms *burra sahib* (that is 'the big master') or in *mem-sahib* (that is literally the madam master, a mode description in which however the gender is patently mistaken, since, unless a transsexual, the expatriate lady thus addressed should surely be a *sahiba*).

The strange case of the *Guru Granth Sahib* must be thus unique not only in the history of the 'Book', but equally in book history. This sacred volume bears several marks of the human and hybrid ways in which mere artefacts can effectively erase the difference between book and Book. It stands, for example, midway between the oral and the scripted. Written down as soon as its text was finalized, except for a few identifiable interpolations inserted in some of the approximately 100 copies permitted to be made by hand between 1604 and 1675, it is equally a triumph of textuality and orality. As the reciting priests (and all Sikh priests are known as *granthis*, i.e., men of the book) sit before a holy and consecrated copy, they do not actually read out the text, but recite from memory. It is essential to the mystique of the *Guru Granth Sahib* that it remains wrapped up, even while it is being read aloud. And the sole portion of the text that every self-respecting Sikh knows by heart and may herself/himself recite is a composition by the first of the Sikh gurus, Nanak (1469–1539). It is called the *Jap-ji*, i.e., the part that is to be ritually recited or chanted, again addressed with an honorific *ji* normally reserved for human beings, such as *sahib*.

V. The 'English Book' and Indian resistance

Few books could provide a greater contrast to the *Guru Granth Sahib* than the Bible, the cherished Book of the West, propagated in India just as soon as it arrived. Some of the earliest works printed in the Indian languages were issued from missionary presses, translations of selected books of the Bible, especially from the New Testament. The history of the sustained, resolute and long-suffering missionary effort to convert India to Christianity, especially under colonial auspices, is not better known because it turned out to be largely a history of failure, almost against divine prognostication. It still provides remarkable examples of what an enormous difference a single imported and translated book was expected to make to a huge country.

As it happens, postcolonial discourse already contains a dazzling, theoretically innovative and widely known discussion of a particularly dramatic account of an early Indian encounter with the Christian Book. It may therefore be of interest to revisit the said site from the specific point of view of the history of the book in India. I refer to 'Signs Taken for Wonders: Questions of ambivalence and authority under a tree outside Delhi, May 1817', an essay by Homi Bhabha. In it he discourses upon an elaborately recorded episode in the history of British attempts to propagate Christianity in north India, through the circulation of copies of the Bible in translation. Though he does not identify or explicate it, the title of Bhabha's essay is of course itself drawn from the Bible ('And I will ... multiply my signs and my wonders in the land of Egypt' from Exodus 7:3, or more relevantly 'Except ye see signs and wonders, ye will not believe' from St John 4:48). Bhabha himself, though, seems rather more interested in looking at Saussurean signs as Derridean and Lacanian wonders, as when he says that colonial authority is 'a sign of difference' (and how one wishes it had been no more oppressive and exploitative than that), or when he suggests that 'the presence of the book has acceded to the logic of the signifier and has been "separated", in Lacan's use of the term, from "itself"'.[14] Yet Bhabha's reconstruction of the whole episode as recounted contemporary missionary sources represents an inspired piece of archival recovery vividly bringing alive some of the ways in which the Western book/Book was early received in India.

Bhabha himself begins as if the focus of his interest is not so much the ambivalent and hybridizing nature of colonial authority as colonial book history, though this initial impression is soon dispelled:

> It is the scenario played out in the wild and wordless wastes of colonial India, Africa, the Caribbean, of the sudden, fortuitous discovery of the English book. ... It is with the emblem of the English book – 'signs taken for wonders' – as an insignia of colonial authority and a signifier of colonial desire and discipline, that I want to begin this chapter.[15]

Yet this phrasing already inclines towards ambivalence. To speak of 'the wild and wordless wastes of colonial India' seems on the face of it to reiterate, with beguiling alliteration, the Anglicist (and not Orientalist, as is often mistakenly thought) prejudice that, before the British came to colonize, locations such as India were utterly uncivilized, illiterate and inarticulate. It is also, of course, to assume that all kinds of evidence to the contrary (such as those cited in this chapter) simply do not exist.

It is therefore to be surmised that Bhabha is being ironical when he speaks of 'the wild and wordless wastes' of the colonies. It would, however, have reassured literal-minded readers of his subversive intention had Babha named in the rest of his chapter one single sign or emblem of Indian literacy and civilization to juxtapose with the vaunted 'English book'.

Having set the scene, Bhabha proceeds to narrate how about 500 Indian men, women and children, returning from a pilgrimage to Haridwar – a holy place where the Ganga (or Ganges) descends from the Himalayas to the plains – are espied carrying copies of the Bible given to them by Christian missionaries there. This rouses great expectations of conversion in the local missionaries and catechists, one of whom, an Indian convert himself, now goes running from Meerut, a hundred miles away, to waylay them and engage them in proselytizing dialogue. Bhabha thereupon quotes an observation by the British missionary who later recorded this episode in *The Missionary Register*: 'The ignorance and simplicity of many [of these Indians] are very striking, never having heard of a printed book before; and its very appearance to them was miraculous.'[16] It may be noted that what the missionary, through his patently patronizing attitude and creaky syntax, is unwittingly acknowledging is that it is the book as a physical object that has impressed these simple Indians as a novelty, and that its 'very appearance' is thereby deemed miraculous rather, apparently, than the message it contains.

But these Indians turn out to be not quite so ignorant or simple. An elder among the Hindu pilgrims comes forward to be their spokesman and remarks, 'We are poor and lowly, and we read and love this book'[17] – a statement which signals, inter alia, an impressive rate of literacy among the poor and lowly in India in the early nineteenth century. And then it turns out that of the many copies of the Bible that the group is carrying, 'some were PRINTED, others WRITTEN by themselves'.[18] This observation shows, firstly, a devotion to reading and writing of an exceptionally high order, since 'writing' the Bible all over again must have involved a major investment of time and effort, to say nothing of the degree of multicultural and multi-faith liberality required. But it also demonstrates something else: in India at that time there apparently existed an easy two-way traffic between writing and printing, indicating that print was not treated as such a new and alien wonder that it could not be promptly domesticated back into traditional script. Bhabha himself, on the other hand, prefers to underline the talismanic quality of the printed book, almost fetishized in the colonial context, by adducing a fairly far-flung comparison with the one printed book possessed by a solitary trader whom Marlow comes across in Conrad's *Heart of Darkness*. Merely a practical guide entitled *Inquiry into Some points of Seamanship*, this is regarded nonetheless in this remote location as no less of a wonder: 'Was it a badge – an ornament – a charm – a propitiatory act?'[19]

The Book from the West, however, has already been subjected to an even more thoroughgoing act of domestication in India, since we find as we proceed with this episode that the copies the pilgrims are carrying, both printed and written, are all 'Hindoostanee' translations.[20] In short, the Bible has been re-written twice over and doubly appropriated. That is why these simple men were able to 'love' reading it. The episode occurs a couple of decades before Macaulay's famous Minute of 1835 endorsed a policy of providing officially for the teaching of English to Indians. And yet, Bhabha is right to insist that this remains an 'English book', even when translated and locally manuscribed.[21] Bhabha's case for its Englishness depends on its appearance, the result 'a print technology calculated to produce a visual effect [through its Hindustani printing] that will not "look like the work of foreigners"'.[22] Yet this book seems even more patently English when we consider its origin and contents. It is the Indian-convert-turned-catechist, Anund Messeh (so spelt, in unmistakably British orthography), who raises the stakes here and seeks, for his own reasons of ulterior strategy, to alienate the pilgrims from a too cosy sense of owning and loving the book. He says to them:

> 'These books ... teach the religion of the European Sahibs. It is THEIR book; and they printed it in our language, for our use.' 'Ah! no,' replied the stranger [the elder pilgrim], 'that cannot be, for they eat flesh.'[23]

This proves to be the breaking point that cannot be negotiated. Under further persuasion, the pilgrims say they may not object to being baptized (perhaps because bathing in holy water or sprinkling it over oneself was a common Hindu ritual anyhow), 'but we will never take the sacrament ... because the Europeans eat cow's flesh, and this will never do for us'.[24] That is the utterly non-textual note on which the encounter with the Book ends, and the parties to it irreconcilably part. (It may be added that conversions to Christianity in India remained low and the proportion of Christians in the Indian population, as high now as ever, is a little over 3 per cent; it may also be recalled that one of the immediate provocations for the Indian 'Mutiny' of 1857 was the introduction of a new kind of rifle cartridge which was greased with cow and pig fat.)

Finally, then, the miraculous power of print and press seem to avail very little; they had in any case already been neutralized in part through old-fashioned manual re-inscription. Among the many inferences to which this episode leads is that the emphasis on forms and technologies of production that constitutes a defining element of studies in book history, interesting and illuminating in its own way, can hardly supersede the importance of textual content. The reception of a book is rightly determined far more by the second than the first. It is ultimately more of a medium than a commodity. The printed book here is rejected as holy not because of any printing deficiencies but because it has come out of the wrong kind of mouth, a mouth polluted and unsanctified by its eating of bovine flesh. For the Indian recipients of this book, beef overrides Bible. This is also relatable perhaps to the notion of oral purity in a different and profounder sense, the purity of enunciation through generations of unpolluted vegetarian mouths that traditionally guarded and preserved the integrity and sanctity of the Indians' own scriptures. Even when technology changed and the oral or the written were printed, the old taboos seemed to have remained in place. As Kesavan has pointed out, books in India remained strictly vegetarian even in their form and appearance, with no use of parchment or vellum.[25] They are thus exempt from the brutally basic definition of the book offered by a Dean of Architecture at the Massachussets Institute of Technology: 'tree flakes encased in dead cow'.[26]

But the last word on the less than overpowering impact of the 'English Book', illustrated through this episode in 1817, belongs to the British missionary who composed and published a salutary narrative of it, complete with sobering moral.

> Still everyone would gladly receive a Bible. And why? That he may store it up as a curiosity; sell it for a few pice; or use it for waste paper. ... Some have been bartered in the markets. ... an indiscriminate distribution of the scriptures, to everyone who may say he wants a Bible, can be little less than a waste of time, a waste of money and a waste of expectations.[27]

Having received the colonial English Book, it would seem that the wild and wordless wastes of India were left with even greater waste, contributed now by the sahibs.

VI. Print (post)colonialism

But one must remember to distinguish between the Book and the book, and to proceed to acknowledge that the latter has succeeded in India far better, enjoying a much more transformative impact than the former ever could. So much so that for some decades now, India has been the third largest producer of English-language books in the world, behind only the USA and the UK. (It is of course by far the largest producer of books in about half a dozen more of the most widely spoken languages on earth, each with more speakers than the total population of Britain, though in Anglophone discourse this fact is sometimes overlooked.) And it is one of the largest consumers of books in the world too, as indicated by the fact that, unlike so many produced in the USA and the UK, books produced in India are nearly all for domestic circulation and seldom travel abroad.

The development of printed book production in colonial India served to change the subcontinent in ways almost unique in the Empire. For one thing throughout colonial rule, and notwithstanding the civilizing mission, a very small minority of the population achieved any kind of functional literacy, and that nearly always in their mother tongue alone. The literacy rate even now stands at not much above 60 per cent. However, several Indians attained both high literacy and intellectual competence, often through the medium of English, through education obtained in India, and in some cases in England too. This was especially the case after the 1870s, when Oxford and Cambridge reformed themselves to admit students who did not conform to the Christian creed and the Thirty-nine Articles of the Church of England. Some of these Indians became, in Kipling's mocking phrase, more English than the English, while others arrived at a stage of political awakening and alienation through which they became articulate and ardent champions of Indian freedom. Gandhi, trained as a lawyer in London, challenged English judges in India in the courts where he was repeatedly put on trial in masterly English prose, and corresponded with successive viceroys in an English style and idiom more than matching their own, while continuing to write all his books in his mother tongue, Gujarati, and addressing the masses at public meetings in the simple form of Hindi or Hindustani, which he was keen to project as a common national language.

Thus to describe English education in India as a 'mask of conquest' is to tell only half the story, for what began as a form of colonial imposition was soon turned around to be deployed as an effective instrument of resistance to colonial rule. As Rimi Chatterjee states in her recent history of the Oxford University Press in India, the 'only possible answer' to the question whether the Press in India operated as a mask of conquest is 'yes and no'.[28] Furthermore, there had already arisen numerous presses in India as a result of indigenous enterprise, publishing in the Indian languages and soon acquiring by this means the kind of reach and circulation that Oxford in India could but dreamingly aspire to. One such was the Naval Kishore Press of Lucknow, a phenomenally productive and influential publishing house in both Urdu and Hindi which dominated book production in north India throughout the second half of the nineteenth century and well into the twentieth, the subject of an incisive and eagerly anticipated study by Ulrike Stark.[29]

In fact, many books in the Indian languages were so potently anti-colonial that they were declared to be seditious and were banned by the British government. These included *Soz-e-Vatan* (*Lament of the Nation* of 1907), by the greatest fiction writer ever in both Urdu and Hindi: Munshi Premchand (1880–1936). Later, when at the very apex of his fame, Premchand repeatedly ran foul of the government for the contents of the two literary-political journals he owned and edited, *Hans* and *Jagaran*.[30] In 2007, to mark 60 years of Indian independence, the British Library mounted an exhibition entitled 'Countdown to Freedom'. As the surrounding publicity declared, from 'one of the largest accumulations of literature and ephemera reacting to India's fight for freedom from colonial rule: which it holds, mainly in its India Office Library which was formerly a government department, [the Library] proposes to put on display for the first time a selection, much of which was banned by the British Government in India between the 1910s and the 1940s'.[31] To make an unembarrassed exhibition of such materials on such a patently postcolonial occasion is to acknowledge that they constitute as memorable and significant a part of British colonial history as any other.

In postcolonial India not many books are banned (though some still are, alas, mainly for reasons again of purported nationalism), but a larger and more visible number are now pirated. Most of these are books produced not in India but abroad, and the main reason for the piracy appears to be, besides illegal gain for the pirates, the need felt to supply a demand for an excessively and unreasonably expensive object of legitimate desire. When Salman Rushdie came on a triumphal tour of India in 1982, following the award of the Booker prize for *Midnight's Children* the previous year, he refused to sign any pirated copy of the book, which sold for 10 rupees while the next cheapest edition, the American paperback, sold for 50. In a huge postcolonial paradox, there still exists no edition of *Midnight's Children* published in India at an accessible Indian price (if we do not count the Hindi translation published finally in 1997). It is a feasible sign of some sort of globalization of the Indian book market that now J. M. Coetzee and Orhan Pamuk too are available in Indian pirated editions.

It might be scandalous, if not possibly actionable, to suggest that the opposite of banning a book may be to pirate it, but a book priced in pounds and dollars and calculated to tap into the incomparably higher per capita purchasing power in some of the most affluent countries of the world is effectively debarred from any significant circulation in India. There is even a degree of internal neo-colonization in this regard, for books published in English in India are as a rule priced considerably higher than those published in the Indian languages. For example, the classic postcolonial Hindi novel *Raag Darbari* sells in Hindi for about half the price of its English translation published locally by Penguin India (even though the English version has cut out about 70 pages from the original, in a common enough phenomenon no less worthy of investigation in studies of book history). The reason often adduced for such disparity in pricing is not the volume of sales but higher overheads; it is true enough that English-speaking heads in India tend to belong to a higher economic bracket than Hindi-speaking heads. There is thus no one book market in India and no one history of the book, for India in this respect is two nations: an anglophone 'postcolonial' India and an Indian-language indigenous India. But the twain have, of course, met and constantly transacted with each other in all kinds of historical and textual situations, as indeed have orality and textuality.

It may be apt, then, to conclude with one last engagement that illustrates quite a different aspect of this interaction. At about the same time the English Book was running into heavy spiritual weather under a tree (or, more accurately, in a grove) outside Delhi in 1817, a lieutenant in the British army in India had just put together, in 1814, a very different kind of book, which forms the last of the three emblematic or exemplary books in this discussion, together with the *Guru Granth Sahib* and the Hindustani Bible. This was the army officer and Old Etonian Thomas Duer Broughton (1778–1835), who found that the native sepoys under his command were in the habit of citing highly literary Hindi verses in the middle of their ordinary daily conversations: not just half-line or one-line tags of which such quotations normally consist, but often full quatrains. He was so struck by this presumably non-British practice of the low and poor among his subordinates (many of whom came from broadly the same class and the same region of north India as the pilgrims debating the Bhabha's notorious Book in Delhi) that he began to take down such verses from the mouths of his soldiers. Soon he had a substantial enough collection which he transcribed into roman, translated into English, and then published as a book titled *Selections from the Popular Poetry of the Hindoos.*[32] It was the first anthology of Hindi poetry to be printed and remained so for several decades afterwards.

What Broughton achieved, out of his commendable Orientalist fascination with a distinctly indigenous practice, was to make a 'book' out of the kind of materials that in Western cultures would by then have been found almost exclusively inside the covers of a book in the first place. For what he had collected were not folk songs or ballads, which one associates with the oral tradition in most cultures. These were some of the finest examples of canonical Hindi poetry written over the previous couple of centuries by poets, many of whom produced their works under royal or other aristocratic patronage, in a period-style called the *riti-kavya,* recognized as highly ornate and courtly. What would have been called high culture in many societies was in India not only 'popular' poetry, as Broughton rightly described it, but came trippingly off the tongues of common soldiers. There was apparently an egalitarian democracy of literary taste which orality facilitated and which the coming of what Benedict Anderson has aptly called 'print capitalism' then served to restrict, at least in an Indian context palpably different in this regard from the European model.

Nor is this practice moribund, even today. I realize as I write this that a fair amount of the verse I myself remember and find myself re(-)citing to like-minded friends, or sometimes alas to no one in particular, was never encountered on a printed page. Not only do I myself dispense it orally, but it has come to me through oral transmission in the first place: from my parents (not only when I was a child, but occasionally even now), from teachers and from friends, through mutual give and take. And if someone even today trots out a Sanskrit *shloka* or a Hindi *chaupai* or *doha* or an Urdu *she'r* in the middle of something else, the done thing for anyone particularly struck with it is not to be seen taking it down but to repeat it to himself in the hope that it will stick. That, at least, is the expected code of honour, rather than pulling out pen and paper. Nor is the method irredeemably ethnocentric, for it seems to work equally well with English verse too, the only difficulty here being that there is not, in Delhi where I live, too much English verse floating in the air.

Orality is supposed to have been dead for some time, rather like the novel or Sanskrit, but like them it goes on emitting signs of vitality at least in some parts of the world, notably in India. The printed book is now believed to be in not much better health among a generation for whom television and computer screen constitute preferred sources of information and entertainment. Oral, or minimally 'text'-ual communications on the mobile phone are, in any case, their principal modes of remote human contact. 'Book history as a field of study marks both an end and a beginning', claim the editors of *The Book History Reader*,[33] and aptly too, for it is only a phenomenon that has more or less run its course, that offers itself as a fit subject for retrospective survey and historicization. The Gutenberg revolution that began with the Forty-two-line Bible in 1450–5,[34] was not it seems a humanistic revolution like the Renaissance and the Reformation or even the French revolution, each issuing in a new scheme of human values. Literacy, literature, forms of communicating and preserving literature orally or through the written book, had all existed for a long time before the printing press was invented. What Gutenberg brought in was merely a new technology, one that facilitated not the production of books as such but rather their large-scale reproduction, resulting, among other effects, in the introduction of copyright and resulting financial control and gain. It is a nice irony, therefore, that one of the major ongoing cyber enterprises of our post-book era, which seeks to make available free of cost in a non-printed digital form some of the best books that have been ever printed, should be called the Gutenberg Project.

Notes

1. Lucien Febvre and Henri Jean-Martin, *L'apparition du livre* (1958), tr. as *The Coming of the Book: The Impact of Printing, 1450–1800* (London: NLB, 1976), cited in 'Book History and Print Culture: An exhibition ...' at the Thomas Fisher Rare Books Library, 1 March 2001–25 May 2001, University of Toronto Library.
2. David Finkelstein and Alistair McCleery, *An Introduction to Book History* (New York: Routledge, 2005), p. 91.
3. Brijraj Singh, *The First Protestant Missionary to India: Bartholomaeus Ziegenbalg (1683–1719)* (New Delhi: Oxford University Press, 1999), pp. 31–4, 82.
4. Raymond Schwab, *Oriental Renaissance*, cited and discussed by Harish Trivedi, in *Oxford History of Literary Translation into English, Volume 4: 1790–1900*, Peter France and Kenneth Haynes, eds (Oxford: Oxford University Press, 2006), pp. 340–54.
5. N. Jha and N. S. Rajaram, *The Deciphered Indus Script: Methodologies, Readings, Interpretations* (New Delhi: Aditya Prakashan, 2000), p. xi.

6. Finkelstein and McCleery, op. cit., p. 29.

7. At the Department of South Asian Languages and Civilizations at the University of Chicago, a graduate student had in 1999 proposed a Ph.D. project, which was formally approved by the faculty, to videograph and analyse such vedic recitations, but the project seems not to have fructified.

8. B. S. Kesavan (ed.), *The Book in India: A Compilation* (New Delhi: National Book Trust, 1992), p. 3.

9. "Chanakyashatakam" [One Hundred Verses by Chanakya], in *Subhashitasamgrahe: An Anthology of Subhashitas*, Part II, compiled by V. Raghavan (New Delhi: Sahitya Akademi, 1983), verse 83, p. 96.

10. When the British set up their own kind of legal system in India, one question that came up was regarding the Book Hindus should be asked to hold in hand when required as witnesses in court to swear to tell the truth, the whole truth and nothing but the truth. Among several equally unsatisfactory solutions tried, the most remarkable perhaps was to ask the witness to hold in hand not a book at all but a *gangajali*, a pot full of the water of the holy Ganga.

11. British Library, *What's On: What's Here*, July–September 2007, p. 12.

12. Though there could obviously be no influence of the Bible on the Book-like features of the *Guru Granth Sahib*, for the Bible was virtually unknown in north India at the time, the Qu'ran, dominantly present in north India as the Book of the Muslim rulers since the twelfth century, must have been some kind of a model. There is of course a tradition of the Qu'ran too, like the *Guru Granth Sahib* and indeed the Vedas, being recited from memory by priest-scholars who are called *hafiz* (custodians) of the Book that they keep safe in *hifazat*, i.e., in their mnemonic custody. Incidentally, this term is used loosely and inappropriately by Anita Desai as the title of her novel of 1984, *In Custody*, which is about an ageing and somewhat dissolute Urdu poet.

13. Duncan Greenlees, *The Gospel of Guru Granth Sahib* (Madras: The Theosophical Publishing House 1952), p. lxxv, and Sahib Singh, *About [the] Compilation of Sri Guru Granth Sahib* (Amritsar: Lok Sahit Prakashan, 1996), n.p., respectively.

14. Homi K. Bhabha, *The location of culture* (London: Routledge, 1994), pp. 108, 119.

15. Bhabha, p. 102.

16. Bhabha, p. 103. Bhabha's own source is *The Missionary Register* (London: Church Missionary Society), January 1818, pp. 18–19.

17. Bhabha, p. 103.

18. Bhabha, p. 103.

19. Bhabha, p. 105.

20. Hindustani was a major bone of linguistic contention in the early nineteenth century. Generally understood to consist of a Hindi-Urdu continuum, written either in the Devenagari or else in the Nastaliq Persian script, it remained for the better part of the period the subject of urgent disagreement between those who, like John Gilchrist (1719–1841), regarded it as consisting essentially of one language, and others who considered it an abstraction from an existing, and myriadic, linguistic spectrum (Editors).

21. It is highly likely, however, that the Bibles these early converts have got hold of are from one of several editions published since 1800 by the Baptist mission in Danish-occupied Serampore. If that indeed is the case, they had been translated by teams of local pandits not from English at all, but directly from

Hebrew in the case of the Old Testament, and directly from Greek in the case of the New, thus further weakening Bhabha's case concerning their Englishness. See *The Baptist Magazine* IV (London, 1912), pp. 443–4 (Editors).
22. Bhabha, p. 117.
23. Bhabha, p. 103.
24. Bhabha, p. 103.
25. Kesavan, p. 9.
26. Quoted in Finkelstein and McCleery, p. 2.
27. Bhabha, p. 122.
28. Rimi B. Chatterjee, *Empires of the Mind: A History of the Oxford University Press in India Under the Raj* (New Delhi: Oxford University Press, 2006), p. 11.
29. See Ulrike Stark, *Empire of Books: The Naval Kishore Press and the Diffusion of the Printed Word in Colonial India, 1858–1895* (New Delhi: Permanent Black, forthcoming). The uncanny similarity between the titles of Stark's book and Chatterjee's, though they treat of very different kinds of presses and reader-ships, serves to underline the close nexus between colonial rule and the printed book in India, even as seen from different sides of the fence.
30. See Amrit Rai, *Premchand: His Life and Times*, tr. from Hindi by Harish Trivedi (Delhi: Oxford University Press, 1991), passim.
31. British Library, *What's On*, p. 14.
32. Thomas Duer Broughton, *Selections from the Popular Poetry of the Hindoos* (London: John Martin, 1814). A Hungarian scholar of Hindi, Imre Bangha, has recently re-edited this work, supplying an introduction, the texts in the original devanagari script, and a bibliography, published in New Delhi by the Mahatma Gandhi Antarrashtriya Hindi Vishvavidyalaya and Rainbow Publishers in 2000.
33. David Finkelstein and Alistair McCleery, eds, *The Book History Reader* (London: Routledge, 2000), p. 3.
34. John Feather, *A Dictionary of Book History* (London: Croom Helm, 1986), p. 126.

2
The Many Worlds of the Vernacular Book: Performance, Literacy and Print in Colonial Bengal

Anindita Ghosh

Writing in the early twentieth century, Saralabala Sarkar recalls her childhood experience of listening to popular religious tales:

> A flood of affection and sweet lament inundated us during the scene when Yashoda dresses the young Krishna prior to sending him into the forest. ... At other times the *kathak* (narrator) would ... describe the sacrificial scene of King Daksha with such tremendous ferocity and intensity that children in the audience would become fearful. ... During scenes describing the marriage of Sita, the *kathak* would be honoured with vermilion and conch-shell bangles (the marks of the Bengali married woman) ... it was as if he had become everyone's very own.[1]

The reading sessions young Sarala remembers were typical *kathakata* renderings where religious texts were (and still are) read out by professional Brahmin narrators to an assembled audience.

How texts are read and assimilated has been the subject of much recent scholarship on the book. Leaving statistics and socio-economic indices behind, newer studies have moved on to examine specific reading contexts and practices, the physiology of reading and the materiality of the reading matter itself.[2] Given the notorious difficulty of finding definitive information on reading audiences, that scholars of the book are only too aware of, the task assumes greater significance.

A key area that has begun to emerge in this literature is the role of performance or orality in the consumption of written texts.[3] In the case of Spanish romances it has been shown how a genre could inhabit multiple trajectories and form the base of literary culture of nearly all social levels, because they were simultaneously heard, read, sung and memorized.[4] The body as a medium of textual experience has also been exposed as being central to early modern reading cultures in Europe, where passions and visions mingled to produce complex configurations of knowledge and reading.[5]

This is pertinent for us. Print cultures, when they emerged in modern India, rode on the crest of rich pre-print literary traditions, written and also oral. The resilience and vivacity of such traditions ensured their survival long after the first printing press was established on Indian soil. And one of the principal indices of their endurance is the continued practice of oral rendition of texts, in both formal and informal settings, well into the early twentieth century. Printed texts were widely sung, read and performed in India, adding to the written matter a rich repertoire of bodily languages, musical traditions and folk and popular motifs. Customary interpolations and interventions both by performers and audience further thickened the original narrative.

The easy disjunction often made between pre-modern and early modern on the one hand, and the modern on the other, in Indian literary studies, has been noted in a recent study.[6] Such periodization is faulty on many counts, but the one that we are concerned with here is that which overlooks vital connections between printed and pre-print literary forms. The intimate relationship between orality and print in modern India tends to be overlooked.[7] Unless dealing with texts specifically meant for performance – like dramas and songs – studies take silent reading in private to be the dominant model of literary consumption.[8] And yet, as this essay shows, textual printed matter in nineteenth century Bengal circulated in a wide range of performative arenas from the relative privacy of drawing rooms and inner courtyards to wider public spaces of the streets, fields and fairs.

Performance and textual matter have academically tended to shy away from one another, the former serving as the exclusive preserve of anthropologists and the latter of literary historians. But just as no performance can ignore the narrative force that propels performance, no text that is orally rendered can afford to be allergic to its performative context. In the case of Africa, this argument has already been stated forcefully by Ruth Finnegan, Isidore Okpewho and Eileen Julien; in the context of Southern India, by Stuart Blackburn among others.[9] My specific concern here is with the local, but exceedingly variegated, setting of Bengal. Here too, fixed written texts are not always inconsistent with oral performances. Built-in space for interjection and explanation within certain narrative structures and genres, the ritual context of renderings, and the persona of the reader and interpreter – all allow for more variable appropriations of written matter.

There are a few things I wish to do in this essay. One is to highlight the intimate connections between printed texts and their performative contexts. Given the rich oral cultures that attended the arrival of print in Bengal, this is indispensable. Secondly, I am interested in complicating some implicit assumptions often made about print and literacy in India. As I demonstrate, knowledge of the written word did not necessarily translate into readership, while conversely, even illiterate and semi-literate audiences could share written texts in communal reading sessions. And finally, I would like to show how a shift in perspective enables us to understand the ways in which a literate pre-print readership dictated the shape of the popular print market in nineteenth century Bengal. Going against the grain of scholarly literature on print in the modern era, this essay establishes how, far from fixing languages, formats, and contents, the printed book had to swim in a sea of multiple meanings and interpretations that severely compromised its textual message.[10] Indeed, the printed text acquired real significance only when rendered orally and publicly in front of large groups, as I show below.

One of the chief reasons why the book in nineteenth-century Bengal has to be treated differently from its contemporary European counterpart is the continuing importance of oral and pre-print traditions that prevented the printed text from being fixed in certain ways. Shared imagination, collective aspirations, and multiple reading practices mingled in complex ways to encourage differentiated uses and multiple appropriations of the same material objects and ideas. Roger Chartier's observations in the context of the uses of print in early modern France are helpful here, although its more specific 'cultural uses' in India were quite different. As he comments while discussing the efficacy of the written text vis-à-vis its orally (ritually or otherwise) rendered form: 'Once proposed, these models and messages were accepted by adjusting them, diverting them to other purposes, and even resisting them–all of which demonstrates the singularity of each instance of appropriation.'[11]

I. Literacy, reading and listening in the pre-print world

There is a longstanding assumption about pre-colonial (il)literacy in India.[12] The general understanding is that only the higher Hindu castes, Brahmins and Kshatriyas, dominated literate society, with great masses of illiterate low-castes forming its underbelly.[13] Part of this belief stems from prevalent European depictions of Indian literary cultures – as evident in colonial travel writings and fiction – which discounted serious investment in reading by Indians.[14] But literacy and reading does not allow for easy correlation in India. Ritual proscriptions, oral renderings and the problem of representation of literary cultures – all add to the difficulty of equating readership and literacy with any certainty.

Traditionally constituting the personnel for literate profession – priests, pundits, and physician – it is true that these high-caste groups used their knowledge of Bengali and Persian to man the higher rungs of the government and smaller feudal establishments. In reality, however, access to the written word was not limited to the high castes only. Contrary to common wisdom, and notwithstanding adverse colonial representations, print in Bengal met a widely dispersed reading and writing culture in the nineteenth century. Unlike in Europe, where a high proportion of the books produced before 1500 were in Latin, and as such inaccessible to vernacular readers, printed Bengali literature when it appeared presented itself to a significantly large literate audience.[15]

A wide network of Persian and Bengali schools had existed in Bengal since the seventeenth century. *Pathshalas* or elementary indigenous vernacular schools are frequently mentioned in Bengali literature of the period[16] and noted occasionally in eighteenth century English accounts.[17] *Pathshala* education was predominantly vocational, consisting of simple arithmetic, commercial and agricultural accounts, reading and writing knowledge of Bengali, and rules of formal correspondence. It was enough, however, to foster a fairly vibrant pre-print literary culture.

Social life as depicted in Bengali poems of the seventeenth and eighteenth centuries suggests that learning was no longer confined to the brahmins. A thriving money economy and tremendous opportunities provided to petty enterprise in land and commerce actively encouraged knowledge of reading and writing among other castes and social groups. Almost anyone with an elementary vernacular education could participate in trade and business and reap the fruits of the flourishing eighteenth-century economy.[18] Not unsurprisingly therefore, educational surveys conducted by British officials in the early part of the nineteenth century found primarily non-brahmin groups engaged in imparting and receiving elementary vernacular education at the *pathshalas*.[19]

Unlike writing in Sanskrit, writing in Bengali was open to all, irrespective of caste status. Dinesh Chandra Sen, the Bengali scholar and manuscript collector, traced some fine eighteenth-century calligraphy to individuals from the lowest sudra, the milkman and washerman castes.[20] Authors as well often came from non-brahmin groups.[21]

Among the most learned and literate lower-caste groups in eighteenth-century Bengal were the Vaishnavas, the rebellious medieval sect that opposed orthodox Hinduism.[22] Vaishnava *tols* (centres for higher learning) provided access to all castes, and a lot of Vaishnava scholars themselves came from non-brahmin caste groups.

Interestingly, despite a sizeable population who could read and write in the language, Bengali in the eighteenth century did not enjoy much prominence and prestige as compared to Persian and Sanskrit, which received official patronage and inspired a lot of creative writing within courtly and elite circles. Sanskrit was the language of Hindu priests and scholars, and the medium of instruction at *tols*. Knowledge of Persian, the official language of the Mughal administration, was required not only at the highest levels of administration and commerce, it also played an important social and political role in preserving rank and hierarchy through the intricate cultivation of etiquette among the genteel.

Bengali, by contrast, was the written language of predominantly functionally literate lesser clerical and commercial groups, as well as poor low-caste masses. Apart from everyday commercial transactions and record keeping at the lower levels of the bureaucracy, the language found its most creative expression in verse compositions. The more demotic profile of Bengali readership spawned a variety of earthy literary genres, based on rural local ballads and religious cults. The texts were invariably rhymed and closely adhered to the spoken form of the language.

Most of such poetry of the period was composed in *payar* (rhymed couplets of fourteen syllables) or *tripadi* (a lengthened form of the couplet being divisible into three parts) metres. It was read or often sung to the accompaniment of musical instruments in public performances. *Panchalis*, or rhythmic couplets set to tune, based on mythological themes and favourite epics, featured prominently on such occasions, as did a particularly popular genre of religious literature in the form of lengthy narrative poetry, spun around local deities, known as *mangal kavyas*.[23] The ritual barring of certain castes from reading publicly and from reading religious texts added to the strength of oral cultures in contemporary Bengal and forged intrinsic relationships between written texts and the spoken word.

There is an important point to note here. Literacy and reading in this age do not map themselves on to predictable populations. In pre-print Bengal, literates could not read indiscriminately. They were bound by strict caste rules concerning the choice of texts and location of readings. Thus only the higher castes – Brahmins and Kayasths – could engage in public reading, while only Brahmins could recite from religious texts. Although many among the lower castes were literate, customarily they would join the illiterate lower classes at collective reading sessions of religious works by a Brahmin reader.[24] Writing in the late eighteenth century, the missionary William Ward found lower castes being able to read and write Bengali with ease.

> Many weavers, barbers, farmers, oilmen, ... can read the translations of the pooranus in the Bengalee. ... [Brass founders or *kasharees*] read and write better than any other shoodrus; and a few read the Bengalee translations of the Ramayana, Mahabharata ...[25]

And yet it is significant that these groups were disenfranchised as far as the ritual reading of sacred texts was concerned. The mediation of holy men and Brahmins, symbolic and otherwise, was indispensable in the interpretation of sacred literature. As a Tantric text warned its readers: 'The fool who, overpowered by greed, acts after having looked up [the matter] in a written book, without having obtained it from the guru's mouth ... will be certainly destroyed.'[26] The ritualized context of reading in such cases transformed the book or written text itself into a ritualized and sacred object.[27]

The act of reading then was invested with considerable ritualistic, symbolic and social significance, and unlike in Europe, fragmented readers into separate parallel domains.[28] This did not exclude more secluded reading in private spaces by the lower castes. As seen above, contemporary manuscripts frequently show a lower-caste hand. Such hidden and relatively unknown taxonomies of reading went unreported in most European accounts and helped in perpetuating myths of limited literacy in pre-colonial India.

Conversely, the written word was not just available to literate audiences. Nor was the dissemination of the written text limited by the personalized interpretation of a few privileged individuals. It was accessible to even wider illiterate groups through communitarian ceremonial reading sessions and local performative traditions, to which we now briefly turn.

Kathakatas or collective narrative sessions, where religious works based on Hindu religious epics and mythology were read out by professional Brahmin narrators or *kathaks*, were in great demand during the period, and survived as a legacy well into the print age. The texts were brahmanical in spirit and content, and almost invariably done in an ornate classical style of composition, with resounding alliterative words and elaborate metaphor. Not surprisingly, the reading event was divided into two sessions – morning and afternoon.

In the first half, the reader merely read from old tattered volumes, and sometimes more primitive wooden tablets. In the second half, the explanation of what had been read before was given in simple Bengali. The *kathak* retold the existing story, interspersing the narrative with suitable songs, poems, popular tales, and moral lessons, heightening the experience of listeners.[29] The text remained inseparable from the telling throughout, with the manuscript carrying ritual and cultural value before and after, and even during, the performance.[30]

The *kathaks* sat under a small awning erected upon a vacant space, and poured out, sometimes for hours together, familiar tales from the *Ramayana* and *Mahabharata*. William Ward graphically describes a typical *kathakata* session hosted by a householder on an auspicious occasion, although the village *chandi-mandap* (the communal worshipping pavilion), or even the shade of the roadside banyan tree, could provide alternative venues:

> A shed covered with thatch and open on all sides, is prepared, sufficiently large, if the ceremony be on a grand scale, to accommodate four or five thousand people. At one end, a place rather elevated is prepared for the person who is to read; and the other end, if there be a portico to the house, is enclosed by a curtain, from whence the women hear and peep through crevices. Mats are spread for the people to sit on, the bramhuns in one place, and the kayusthus in another, and the shoodrus in another. On the appointed day all take their places. ... The reader (Pathuku) ... sits on the elevated seat ... (and after a brief ceremony, about 9 or 10 in the morning) begins to read ... The first day they sit about an hour; but on succeeding days they begin at seven and continue till twelve; and in the afternoon meet again, when the meaning of what was read in the forenoon in Sungskritu is ... given in Bengalee, by the Kuthuku, or speaker; who takes the seat of the Pathuku ... The whole is closed at dusk, when the people retire, and converse upon what they have heard. This method is pursued from day to day till the book is finished.[31]

The *kathakata* events provided a focal point to community living. The moral authority accorded to the narrator and the deep faith of the attending audience gave him an extremely involved role.[32] The people sitting around evidently acceded their full and implicit belief to the prodigies related, for, as a contemporary observed, 'frequently the whole crowd makes some sudden impulsive gesture, illustrative of the progress of the story'.[33] Young and old, men and women would flock every day to such gatherings, which sometimes continued for months on end.[34] One study rightly underlines the participatory nature of *kathakata* renditions. Everyone had a share: the patrons, the performer, and the listeners were all expected to play their respective parts in it.[35] This was undoubtedly an extraordinary celebration of shared emotions and listening experiences, cementing the community and inculcating piety, virtue, and conformity.[36]

The oral traversed the domain of the written through other significant routes as well. Performances based on the *mangal kavya* and *panchali* texts offered multifarious points of intervention and negotiation between the written text and its audience. Religious ballads celebrating the various forms of the goddess Shakti – Manasa the snake goddess, Sitala the goddess of fever and smallpox, Chandi, and others[37] – seem to have sprung from oral traditions of nomadic lower castes that then became gradually sanskritized over time.[38] As Edward Dimock points out, the *mangal kavya* poems were simultaneously part of written and oral traditions, and thus continued to be recited during worship and festive gatherings.[39] While some of them were sanitized and drawn into brahmanical circles, the popular performative tradition continued to thrive and almost invariably escaped fixation by writing. Writing at the end of the eighteenth century, Francis Buchanan-Hamilton discovered at least 350 such performing groups. There were usually seven or eight songsters, with anklets tied to their feet, led by a chief or *sardar*. They sang and danced at the same time, clapping a pair of cymbals. Two others accompanied on the drum.[40]

Prolific written and orally shared vernacular literary cultures in Bengal from the mid-sixteenth century onwards thus had already established clear tastes and preferences in reading when the printed book arrived in the region. The poor socio-political and cultural status of the language encouraged an unrestricted, fecund, and highly productive life outside narrow literary circles, while a lack of ritual prescriptions surrounding its private reading and writing ensured the widest possible circulation. The most common of these genres existed as rhymed poetry – read and performed – composed in a vibrant and colloquial Bengali idiom, and relating to the life of ordinary people. Such energetic sociologies (and physiologies) of reading could not just disappear with the advent of print.

II. The new print: negotiating the oral

In 1822 the *Friend of India*, a missionary newspaper, published the following report from a correspondent:

> I am glad to perceive, that everyday the natives are increasing in their sales of native books: there are now in and near the city of Moorshedabaad no less than four walking booksellers that I know of. In speaking to one last week, he informed me, that upon an average he sold to the amount of 30 Rupees per month. Two of the four are in the employ of a native of Calcutta, the other two are selling for another native, who has established a press near Agrudeep. [41]

One estimate offered in 1854 is that not less than two million books had issued in Bengal over the previous ten years.[42] Even given that this is an unsubstantiated figure, there is no denying that, by mid-century, print in various forms had made remarkable inroads into the Bengali cultural world.

Bengal's prodigious printing and publishing industry flourished from the middle of the nineteenth century onwards.[43] Between 1868 and 1900 the number of magazines and newspapers in circulation in the vernacular rose from 255 to over 1000.[44] Of all the administrative divisions producing books, including the Presidencies of Bombay and Madras, it was undoubtedly Bengal, statistically speaking, that proved the most explosive.[45] The Bengal Library Quarterly Reports catalogued on the basis of the publications registered, return about 200, 000 titles between 1868 and 1905 – that Robert Darnton estimates was 'more, by far, than the total output of France during the Age of Enlightenment'.[46]

At the centre of this remarkable phenomenon lay the numerous small presses huddled close together in the narrow lanes and by-lanes of the Battala area, part of the teeming 'Native Town' in north Calcutta.[47] In 1857, the average annual production figures of the individual presses ranged from 8000 to 47,000 copies, depending on their size.[48] While textbooks for schools sold very well and formed a staple of the trade, the presses vied with each other for producing the latest in recreational and religious literature. Despite reformist disapproval, they did a particularly brisk trade in cheap ephemeral pamphlets, which enjoyed a large readership in both urban and rural homes.

Mid-nineteenth century onwards there seems to have existed a congenial climate for books. The number of literates in Bengal at this time increased significantly. Prospect of jobs in the mushrooming government and mercantile establishments combined with the spread of vernacular education provided the initial impetus.[49] In addition, economies of scale following from increasing print-runs and a competitive market made for extremely affordable prices of books.

The burgeoning vernacular print market was thus apparently perfectly poised for a smooth take-off. Indeed the runaway figures of book production seen above seem to confirm that proposition. But there is compelling evidence to suggest that printed books had to struggle to break into the contemporary reading world. Statistics alone does not unveil the entire picture. Books in Bengal need to be understood within their specific contexts of usage.

The printing revolution and its impact on the reading audience must not be exaggerated. Chartier's pioneering research has gone a long way in establishing lines of continuity between the worlds of print and manuscript in early modern Europe.[50] Much the same could be said for nineteenth-century Bengal. The printed book was the direct heir of the manuscript, and preserved on many occasions its formats, genres, and uses. Besides, as in Europe, manuscript publication continued to flourish alongside printing for a long time.

The experience of the missionaries can be taken as an interesting case in point. Christian missionaries who came to Bengal in the early half of the nineteenth century registered an enormous demand for their gratuitous religious vernacular tracts and books. Initial jubilation at the eager reception, in the reports back to parent institutions, was, however, soon replaced by despondence, as it was discovered that the literature taken away was not always read. The paper on which it was printed could be put to a range of practical uses – from wrapping medicines to lining baskets carrying scented oil bottles, and even flying kites.[51]

Undoubtedly, print appeared as a difficult medium to many readers at first. Early *Native School Reports* testify to the halting recognition of printed texts among Bengalis: 'As they have previously never seen anything but manuscript, and that possibly in small quantity, it is not easy to find a man who can read the printed character with any readiness, not withstanding its superior clearness and regularity.'[52] In 1818–19 the vernacular indigenous schools of Calcutta were using only manuscripts of well-read poetical compositions. The School Book Society often found them reluctant to switch to printed works: out of the 42 schools offered a free supply of the Society's publications, only 17 readily accepted.[53] The first official survey of vernacular education in Bengal by William Adam too reported the predominant use of manuscripts in schools in Murshidabad. One teacher, previously in the employment of a European, who used to support a Bengali school, retained only a few printed books that were 'preserved as curiosities, or as heirlooms to be admired, not used'.[54] Much of the teaching in Bengali schools was still conducted orally and committed to memory.

Visually the printed text proved a challenge to the new reader. Thus Rassundari Debi, a self-taught Bengali housewife, whose surreptitious project to educate herself has attracted much scholarly attention in recent times,[55] found it difficult at first to read printed books. Having eagerly waited for her son to buy and post a particular book from Calcutta, she found to her dismay that she was unable to read it:

> Some days later the book reached me. On receiving it I joyously took the book in my hands and opened it, only to discover that the print was too small for me. I could not read it.[56]

The problem manifested itself to the earliest pioneers of printing in Bengal. The missionaries of Serampore, responsible for setting up the first Bengali press in 1800, were faced with the dilemma of choosing between the cost of production and readers' convenience, during the incipient stages of printing the scriptures. While larger types meant more expenses because of the bulk, it allowed for an easier transition from manuscripts to printed texts.[57] After a series of experiments in 1832 they evolved a reduced typeface that allowed for a pocket version of the Testament of duodecimo size. However, the original problem persisted:

> While these reduced types bring both the Old and New Testament into a volume so portable and so well suited to the young among the population of Bengal … there are many among those of the middle age as well as older, who cannot read this small type with pleasure, and who, accustomed from childhood to a very large character … will never be able to enjoy the perusal of a book in this smaller print.[58]

The cannier commercial publishers in Calcutta had anticipated the same problem and responded to it in quite a different way. The early Battala publications closely shadowed the manuscript font and style while preparing typefaces. Some genres in fact continued to hold on to bolder sized typescripts well into the turn of the century.

The change from a listening, sharing oral culture to a private, silent mode of reading could be abrupt and stifling. Such participatory and expositionary forms of narration as in the tradition of *kathakata* and the modes of addressing the standing spectators inherent in narrative structures of *panchalis* had allowed a lively and active role for the pre-print audience. Linear development of narrative, objectivity, and clarity of expression – the general rules of written style – were not going to appeal to such readers. Commercial presses therefore took care to preserve enclaves of performative oral traditions within the format of the standard prose narrative. It shows through in the imitation of speech patterns in the narratives, the first-person authorial voice, the abundance of conversational didactic messages and explanatory comment, as well as the preservation of folkish motifs and their variants.

Poetry and songs constituted the bulk of the book trade, and this is where earlier performative traditions left their clearest trail. While contemporary elite Bengali poets like Madhusudan Dutt experimented with the more complicated rhyming patterns of the sonnet, *payar*, the preferred metre for much traditional Bengali poetry, was the favourite of Battala's composers. The rhythmic couplets were harnessed to the service of religious and love poetry alike, and rendered in a catchy sing-song manner when read aloud to a gathered audience.[59]

Songs, wherever possible, made cameo appearances in prose works to spice up a storyline, or simply to break the monotony of the narrative format. They could be used rather imaginatively to emphasize a point or reveal the deepest emotions of the characters involved. But more often than not their inclusion was rather arbitrary, following no standard rules of grammar, and sometimes entirely unconnected to the main plot. The readers did not seem to mind this, judging by the author's anticipation of active involvement on their part.

Elaborate instructions as regards the mood (*raga*) and rhythm (*tala*) in which the song should be sung invariably accompanied every musical piece in the text. Evidently this was intended for not just the lead singer, as choruses frequently intervened to allow for more demotic rendering of the narrative. Readers and/or listeners were thus grafted onto the text, making reading the printed word a highly participatory experience. Perhaps these texts were most effective when sung and read in collective gatherings. So naturalized did the structural juxtaposition of song and prose become that, from the mid-century onwards, they appear as organic to contemporary literature, deployed with great flair in a wide range of prose genres from dramas to novels.

For first-generation readers of print, the simple language of literature set out in the form of dialogues was very welcome. Early print culture was therefore closely linked to speech. Dramas based on pseudo-historical, mythological, and social themes were particularly successful in mobilizing such narrative techniques, and they consequently enjoyed a large reading population. Social farces, composed in a coarse colloquial, and offering caustic critiques of contemporary moral decadence were particularly popular 1860s onwards.

It must be emphasized that even with the coming of the book, personalized reading in private by no means exhausted the possible use of the printed text. Silent reading was, in fact, a rather rare practice in the mid-nineteenth century. The sight of a man poring over his book was not uncommon, but listening was more prevalent. A report in the *Calcutta Review* carried a vivid description of such gatherings at small shops at the end of the day:

> The reader, sitting on his haunches, with his book laid on the floor before him, spells out couplet after couplet; for all the popular books are in verse, or are read as if they were in verse. His skill, generally, is not very great [compounded by printing errors]. ... It is always carried on aloud, and according to a sing-song tune, ... [to which] the head beats in time.[60]

Two of the earliest Bengali periodicals, produced by missionaries from Serampore, the *Digdurshun*, an informative journal mainly intended to be a textbook in native schools, and the *Samachar Darpan*, a weekly publication featuring mainly news items, gained immense popularity when they first appeared and were primarily consumed by a listening audience. Readers apparently took home copies to read in leisure to their families and neighbours:

> A copy each [of the *Samachar Darpan*] is sent to the schools for reading out by monitors and elder boys. The master then takes it home and is thereby enabled to indulge his neighbours with a perusal of it. ... The number of those ... who flock around a man who has one of them, to become acquainted with its contents and read it in their turn ... is highly pleasing ... There is a reason to suppose that each paper on an average obtains ten readers or attentive hearers.[61]

The *kathakata* sessions also continued alongside. Mahendranath Dutta, a retired engineer in a government department, recalled in his childhood memoirs how such reading sessions were a source of moral inspiration and guidance for one and all.

A lot of people came for such sessions, from the Brahmin pundit to the lowest of castes such as the cobbler and *hnadi*. It was open to all. One good thing deriving of these events was the fact that it bred a sense of morals amongst the audience. The impact was the same on all. There was no difference between rich and poor, learned and ignorant. The idea of the 'good' and 'bad' was the same for everyone.[62]

Rather than displacing earlier reading worlds and unleashing its own irreversible dynamics, print made modest and hesitant inroads into earlier pre-print cultures. As elsewhere in India, strong traditions of oral cultures survived in Bengal well into the nineteenth century.[63] Availability of multiple copies of the same work did not inevitably prompt the demise of communal reading. Reading as a collective act of performance is manifest in the shared readings of all kinds of works – religious, political, literary and scandalous – by diverse reading communities, and not necessarily bound by knowledge of the written vernacular.

III. Print in performance

Print in Bengal in the nineteenth century existed alongside rich performative cultures. Songs sung within the generic structures of *panchalis* and *mangal kavyas*, or specific to events and occupations such as fishermen's songs (*bhatiali, sari*), devotional songs (*keertans*), or wedding and harvesting songs, were an important part of contemporary folk repertoire. They were usually performed in communal gatherings – singly or collectively – and reflected the quotidian concerns of their highly involved audiences, alongside their generic thematic contents. With the burgeoning of Calcutta as an urban centre, migrants from rural areas carried such traditions to the city, over time adapting them to more urban settings, and even giving birth to newer ones. The street culture of Calcutta in the early part of the nineteenth century was a vigorous one, consisting of the verbal duels of urban folk poets or *kobis*,[64] the lampooning *sawng* pantomimes and jaunty *khemta* dances.[65] Traditional folk humour was interlaced in these performances with pungent lower order hatred of the urban successful, and evoke images startlingly similar to the Rabelaisian carnival world. Basic to all of them was mocking laughter, sometimes light-hearted, but often pointed and taking the form of hostile derision.

Folk dramas or *jatras* were an integral part of this oral culture. Originating from song and dance rituals associated with certain religious festivals, *jatras* evolved over time to become longer events including dialogues, narrators and even comic relief.[66] They were performed on open ground where actors were entirely surrounded by the audience, with a musical chorus placed on one side. While the earlier *jatras* were based on mythological and religious themes, mid-nineteenth century onwards they tended to include more contemporary themes and events. Lower order involvement was characteristic to the original *jatra* form, and was reflected in the subject-matter of songs sung by the artistes. Characteristic songs (*ad-khemta*) and dances (*khemta*) set to a lively tempo added to their popularity. Being sung over and over again in everyday locations like the marketplace and fields, these were rendered almost commonplace.[67]

Jatra troupes multiplied in the nineteenth century, and registered growing involvement from the upper social brackets, even as they remained an indispensable feature of religious festivals.[68] Bepin Pal, the prominent revolutionary nationalist from Bengal, mentions his family's active participance in such performative cultures in Sylhet and Jessore in his childhood, and records the hosting of *jatras* and *puran paths* in the family home. The sets were simple and devoid of much theatrical paraphernalia. But so dear were the themes to the hearts of the audience, he recalls, that the lack of these 'did not at all interfere with the inner enjoyment of it'.[69] Newspapers reported *jatras* and *khemta* dances being put up at all kinds of events, from more private occasions like birth in a family to public ones like annual meets of local sports clubs and agricultural fairs.[70] Audiences voiced their approval and continuing support of the dramatic form.[71] As the experience of one village attests, *jatras*, nautches, festivals and songs of *neda-nedis* (Vaishnava singers) constituted the staple of entertainment for the residents.[72]

The printed text was in close communion with this performative world. In the print market cheaply produced pamphlet dramas proliferated from the mid-1870s onwards. They were published in pages of about 20 to 40, with an average print-run of 1,000 to 2,000. Written in a racy colloquial and dwelling on themes of urban decadence and moral corruption, the plays hovered between the boundaries of social censure and pure sensation. Those that were received well invariably ran into two or three editions. Sold at attractively cheap prices, these works were hawked by pedlars on the streets of Calcutta and in distant villages. Although they made for a large reading population, some of these dramas were also put up on stage, adding to their charm. Small town theatres in the suburbs surrounding Calcutta would often put them up as minor supplements to other dramas.

Among the factors contributing to the popularity of the dramatic form, were the numerous theatres emerging in the northern part of the city. Theatre reviews, playbills and letters to the editor, frequently carried in Bengali newspapers, indicate the remarkable appeal of this form of entertainment in the new metropolis. By the end of the century, dramatic clubs and societies had mushroomed all over Bengal, catering to mainly a suburban and small town population. In 1910, the Burdwan District Gazetteer reported that almost every village in the district had a theatrical society.[73] In the Nadia district too amateur dramatic societies had mushroomed, particularly in the towns. In Ranaghat alone there were four such societies, each with its own stage and props.[74]

The intimate connection between the on-stage performances and the printed texts was noted by a contemporary artiste. Gratuitous distribution of the printed texts of the dramas, accordingly, boosted the numbers attending the theatres.[75] Kathryn Hansen notes the same practice in the Parsi theatre in Bombay in the nineteenth century. Accordingly, theatrical companies regularly commissioned playwrights to compose dramas for their productions, and later published them in book form.[76] The literate section of the audience for the plays consuming such printed book versions overlapped with wider emergent readerships for popular fiction, novels and the general run of cheap recreational literature.[77]

The experience of the colonial state in trying to stamp out sedition within its territories can serve as an illustrative case in point. The tremendous potential of performance vis-à-vis print in rousing unrest was noted by the British government as early as the 1870s, even as vernacular print was being closely scrutinized in the wake of the 1857 uprising. The ability of performances to inflame political passion, much more than printed texts, became apparent when the Great National Theatre of Calcutta staged the controversial *Nildarpan* – a charged historical play against indigo planters – in Lucknow in 1872. The play had earlier raised a storm in Calcutta in 1861 when it first appeared in printed form, highlighting the plight of peasants forcibly required to cultivate indigo.[78] But the disquiet soon died down as the government acceded to the demands of the campaigners and rebels, and took legal action to check the atrocities of the planters. When the play was performed almost a decade later much of the heat had dissipated. And yet it created a stir among the local English audience. During a scene where an English planter attempting to rape a peasant woman was being humbled by a Muslim peasant – an actress in the play recalls – some British soldiers even tried to disrupt the performance by climbing on to the stage with swords in their hands.[79] The show had to be finally cancelled and the troupe asked to leave town by the district magistrate.

As the newly formed Bengali public stage began to reflect the political concerns and aspirations of its mostly middle-class patrons, the government became very watchful. While frontal attack on the regime was rare, tongue-in-cheek references to the oppression of the colonial state became quite popular. In 1875, two plays, about the brutal treatment of the Assam tea plantation workers by the English planters, and the victimisation of the Raja of Baroda by the English Resident, were staged.[80] The following year the Great National Theatre staged a farce lampooning a local lawyer, who had allowed the Prince of Wales into his inner chambers or the *andarmahal*, thereby apparently exposing the women of the household to the public – and more explicitly male – gaze. The Government responded this time with an ordinance prohibiting dramatic performances which were 'scandalous, defamatory, seditious, obscene or otherwise prejudicial to public interest'. The answer to this was another farce, *The Police of Pig and Sheep* – referring to the then police superintendent Lamb, and the Police Commissioner Sir Stuart Hogg – at the same theatre. Three days later, the manager, Amritalal Basu, and the director, Upendranath Das, were arrested on concocted charges of 'obscenity' and sentenced to a month's imprisonment.[81]

I would like to conclude by referring to another extremely relevant example. Robert Darnton in a recent essay has highlighted the case of a *jatra* performer, Mukunda Lal Das, who was charged with sedition for attacking the British presence in India.[82] Mukunda had rendered into *jatra* form and had been performing for some time a printed play called *Matri Puja*. While ostensibly a Puranic tale of conflict between the gods and demons, the work assumed threatening proportions for the authorities in Mukunda's performances, where he would regularly improvise to ridicule local officials and even the king emperor. It proved very popular, with the court documents recording 168 performances. Mukunda also published a songbook, *Matri Puja Gan*, which consisted of 53 songs, many of them from his *jatra* version. After several unsuccessful attempts to catch him, Mukunda was finally arrested and brought to trial in 1908.

Even though the printer (in the absence of the author, Kunja Behari Ganguly, who had fled) was fined 200 rupees, clearly it was Mukunda who was the principal culprit in the eyes of the court. It was his performances – which included acting, singing and miming – that had made the text come alive to the audiences. More significantly, Mukunda received twice as long a prison term for his singing as for his songbook. The judge's verdict is testimony to the primacy of oral culture in contemporary Bengal: 'There can be no question that the harm done by the accused by penetrations into remote villages with his mischievous propaganda was infinitely greater than the harm done by him in publishing a printed book.'[83]

Access to the written word was thus a process much more broadly defined than simply the silent reading of an individual in isolation, literacy in its classic sense. Reading cultures in the print era were wholly immersed in pre-print practices of sharing the written word. Plural uses and interpretations of printed texts used in common, rather than internalized and private reading experiences, broadened the possibilities and patterns of print consumption. Collective exposure to print entailed decipherment in common, with those who knew how to read leading those who did not. It invested the printed image or text with values and intentions that had little to do with those of solitary book reading.

In its early years, then, the printed book 'disappeared' into the labyrinthine world of Bengali readership, being appropriated and internalized in diverse ways by lively groups of both intermediary and primary readers, through performance and ritual. The location of the printed book in a culture that was still primarily oral prompted it to appeal to pre-print sensibilities both in the choice and style of the reading matter as well as in its flexible patterns of consumption. In fact, it was the adaptability of the printed book that ensured its commercial survival in an environment where oral entertainment ruled. Missing the importance of performance in this print world would be tantamount to losing half the picture.

Notes

1. Chitra Deb (ed.), *Saralabala Sarkar Racanasangraha*, vol. 1 (Calcutta, 1989), p. 774.
2. As selected readings see, Roger Chartier and Guglielmo Cavallo (eds), *History of Reading in the West*, trans. Lydia G. Cochrane (Cambridge: Polity, 1999); Robert Darnton, 'History of reading' in Peter Burke (ed.), *New Perspectives on Historical Writing* (Cambridge: Polity, 1991); Paul Saenger, *Space Between Words: The Origins of Silent Reading* (Stanford: Stanford University Press, 1997); Lisa Jardine and Anthony Grafton, '"Studied for action": How Gabriel Harvey read his Livy', *Past and Present*, 129 (November, 1990), pp. 30–78; Alberto Manguel, *A History of Reading* (London: Harper Collins, 1996); James Raven, Helen Small and Naomi Tadmor (eds), *The Practice and Representation of Reading in England* (Cambridge and NY: Cambridge University Press, 1996); Martyn Lyons, 'What did the peasants read? Written and printed culture in rural France, 1815–1914', *European History Quarterly*, 27/2 (1997), pp. 165–197; Michele Moylan and Lane Stiles (eds), *Reading Books: Essays on the Material Text and Literature in America* (Amherst: University of Massachusetts Press, 1996).
3. Martyn Lyons has shown how oral reading habits persisted well into the nineteenth century in Europe. See his 'New readers in the nineteenth century: Women, children, workers', in Chartier and Cavallo, *A History of*

> *Reading in the West*, pp. 342–4. Also see Roger Chartier, 'Reading matter and "Popular" reading: From the Renaissance to the seventeenth century', ibid., pp. 276–8.

4. Roger Chartier, 'Reading matter and "popular" reading', p. 273. See also, B. W. Ife, *Reading and Fiction in Golden-Age Spain: A Platonist Critique and some Picaresque Replies* (Cambridge and NY: Cambridge University Press, 1985).

5. Adrian Johns, *The Nature of the Book: Print and Knowledge in the Making* (Chicago and London: University of Chicago Press, 1998). See Chapter 6, 'The physiology of reading'.

6. Stuart Blackburn and Vasudha Dalmia (eds), *India's Literary History: Essays on the Nineteenth Century* (New Delhi: Permanent Black, 2004).

7. Stuart Blackburn's study is an interesting exception. As he shows in the case of the bow-song tradition in Tamilnadu, written texts drive the actual performance of the songs. See his *Singing of Birth and Death: Texts in Performance* (University of Pennsylvania Press, 1988).

8. Even Priya Joshi's otherwise meticulous study of readers and literary consumption of English novels in India takes silent reading as the basic premise. See Priya Joshi, *In Another Country: Colonialism, Culture and the English Novel in India* (New York: Columbia University Press, 2002).

9. For Africa see, *inter alia*, Ruth Finnegan, *Oral Literature in Africa* (Oxford University Press, 1970) and *The 'Oral' and Beyond: Doing Things With Words in Africa* (Oxford: James Currey; University of Chicago Press; University of Kwa-Zulu Press; 2007); Isidore Okpewho, *The Epic in Africa: Towards A Poetics of Oral Performance* (New York: Columbia University Press, 1979) and *African Oral Literature: Background, Character and Continuity* (Bloomington: Indiana University Press); Eileen Julien, *African Novels and the Question of Orality* (Bloomington: Indiana University Press, 1992) and Stephanie Newell, *West African Literatures: Ways of Reading* (Oxford University Press, 2006). See also, most recently, Letitia Adu-Ampoma, 'What's it all about?', *Wasafiri* 52 (Autumn 2007); The Book in the World: Readers, Writers and Publishers, Robert Fraser and Susheila Nasta (eds) (London, New Delhi and New York: Routledge, 2007), pp. 45–51. For South India, see especially Stuart Blackburn, *Print, Folklore and Nationalism in Colonial South India* (New Delhi: Permanent Black, 2003).

10. Much scholarship on print is based on ideas of closure and fixity in the printed text. Lucien Febvre and Jean-Henri Martin, *The Coming of the Book: The Impact of Printing, 1450–1800*, trans. G. Gerard (London/NY: Verso, 1997), and Elizabeth L. Eisenstein, *The Printing Press as an Agent of Change*, 2 vols (Cambridge University Press, 1979) have principally set the trend in this regard.

11. Roger Chartier, *Cultural Uses of Print in Early Modern France*, trans. Lydia G. Cochrane (Princeton, New Jersey: Princeton University Press, 1987), p. 7.

12. This is despite the Orientalist fanfare about ancient Indian Sanskrit scholarship.

13. C. A. Bayly thus argues that village education in Bengal catered to 'clean caste' male children only. See his *Empire and Information: Intelligence Gathering and Social Communication in North India, 1780–1870* (Cambridge: Cambridge University Press, 1996), p. 37. Historians for other parts of eighteenth-century India tend to agree. Karen I. Leonard, in *Social History of an Indian Caste: The Kayasths of Hyderabad* (Berkeley and Los Angeles: University of

California Press, 1978), traced a close connection between the scribal monopoly of the upper writing castes and politico-economic power in early nineteenth-century Hyderabad.

14. Amazingly, such literary stereotyping continued into the nineteenth and twentieth centuries as well. See Priya Joshi, 'Reading in the public eye: The circulation of British fiction in Indian libraries, *c.* 1835–1901, in Blackburn and Dalmia, *India's Literary History*, pp. 280–1.

15. Even though literacy is not adequately reported in official Indian records during this period, a significant portion of the population had an elementary knowledge of reading and writing. See the outstanding study by Parames Acharya, *Banglar Deshaja Sikshadhara* (Calcutta: Anushtup Prakashani, 1989).

16. Indigenous schools find mention in the *mangal kavyas* or religious ballads of the period. The earliest reference probably is that by Rupram Chakravarti in his *Dharma Mangal*, dating back to the seventeenth century. See Acharya, *Banglar Deshaja Sikshadhara*, Chapter 2.

17. Edward Ives, *A Voyage From England to India* (London, 1773), p. 29; Q. Craufurd, *Sketches Chiefly Relating to the History, Religion, Learning and Manners of the Hindoos with Concise Accounts of the Present States of the Native Powers of Hindostan* (London: T. Cadells, 1792), vol. 2, pp. 12–13; William Ward, *A View of the History, Literature and Mythology of the Hindoos*, 4 vols, 3rd ed. (London: Black, Parbury, and Allen, 1817–20), vol. 3, p. 160; Francis Buchanan-Hamilton, *History, Antiquities, Topography and Statistics of Eastern India*, M. Martin (ed.) (London: W. H. Allen & Co., 1838), vol. 2, pp. 705–6.

18. Ronald Inden's close study of the genealogies of the clans demonstrates a remarkable social mobility whereby lower ranking *jatis* (clans) rose through trade, landholding, administration and marriages. See Ronald Inden, *Marriage and Rank in Bengali Culture: A History of Caste and Clan in Middle Period Bengal* (Berkeley and Los Angeles: University of California Press, 1976), pp. 135–37; Hitesranjan Sanyal, 'Continuities of social mobility in traditional and modern society in India: Two case studies of caste mobility in Bengal', *Journal of Asian Studies* 2 (February 1971).

19. William Adam's earliest surveys produced three invaluable reports between 1835 and 1838, reprinted in Anathnath Basu (ed.), *Reports on the State of Education in Bengal* (Calcutta: Calcutta University, 1941).

20. Dinesh Chandra Sen, *History of Bengali Language and Literature* (Calcutta: Calcutta University, 1911), p. 599.

21. See for instance the colophons published in Panchanan Mandal (ed.), *Punthi Parichay*, (6 vols) (Santiniketan, 1951–1990). Also see Acharya, *Banglar Deshaja Sikshadhara* (Calcutta: Anushtup Prakashani, 1989), p. 74.

22. Not only Bengali but also Sanskrit featured in their accomplishments. Francis Buchanan-Hamilton, the eighteenth-century ethnographer-cum-travel-writer, found the Vaishnavas (he refers to them as 'religious mendicants') among the most literate and learned in Bengal. Buchanan-Hamilton, *History, Antiquities, Topography*, pp. 708–09, 755.

23. Literally meaning 'songs of blessing', they were dedicated to various local forms of the mother-goddess Shakti, worshipped as a source of divine female power.

24. See William Ward, *A View of the History*, vol. 1, p. 85.
25. Ward, *A View of the History*, vol. 3, pp. 95–8.
26. Cited in P. Heehs (ed.), *Indian Religions: A Historical Reader of Spiritual Expression and Experience* (London: Hurst, 2002), p. 194.
27. William Ward mistakenly refers to the Puran reading sessions as 'the worshipping of books'. Although the books were sacred, they themselves were not the objects of veneration. Ward, *A View of the History*, vol. 1, p. xlv.
28. See Benedict Anderson, *Imagined Communities: Reflections on the Origins and Spread of Nationalism* (London: Verso, 1983) for the European experience.
29. Nabin Sen remembered how his own father, reading out the *Manasa punthi* (manuscript), was able to move the audience to tears, especially the women. Nabin Sen, *Amar Jiban*, 2 vols (Calcutta, 1907), vol. 1, p. 124.
30. Stuart Blackburn rightly points out how the intimate connection between the written and the oral is not unique to any particular tradition in South Asia, but much more generic. See Stuart Blackburn, *Singing of Birth and Death*, p. 29.
31. Ward, *A View of the History*, vol. 2, pp. 85–6.
32. The importance of embodied knowledge, with texts assuming importance only when incorporated in the person of the narrator, has been studied in other religious contexts. See W. A. Graham, 'Quran as spoken word: An Islamic contribution to the understanding of scripture', in R. C. Martin (ed.), *Approaches to Islam in Religious Studies* (Tucson: University of Arizona Press, 1985).
33. 'Brahmanism and the Ramayun', *Calcutta Review*, vol. 13 (January–June 1850), p. 49.
34. Ward, *A View of the History*, 2:85, noted that while the *Shribhagawat* recitation took only one month, the narration of the *Mahabharata* spanned four months.
35. Gautam Bhadra, 'The performer and the listener: Kathakatha in modern Bengal', *Studies in History*, 10 (July–December 1994), p. 246.
36. The shared imagination among communities of pre-print listeners has also been highlighted in other Indian contexts. See Allison Busch, 'The anxiety of innovation: The practice of literary science in the Hindi/*Riti* tradition', *Comparative Studies of South Asia, Africa and the Middle East*, 24:2 (2004), p. 54.
37. See Buchanan-Hamilton, *History, Antiquities, Topography*, 749; Ward, *A View of the History*, 1:232–38. For an account of these legends see Sen, *History of the Bengali Language*, pp. 48–55, 257–76. Also see Edward Dimock, trans., 'Ketakananda Das' Manasamangal', in *The Thief of Love: Bengali Tales from Court and Village* (University of Chicago Press, 1963), pp. 197–294; and the translated excerpts by Aditi Nath Sarkar and Ralph A. Nicholas in 'The fever demon and the census commissioner: Sitala mythology in eighteenth and nineteenth century Bengal', in Marvin Davis (ed.), *Bengal: Studies in Literature, Society and History*, Occasional Papers on South Asia, no. 27 (Ann Arbor: University of Michigan Asian Studies Centre, 1976).
38. As Dinesh Sen has observed, this higher-caste involvement in *mangal* works led to a gradual brahmanization of the local cults and a sanskritization of their literature by the end of the eighteenth century. Sen, *History of the Bengali Language*, pp. 296–97.

39. Edward C. Dimock, 'The Goddess of Snakes in Medieval Bengali Literature', *History of Religions* 1:2 (Winter 1962), p. 308.
40. For a vivid account of such *mangal* recitals in Dinajpur, see Buchanan-Hamilton, *History, Antiquities, Topography*, p. 929.
41. *Friend of India*, Monthly series, 5 (1822), p. 86.
42. James Long to G. F. Cockburn, Chief Magistrate of Calcutta, 23 June 1854, quoted in Jatindranath Bhattacharya, *Bangla Mudrita Granthadir Talika, 1743–1852* (Calcutta: A. Mukherjee, 1990), p. 161.
43. See Anindita Ghosh, *Power in Print: Popular Publishing and the Politics of Language and Culture in a Colonial Society* (New Delhi: Oxford University Press, 2006) for a fuller discussion of this print market.
44. Figures are approximate only, based on a list of periodicals provided in B. N. Bandyopadhyay (ed.), *Bangla Samayik Patra*, 2 vols (Calcutta: Bangiya Sahitya Parishat, 1972–7).
45. Bengal's leading position in the world of publication had not changed even towards the end of the nineteenth century. Thus in 1898, Bombay and Madras taken together (counting 1, 834) could not match the annual production figures for Bengal (2174) that year. See table in Darnton, 'Literary surveillance in the British Raj', *Book History*, 4 (2001), see pp. 148–9.
46. Robert Darnton, 'Literary surveillance', p. 134.
47. The original name 'Battala' (literally, 'under the banyan tree') stemmed from the location of the first few presses in the vicinity of a real living or once existing banyan tree in the Shobhabazar area in north Calcutta. See Sukumar Sen, *Battalar Chhapa O Chhobi* (Calcutta: Ananda, 1989), p. 44. However, it soon came to stand for the entire area sprawling across the Garanhata, Ahiritala, and Chitpur areas, and even further.
48. See James Long, *Returns Relating to Publications in the Bengali language in 1857*, Selections From the Records of the Bengal Government, vol. xxxii (Calcutta, 1859).
49. This phenomenon has been studied in detail by historians. See e.g., Aparna Basu, *The Growth of Education and Political Development in India, 1898–1920* (New Delhi: Oxford University Press, 1974).
50. Roger Chartier (ed.), *The Culture of Print: Power and the Uses of Print in Early Modern Europe*, trans. Lydia G. Cochrane (Cambridge University Press, 1989); Guglielmo Cavallo and Roger Chartier (eds), *A History of Reading in the West*, trans. Lydia G. Cochrane (Cambridge: Polity Press, 1999).
51. For a fuller discussion of this see Anindita Ghosh, 'Between the Text and Reader: The Experience of Christian Missionaries in Bengal (1800–1850)', in James Raven (ed.), *Free Print and Non-Commercial Publishing Since 1700* (Aldershot: Ashgate Press, 2000), pp. 162–76.
52. *First Report of the Institution for the Encouragement of Native Schools in India* (1817), p. 32.
53. *First Report of the Calcutta School Society* (1818–19).
54. William Adam, 'Third Report' (1838), in Basu, *Reports on the State of Education*, p. 234.
55. See for instance, Tanika Sarkar, *Words to Win: The Making of Amar Jiban; A Modern Autobiography* (New Delhi: Kali for Women, 1999). Rassundari pursued this project with much difficulty in the secrecy of her kitchen, and unknown to her husband and family, by scratching letters from torn

manuscript pages on the blackened walls of her kitchen. Although the more progressive families of the time encouraged learning among women, Rassundari's location in a rural landholding family did not allow her that opportunity.

56. The book mentioned was the *saptakanda* (seventh episode) of the *Valmiki Purana*, a sacred text. But so determined was Rassundari to read it, that she continued to endeavour, and had managed to master the print within a few days. See Rassundari Debi, *Amar Jiban* (Calcutta, 1898), p. 91.

57. *A Memoir of the Serampore Translations for 1813*, p. 21.

58. *Tenth Memoir Respecting the Translations and Editions of the Sacred Scriptures, Conducted by the Serampore Missionaries*, 2nd ed. (London: J. S. Hughes, 1834), pp. 13–14.

59. In an interesting case of reversal, Adam Fox has shown how manuscript ballads in Jacobean England written to be distributed, sung and signposted on walls, replicated the form of the printed ballads, including the two-column lay-out and melodies. See Adam Fox, 'Ballads, libels and popular ridicule in Jacobean England', *Past and Present*, 145 (November 1994), pp. 47–83.

60. 'Popular literature of Bengal', *Calcutta Review*, 13, p. 258. Christian missionaries distributing their tracts in Bengal found books thus being read aloud to groups in shops, open fields, and other places. See *Second Report of the Calcutta Christian Tract and Book Society* (1829), p. 7; and *Fourth Report of the Calcutta Christian Tract and Book Society* (1832), p. 16.

61. *Second Report of the Institution for the Support and Encouragement of Native Schools*, 1818.

62. Mahendranath Dutta, *Atmakahini* (Calcutta, 1924), vol. 1, p. 23.

63. See A. R. Venkatachalapathy, 'Reading practices and modes of reading in colonial Tamilnadu', *Studies in History*, 10, July–December (1994); Pragati Mohapatra, 'The making of a cultural identity: Language, literature and gender in Orissa in the late nineteenth and early twentieth centuries', unpublished Ph.D. thesis, School of Oriental and African Studies, University of London (1997); Farina Mir, 'Imperial policy, provincial practices: Colonial language policy in nineteenth century India', *Indian Economic and Social History Review*, 43:4 (2006), p. 422.

64. These were verbal duels of folk poets in urban settings. Starting with gentle banter and witticisms based on traditional devotional poetry, over time they began to draw on their immediate urban contexts and became more confrontational and abusive in nature.

65. For a rich and evocative account of such street cultures see Sumanta Banerjee, *The Parlour and the Streets: Elite and Popular Culture in Nineteenth Century Calcutta* (Calcutta: Seagull, 1989).

66. Ibid., pp. 103–7.

67. Dineshchandra Sen, *Bangabhasha O Sahitya* (Calcutta, 1896), p. 376.

68. Sumanta Banerjee, *The Parlour and the Streets*, pp. 106–7.

69. Bepin Pal, *Memories of My Life and Times, 1857–1884*, 2 vols (Calcutta: Sanyal & Co., 1932), vol. 1, p. 85.

70. *Sadharani*, 2 Ashad, 5 & 16 Magh, and 4 Falgun, 1286 B.S. (1879); *Sulabh Samachar*, 20 March 1880.

71. *Sadharani*, 27 Poush, 1281 B.S. (1874).

72. Letter to the Editor, *Someprakash* (7 September 1863).

73. *Burdwan District Gazetteer* (Calcutta, 1910), p. 72.

74. *Nadia District Gazetteer* (Calcutta, 1910), pp. 54–5.
75. Apareschandra Mukhopadhyay, *Rangalaye Trish Batshar*, pp. 42–3.
76. See Kathryn Hansen, 'Language, community and the theatrical public: Linguistic pluralism and change in the nineteenth century Parsi theatre', in Blackburn and Dalmia, *India's Literary History*, pp. 62, 64.
77. See Anindita Ghosh, *Power in Print*, Chapter 5.
78. The original play by Dinabandhu Mitra was translated by Michael Madhusudan Dutt in English in 1861, at the request of Rev James Long, who then sent the English version on to authorities in London in the hope that it would prompt sympathetic legislation on their part. But the project boomeranged when Long was accused of sedition, and had to pay a fine of one thousand rupees (dramatically paid up on his behalf by Kaliprasanna Sinha). See Sumanta Banerjee, *The Parlour and the Streets*, pp. 185–7.
79. Kironmoy Raha, *Bengali Theatre* (New Delhi, 1978), pp. 26–8 (cited in Sumanta Banerjee, *The Parlour and the Streets*, p. 187). The actress concerned is the famous Binodini Dasi.
80. These were the *Cha-kar Darpan* and the *Gaekwad Darpan*, respectively.
81. Hemendranath Dasgupta, *The Indian Stage*, vol. 2 (Calcutta, 1946), cited in Rabindranath Bandyopadhyay, *Bangla Natya Niyantroner Itihas* (Calcutta, 1976), p. 17. In 1911, at least 13 dramas were prohibited under the provisions of the Act. See 'Short notes on some proscribed books and a list of prohibited dramas', Paper no. 50, Bundle no. 15 (West Bengal State Archives).
82. Robert Darnton, 'Literary surveillance in the British Raj', pp. 161–7.
83. Ibid., p. 167.

3
Publishing and Translating Hafez Under Empire

Kitty Scoular Datta

The publication history of the Persian poet Hafez, contemporary of Petrarch and Chaucer, in England and India from the late eighteenth century to the early twentieth is a fascinating test-case for Edward Said's theory of western orientalism and illustrates both orientalism's apparently innocent aesthetic surface and its internal complexity in the shifting power-relations between cultures. This involves not only imperial interventions, but the Persianate Asian world's varying appraisal of one of its own unconventional and ambiguous writers, who called himself *rind* and *qalandar*, 'vagabond'. Even so, throughout the Islamic world Hafez was regarded as the supreme poetic craftsman, whom to quote was a sign of the cultured Ottoman or Mughal courtier. So for an Englishman to know and refer to him was a badge of diplomatic ability as well as linguistic skill and informed taste.

Our story begins in Oxford, where the young William Jones (b. 1746), precocious classicist and wide-ranging multi-linguist, in hope of a diplomatic job (maybe an ambassadorship to Ottoman Constantinople), inspected Hafez manuscripts in the Bodleian Library and British Museum, as he studied Arabic and Persian and corresponded with the Continental Persianist Count Reviczky. As he later wrote, it was political and commercial ambition that encouraged the study of a language for which simple scholarship had failed to find public patronage. 'Interest was the charm which gave the languages of the East a real and solid importance'.[1] A Latin version by Reviczky of 15 Hafez poems appeared in the same year, 1771, as Jones's celebrated rendering of his third *ghazal* or ode which burst upon English readers in nine six-line stanzas, six lines to one of Hafez's nine *bayt* or lines,

each composed of two hemistiches, rhyming a a b a c a d a over four
bayt:

> Sweet maid, if thou would'st charm my sight,
> And bid these arms thy neck infold;
> That rosy cheek, that lily hand
> Would give thy poet more delight
> Than all Bokara's vaunted gold,
> Than all the gems of Samarcand.
>
> Boy, let yon liquid ruby flow,
> And bid thy pensive heart be glad,
> Whate'er the frowning zealots say:
> Tell them, their Eden cannot show
> A stream so clear as Rocnabad,
> A bower so sweet as Mosellay.

Jones's first 12 lines equal Hafez's first two, expanding his compressed
hyperboles, for which a modern prose rendering would be: 'If that Turk
of Shiraz wins my heart, I will give Samarqand and Bukhara for her
black mole. [No 'rosy cheek' or 'lily hand' here]. Boy, bring the rest of
the wine! For you will not find in Paradise the banks of Ruknabad river
or the pleasure-walks of Musalla'. The celebration of love and wine
seems entirely secular, calling up the classical Anacreon or Horace, as
Jones and others noted, and banishing solemn thoughts.

> Speak not of fate – ah! change the theme,
> And talk of odours, talk of wine,
> Talk of the flowers that round us bloom:
> 'Tis all a cloud, 'tis all a dream;
> To love and joy thy thoughts confine,
> Nor hope to pierce the sacred gloom.[2]

This poem, which first appeared as the prime illustration of Persian
poetry in Jones's *A Grammar of the Persian Language* (London, 1771) set
flowing a rush of Hafez translations by the East India Company officials
for whom the study of Persian for trade or diplomacy was a requirement, embellished by literary knowledge. As soldier and envoy Sir John
Malcolm noticed of Persian speakers, 'Allusions to works of fancy or fiction are so common in conversation, that you can never enjoy their
society if ignorant of such familiar topics'.[3]

Individuals in Company service had studied the language long before Jones. A striking example was the Highlander James Fraser, posted in 1730 at Surat, the trading-port north of Bombay, whose expertise was in demand for negotiation with local Mughal officials, and who collected manuscripts of Persian poetry, including two of Hafez now in the Bodleian Library.[4] Another was Malcolm, who spouted Persian poetry to Sir Walter Scott in 1811, though his taste was rather for the heroic narrative of Firdawsi, while other Company men read Nizami's tales or Sa'di's moral verses. Such men were not in basic need of Jones's *Grammar* or John Richardson's *A Specimen of Persian Poetry* (1774), as they had already had private tutors or *munshis* to instruct them. In fact it is likely that Jones benefited from the six months in Oxford of I'tisam-al-Din, a Persian Secretary accompanying Company officials to England in 1767, with whom he discussed manuscripts and language, and Jones did recommend learning from a 'native', 'living instructor'.[5]

The presence of such indigenous experts was not exactly suppressed, rather publicly played down. So when the world's first printed edition of Hafez in Persian script appeared in 1791, edited by Mirza Abu Talib Khan, and printed in Calcutta by Aaron Upjohn (Figure 3.1), credit was given to Richard Johnson, an English official with the reputation of a connoisseur, for his patronage of it. Abu Talib Khan, son of a Persian gentleman in the service of the Mughals, and himself a poet, scholar and man of taste, not only drew on a range of manuscripts for his edition, but was sceptical of the value of Jones's *Grammar*, and advocated learning direct from the expert.[6] It is noteworthy that when Samuel Rousseau, formerly British agent at Ispahan, published *The Flowers of Persian Literature* in 1801 (repr. 1805) including 25 earlier translations of Hafez, described as a supplement to Jones's *Grammar* and printed at the Arabic and Persian Press, Spa Fields in London, it was dedicated to Mirza Abu Talib 'as a token of respect and friendship', with a full-page portrait of him.

Even so it was Jones, as founder and President of the Asiatic Society of Bengal in Calcutta, who mediated to Europe a view of Hafez's poetry as mystical and allegorical already established in Sufi commentary, in his essay for the Society, 'On the Mystical Poetry of the Persians and Hindus'.[7] Other British Persianists countered this view, such as Edward Scott-Waring in his *A Tour to Shiraz* (Bombay: Courier Press, 1804), though he did recognise certain Hafez poems as mystical. Indeed elsewhere Jones had accepted the ambiguities of Hafez, and described the literal impression his poems often gave as 'the sentiments of a wild and

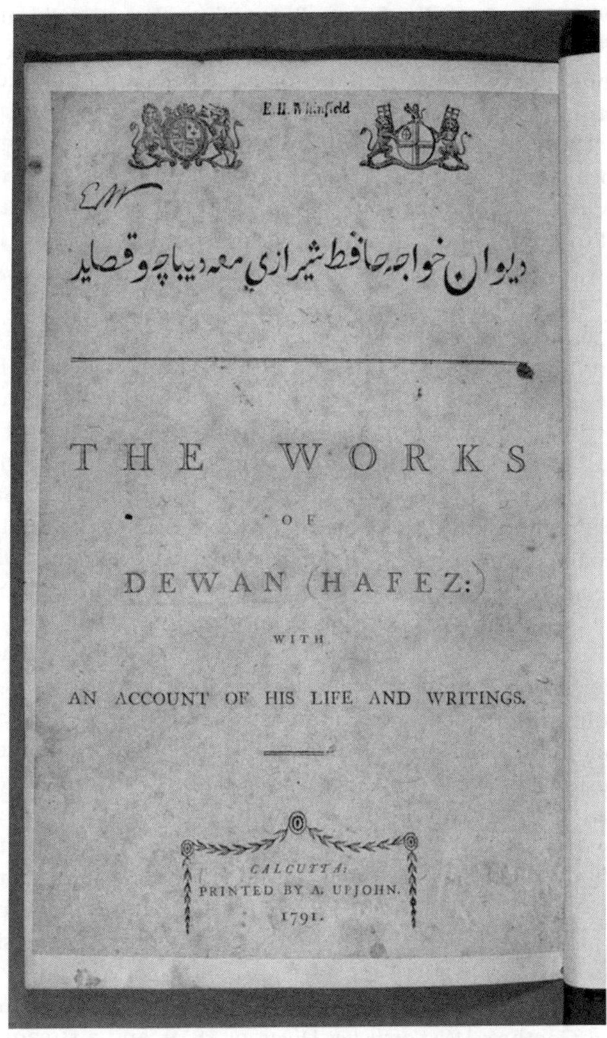

Figure 3.1   Diwan-i-Khwajah Hafez-i Shirazi: The Works of Dewan Hafez; With an account of his life and writings Ed. Mirza Abu Talib Khan (Calcutta: Printed by A. Upjohn, 1791), in Nastaliq type cast by Stuart and Cooper, 1787. Title page. Bodleian Ind. Inst. Persian D237

voluptuous libertinism'. The *Encyclopaedia Iranica* (2003) presents a similar range of view, while it stresses that many of his poems are a direct assault on narrow institutional religion and its professionals.[8] This was the spirit in which the Bengali reformer Rammohun Roy quoted Hafez twice in his Persian essay critical of legalism, *Tohfat 'ul muwahhiddin* (1803–4): 'The disputes of seventy-two sects are to be excused. Since they did not see the truth they took to falsehood'; 'In our Way there is no sin except doing injury to others'.[9] Yet in Indian Sufi circles during Mughal pre-eminence, certain local saints from the sixteenth to the nineteenth century were known for their devotional recitation of Hafez poems in an ecstatic state grounded in a symbolic, not a literal, understanding, and the Emperor Jahangir was known to believe the poems gave him practical spiritual guidance when randomly opened.[10]

When Company cadets read Persian poetry privately with their *munshis*, or at Fort William College in Calcutta or Haileybury College in England, they were entering a Middle Eastern thought-world which had from medieval times spread both west and further east, wherever Islamo-Persian culture and its splendid manuscript tradition had been carried. Influential accounts of European orientalism before and after Said have emphasised its Sanskritic element, and neglected adequate discussion of its Persianate element or its regional vernacular element, which for most officials took precedence because of the need for local communication.[11] More than this, the significance of the *pandits* and *munshis* who were main sources of knowledge have, in post-colonial accounts, been underplayed as 'imperial collaborators', as they were earlier underplayed from notions of western supremacy. Since both before and after 1800, diplomatic relations with Mughal and other Indian territories under Muslim rule were as important as relations with the larger Hindu population, practical necessity combined with literary taste among Company officials, so differentiating their concerns from the philosophical and poetic enquiries of German scholars and writers into grounds for a unified world culture, with a Vedantic slant. Yet this too is to overlook Joseph von Hammer's important complete translation of Hafez into German in 1812–13 (he had met Mirza Abu Talib Khan in Istanbul, and accompanied Napoleon's Egyptian invasion). This deeply influenced Goethe's *West-ostlicher Divan* of 1819, and a stream of other 'imitations' of Persian poetry followed, indebted as much to Rumi, Jami and other lyricists as to Hafez.[12] Edward Said did concentrate on the Middle Eastern aspect of western orientalism, but without giving attention to the ambiguous complexities of interpretation of particular texts in a varying historical climate.

John Nott's dedication of his Hafez translations in 1787 articulated the aims of his generation of Company officials in relation to populations under British governance through military and diplomatic expansion: 'We should draw our knowledge of the laws, the customs, and the manners, under which they live, from the fountain-head. Power may produce obedience; but it is a similar communication of thought, which can reconcile and subdue the mind'.[13] This repeats the terms in which Warren Hastings in 1785 recommended the Charles Wilkins translation of the *Bhagavadgita*, articulating an imperial policy of 'conciliation' to palliate the subjects' sense of defeat.[14] Two errors of judgment are implicit in the 'conciliation' argument – one that any conquered society will under occupation be won over by means of acquired and shared language and literature; and another, that British officialdom will itself embrace this policy wholeheartedly. That it did not is clear in the complaint in 1846 by the Oriental Translation Committee of London's Royal Asiatic Society that devotion to Asian languages and literatures was very much a minority matter: 'Very many manuscript works, which contained useful and curious information, and which might elucidate history, clear up doubts, remove errors, explain different religions, amuse and entertain the mind, and, at all events open to all new subjects for profitable reflection and interesting research, remained neglected, the food of worms, in various collections, and having been conveyed from lands where they were valued and studied, were left about unnoticed and unknown'.[15]

Manuscripts of Hafez contain a varying number of his poems, usually over 500, so he was treated very selectively by most of his translators, such as John Nott, who did versions of only 17 'odes', with the Persian text and a Roman-type transliteration on pages facing his English translations. Nott was a doctor on Company ships plying the eastern trade who retired to Bath and shared knowledge with his friend Charles Fox of Bristol.[16] This student of oriental languages and manuscript-collector had travelled to Caspian Russia where he met Shi'a Muslims who impressed him, and wrote, under the pseudonym of Ahmed Ardabili, a set of Persianate lyric poems, besides doing extensive Hafez translations of his own between 1802 and 1804, now in the John Rylands Library.[17] He was also in touch with John Haddon Hindley who described, compared, and translated 22 poems on the phases of love from a Hafez manuscript in the Chetham Library, Manchester.[18] In other words, as soon as the Hafez bug bit, a group of enthusiastic friends, several of them based in the West Country, shared and published their enthusiasms, and bought and sold manuscripts to each other. Southey, Coleridge and Wordsworth were on the edge of this group – but that is another story.[19] This was a period of random translations in *Miscellanies*, some of which Professor Arberry of Cambridge in 1947 considered good enough to be reprinted in his anthology of Hafez in English.[20] Here is a snatch of a typical John Nott production:

> Hither, boy, a goblet bring
> Be it of wine's ruby spring!
> Bring me one, and bring me two;
> Nought but purest wine will do.
>
> It is wine, boy, which can save
> Even lovers from the grave;
> Old and young alike will say–
> 'Tis the balm that makes us gay …
>
> If the nightingale's rich throat
> Cease the music of its note;
> It is fit, boy, thou should'st bring
> Cups that will with music ring. …[21]

Has any Keats critic noticed that his association of nightingales with wine is Persian?

Anglo-Persian relations after 1800 became intense because of the fear of French or Russian invasion of India from the north-west, and Sir John Malcolm and the Ouseley brothers, Sir Gore and William, went on diplomatic mission to Persia, where they picked up splendid Hafez manuscripts. Sir Gore also possessed a Hafez which had belonged to Nawab Asaf-ud-Daula of Awadh, where he had served as a free-lance military officer, with the Nawab's seal on every page.[22] Malcolm's account of his acquisition of a manuscript from the environs of the poet's tomb in Shiraz emphasises its authenticity, transcribed from the ancient copy that 'was collated from a hundred copies by Sharan Khan and consecrated at the author's tomb by that prince'. Malcolm had his own copy checked against it by 'three Moullahs' whose 'seals are affixed'.[23] Modern Iranian editions have gone to the earliest extant copies, from the early fifteenth century, including one of Malcolm's, dated 1410–11, now in the British Library, and one of its most celebrated Persian items, with a range of texts and miniatures.[24] Lest one should suppose that these books were collected largely for their visual splendour, there is evidence of interest in the spiritual meaning of Hafez in several manuscripts of symbolic commentary once possessed by Company officials and now in the British Library – one made for Malcolm in 1811, five earlier Mughal commentaries owned by John Leyden, Malcolm's Scots linguist-friend, and two belonging to Claudius Rich, who had learnt his first Persian and Arabic in Bristol as a boy from Charles Fox, and became British resident in Baghdad.[25]

The next phase in the publication-history of Hafez under empire belongs to the establishment of colleges and universities in South Asia, and academic study of Persian, by Muslims and Parsis certainly, but not exclusively. From 1828 onwards appeared a stream of Persian-script editions, some of them with prose versions in English, prepared for both British officials and Indian undergraduates – this in spite of Macaulay's denigration of oriental literatures in his 1835 Education Minute. Even so editions appeared in Bombay, Calcutta, Lucknow, Kanpur and Lahore, covering the whole range of Hafez poems, sometimes in groups of 50 with a crib.[26]

Nor was the study of Persian poetry in India confined to the Muslim or Parsi communities. Lal Behari Gupta, a Bengali studying for an Indian Civil Service post in 1868–71, read Persian literature at University College, London.[27] Even more significantly, the Bengali poet Rabindranath Tagore wrote of his father Devendranath that 'in his heart the poems of Hafiz and the *Upanishads* were in confluence'. Devendranath, in the spirit of Mughal Sufism and Brahmo religious reform, had quoted him in Persian with a Bengali translation in his autobiography at points of particular importance, such as family loss of financial stability ('In that desire, may there be no other prayer than the prayer for lightning – if lightning were to fall and destroy my hoard and harvest, then I should not be surprised') and uncertainty about his future, as well as his sense of divine presence during mountain travels and other times of insight ('henceforth I shall radiate light from my heart upon the world, since I have reached the sun and darkness has vanished').[28] That generation's sense of a composite south Asian literary culture, drawing on both ancient Sanskrit spiritual texts and similar tendencies in Persian poetry and Mughal religious thinking, especially Prince Dara Shikoh's *The Confluence of Oceans* (owned and partly translated in early eighteenth-century Surat by James Fraser) was not stifled by imperial educational trends.[29]

The first complete English translation of Hafez in 1891, by the soldier-translator of the Raj, H. Wilberforce Clarke, incorporating in the English prose text a mystical interpretation dependent on a famous Turkish Sufi commentary, was still considered by the great twentieth-century Indian poet Iqbal as valuable, as was H. Brockhaus's edition of the Persian text (Leipzig, 1854), also with Sudi's commentary.[30] The first printed edition in Persia itself appeared only in 1838. And in South Asia editions have continued to appear – in 1988 a scholarly edition by

Nadir Ahmed from New Delhi, and in 2000 an Urdu version by Khalid Hamid from Karachi.

When Sirdar Iqbal Ali Shah, friend of the ruler of Afghanistan, published *The Oriental Caravan: A Revelation of the Soul and Mind of Asia* (London, 1933), to represent Hafez he chose some of Gertrude Bell's translations. They had first appeared in 1897, and again in 1928.[31] One of Bell's uncles was a diplomat to the Ottoman Empire, and after studying history at Oxford she had strong archaeological interests, learned Persian in London and Tehran, and eventually settled in post-Ottoman Baghdad as a searcher for antiquities. Professor Arberry, from his mid-twentieth-century vantage, considered her selected versions of Hafez the best ever into English. This is due in part to her choice of a more spacious seven- or eight-lined rhyming stanza, usually iambic, though with an occasional Browningesque anapaestic rhythm and turn of phrase:

> The rose has flushed red, the bud has burst,
> And drunk with joy is the nightingale -
> Hail, Sufis! Lovers of wine, all hail!
> For wine is proclaimed to a world athirst,
> Like a rock your repentance seemed to you,
> Behold the marvel! of what avail
> Was your rock, for a goblet has cleft it in two!
>
> Bring wine for the king, and the slave at the gate
> Alike for all is the banquet spread,
> And drunk and sober are warmed and fed.
> When the feast is done, and the night grows late,
> And the second door of the tavern gapes wide,
> The low and the mighty must bow the head,
> 'Neath the archway of life to meet what … outside?[32]

Bell was much more varied and adventurous in her roving choice of poems, with a particular talent for matching poem to form, well-heard in a poem in an idiom resembling Petrarch's which links with the early death of the man she loved, a diplomat posted in Tehran:

> When I am dead, open my grave and see
> The cloud of smoke that rises round thy feet:
> In my dead heart the fires still burn for thee;
> Yea, the smoke rises from my winding-sheet!

> Ah, come, Beloved, for the meadows wait
> Thy coming, and the thorn bears flowers instead
> Of thorns, the cypress fruit, and desolate
> Bare winter from before thy steps has fled.
>
> Hoping within some garden ground to find
> A red rose soft and sweet as thy soft cheek,
> Through every meadow blows the western wind,
> Through every garden he is fain to seek.
> Reveal thy face, that the whole world may be
> Bewildered by thy radiant loveliness;
> The cry of man and woman comes to thee,
> Open thy lips and comfort their distress.[33]

This is hardly the vagabondish tone of the *qalandar*, the flouter of convention who is Hafez's most recognisable persona. Something of that persona passed on to India's Persian and Urdu poets, particularly to Muhammad Iqbal, who wrote in both languages, in his early poems the questioner in Sufic vein of conventional pieties. Yet by the time he wrote *Payam-i-Mashriq* (1923), his preface, surveying the influence of Hafez on German poetry since Goethe, expresses his doubt over the decline in European life and letters, as he put it, 'the danger of the domination of that enervating and escapist Persian ease and indolence which can hardly differentiate between emotion and thought'.[34] In his view, if Europe had given way to materialism and love of expansionist power, Asia had declined into inactive lethargy. So Hafez, however much his poetry has been traditionally admired, is the worst model for both life and art. Yet Iqbal did not avoid the metaphorical language of Hafez in which he and his audience were soaked, but rather gave it a new activist and forward-looking turn, for example in both the form and imagery of his Persian *ghazals Zabur-i-'Ajam* (1927).[35] Earlier, by wittily calling Kemal Ataturk the reformist Turkish president 'the Turk of Shiraz, who has ravished the heart of Tabriz and Kabul' [that is to say, admired by Iran and Afghanistan], he turned a celebrated love-poem into a political statement of pan-Islamic solidarity ('The rise of Islam', 1923). The same poem ended with a couplet taken straight from Hafez:

> Come, in order that we may strew roses and pour wine into the cup
> Let's split the roof of the sky, and find a new way of doing things.

He continued this kind of ingenious misquotation in support of newness in an ironic epigram of 1923, 'To England', praising Asia for drinking from the western cup of national self-respect, and becoming intoxicated with a new self-consciousness. So the nightingale's love of the rose as a metaphor for inspiration is transformed into a political statement of longing for the garden of national freedom learned from England, the land of the rose:

> The rose's scent itself had first the garden's pathway shown.
> How else the nightingale a garden's presence could have known?[36]

Iqbal, like Rabindranath Tagore, was a shrewd critic of militaristic and imperial nationalism and well aware of the India-wide call for *swaraj* as inner discipline and social reform, so his personal reading and modernist transcreation of Hafez is an index of world-transforming post-imperial changes of spirit.[37] Yet his universalism had a Muslim League pan-Islamic perspective, whereas Tagore's, in Brahmo or Sufi mode, was one crossing specific communal boundaries in pursuit of what he called a 'confluence', a conjunction of differences necessary to creativity.

Notes

1. *The Works of Sir William Jones in Six Volumes* (London, 1799), II, 126, from *A Grammar of the Persian Language*, 'Preface'; [Count Reviczky] *Specimen Poeseos Persicae, sive Muhammedis Schems-Eddini notioris agnomine Haphyzi Ghazelae, sive Odae* (Vienna, 1771), bilingual edition (Persian/Latin) of 15 odes of Hafez (or 'Hafiz', as he was often spelled).
2. Jones, *Works*, II, 141–6, presents each *bayt* in 2 lines of Persic script followed by 2 lines in Roman transliteration, with English prose version, 242–3, and verse, 244–6. *Poems, consisting of Translations from the Asiatick Languages*, repeats this Hafez lyric, with Roman-type transliteration of Persian text at foot of each page, in *Works*, IV, 449–52. Evidence that Jones translated with one eye on Reviczky's Latin is his use of the word 'Fate' (*arcana fati*).
3. [Sir John Malcolm] *Sketches from Persia* (1827), I, 128.
4. James Fraser (1703–1754) is referred to as Persian translator at Surat in BL. India Office Records G/36/24 (1739), 69–72. Bodleian Fraser Persian MSS 71 and 72 are of Hafez.
5. I' tisam-al-din, *Shigarf-nama-i wilayat* (written 1785, Bodleian MS Caps. Or. A.8, fol. 187) refers to his visit to Oxford after arrival in Britain, 1767, as Archibald Swinton's Persian Secretary, and meeting with William Jones, who showed him there 'numerous books in Persian and Arabic'. See Gulfishan Khan, *Indian Muslim Perceptions of the West during the Eighteenth Century* (Karachi: Oxford University Press, 1998), 72–78, 248–9.
6. *Diwan-i-Khwajah Hafez-i Shirazi: The Works of Dewan Hafez; with an account of his life and writings* (Calcutta: Printed by A. Upjohn, 1791), in Nastaliq type cast by Stuart and Cooper, 1787 (Graham Shaw, *Printing in Calcutta to 1800* [1981], 65, 145). Mirza Abu Talib Khan (1752–1806) wrote in Persian his

Travels ... in Asia, Africa, and Europe (1799–1803), tr. Charles Stewart (London, 1810; enlarged, 1814). See G. Khan, *Indian Muslim Perceptions*, 95–100, 249–54.

7. Jones, *Works*, I, 445–61.

8. *Encyclopaedia Iranica*, XI, fasc. 5 (2003), 'Hafez'. Also J. Christoph Burgel, 'Ambiguity: A Study ... in the Poetry of Hafiz', ed. M. Gluntz & Burgel, *Intoxication Earthly and Heavenly* (Bern, 1991). All references are to the standard modern text, ed. Muhammad Qazvini & Qasim Ghani (Tehran, 1941; hereafter referred to as QG).

9. *The English Works of Rammohun Roy*, ed. J. C. Ghose (4 vols, 1906; repr. New Delhi, 1982), IV, 941–58, 'A Present to the Believers in One God, being a translation of *Tuhfatul Muwahiddin*', 951 (QG, clxxxiv); 957 (QG, lxxvi).

10. Examples are in Sayyid Athar Abbas Rizvi, *A History of Sufism in India* (2 vols, New Delhi, 1978), I, 238, II, 114, 131, 314; Muhammed Umar, *Islam in Northern India during the Eighteenth Century* (New Delhi, 1993), 68.

11. Examples are Raymond Schwab, *The Oriental Renaissance: Europe's Discovery of India and the East, 1680–1880* (Paris, 1950; tr., New York: Columbia University Press, 1984); J. J. Clarke, *Oriental Enlightenment: The Encounter Between Asian and Western Thought* (London, 1997); Richard King, *Orientalism and Religion* (London, 1999) But see Farhang Jahanpour, 'Western Encounters with Persian Sufi Literature', *The Heritage of Sufism III*, ed. L. Lewisohn (Oxford, 1999), 28–59.

12. Joseph Hammer[-Purgstall], *Der Diwan von Mohammed Schamsed-din Hafis* (2 vols, Stuttgart and Tubingen, 1812, 1813), has 576 poems, with Latin analogues noted. Johann Wolfgang von Goethe, *West-ostlicher Divan*, tr. John Whaley as *Poems of the West and East* (Bern, 1998), introduction by K. Mommsen, includes some of Goethe's commentary. G. Khan, *Perceptions*, 252.

13. 'Dedication to the Duke of Richmond' by John Nott, *Ketab-i Lalehzar az Divan-i Hafez: Selected Odes, from the Persian Poet Hafez* (London, 1787), ii.

14. Warren Hastings, Preface to *The Bhagavad-Geeta*, tr. Charles Wilkins (London, 1785), on 'the cultivation of languages and science', which 'conciliates distant affections' and trains rulers in 'benevolence'.

15. Account of the formation in 1828 of Oriental Translation Committee, in Sir Gore Ouseley, *Biographical Notices of Persian Poets* (London: Oriental Translation Fund, 1846), ccxx.

16. John Nott, *Selected Odes, from ... Hafez* (1787); ODNB.

17. [Charles Fox], *Aks-i-Partaw: Poems, Containing the Plaints, Consolations, and Delights of Ahmed Ardebeili* (Bristol, 1797); John Rylands Library Persian MSS 355–56 (1802–04).

18. John Haddon Hindley, *Persian Lyrics, or Scattered Poems from the Diwan-i-Hafiz* (London: Oriental Press, 1800).

19. See Kitty Scoular Datta, 'Before the Deluge', *Times Literary Supplement*, 20 August 2004, 114–15.

20. Arthur. J. Arberry, *Fifty Poems of Hafiz* (Cambridge University Press [1947]).

21. Nott, Ode 2, reproduced Rousseau, 167–8. William Ouseley, *Persian Miscellanies: An Essay to Facilitate the Reading of Persian Manuscripts* (London, 1795) abounds in references to Persian nightingales, marked up by bibliophile Francis Douce in his copy, now in Bodleian Library.

22. Sir Gore Ouseley, *Persian Poets* (1846), 41–2. Bod. Ouseley MS 148, dated 1439, is one of several Hafez MSS.

23. J. W. Kaye, *The Life and Correspondence of Major General Sir John Malcolm* (2 vols, 1856), I, 128. Claudius Rich's Hafez MS, BL Or. 2195, notes similar checking of text at Hafez's tomb by his secretary, 1821; BL 7759 is Rich's 1451 Hafez, written for Shahrukh.

24. *Encyclopaedia Iranica* XI, 5, refers to use of Malcolm's MS, now BL Add. MS 27261.

25. BL Add. 27264 (Malcolm), BL Add 7765 (Rich). Leyden's Mughal commentaries are listed by H. Ethe, *Catalogue of the Persian Manuscripts in the India Office Library* (Oxford, 1903), nos. 1269–74.

26. British Library has educational editions, Bombay 1829, 1886, 1889, 1891, 1895; Kanpur 1831; Calcutta 1858, 1881; Lucknow 1876, 1886; Poona 1896; Lahore 1921.

27. Information from Gupta's great-grandson Sunanda Datta Ray.

28. *Selected Letters of Rabindranath Tagore*, ed. Krishna Dutta and Andrew Robinson (Cambridge University Press, 1997), 283, to Brajendranath Seal, 1921. *The Autobiography of Maharshi Devendranath Tagore*, tr. Satyendranath Tagore & Indira Devi (Calcutta, 1909), 65, 104–5, 106, 127, 133(2), 135 quotes Hafez's Persian (QG, cccxlv, 6–8; cccxlii, 5–6; lxxxvi, 13–14; v, 1–2; ccxxiii1, 9–10; lxvii, 1–2; xlvi, 3–4; lxxxvii, 5–6). *The Golden Book of Rammohun Roy* (Calcutta, 1997), 155, records Devendranath's youthful witness of Rammohun's daily prayers using Sanskrit, Arabic, Persian verses.

29. Bodleian MS Fraser 260, *Majma'ul Bahrain* (Persian); MS Fraser 274*, f. 50, translation.

30. H. Wilberforce Clarke, tr., *The Divan, Written in the Fourteenth Century by Khwaja Shamsud-Din Muhamad-i-Hafiz-i-Shirazi* (2 vols, London, 1891, repr. 1974), noted by Anne Marie Schimmel, *Gabriel's Wing ... the Religious Ideas of Muhammad Iqbal* (Leiden, 1963; Karachi, 2000), 339.

31. Gertrude Lowthian Bell, *Poems from the Divan of Hafiz* (London, 1897, 1928).

32. In Arberry, p. 91 (QG, xxv).

33. In Arberry, pp. 127–8 (QG, ccxxxiii); H. V. F. Winstone, *Gertrude Bell* (London, 1975), 33–7.

34. Sir Muhammad Iqbal, 'Preface' to *Payam-i-Masriq* (1923), tr. Syed Abbas Ali Jaffery as *The Moonbeams over the East* (Karachi, 1996), 58–66.

35. Arthur J. Arberry, tr., *Persian Psalms (Zabur-I 'Ajam)* (Lahore, 1948).

36. D. J. Matthews, *Iqbal: A Selection of the Urdu Verse* (London, 1993), 168; Jaffery, tr., 133; Schimmel, *Iqbal*, 46, 63–5, 71, 77, 339–40.

37. On Iqbal's vision of South Asia, Ayesha Jalal, *Self and Sovereignty: Individual and Community in South Asian Islam Since 1850* (London and New York, 2000), 166–79; Mushirul Hasan, *Islam in the Subcontinent* (New Delhi, 2002), 198, 347. Rabindranath Tagore's critique of empire includes *Nationalism* (London, 1917).

4

Missionary Writing and the Self-Fashioning of Assamese Cultural Identity in Colonial India: Revisiting the Past, Understanding the Present

Hemjyoti Medhi

I. Prologue

On 27 February 2006, the state government of Assam took a far-reaching and controversial decision. It changed the spelling and thus the accentuation and pronunciation of the state's name from its conventionally accepted English-influenced form to 'Asom' in order to 're-christen itself' to convey a more authentic-sounding identity. The decision was a response to an appeal in the literary magazine *Goriyoshi* by Chandra Prasad Saikia, Assamese author and former president of the Assam Sahitya Sabha, the premier literary association of Assam, who had argued that 'It is perfectly desirable that the name by which a particular people identifies their State should also be the name of that State for all purposes.'[1] Immediately the Association of Tai–Ahoms, linear successors to the Ahom kingdom that had ruled large parts of present day Assam for some 600 years (1228–1826 CE), prior to its accession by the British, issued a press release opposing the move, adding that they were in favour of retaining the anglicized name. Several other bodies followed suit in this act of disavowal.[2]

II. The nation and its Books

In an eloquent and largely convincing keynote opening chapter to Volume 1 of *Books Without Borders*, the scholar and printer Sydney Shep calls for a paradigm shift in the prevailing methodologies of the National Book History projects which, she argues, tend to reinforce the dominant ideology of the nation state. In this process the book – an otherwise neutral 'commercial commodity' – becomes a signifier of movements, ideologies, and of forms of hegemony and power that unproblematically reproduce existing hierarchies rather than challenging them.[3] Such a repudiation of existing indices of the nation as a category for the study of book history is understandable. It may, however, prove problematic in certain contexts precisely because of its invocation of the artificiality of national geographical boundaries. To some ears such an anticipatory celebration of a nation-less or border-less world will sound liberating and welcome. It possesses nonetheless extra implications when applied to particular local frames. In certain contexts it may even be viewed as reinforcing the very hegemony of transnational capitalism in production and dissemination of which it apparently complains. In my view there are other priorities that need to be heard alongside this globalized argument. Instead of dissolving the nation as a category of enquiry from book history, there is a counter-balancing necessity to intervene in the ways the nation has been formulated in postcolonial studies. This is especially the case with the influential binaries set up by Edward Said in his seminal study *Orientalism* and elsewhere between the colonized and the colonizer, black and white, nationalism and colonialism.

A vital case in point is Assam, in the north-eastern region of India. Here there have been historically, and are at present, pressing questions of culture and identity each of which is intertwined with the politics of insurgency and immigration. An informed consideration of these factors should not lead us to write off the nation as such. The need here is quite otherwise: constantly to reinvent the concept of nationhood with an eye to bearings both nuanced and complex. Book history and the transportation of print medium, as it happens, throw an unusually sharp light on this narrative. This paper accordingly represents an attempt to explore a particular interdisciplinary terrain defined by book history, missionary writings, colonial power structures and nationalism, through two particular parameters. First there are the publications, letters, writings, memoranda etc., of the American Baptist Mission in Assam during the colonial period. Second, and related to it, is the self-fashioning of Assamese cultural nationalism in nineteenth-century colonial India. It is my contention that 'print capitalism' and the production of books in colonial Assam are inseparable from the history of the 'celestial mission' of the American Baptist Mission, the layered power structures of colonial administration, the prevalence of the Bengali language in the schools and courts of the province, and the question of linguistic and cultural affirmation by the newly Western educated Assamese intelligentsia.

The present study tells the neglected story of the self-fashioning of Assamese identity, independent and unique, and examines the claim of a language and culture repeatedly threatened from neighboring Bengal. It acknowledges tangentially the Saidian view of Orientalism as 'a western style for dominating, restructuring and having authority over the Orient'.[4] It likewise acknowledges variations or redefinitions of this hegemonic relationship in terms of 'hybridity,[5] 'transaction',[6] or 'consumption'.[7] Lastly it responds to the well-known criticism of Said voiced in 1992 by the Indian critic Ajijaz Ahmad for his poignant silence about the ways in which Western texualities may have been 'received, accepted, modified, challenged, overthrown or reproduced by the intelligentsias of the colonized countries'.[8]

I mean to extend Ahmad 's position to accommodate an instance of cultural nationalist self-fashioning bearing powerful witness to the agency of the native intelligentsia in fashioning a linguistic and cultural identity in the face, not merely of the Western colonizer, but of another native group, the Bengali. In his book *The Nation and Its Fragments*, Partha Chatterjee has issued a challenge to the monolithic stereotype of nationalism stemming from Benedict Anderson's earlier, and highly influential, study *Imagined Communities*. Anderson's paradigm, for all its apparent subtlety, had advanced a fundamentally monolithic model of the evolution of national consciousness and it relation to print capitalism. Chatterjee by contrast champions forms of cultural production that separate the inner from the outer, the private from the public domain. He calls for the study of nationalism as a 'cultural construct' that enables the colonized to conceptualize their difference and autonomy. He adds that this 'hypothesis for nationalist thought' represents 'a different discourse, yet one that is dominated by another'.[9] It is my further contention that the impediment of binaries remains even in Chatterjee's informative hypothesis, since the interpretation of nationalist expressions as cultural constructs opens up a far more radical way of exploring them, unconstrained by the straight jacketed discourse of 'orientalism'. The additional question is this: if nationalist thought is a cultural construct, can we locate expressions of such thought in the 'othering' of a different native group rather than the colonizer? The assertion of a unique Assamese identity in the face of the hegemony of Bengal may well be a case in point.

III. Mission (im)possible[10]

This study postulates certain dialectical possibilities that may help to refine discussion of such issues. In the process of decolonization, I believe, new categories come into play and, along with them, recognition of challenges once encountered by the very missionary writing and colonial education that has come under such severe attack in recent times. In the context of Assam, the displacement of the hegemony of the Bengalis was achieved by invocation of a 'unique', 'different' and self-sufficient Assamese language, bolstered by claims of a literary tradition specific to Assam: first in its spiritual writings (that is in the *Bhakti* cult) and, second, in its secular writings such as its *buranji* or historical chronicles, published for the most part in the region's first monthly 'paper' *Orunodoi* (1846) by the American Baptist missionaries in the Mission Press at Sibsagor in Upper Assam.

Through such means missionary writing and associated activities played an essential role in the salvaging of language and culture.[11] The reputation of the missionaries has of course been subjected over the decades to a sort of seesawing effect. The traditional understanding of the missionary work had been as an *'abadan'*, a gift or contribution. Several recent outbursts in postcolonial studies have excoriated this easy acceptance of the myths of enlightenment as a colonial legacy artfully presented as a version of 'modernity'. Thus, whereas the politics of Christian missions scarcely used to be challenged, the new consensus implicates almost all missionary work within the framework of orientalism invoked by Said and his followers, weaving a continuous narrative of the complicity of missionaries with the colonial administration. This very view, however, ignores instances where the missionaries came to be regarded by their political overlords as troublemakers who constantly interfered with 'native life'. Take, as just one instance, the following newspaper item. 'News of a terrible massacre of British troops at Vellore ... the outbreak was seen as a result of missionary interference with the natives ... As a result of this, the Governor wrote a strong letter to the Serampore missionaries demanding the immediate closing of the Calcutta Chapel and the cessation of all publications that aimed at the conversion of the native.'[12]

Now while I accept that the ideology of the 'civilizing mission' needs to be located in colonial discourse, it is equally important to try and understand the contribution made by the missions to shifting power relations, together with forms of agency and appropriation. I refer to the vigorous debate in missionary writings concerning the relative merits of Bangla and Assamese, conducted via letters to colonial government and memoranda by local people. By such means alternative discursive practices and choices were played out and contested. The debate produced a spate of relevant publications. Among them were the first Biblical translation into Assamese, *Dharmapustaka* (1813), William Robinson's

Grammar of the Assamese Language (1839), Mrs. H. B. L. Cutter's two-part *A Vocabulary and Phrases* (1841), Nathan Brown's *Grammatical Notices on the Assamese Language* (1849), Miles Bronson's *A Spelling Book and Vocabulary in English, Assamese, Singpho and Naga* (1839), *A Dictionary in Assamese and English* (1867) and the first monthly 'paper' in Assamese *Orunodoi* (1846). Every one of these played a part in shaping a coherent linguistic category and homogenous cultural identity for the Assamese in print.

The initial steps in this process were taken by the British Baptist Missionary Society's station in Danish-administered Serampore, who published a New Testament in Assamese, the *Dharmapustaka*, in 1813. Thirteen yeas later the Yandaboo Treaty of 1826 facilitated the British annexation of Assam. As Assam was absorbed into an extended Bengal Presidency, Bengali was established in 1837 as the language of the court, schools and administrative correspondence, much to the irritation of later Assamese intellectuals. Phookan wrote in his *Observations on the Administration of the Province of Assam* in 1853, 'Under the Provisions of Act XXIX of 1837, the Vernacular language of a District was directed to be used in the courts. We find, however, with regret, that notwithstanding the provisions of this wholesome law, a foreign language, viz., the Bengallee, has been introduced into the courts of Assam'.[13] Printed at the American Baptist Mission Press at Sibsagor, his book *A Few Remarks on the Assamese Language and on Vernacular Education in Assam* is referred to in this debate again and again, the patronage of the missionaries remaining integral to the formulation of his claim. This book was possibly the first in English by an Indian published in by the Sibsagor Mission Press in Assam. Its title is itself suggestive. Reading it, one realizes just why the nation remains so integral to book history, even if it is not always the nation as rehearsed in the postcolonial field. Nonetheless, it would be politically naïve to suggest that the philanthropy of such ventures rose above the politics of mission. For the Baptists the spreading of the Christian message was all-important: they saw the imposition of Bangla as a deterrent to a successful evangelization of the Assamese people. Miles Bronson, for example, drew on the precedent of the great Vaisnavite saint of Assam, Sankardev, who had successfully connected with the masses by transcreating Sanskrit text into the vernacular. In a letter to the editor of *Friend of India* on May 25, 1855 he wrote: 'The Mission ... found ... that the employment of educated Bengali assistants and the use of Bengali books are nearly useless. The Assamese don't really understand them.'[14] The mission at Sadiya was seen as a launch pad for a further mission to Shans, contributing to an eventual, and wider, 'celestial empire'. Language, and authentic local language at that, was to be its vehicle.

The battle was now to confront the administration directly. When in 1853 Judge Moffat Mills was sent to investigate the administration of Assam, he was approached directly by the missionaries. In an appendix to his resulting report Mills included a letter by A. H. Danford, a missionary from Gowhatty, dated the 19th of July 1853, vindicating the use of the vernacular in elementary teaching. Danford opined, 'That the Bengalee should be an impediment in acquiring a knowledge of the sciences is evident from the nature of the case; moreover this knowledge when acquired will lie as foreign material in the mind, and being unnaturalized will never be appropriated for the good of the country'.[15] Mills' conclusion ran thus: 'I think we made a great mistake in directing that all business should be transacted in Bengalee and that Assamese must acquire it.'[16] Another such initiative was a memorandum submitted to George Campbell in March 1872, by Miles Bronson and over two hundred high-ranking Assamese. Eventually on 19 April 1873 a Resolution was taken by the Bengal Government's Education Department noting that 'Since Mr. Mills and Anundaram Phookan wrote in Assam, more or less agitation has gone on time to time for the recognition of Assamese as the language of the courts'. The then commissioner Col. Henry Hopkins is said to have commented: 'the Seebsagur Missionaries to whom we are chiefly indebted for the agitation in favor of the creation of the Assamese language'.[17] It would be disingenuous to suggest that the missionaries alone were responsible for the fact that Assamese was thus reinstated. Rajel Saikia for one has argued that administrative convenience was a weightier consideration.[18] Despite this caveat, the role that the missionaries played in shaping Assamese nationalist vocabulary in the nineteenth century is a story well worth the telling.

Anglicization or sanskritization?[19]

The history of the reconstruction of the Assamese language became ever more energized once the newly educated Assamese took up the project. The missionaries had maintained the vocabulary and pronunciation of earlier Assamese texts. In their monthly paper the *Orunodoi* for example they maintained the nuances of colloquial everyday speech.[20] Bronson wrote in his Foreword to *A Dictionary in Assamese and English* (1867), 'The system of Orthography adopted in this work is that of Jaduram Barua a learned Assamese pundit which it is believed much better corresponds with the actual pronunciation of the people than any other system met with'. He added that 'unfortunately an impression has prevailed that Assamese and Bengali are identical or nearly so ... The higher class, seeing their own language ignored, strive to obtain a sufficient knowledge of Bengali to fill Government Offices; but they never feel at home in the language ... Both Assamese and Bengali borrow largely from Sanskrit but the grammars are quite different'. He went on to say, 'A very prominent characteristic of this language is the pronunciation of Sanskrit letters like the guttural h or kh, corresponding with the Greek *chi*, a sound unknown in Bengali.'[21]

However, missionary printers preferred to adapt Bengali script with a modicum of modification rather than to create a fresh font for Assamese. This is one of the reasons that Assamese continues to be regarded popularly as a dialect of Bangla to this very day. The repercussions were to recur in the twenty-first century in a completely different guise, one that was equally pivotal for redefining Assamese nationality. It was only in 1900 that *Hemkosha or An Etymological Dictionary of the Assamese Language* evidenced an elaborate attempt at locating and standardizing Assamese on Sankskrit foundations. In it its editor Barua, in conformity with the views of an increasing number of educated Assamese people, rooted his dictionary in grammatical subsoil in keeping with other Sanskrit cognates such as Bengali and Oriya. For example he reinforced three different forms of the phoneme ' b a', even though the Assamese today do not distinguish between these three varieties. (Nor indeed do they pronounce it in the manner of most other Sanskrit cognates, being a glottal fricative in Assamese.) The Assamese script in earlier manuscripts had mostly 'a'.[22] But the *Hemkosha* began to make distinctions not always maintained in old Assamese texts.[23] In refutation of the familiar argument that the missionaries were largely responsible for the Sanskritization of many Indian languages,[24] I would like to cite this as one case where initial attempts by missionaries to retain the common speech patterns found in old manuscripts were reviewed by growing numbers of newly educated indigenous scholars.

There were political reasons for this shift from an earlier antagonism to Bengal to an attempt at the turn of the century to assimilate with the mainstream Indian language family. It can most helpfully be construed against the backdrop of the nationalist movement once the geographical mapping of colonial India came under scrutiny from the nationalist press. The Assamese intelligentsia readily co-opted a standard used in other Sanskrit cognates like Oriya and Bangla without really considering the speech/written dichotomy. In another context Jayeeta Sarma argues that 'Such attempts at affiliating to larger Indic Tradition were an integral part of fitting in with the power realities of the British-ruled subcontinent, within which Assam was being formally incorporated for the first time.'[25] They can further be contextualized in the parallel context of the literary cultures and their formation in a multilingual country like India. Here the hegemony of Sanskrit has either been actively denounced or carefully incorporated in the claims of a linguistic culture by different regional languages at different points in time, precisely in the interests of shaping a national literary tradition. In the case of Tamil, as Norman Cutler explains, 'the term "Tamil Renaissance" is often applied to the period beginning in the later half of the nineteenth century when Tamil literary culture was altered through the recovery, editing and publication of early Tamil classics. This period coincides with the development of a Dravidianist political agenda, popular among certain sectors of the Tamil population, that emphasized the antiquity of the Tamil civilization and, most importantly, its essential independence from Sanskritic culture'.[26] In Kannada by contrast, according to D. R. Nagaraj, 'The idea was to build a common area of cultural referentiality that could integrate Kannada into the complementary circles of the Sanskrit cosmopolitan cultural order.'[27] And as Sudipta Kaviraj argues in his essay 'The Two Histories of Literary Cultures in Bengal': 'As British rule extended westwards, extensive Hindustani speaking territories were added to the Bengal Presidency. Bengalis duly developed subimperialist delusions about themselves and considered other groups within the larger territory of the presidency their natural inferiors ... Other linguistic groups could regard the lighted circles of Bangla literary culture with admiration or resentment, but they were not serious interlocutors. The delineation of the *cultural* boundaries of Bengal was the work of not the colonial state but of the new Bengali intelligentsia'.[28] Though Kaviraj doesn't explore the example of the Assamese, the educated people of Assam undeniably came to regard Bengali 'subimperialism' precisely in these terms. The antagonism to Bengali found expression in various ways, yet the tenor of the argument consistently retained that of 'othering'. In a series of letters written to *Orunodoi*, 'a prominent Assamese' wrote about the 'Duties of parents towards their children' to protect them against the sinful influences of Bengali culture. 'Earlier these sins were limited to only a few numbers, when there was hardly any Bengali around. Now that these people have come in hordes our youth have gone astray and have started indulging in sins such as drinking, prostituting, treachery, false litigation etc. The native Assamese has been spoilt by his evil companion.'[29] This process of demonizing the Bengali continued even after the expulsion of the

Bengali language from courts and schools in 1873. It persisted well into the twentieth century in popular discourse, up to and including the Assam Agitation of the 1970s and 1980s.

IV. *Asom Buranji*: a nationalized history

The establishment or 'construction' of a language by the missionaries of which we have spoken above might be read as instrumental towards a religiously conceived 'celestial empire', were it not for its nurturing of one of the key elements of nationalist consciousness. The claims of a distinctive Assamese history were themselves first aired in the pages of the journal *Orunodoi*. Partha Chatterjee has delineated the invention of a tradition of nationalist history as crucial to the conceptual framing of the nation. Moreover, Bankim's celebrated outcry 'We have no history. We must have a history ...' has found echoes in selective appropriation of a Hindu past into the myths of Indian Nationalism. It was in August 1850 that the *Orunodoi* first published an item entitled '*Purani Asom Buranji*: Ancient Assamese History – No. 1', beginning with the interesting announcement: the mission had come across some original historical writings of the Ahoms in the shape of *Ahom Buranji*, a text it was now intent on 'reproducing ... in its original form'.[30] As I have already explained in the opening paragraph to the present chapter, the Ahoms were a Tai-Shan people, that is an originally Tai-speaking group who later took on the Assamese language and ruled in Upper Assam for 600 years before the British annexation that merged Ahom-ruled and non-Ahom ruled areas into one. As Sanjib Barua has argued, the geographical mapping of colonial Assam by no means corresponded to the pre-colonial Ahom kingdom.[31] Despite this discrepancy, the local history of the erstwhile kingdom of the *Ahoms* was readily appropriated by this act of publication into the greater history of colonial *Assam*. What is more, the publication of '*Purani Asom buranji*' in a series of entries over succeeding months would prove indispensable to claims of a 'unique' Assamese history that were to fit in so well to a narrative of nation.[32]

In his *A Few Remarks on the Assamese Language and Vernacular Education in Assam* Anandaram Dhekial Phukan wrote: 'In no other department of literature do the Assamese appear to have been more successful than in History ... In 1829 Haliram Dhekial Phukan printed and published in the Bengali Language a brief compilation from the Buranjis; and in 1844 Radhanath Bor Borua and Kassinath Tamuli Phukon published at the American Mission Press, a somewhat more comprehensive work on the History of Assam in Assamese. A portion of the History of Kamroop has been also since published by the Missionaries in the *Orunudoi* Magazine'.[33] In contemporary critical discourse the *buranjis* have aroused interest as one of the pre-modern narratives in prose that qualify as chronicle rather than history. However, the continuation of the use of the term *buranji* against the more acceptable *itihas* as in other Sanskrit cognates, strongly suggests a process of constituting an identity with specific and unique markers. Joyeeta Sharma has illustrated how the *buranjis*, originally written in the Tai language, were gradually made available in the *ujonia* variety of Assamese, and this process acquired 'the status of [a] local ancestor for modern history'.[34]

The etymology of the word *Bihu*[35] affords us with another clear instance in which tribal practices, in this case a form of agricultural ritual, were subjected to sanskritized interpretation. The vital input here was from Lakshminath Bezbaroa in the pages of the periodical *Bahi* that ran from 1909 through to 1945. In the seventh year of the magazine's existence we find him writing: 'The word Bihu has come from *Bixub/Bishub*. Or what is called the Equator. *Bishuboshou Dibakara*. This is the day when the sun enters the *Mesh* (Aries), *Tula* (Libra), and *Makar* (Capricorn) signs ... This is the day of *Sankranti*. In our neighbouring Bengal (*Bongodesh*), this *sankranti* does not have a name after *bishu* or bihu nor can we find it in any other province (pradesh) (If it is there in some nook and corner of India, I don't know. *But in Assam, the ancient astrological concept bishu is prevalent as Bihu. Don't you understand from this, that the most ancient of the ancient Aryan civilization has been active in Assam for ages now'* (1569, my translation, emphasis added).[36] Bezbaroah's claim of an ancient sanskritic astrological etymology for a local custom proved richly connotative. On the one hand the Assamese was instantly established as richer in tradition than neighboring Bengal; on the other hand, a sanskritic legitimacy was proposed for what was otherwise considered a mere folk ritual. The second has far reaching consequences since in effect it placed animism and other arcane rituals within a Hindu tradition. Henceforth the ritual bathing of the cow during this folk festival could be regarded as synonymous with the Hindu worship of the cow. Nonetheless Abhay Barua in a much later analysis does mention the possibility of an extra-aryan origin for the term *bihu*. He writes: 'In the 13th century, when the Mongoloid Thai/Tai came to Assam and saw the folk practice ritual bathing of cows they called it Boihoo. In the Tai language, Boi means to pray and Hoo stands for cow.'[37] Nor would twentieth-century anthropological and sociological studies endorse a sanskritized interpretation of the rite perpetuated in official discourse through the medium of school textbooks and the like.

V. Epilogue

The story of national consciousness we have traced out is illuminating because in it we can observe the idea of a nation being formulated, not out of one Manichean binary of self and other, but according to a welter of replicated and ramifying oppositions. Essentially the language of the nation was constructed out of two materials. One privileged the grammar of a cosmopolitan culture that marginalized and appropriated histories, cultural practices and rituals. It was these very suppressed and assimilated elements that then would begin to fight back by forwarding their own claims for separate homelands, an identity, and a script so cavalierly diverted into the mainstream of the 'greater Assamese community'.[38] To write off the nation is thus to write off the politics of identity formation from Indian book history. We need to be conscious of the category of the nation precisely *because* we have grown so precociously wary of its ideological overpowering of spaces, histories and identities.

Even more pertinent to the project of book history are the changing dynamics of print capitalism in the cyber world. Chandan Sharma has posed a pertinent question regarding the script of the Assamese language. The commonly used UNICODE for Assamese is a derivative from Bengali, the derivation made easier because the missionaries transplanted the Bengali script onto the Assamese language. However every time the computer version is updated a problem arises of transferring documents typed in the earlier format to the new programme because the inherent code of conversion formula is that of Bengali. Recently, materials typed in the Assamese 'Ramdhenu' typeset refused to open in the latest Microsoft XP. The question arises as to whether such present and future incompatibilities will involve the non-availability of texts that were typed in Ramdhenu or another typeset each time a new version of computer software arrives to replace earlier ones.[39]

The issue at stake is not just one of technology vis-à-vis tradition. Imperialism of a very different order is about to engulf the book, monopolizing and establishing a transnational hegemony in the production and dissemination of texts. Book history, even in the cyber age, has perforce to situate itself between residual or growing forces of ethnic nationalism on the one hand, and the empire of global transnational capitalism disguised as technological advancement on the other. To attempt to disengage the two would be to deny living history.

Notes

1. 'Assam is Asom', *The Hindu*, 28 Febuary 2006 (http://www.hinduonnet.com/2006/02/28/stories/2006022806151200.htm).
2. 'Gogoi defends change of name to Asom'. *The Assam Tribune*, 2 March 2006 (www.assamtribune.com/mar0206/main.html).
3. Sydney Shep, 'Books Without Borders: The Transnational Turn in Book History' in *Books Without Borders, Volume 1: The Cross-National Dimension in Print Culture* (Basingstoke: Palgrave Macmillan, 2008), pp. 13–37.
4. Edward Said, *Orientalism* (London: Routledge, 1978), p. 3.
5. See Homi Bhabha, *Nation and Narration* (London: Routledge, 1990).
6. See Harish Trivedi, *Colonial Transactions: English Literature and India* (Calcutta: Papyrus, 1993).
7. See Priya Joshi, *In Another Country: Colonialism, Culture and the English Novel in India* (New York: Columbia University Press, 2002).
8. Aijaz Ahmad, *In Theory: Classes, Nations, Literatures* (Delhi: OUP, 1992), p. 172.
9. Partha Chatterjee, *The Partha Chatterjee Omnibus* (Delhi: OUP, 2004), p. 42.
10. It is important to state at the outset that the purpose of large-scale migration of the Bengali *babu* to Assam after British annexation was to fill clerical positions in colonial administration, jobs that the Assamese initially were not ready in educational terms to undertake. Thus any reliable account of nationality- culture- and identity-formation and resistance to Bengali domination would also need to consider the Assamese educated middle class's desire to replace the Bengali 'babu'. There is another interesting story of Assamese cultural Renaissance as influenced by the nineteenth-century Bengal Renaissance. See to Hiren Gohain, *Oitijhyor Rupantar aru Annyannya Prabandha* [Transition of Tradition and Other Essays] (Guwahati: Student's Stores, 1993) for a fuller account.
11. Another interesting sidelight is afforded by gender construction in the conceptualisation of Assamese cultural nationalism, for which regrettably I have no room in the present publication.
12. E. A. Annet, *Splendid Lives Series: William Carey: Pioneer Missionary to India* (London: Indian Sunday School Union, 1914), p. 100.
13. A. J. Moffatt Mills, *Report on the Province of Assam, 1853* (Assam and Calcutta: Publication Board, 1984), p. 131.
14. H. K. Barpujari, *The American Missionaries and North-East India (1836–1900): A Documentary Study.* (Guwahati and Delhi: Spectrum, 1986), p. 143.
15. Mills, Report on the Province of Assam, p. 91.
16. Mills, ibid., p. 28.
17. Maheswar Neog, 'Asamor Jatiya Jibanat Baptistar Bhumika', *Prakash*, November 1983, p. 128.
18. Rajen Saikia, *Social and Economic History of Assam, 1853–1921*, (Delhi: Manohar, 2000), p. 202.
19. The concept of Sanskritization is largely acknowledged as a principal theoretical contribution to sociological study in India by M. N. Srinivas. Srinivas

defines it as 'the process by which a 'low' caste or tribe or other group takes over the customs, rituals, beliefs, ideology and style of life of a high and, in particular, a 'twice born' (*dwija*) caste. (M. N. Srinivas, *Village, Caste, Gender and Method: Essays in Indian Social Anthropology*, New Delhi: OUP, 1996, p. 88). Though this paper discusses sanskritization within the context of colonial power structures in the nineteenth century that paved the way for a hegemony of the Assamese educated middle class, it is important to register here that the process of Sanskritization in religious and cultural spheres had already begun much earlier and the Ahom kings were initiated into sanskritized titles like 'Swarganarayan' in the fifteenth to sixteenth centuries.

20. Maheswar Neog, 'Introduction' in *Orunodoi_1846–1854*, Dr Nathan Brown (ed.) (Assam and Calcutta: Publication Board, 1983), pp. 111, 125.
21. Neog, ibid., p. 124.
22. Samiran Das, 'Saptadah sotikar asomiya bhasha aru Raghunath Mahantar Katha-Ramayan' in NagenThakur and Khogesh Sen Deka (eds) *Bhasha Chinta Bichitra* (Guwahati: Puberun, 2000).
23. Maheswar Neog, 'Asamor Jatiya Jibanat Baptistar Bhumika', *Prakash*, November 1983, 111.
24. Svati Joshi, *Rethinking English: Essays in Literature, Languages, History* (Delhi: Trianka, 1991), p. 17.
25. Jayeeta Sarma, 'Heroes for Our Times: Assam's Lachit, India's Misiile Man' in Zavos et al. (eds) *The Politics of Cultural Mobilization in India* (Delhi: OUP, 2004), p. 173.
26. Norman Cutler, 'Three Moments in the Genealogy of Tamil Literary Culture' in Sheldon Pollock (ed.) *Literary Cultures in History: Reconstructions from South Asia*.(Berkeley and Los Angeles, University of California Press, 2003), 288.
27. D. R. Nagraj, 'Critical Tensions in the History of Kannada Literary Culture' in Pollock (ed.), 327.
28. Sudipto Kaviraj, 'The Two Histories of Literary Culture in Bengal' in Pollock (ed.), 537–8.
29. *Orunodoi*, July 1853, 105, my translation.
30. *Orunodoi*, August 1850, 59.
31. Neog, p. 19.
32. Sanjib Barua, *India Against Itself: Assam and the Politics of Nationality* (Delhi: OUP, 1998).
33. Maheswar Neog (ed.), *Anandaram Dhekial Phukan: A Plea for Assam and Assamese.* See also *The Complete Text of Observations on the Administration of the Province of Assam and A Few Remarks on the Assamese Language and on Vernacular Education in Assam* (Jorhat: Assam Sahitya Sabha, 1977), pp. 163–4.
34. Joyeeta Sharma, 'Heroes for Our Times: Assam's Lachit, India's Misiile Man' in Zavos et al. (eds) *The Politics of Cultural Mobilization in India* (Delhi: OUP, 2004), p. 172.
35. Bihu is the 'national' festival of the Assamese, celebrated thrice yearly. The most popular and elaborate celebration, 'Rongali Bihu', occurs during the spring.
36. *Bezbaroa Granthawalee*, Vol. II, (Guwahati: Sahitya Prakash, 1988).
37. Abhay Barua, *Bihu Janakrishtir Boishishtya*, (Guwahati: Students Stores, 1989), p. 26, my translation.

38. The late twentieth century has seen formation of several associations by ethnic groupings in Assam demanding autonomous states so as to pursue their own nationalist projects. The Bodo Movement, the Karbi Anglong Autonomous State Demand Council and others are burning examples. The enormous popular participation in these movements is indicative of a living history in which nationhood no longer remains a mere 'construct'.
39. Chandan Kumar Sharma. *Asomiya Kon? Ek Rajnoitic aru Samajtatwik Abalokan* [Who is an Assamese? A Political and Sociological Perspective] (Guwahati: Spani, 2006), p. 17.

5
Futures Past: Books, Reading, Culture in the Age of Liberalization

Priya Joshi

A mutual wariness exists between book historians and literary scholars, between those who study the production, circulation, and consumption of texts, broadly conceived, and those who study the content of some carefully chosen texts, narrowly conceived. Book history and literary study remain two robust fields separated by a common research agenda, with many literary scholars unwilling to embrace the empirical methods of book history and its pursuit of exploring context over text. The few scholars who have stepped across the great divide often find themselves at the vanguard of literary and cultural studies, discovering in the methods of the Great Satan approaches that have helped revise many cherished chestnuts on gender (Tuchman, M. Cohen), class (Rose), nation (St Clair), empire (Joshi), and social formation.[1] This essay draws upon a series of research vignettes in order to reflect upon the contributions book history continues to make to more traditional literary study, by introducing new vistas that open the practice of close reading so cherished in the Anglophone literary academy.

When the French historian Roger Chartier asked whether books made revolutions, he was only half serious. His response, though, that ways of reading just might be responsible for revolutions, is a gauntlet that has yet to be seriously taken up.[2] It seems time now to address the many opportunities and challenges that research into readers and institutions of readings, such as libraries, present to literary studies. Our focus will be on the social lives of readers as well as on the institutions that shaped readers and reading in the nineteenth and twentieth centuries. My comments will attempt to bring a comparative dimension into play, integrating insights from the relatively well-studied archives of metropolitan libraries such as those in England and Scotland, with libraries being uncovered in the peripheries (Canada, India, and Nigeria).

There is another 'comparative' dimension to introduce here and that is a transhistorical one. Having worked quite extensively with nineteenth-century archives of British and Indian publishing and book culture, I'd like now to extend these findings into the twentieth century.

The chapter proceeds in three parts, each exploring a term from the subtitle (Books, Reading, Culture) and weaving them together toward the conclusion. India is the primary case, but as is clear in this and my previous work on the subject, to conceive of 'India' as a discrete national identity or limited geographical space is a grave error, especially when it comes to studying the circulation of print and ideas. For 'India' was involved in the global commerce of ideas and ideologies well before the Raj, when a tax was placed on all print originating from outside the British metropolis. There are many legacies of the Raj's century-long effort to monopolize print in the former colony, but the robustness of the global marketplace prior to and since Independence has obviated the once-bipolar colonial relationship and cemented an entity far greater than the national.

I. Books

Walking the streets of Bombay is quite possibly one of the most spectacular of urban activities. Unlike London or Paris, and maybe even New York, whose downtown streets seem to have given way altogether to an undistinguished global economy of Gaps, Starbucks, and Tie Racks, Bombay seems to have held out a little better. The city bears it colonial past with fading indulgence: the neo-Gothic Churchgate Station is among the most photographed site among nostalgists of the British Raj. Right beside Churchgate's magnificent façade, however, lies the other Bombay, jostling for attention and inevitably getting it. Surrounding the heart of this Bombay are hundreds of book vendors selling everything from Marie Corelli's bestselling Victorian novels to multiple biographies of that other Victorian victim-goddess Diana, the Princess of Wales (the titles are almost entirely in English). Bombay's bouquinistes are a hardy group, and they are to be seen even during the torrential monsoon months, covering their wares with flimsy blue tarps, but still purveying bestsellers of all ages to readers of all ages (see Figure 5.1 [(a) and (b)]).

My first real memory of book buying and bookselling came from this textual cornucopia, and years later when I saw Giuseppe Arcimboldo's painting 'Librarian' (1566), with its subject's face and figure entirely constituted by elements from the codex (Figure 5.2), I was convinced

Figure 5.1   Book vendors outside Churchgate Station, Bombay (©Priya Joshi)

Source: Public domain.

Figure 5.2   Giuseppe Arcimboldo, 'Librarian' (1566)

that Arcimboldo must have been a ganja-smoking hippie in India and not a sixteenth-century Italian painter in the Habsburg court. For the feast of books is unavoidable in this coastal city, so visually prevalent and enticing that even in the heart of one of Asia's most bustling commercial metropolises, businessmen and women are routinely 'caught' browsing among wares whose diversity could probably put Amazon's warehouses to shame (see Figure 5.1 [(a) and (b)]).

If one were to study India's contemporary metropolitan book culture, it would surely have to take the urban, public, display of books and their urban, public consumption as a starting point. For despite Benedict Anderson's charming formulation that reading is an utterly private activity that takes place entirely in the 'lair of the skull', invisible from public scrutiny or intrusion, the Bombay example reveals something quite different.[3] In this city, one reads as one eats (the irresistible street food is often packed in newsprint, and magazine stories vie with mustard and fenugreek for spice). In Bombay, one reads as one sleeps (covering one's face with a paper as a flyswatter), and sometimes one eats what one reads, as does the holy cow – in the trash heaps that characterize all metropolises in the developing world. The activity of reading lies open to public gaze, though reading's effects – the subject of this essay – are another story.

The feast of print that presents itself outside Churchgate Station is by no means anomalous or one of recent invention. It is embedded in the literary culture of colonial and ex-colonial India where books have been prized, often in inverse proportion to literacy. One of the arguments I presented in my previous work on the subject was to study not just what was available to Indian readers, but what of it was read, how it might have been read, and possibly why.[4] That work focused largely on the nineteenth century, a period of great social and political turbulence in the colony, when the arrival of the British was accompanied by that of an imported literary form, specifically the novel. If the British were not terribly welcome in India, their cultural import was, and the English novel became massively popular among Indian readers who turned to it with avid enthusiasm for their leisure reading.

In tracking the fortunes of the English novel in India, I spent a considerable amount of time working on Indian public and circulating libraries extant from the period, which were the spaces where Indian readers availed of titles for their leisure reading that they either could not or would not purchase. Consider a few statistics about libraries from this period: between 1887 and 1900, the number of scientific and literary societies in the Madras Presidency increased almost threefold, from

146 institutions in 1887 to 401 in 1900. Annual membership figures varied greatly in these institutions, from 5 members or visitors to 14,532 (a considerable range of readers that nonetheless remained relatively consistent across time). There were proportionate increases in the number of libraries and reading rooms for other regions as well: the Bengal Presidency went from having 49 libraries and reading rooms in 1886 to 137 in 1901, an almost threefold increase; while the number of such institutions in the Bombay Presidency increased over fivefold, from 13 in 1886 to 70 in 1901.[5]

Under these circumstances, it would be accurate to claim that there was a discernible continuity between the metropolitan, urban culture of libraries in Victorian England and in Victorian India – that libraries were an important pillar of liberal imperialism, places of enlightenment and some freedom of learning.[6] Of course there are a number of caveats we could include: that unlike public libraries in England, India's were still largely utilized by male readers, at least officially;[7] but it is equally accurate that the Indian library 'system' in the nineteenth century was distributed between urban centres such as Bombay, Madras, Calcutta and smaller towns and rural outposts, much as it was in England.[8]

It would *not*, however, be accurate to claim that libraries as a cornerstone of book culture were to be found widely elsewhere in the British Empire. The Canadian scholar, Carole Gerson, notes the lamentable state of public libraries in nineteenth-century Canada, where one informant reported that in 1867, there was 'no public library in any of our chief towns.'[9] Meanwhile, the sociologist Wendy Griswold has documented the relative paucity of libraries in contemporary Nigeria. As Griswold reports, 'Nigeria [with a population of 137 million] officially reports having 92 public libraries. By way of comparison, Mexico, a bit smaller in population [105 million], has 2,269 libraries, and a fully literate country like Britain [population ca. 60 million], with a little more than half the population of Nigeria, has 5,270 libraries.'[10] Griswold's data seem to indicate a real tension between the absence of a fully formed 'book culture' and an uneven, though palpable, presence of a reading culture. It is, of course, only fair to add that Griswold's own predetermined notion of what constitutes a 'reading culture' has been strongly criticized, as have her Anglophone orientation and reliance on UNESCO-derived data.[11] In verifiable fact, Nigeria possesses a fairly lively network of local popular publishers – the presence of which has been documented for Hausa literature by Graham Furniss, and for writing in Yoruba by Karin Barber – as well as of booksellers and channels for review: all aspects of what may be termed, in the broader sense, a 'book culture'.[12] For all of that, Nigeria's evident pride at having produced a Nobel laureate for literature – Wole Soyinka – plus an illustrious recipient of the biennial Man Booker International Prize – Chinua Achebe – is tempered by metrics revealing a total novelistic production of approximately 500 titles since independence in 1960 (Griswold, 275ff.).

The remainder of this chapter spells out the distinctions between these two cultures – that of books and of reading – and draws out some implications for further research.

II. Reading

Up to the account of the Indian story, there seemed to be a correlation between the robustness of book culture in a country (specifically, the presence of domestic publishers and libraries primarily, but also bookstores, reviews, literary journalism, literary societies) and reading culture. If one had the former, one had the latter as well. However, Griswold's research in post-Independence Nigeria suggests that such a correlation is not necessary. Nigeria's patchy book culture (few libraries and relatively sporadic book distribution) nonetheless produces a devoted sector of readers who often go to considerable lengths of procure and read books. Despite the distractions to reading in tranquility, urban Nigerians seem to have found a salubrious solution: 'probably the best spaces for reading outside the home', Griswold reports, 'are in offices ... but even the most devout – and irresponsible – bookworm is likely to be interrupted in this environment' (Griswold, 107). Indeed, Griswold's research sensitizes an important fact sometimes overlooked: that the absence of a book culture may tell us very little about the presence of a reading culture.

In his recent memoir, Gabriel García Márquez describes the vibrant café life in Bogotá where he received his formative literary education: 'For the most part, these new works [such as those by Borges, Graham Greene, Lawrence, and Katherine Mansfield] were displayed in the unreachable windows of bookstore, but some copies circulated in the student cafés, which were active centers of cultural dissemination for university students from the provinces.'[13] The weakness of a book culture in Bogotá may have thwarted a reading culture, but rather than obliterate reading, it simply moved reading elsewhere: from libraries to cafés in the case of Bogotá, and to office buildings in the case of Nigeria.

Similarly, the presence of robust institutions that characterize a book culture may not indicate a 'reading' culture as such, as I discovered when researching the social lives of libraries in India. A bit of background to this remark: I had been looking for circulation records from the nineteenth century at the Connemara Public Library in Madras (est. 1855). As a public library, the Connemara is both more and less than typical: initially appended to the Government Museum in Madras in 1855, it was modelled loosely upon the British Library. Like the British Library, the Connemara too had a deposit mandate (it remains in fact one of four deposit libraries in India). Visitors and readers at the Connemara were welcome to read books and periodicals provided they were over 17 years of age. Because neither fees were charged nor membership restrictions placed in this library (a fairly unusual practice among Indian public libraries), the Connemara tended to draw a broad cross-section of the literate community to its reading rooms. The deposit mandate meant that readers encountered a large and varied collection, which in turn attracted both scholar-specialists and lay figures looking for light reading (or a quiet place to sleep).

Perhaps because of the Library's association with the Government Museum, its collection inevitably reflected the scholarly bent of the affiliate institution (see Figure 5.3). A large part of the monies provided to the collection in the early years of the last century went to purchasing titles in Anatomy, Biology, Zoology, Arts & Industry, Mineralogy, Botany, Geology, Forestry – all disciplines 'useful' to the economic development of the Madras Presidency. History, Religion, Literature, Languages, and the Arts were not neglected, however, and holdings in these subjects were on average proportional to those found in similar public libraries in the UK, the USA, and France for the period.

What the Connemara archive initially provided were aggregate statistics on borrowing by rough category from 1910 to 1920 and detailed statistics on borrowing by category from 1996 to 2003. The early twentieth-century circulation statistics at the Connemara were virtually identical to those found in libraries in the UK, USA, Canada, and elsewhere in India: fiction comprised less than a third of the library's holdings yet circulated far more often than any other subject (see Figure 5.3). At the Connemara, fiction constituted 20 per cent of total circulation with History a close second. Despite the fact that between 1910 and 1920 the Connemara carried fiction both in English and the 'vernacular languages' (a consequence of the deposit mandate formalized after the 1867 Press and Circulation of Books Act), the bulk of it during this period circulated in English, a detail I will explain presently.

By the 1990s, however, a subtle change became visible at the Connemara Library: the stock of fiction remained the same, yet its circulation was now

92   *Futures Past*

A statement of the number of books issued to readers during the last two years, under the various subject catalogue heads, is subjoined :—

	1912–13.	1913–14.
Anatomy ; biology ; natural history ; zoology	968	1,015
Anthropology ; folklore	472	460
Archaeology ; architecture	583	304
Arts ; industries	1,283	1,000
Atlases ; maps	86	74
Belles lettres	6,010	6,207
Botany ; arboriculture ; horticulture	274	338
Chemistry ; agriculture ; photography	308	284
Classics	157	263
Dictionaries ; encyclopaedias ; gazetteers ; manuals	6,845	7,083
Economic products	263	342
Education ; ethics ; logic	891	976
Exhibitions	27	20
Forestry ; timbers	62	71
Geography ; physical geography ; physiography	119	146
Geology	95	122
History	4,687	4,876
Jurisprudence	380	370
Medicine ; surgery ; pathology	405	384
Microscopy	16	20
Mineralogy ; metallurgy	182	159
Natural philosophy	608	718
Numismatics ; medals ; heraldry	92	82
Philology ; epigraphy	1,308	1,260
Photographs	160	152
Physiology	848	561
Public health	92	84
Religion	1,648	1,607
Sport and games	206	217
Travels ; voyages	206	182
Vernacular languages	68	51
Fort St. George Gazette (other than current issues)	842	964

Source: *Government of Madras Educational Department.*
Madras: Government Museum, 1914.

Figure 5.3 From Connemara Public Library, Madras: annual report showing books issued to readers by subject, 1912–14

largely in 'vernacular languages' – Tamil to be precise, with titles in Telugu and Kannada as seconds. Meanwhile, the novel's popularity was replaced in the late twentieth century by the circulation of titles in Engineering, Mathematics, and Management, which comprised roughly 30 per cent of the total titles in circulation (of which Engineering comprised close to 55%, Management around 32%, and Mathematics approximately 13%).

The following chart (Figure 5.4) graphically documents the manner in which stock in the Library kept abreast of users: before Independence, there were more titles in stock than there were users; after Independence, the number of readers and titles was roughly equal, and then, by the late 1960s, the number of titles in stock towered above the number of

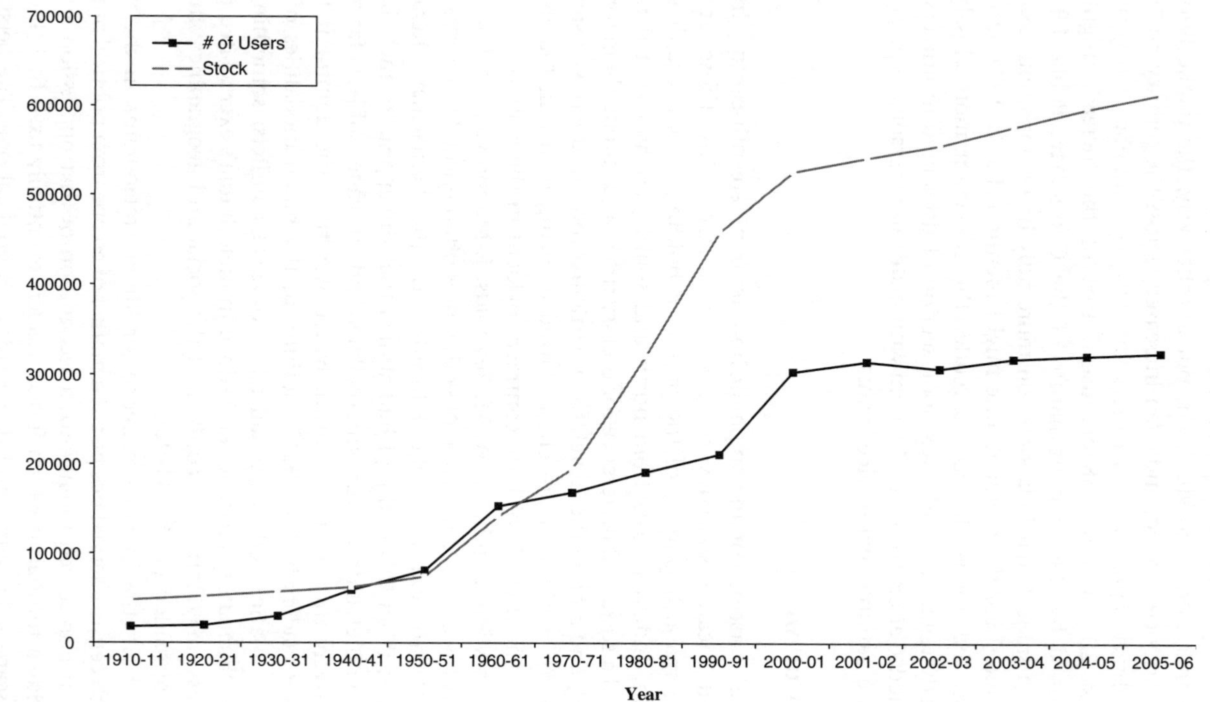

Source: Connemara Public Library, Madras, Annual Reports, 1910-2006.

Figure 5.4 Connemara Public Library, Madras: increases in users and stock, 1910–2006

users (again a trend normative in most libraries of this kind). In short, between 1910 and 2006, while the Library's stock increased tenfold its users increased twentyfold. Or, put another way, the public library's popularity continued, and even increased, across the century. In 1910, the Library reported 18,374 users; by 1997, that number had gone up almost 20 times to 358,993 users. Part of the increase might be explained by the evolving nature of the Connemara Public Library itself, a subject that I elaborate on more fully in a companion essay to this one.[14] For the moment, one might mention that in 1981 authorities at the library decided to render the collection more closely to readerly demands, and a textbook section of titles used in universities was added along with a study room with materials for graduates preparing for the nation's civil service exams.

III. Culture

In the course of working on public libraries in nineteenth-century India, I had located statistics on circulation resembling those at the Connemara. Regardless of the profile of holdings, often regardless of region, Indian readers from north and south, east and west demonstrated a sustained preference for literary titles, and among them for the novel, and among the novel, for a particular form of the novel: specifically, for works that are characterized as being in the melodramatic mode. The rhetoric of stark contrasts, evident in the work of novelists such as Marie Corelli, G. W. M. Reynolds, F. Marion Crawford, among others towered in circulation over the titles often pressed into service by the Department of Public Education or the Vernacular Literature Society. From this finding I had argued that the appeal for melodrama in the nineteenth century interpellated Indian reader-subjects far more effectively than literary realism, which was then the dominant form among readers in the UK. Something in the moral modalities of the melodramatic mode personalized ideological conflicts; something in the hallucinatory anxieties embedded in melodrama's excruciated plottedness imaginatively reconfigured the social and geographical imaginary of readers (Joshi, 83–92).

In short, the Indian preference for literary melodrama in the nineteenth century served not just as a marker of escape from political oppression. It also served to enhance a recognition of that oppression and to provide a tutorial in which Indian readers eventually used their literary landscape to imagine, and then achieve, a political one. The persistent desire for fiction in libraries was an index to the ways in which the novel was put to use in this project. It provided a liberation narrative for readers whose desire for pleasure came to be transformed into one for political change. Readers, I had argued, used libraries and the books therein to discover ways of achieving mastery over their social and political worlds.

In the desire for literary texts from public libraries, we have an account of how a literary form's imaginative possibilities play out among readers. What can we now say about the dramatic shift toward titles in Engineering, Management, and Mathematics that characterizes the Connemara's circulation in the 1990s, half a century after Independence?

This question might be addressed by underscoring the commonplace: that the calculus of modernity in India changed between 1910 and the century that followed. It changed from something inherently implicated with the colonial state and impossible to abstract from it to something that had global reach and inflections. Rather than being a single destination to which India was driving, modernity and its myths evolved significantly between the early decades of the twentieth century and its end. In 1992, India lifted its stringent controls on the free market, 'liberalized' its economy, and ushered in an exuberant embrace of that form of material desire known elsewhere as globalization.

It is arguably the case that in a public sphere dominated less by the preoccupations of anti-colonialism than ex-colonial nationalism and economic mobility, the appeal of imaginative literature in the melodramatic mode, visible in the early decades of the twentieth century, was satisfied more compellingly by popular film than by print culture. This might partly explain the decline of literature in the Connemara's circulation during the 1990s. Meanwhile, the pressures of consumerism and economic advancement manifested themselves among Madras' consumers who turned to civil institutions such as public libraries in an effort at self-cultivation and economic advancement through the acquisition of formal educational credentials. The high technical literacy in the state of Tamil Nadu, of which Madras is capital – and its close integration into the global economy – is both an explanation and a consequence of institutions such as the Connemara that, in responding to readerly demands and establishing textbook collections, extended the institution's reach from a place of leisure to one of social architecture. Readers in the 1990s came to the Connemara Public Library now not to learn how to resist the colonial state by the act of consuming its products as they had with the novel in the nineteenth century. Rather, readers now came to learn how to master a postcolonial modernity in which advancement in the 'knowledge industries' marked a form of liberation from the economic stasis that characterized the Licence Raj of the 1970s and 1980s.

If medical education or the life sciences (such as Biology, Chemistry, or Microbiology) figure less in this new economy of self advancement where Engineering, Management, and Mathematics dominate, it may be because slots in medical schools in the state are far fewer in number than those in engineering or the information technology sector and also because credentials in the IT sector are far more portable globally than those in the medical and life sciences. As agents and actors within a system that they seek to manipulate to advantage, readers at Madras's Connemara Public Library provide a perspective on an economic and social reality. Their readerly preferences gesture both symbolically and materially to a social order in which print capital in general and books in particular are resources of hope for the literate.

IV. Futures past

Just as literacy in English had marked the cadres of Indians joining the colonial employment apparatus in the nineteenth century, now in the 1990s, literacy in Engineering, Management, and Mathematics marked the cadres joining the global economic apparatus under liberalization. In both cases – during empire and globalization – public institutions such as the Connemara became zones of engagement implicated in fashioning then enhancing public culture in modern India. But this time, it was mathematics and not melodrama, engineering and not the novel that characterized the shape of an economic nationalism under the flag of liberalization.

In conclusion, it is worth noting that as the history of reading becomes a growth area in literary studies, as we read readers reading, we might do well to remember that readers read many things in books that are not books themselves. The reading culture that Wendy Griswold and others have noted illuminates both reading and culture, and 'culture' is more often social and economic before it is even remotely literary. As Sydney Shep observes in the opening chapter of the companion volume to this one, print culture is not always synonymous with literary culture, though it can indeed play a key role in illuminating the mentalités of a historical moment which literary scholars have claimed as their territory for too long. Too often, those lamenting the death of the 'book' mean the death of the 'literary' book; yet, as the Bogotá example indicates, the literary book often circulates outside the confines of book culture and thrives there. The challenge of studying book history throws up just such provocations, and one remains hopeful that the literary critic is willing, occasionally, to betray the text in studying its contexts.

Notes

1. Margaret Cohen, *The Sentimental Education of the Novel* (Princeton: Princeton UP, 1999); Priya Joshi, *In Another Country: Colonialism, Culture, and the English Novel in India* (New York: Columbia UP, 2002); Jonathan Rose, *The Intellectual Life of the British Working Classes* (New Haven: Yale UP, 2001); William St Clair, *The Reading Nation in the Romantic Period* (New York: Cambridge UP, 2004); Gaye Tuchman with Nina E. Fortin, *Edging Women Out: Victorian Novelists, Publishers and Social Change* (London: Routledge, 1989).
2. See the chapter, 'Do Books Make Revolutions?' in Roger Chartier, *The Cultural Origins of the French Revolution*, trans. Lydia G. Cochrane (Durham: Duke UP, 1991).
3. Benedict Anderson, *Imagined Communities: Reflections on the Origin and Spread of Nationalism*, 2nd rev. ed. (New York: Verso, 1991), p. 35.
4. See *In Another Country*, especially Chapters 2–4.
5. *Report on the Administration of the Madras Presidency* (Madras: Government Pr., 1887–8 and 1899–1900) pp. clx–clxiv and pp. clxxviii–clxxxix respectively; also *Thacker's India Directory*, (Calcutta: Thacker, Spink, & Co., var. years). Indian public libraries, as these sources document, existed within a constellation of other social institutions around them variously called 'Literary Societies' or 'Reading Rooms'. It ought to be noted, however, that both of these terms are something of misnomers: 'Literary Societies' often had less directly to do with literature or with maintaining print collections than with the 'political improvement of the people of India', as the Triplicane Literary Society indicated in its mission statement; and 'Reading Room' often included the corollary activities, 'to deliver lectures; to afford amusements as billiards, &c.' as the Vizagapatnam Hindu Reading Room maintained in its charter statement. In this regard, many of these reading rooms and societies were more like the Mechanics' Institutes that proliferated (then failed) in Britain in the 1830s and 1840s, motivated by good intentions for civic improvement but indifferent to local needs. Like the Mechanics' Institutes, these Indian institutions too were often what R. K. Webb calls 'clubs to local vanity', and places of essay recitals, rather than public libraries of the kind mentioned in this section. For more on the Mechanics' Institutes, see R. K. Webb, *The British Working Class Reader, 1790–1848: Literacy and Social Tension* (London: George Allen & Unwin Ltd, 1955) p. 64; see also Richard D. Altick, *The English Common Reader: A Social History of the Mass Reading Public, 1800–1900* (Chicago: University of Chicago Press, 1957) pp. 188–212. In contrast, Carole Gerson's research on nineteenth-century Canada cited below indicates that Mechanics' Institutes in Montréal and Toronto often took the place of absent public libraries in these cities.
6. One of the most striking documents using the language of liberalism to oppose censorship of the native press and its institutions such as public libraries came from the pen of Reverend James Long, a respected educator

and civil servant commissioned after the 1857 Mutiny with preparing a *Report of the Native Press in Bengal*. One of Long's conclusions: 'The opinions of the Native Press may often be regarded as the safety valve which gives warning of danger' (iv). See Rev. James Long, 'Report on the Native Press in Bengal', *Selections from the Records of the Bengal Government, No. xxxii. Returns Relating to Publications in the Bengali Language, in 1857, to Which Is Added a List of the Native Presses, with the Books Printed at Each, Their Price, and Character, with a Notice of the Past Condition and Future Prospects of the Vernacular Press of Bengal and the Statistics of the Bombay and Madras Vernacular Presses*, ed. Rev. J. Long (Calcutta: John Gray, 1859).

7. James Long's research in Bengal during the 1850s indicates that while libraries and the print industry were observably male in the public sphere, their users were often women for whom books were borrowed or purchased by male members of the household (Long, xv). Similar findings emerge in the work of Jan Fergus and Paul Kaufmann for eighteenth-century England with Fergus observing '[w]hether or not men were readers, they constituted a sizeable proportion of the borrowers' [of Samuel Clay's Library in Warwick] (Fergus, 178); while Kaufman's data from a Bath circulating library indicate 'with a preponderance of at least 70 per cent, the men loom large in this profile' (Kaufman, 225). See Jan Fergus, 'Eighteenth-Century Readers in Provincial England: The Customers of Samuel Clay's Circulating Library and Bookshop in Warwick, 1770–1772', *The Papers of the Bibliographic Society of America* 78.2 (1984); Paul Kaufman, 'In Defence of Fair Readers', *Libraries and Their Users: Collected Papers in Library History* (London: The Library Association, 1969).

8. See *In Another Country* for a list of public libraries established for Indian readers in remote provincial towns (Joshi, 54ff.).

9. Carole Gerson, citing Thomas D'Arcy McGee, in *A Purer Taste: The Writing and Reading of Fiction in English in Nineteenth-Century Canada*, (Toronto: University of Toronto Press, 1989), pp. 4–5. Mechanics' Institutes apparently filled in for absent public libraries in Canada, and the novel (despite the widespread opprobrium it suffered) circulated robustly in nineteenth-century Canada with fiction comprising from two thirds to three quarters of materials circulated at Mechanics' Institutes in Montréal and Toronto in the 1870s and 1880s (Gerson, 17ff.).

10. Wendy Griswold, *Bearing Witness: Readers, Writers, and the Novel in Nigeria* (Princeton: Princeton UP, 2000), p. 107. Griswold's figures come from Table 7.1 of the *UNESCO Statistical Yearbook* (Paris: UNESCO, 1991). The exception to this picture of public libraries in Nigeria is the British Council, but this has only 5 libraries and one information center in the country (see Griswold, op. cit.)

11. See especially Robert Fraser: *Book History Through Postcolonial Eyes: Re-writing the Script* (London and New York: Routledge, 2008).

12. See especially Graham Furniss, *Poetry, Prose and Popular Culture in Hausa* (Edinburgh University Press, 1996) and Graham Furniss, Malami Buba and William Burgess eds, *A Bibliography of Hausa Popular Fiction* (Köln: R. Köppe, 2004). Also see Karin Barber ed. *Africa's Hidden Histories: Everyday Literacy and the Making of the Self* (Bloomington: Indiana University Press, 2006) and her *The Anthropology of Texts, Persons and Publics: Oral and Written Culture in Africa and Beyond* (Cambridge University Press, 2007). For the colonial Gold

Coast and postcolonial Ghana the case has been put by Stephanie Newell in her *Ghanaian Popular Fiction: Thrilling Discoveries in Conjugal Life and Other Stories* (Oxford: James Currey; and Athens, Ohio: Ohio University Press, 2000) and in her *Literary Culture in Colonial Ghana: How to Play the Game of Life* (Manchester University Press, 2002).
13. See Gabriel García Márquez, 'The Challenge', *New Yorker*, 6 October 2003, p. 100.
14. See Joshi, 'The Social Lives of Institutions', delivered as the Nicholson Lecture at the University of Chicago, May 2007 (forthcoming in print, 2008).

6
Book Circulation and Reader Responses in Colonial India

David Finkelstein

In 1990 in a small bookstore in Stirling, Scotland, I came across an 1880 third edition, one volume reprint of Philip Meadows Taylor's 'Indian mutiny' novel, *Seeta*. The novel, originally published in three volumes by Henry S. King in 1873, had become a staunch and profitable back catalogue seller for King's successors C. Kegan Paul and Co., reprinted in at least ten editions in their standard and Colonial Series between 1880 and 1900. This particular 1880 version, tattered and worn from years of handling, still bore traces of its first owner and evidence suggesting a grand return voyage from London to India and then to Brighton. How it ended up over one hundred years later in Scotland is unknown: perhaps it was as a result of lively trades and sales between readers and various second hand book dealers, or perhaps a wandering victim of country house sales and book stall purchases. What was striking about this volume, though, was physical evidence of its first owner viscerally and actively engaged with the themes of the novel – pages and illustrations had been ripped out, notes scribbled in the margins, newspaper clippings pasted into the front and back covers. The marginalia in this volume offers tantalising glimpses into generally undocumented aspects of the nineteenth-century Indian book trade and of the colonial reader.

This chapter is about the journey of this tattered volume of fiction from Britain to India and back. It is a case study illustrating nineteenth-century colonial book-trade connections, highlighting the role of little known intermediaries in distributing colonial texts and opening a window onto one reader's reception and interaction with his reading material. How had this volume, originally published in London, found its way to India? By what means did its reader encounter it, and what was his response to its contents? What, as a result, can we learn about the colonial book trade in India by following its journey? To provide partial answer to these questions, I will attempt to map out the narrative of production, distribution and reception history found in the pages of this volume.

I. Enter the author

Seeta's author, Philip Meadows Taylor (1808–76), lived and worked in India for almost 40 years as a military and civil advisor to various independent Indian states. Born in Liverpool, he moved to Bombay in 1824 to take up a position in a small retail shop. It was a disagreeable experience, and through contact with his mother's cousin William Newnham, a well-placed civil servant, he escaped by gaining a commission in the independent army of the Nizam of Hyderabad. Thus began a remarkable military and civilian career independent of both the East India Company and the official British civil service establishments.[1] A self-taught individual, Taylor became fluent in six Indian languages, developed skills as a keen amateur archaeologist and engineer and emerged as a significant literary chronicler of Indian customs and life, writing novels, histories and learned journal articles. Known as the 'Scott of India' for his series of historical romances based on Indian history, he gained notoriety in 1839 for his first work, *Confessions of a Thug*, which presented a curiously sympathetic account of the Indian 'Thug' strangler thieves, who during that period infested Indian roads and preyed on pilgrims and travellers. Taylor did not conform to standard British colonial norms – he spent a great deal of time in Indian company, and married a half-Indian woman. His sympathy for his adopted country comes through in the six historical romances he wrote between 1839 and 1875, most of which concentrate on romanticising key moments in Indian history (albeit a history framed by European interests – such as the clashes between Tipu Sultaun and the British featured in his 1840 novel *Tippoo Sultaun*, or the rise of British dominance in the sub-continent as signalled by the 'Battle of Plassey' victory over Indian forces in 1757, the theme of his 1865 work *Ralph Darnell*).

Meadows Taylor's experiences and views on matters of Indo-British relations made their way into his fifth work, the 'mutiny' novel *Seeta*, published in three volumes by Henry S. King in 1873, then reprinted in one volume editions through to the end of the century. It is an idealised portrait of a marriage between a British district officer and a high-caste Indian woman, set against the backdrop of the Indian rebellion of 1857. The heroine Seeta, originally named Savitsee (a direct reference to an Indian legend whose heroine, Savitri, dies in order to save her husband),

Taylor wrote to the Edinburgh publisher John Blackwood, was to be an 'Indian girl full of life and energy, passionate in her love, perhaps capricious and petulant at times, but devoted – even to death.'[2] Taylor spends a great deal of time in the novel arguing in favour of interracial relationships, but in the end gives way to popular taste and conventions by abruptly having Seeta die saving her husband from the thrust of a rebel's spear. The moment is replicated in the frontispiece over the caption 'Faithful unto Death', echoing the theme Taylor had drawn attention to when unsuccessfully promoting the work to Blackwood. Taylor rather unconvincingly closes off the work with the marriage of his protagonist to an English woman more to the liking and approval of his relations.

Recent critical evaluation of Taylor's late experiment in promoting miscegenation has not been kind. B. J. Moore-Gilbert, analysing the work in relation to other historical romances of the period, declares the novel to be 'in the manner of the most sickly romance', concluding that in this way Meadows Taylor 'conveniently avoids the necessity of exploring more fully the painful moral and social issues foregrounded by the relationship'.[3] An 1897 evaluation of the work in *Blackwood's Magazine* concurred that the abruptness of the ending 'strikes us as akin to the action of the player who upsets the chessboard because he can see no way of winning'.[4] Contemporary critical reception found more objectionable the positive presentation of mixed marriage. As one reviewer for the *Calcutta Review* concluded, Seeta's tragic ending was inevitable and a lesson for all British colonial readers who would tolerate such links: '… so long as the "maids of Merrie England", and the lassies of Bonnie Scotland are willing to share with us our joys and sorrows in the East, doubtful and dangerous experiments such as Cyril and Seeta made should by all means be avoided'.[5]

II. The high road to India

Meadows Taylor's historical romances were among a significant number of literary texts popular in nineteenth-century colonialist and Indian circles alike, part of an influx of English language texts into Indian markets after the enactment of the English Education Acts of 1835. The acts, a result of initiatives by Thomas Babington (Lord Macaulay) and other reformers bent on establishing the primacy of English education in India, created new market opportunities for British publishers, and imports of British books and printed matter into India rose accordingly as a result. John Murray was among the first to attempt publishing initiatives specific to India, issuing reprints of his best-selling titles under the Murray

Colonial and Home Library series that ran between 1843 and 1849. Others saw more value in pursuing the educational market: by 1863 Macmillan's, for one, had gained a strong position in India marketing educational texts and profiting from sales to libraries and book clubs. 'What strides education must be making among the natives!' Alexander Macmillan commented to his nephew George Otto Trevelyan that year. 'We sell considerable number of our mathematical books, even high ones, every year to India.'[6] In 1886 Macmillan would reposition itself by launching its successful Colonial Library Series for Indian-based readers, drawing on Murray's past experiment as well as on Richard Bentley's short-lived Bentley's Empire Library (which published 16 titles between 1878 and 1881). Kegan Paul started up its own Indian and Colonial Library Series in 1887 in an attempt to compete with Macmillan (and in which Philip Meadows Taylor's work featured prominently), but the venture proved unsuccessful and was terminated in 1889.[7]

Between 1850 and 1864 alone, the value of imported English language texts jumped a staggering 120 per cent, from £150,000 to £330,000. Subsequent levels of imports dropped but were to hold steady through to 1900 at around £210,000 per annum, with British-produced works accounting for almost 95 per cent of all Western books brought into India between 1850 and 1900, and approximately 80 per cent or more of these arriving in the port cities of Bombay and Calcutta.[8]

The types of texts shipped to Indian shores were multifarious, including grammar and general textbooks, biographies, poetry, histories, plays, novels and literary periodicals. Priya Joshi notes that the British novel, particularly those of 'serious standards', was a dominant textual form imported into India in the nineteenth-century, brought in as a means of supporting and legitimating Englishness in the colony. 'Yet the fiction consumed most voraciously,' she argues – 'discussed, copied, translated, and "adapted" most avidly into Indian languages, and eventually into the Indian novel – was not the novel of "serious standards" but the work of what are often considered minor British novelists whose fortunes soared for several generations among enthusiastic and loyal Indian readers long after they had already waned in Britain.'[9] Meadows Taylor's historical romances were among such 'minor' works that dominated Indian library and book trade lists. A study of European authors available to nineteenth-century Indian readers in 14 public libraries in Bombay, Calcutta, Madras, Delhi, Allahabad and Patna between 1860 and 1901, for example, notes that Taylor's work could be found in 12 of them.[10] Meadows Taylor's novels also appear in a survey of nineteenth-century European works most translated into Indian languages (and in particular his novels *Confessions of a Thug* and *Tara*, the latter of which was trans-lated into four different indigenous languages).[11]

Whether of 'serious nature' or not, print culture, as part of government printed and sanctioned edicts and information, or as part of educational or cultural remits, was seen by nineteenth-century British commentators as key to ruling and changing India. Nicholas Dirks, in his introduction to a collection of essays entitled *Colonialism and Culture*, effectively sum-marises, 'Colonial knowledge both enabled colonial conquest and was produced by it; in certain ways, culture was what colonialism was all about.'[12] As the *Friend of India* noted in 1836, 'Our Empire in India is an empire of opinion', acknowledging the role that information and social communication processes played in upholding and defining the British presence in India.[13] In a speech to the Edinburgh Philosophical Society in 1846, Lord Macaulay, drew similar attention to the effect that expo-sure to British print culture was expected to have in India, offering a toast 'to the literature of Britain ... which has exercised an influence wider than that of our commerce and mightier than that of our arms ... before the light of which impious and cruel superstitions are fast taking flight on the Banks of the Ganges!'[14]

III. The reader

But what of the tattered volume of *Seeta* that sparked off this inquiry into the Indian colonial book trade? First noticeable item of interest was an owner's label stuck in the inside cover of the volume, as well as on the first page of the opening chapter. The label read Surgeon-General F. F. Allen, C.B. Who was Surgeon-General Allen? Little information is available on him, but details that exist suggest Frederick Freeman Allen was a medical surgeon, born in 1825, who in 1848 joined the Bengal Army as an assistant surgeon and over the next 30 years, like Meadows Taylor before him, took on unconventional postings in indigenous services. He rose steadily through the Indian military medical ranks, becoming surgeon to the Fourth Regiment Irregular Cavalry between 1852 and 1857, surgeon to the Second Ghurka Regiment between 1858 and 1876 and retiring in 1880 as Deputy Surgeon-General in the can-tonment of Umballa (now Ambala), about 200 kilometres from Delhi. On his retirement he moved to Brighton (as was common amongst returning civil, military and medical colonial returnees). Knighted a Companion of Bath (C.B.) in 1872, on his return to Britain in 1880, he was awarded the titular title of Honorary Physician to the Queen, a post he kept until his death in December 1888.

Having established who Allen was, let's consider when and where he might have purchased *Seeta*. Allen retired in 1880, just as this third edition was issued. It is conceivable he might have picked up his copy on his return to Britain. He would have been the type of interested reader the book was aimed at, and Kegan Paul & Co. were assiduous in advertising their novels in newspaper and journal ads, as well as in the back of related publications. But Allen had not bought this work in Britain. He had bought it in India; in Bombay, to be exact, at a branch of the well-known Indo-British bookselling and publishing firm Thacker and Co. This much can be established by a faint bookseller's stamp on the inside front leaf of the work. This book, published in London, was part of the flood of books imported into India, shipped thousands of miles from London in a general consignment to Thacker & Co.'s Bombay book-selling wing.

IV. The bookseller

But who were Thacker and Co.? Here is a question that those interested in colonial book history in India should pause to consider. The history of Thacker and Co. (or Thacker, Spink and Co. as they were better known) is one of the least known in nineteenth-century Indo-British print-culture history. Yet it is one of the most important in terms of the Indian colonial book trade, for Thacker and Co. were important intermediaries in the conduit of British texts to Indian shores. Part of the difficulty in understanding the firm's place in Indian cultural-distribution terms is the lack of primary documentation about it: there are no archival records extant, or at least very few that relate directly to the firm's activities or that have been recorded in major public repositories. But for over 100 years, it played a major role in Indo-British circles, and the lack of information and documentation of its activities leaves a gaping hole in our understanding of the circulation of colonial texts in the main cities of India.

What we do know can be gleaned from scattered printed sources – advertisements, newspaper clippings and other ephemeral notes. These suggest that the firm was founded in Calcutta in 1819, serving multiple functions as publisher, printer, bookseller, stationer and banker. Lucrative business links with Britain resulting from these activities led the founder William Thacker to open a branch in Broad Street, London in 1839 under the name W. Thacker and Co. Not much is known of William Thacker, though one brief account notes he was a genial and lenient character, 'noble in appearance, courteous in his manner, and venerable in his long silvering hair'.[15] Thacker shifted premises to 41 Threadneedle Street, in 1842; then 46 Lime Street, in 1846; and finally 87 Newgate Street, in 1851. In 1851 William Spink, nephew of William Thacker, joined the firm in Calcutta, and the company was renamed Thacker, Spink and Co., though it continued to trade in various circumstances as Thacker & Co. The firm also traded in Bombay as Thacker, Vining and Co. from 1860 through to the 1940s. Its most famous employee was Henry Irving, who spent four years as an apprentice in the London office between 1852 to 1856, before forging a successful career as an actor and theatrical entrepreneur.[16]

The firm serviced colonial readers in many ways. Its best-known work was its *Directories*, first published in 1863 and which dominated the market thereafter. The *Directories*, contained commercial and trade lists for Calcutta, and then later for all three Indian Presidencies. From around 1864 onwards the *Directories* also featured advertisements for books sold or printed at their own press, or bought on consignment from London publishers such as Macmillan or specialist firms such as the legal publishers William Maxwell. In addition it acted as a publisher for government sources, producing law codes and acts, military texts and guidebooks. Other publications included general works on topography, Indian religion, flora and fauna, languages and general literature. It did not publish indigenous language texts. Through its bookselling and subscription library branches it distributed its works and material imported from Britain. It also offered banking and general financial services to its Indo-British clients, drawn from the East India Company, the military and the British Indian civil service.

Thacker & Co. was not the only agency to operate such bookselling, publishing and financial services for Indo-British clients. Another competitor was Henry S. King, founder, in 1871, of the London firm that would become the publishing giant C. Kegan Paul, and for a period a partner by marriage in the Smith, Elder publishing firm, who successfully developed the East India agency and banking arms of Smith, Elder between 1853 and 1868. This had emerged out of bookselling activities in India, where in providing books and stationery to East India Company officers anxious for the latest news and material from Britain, Smith, Elder had also tapped into market demands for a range of financial services, from money drafts to banking interchange services between Britain and India. From there they had moved into publishing newspapers for both home and overseas markets: thus the *Overland Mail*, established in 1855, provided home news to Indian-based readers, while the *Homeward Mail*, started in 1857, provided Indian news to British readers. As Leslie

Howsam points out, such lucrative overseas trade subsidised much of Smith, Elder literary publishing work: the funds poured into the founding of their monthly literary journal *The Cornhill Magazine* in 1860, and their newspaper *The Pall Mall Gazette* in 1865 owed a great deal to the turnover generated by King's financial and commercial work (£627,129 in 1866 alone).[17] In 1868, King and George Smith dissolved their partnership, and King took with him the agency and banking concerns, which he continued to run along with new publishing concerns begun in 1871, before selling off the publishing side to Charles Kegan Paul in 1877. He died in 1878.

Thacker, modelled along similar flexible business lines, gained lucrative contracts publishing government manuals and directories, sold books from Britain to Indo-British customers and offered financial and banking services to these same customers. It was able to use the profits generated to operate from comfortable surroundings. One of the few accounts we have of Thacker in the nineteenth-century comes from the travel writer Emma Roberts, who writes in 1835 of visiting Calcutta, where 'the most magnificent establishment in the city is that of the principal bookseller, Thacker & Co.'[18] In the 1920s, the same Calcutta branch was still in operation, providing the Bengali writer Nirad Chaudhuri with French and English publications of limited editions of Anatole France, Arden editions of Shakespeare, and copies of Moliere's plays.[19]

Thacker & Co. is best remembered now for its connection with Kipling – it published his first works, *Departmental Ditties* and *Plain Tales from the Hills*, in 1886 and 1888 respectively.[20] Quiller-Couch recalls the excitement generated in London literary circles by this new talent, which led him to rush off on Henry James's recommendation to Thacker and Spinks' exotic London store in search of Kipling's new works: 'Next morning, following the master's directions,' he wrote years later, 'I found the emporium of Messrs. Thacker and Spink in the City, and dug out from behind piles of cinnamon, aloe, cassia, and other products of the East, a collection of grey paper-bound pamphlets, together with 'Plain Tales from the Hills' in cloth.'[21]

In 1919 the firm split its operations, floating off its London branch as a separate concern. Heavy losses in its banking operations over the following decade, and debts of £13,500 owed to its former London partners for goods supplied, led the Calcutta-based part of the firm to file for bankruptcy in November 1931.[22] The Indian bookselling branches were bought out by a team comprised of local management and former employees, and continued to operate in diminishing circumstances until the 1960s. That more is not known about this firm is due in great part to the loss of British and Indian business records documenting its history – the former due to bombing damage suffered during the Second World War, the latter due to the ravages of climate.

V. Reading the signs

One final point to consider, which I referred to at the start of this, so completing the cycle of production, distribution and reception this paper has loosely adhered to. The tattered volume of *Seeta* that began this discussion has some important clues to impart about readership and reader reception. And it raises questions about how closely Allen identified himself with the work he bought in Bombay in 1880 and brought home with him to Brighton to read. Until recently, very few had seen the value of examining the blank spaces in books for evidence of responses from individual or interpretive communities of readers.[23]

Part of this shift in critical enquiry has been motivated by the hunt for the individual reader, recognition that readers are *different*, thus making it difficult to impose homogeneous identities on readers. Yet at the same time a powerful argument has been advanced for viewing individuals within the contexts of interpretive communities of readers,[24] whose individualistic responses to texts are mediated within shared codes of interpretation, whether of a national, communal or social nature. It is what James L. Machor in *Readers in History* has called 'the exploration of reading as a product of the relationship among particular interpretive strategies, epistemic frames, ideological imperatives and social orientations of readers as members of historically specific – and historiographically specified – interpretive communities'.[25]

In this volume are intriguing signs of readership interaction, signs of additions and omissions. Pasted into the inside front and back of the volume are contemporary newspaper clippings from the *Pioneer* on interracial marriages and relationships. On the inside front, a poem of an amorous encounter between British officer and an Indian woman; on the back, an article bemoaning the lack of understanding of Indian culture and society amongst the British in India, and claiming things were better in the past when Indo-British relations allowed interracial marriage (putting the blame for this separation on the codification and separation of Indo-British social life through the introduction of the British woman in India). The relevant passage noting this is heavily underscored and a comment inked in the side reads, 'true in part'.

Missing is the frontispiece showing the dramatic moment when Seeta saves her British husband from certain death by spear thrust from a 'native' mutineer. Also ripped out of the work is a crucial chapter which includes an impassioned defence of interracial marriage by the main British male protagonist, Philip Mostyn, who argues forcefully for a return to cordial and informal relations with Indians, expresses appreciation for their undervalued cultural traditions and questions the social bar against relationships between British and Indian subjects.

Such examples of readership interaction with the text (the notations and the omissions) are intriguing; they point to an aspect of Surgeon-General F. F. Allen that is difficult to clarify without further knowledge of his personal circumstances. Did he, for example, have a particular reason for identifying with the sentiments and themes of the work? Had he himself personal experience of a miscegenational relationship? The biographical details available do not record his status as being other than single. Like Meadows Taylor, Allen was an individual whose career was spent in general military service, though Allen, acting as physician to indigenous and British troops and stationed in both major and minor cantonments, was less isolated within British Indian military society than Meadows Taylor. British military attitudes to mixed-race relations, as recent commentators have pointed out, were complex, ambivalent and fluctuated throughout the nineteenth-century.[26] Miscegenation, initially condoned in the early part of the nineteenth-century, became problematic as the century progressed, not least because of a groundswell of British popular opinion that was decidedly against encouraging marriage or sexual relations between Indians and Europeans, and an increasingly intolerant British Indian society that drew on racially based categorisation and quantification to maintain social and hierarchical distances between rulers and ruled. But ample evidence exists of the British Indian army condoning acts of miscegenation within certain parameters, and in some instances encouraging it, partly in order to resolve the issue of the continuing lack of single European women of marriageable age in the Indian sub-continent throughout much of the period. Thus, as Young and Peers point out, while racial discourse was always informed by the potential of interracial sexuality, it was done in fragmentary and unstable ways.

F. F. Allen's marginalia comments on miscegenation then are perhaps less surprising in such contexts. They also reveal a misogynistic attitude towards European women that was common among old 'India' hands. The male dominated world of the British military in India in the nineteenth-century was one which often bemoaned the changes brought about by the insertion of British women into contemporary colonial society. Allen was no exception. As far as miscegenation was concerned, though, from the little evidence available, Allen thought the topic significant enough to warrant recording, commentating on and saving relevant ephemera within the covers of this unusual tale of mixed marriage.

VI. Conclusion

The evident physical signs of interaction with *Seeta* noted here only provide tantalising and inconclusive insights into a contemporary reader's engagement with its themes. The trajectory of colonial book production, distribution and reception which this essay has attempted to sketch out as a whole is sadly and frustratingly also incomplete, particularly in terms of understanding the manner in which intermediaries like Thacker & Co. functioned to facilitate the circulation of texts in colonial India. At very least this piece offers an example of the type of unusual information waiting to be uncovered through engagement with such non-standard and secondary source material for clues about colonial print culture.

Notes

1. David Finkelstein, *Philip Meadows Taylor (1808–1876)*. Victorian Fiction Research Guides XVIII (Queensland: University of Queensland Press, 1990): 3–4.
2. Quoted in Finkelstein, 1990, 14.
3. Bart Moore-Gilbert, *Kipling and 'Orientalism'* (London: Croom Helm Ltd, 1986): 52–3.
4. Hilda Gregg, 'The Indian Mutiny in Fiction', *Blackwood's Magazine*. 161 (February 1897): 222.
5. Anon., *Calcutta Review*. 63 (1873): 87.
6. Quoted in Priya Joshi, *In Another Country: Colonialism, Culture, and the English Novel in India* (New York: Columbia University Press, 2002): 96.
7. See Joshi, 2002, 93–138; also Johanson, Graeme, *A Study of Colonial Editions in Australia, 1843–1972* (Wellington, NZ: Elibank Press, 2000) *passim*.
8. Priya Joshi, 'Culture and Consumption: Fiction, the Reading Public, and the British Novel in Colonial India', *Book History* 1 (1998), 200, 201; Joshi, 2002, 41.
9. Joshi 1998, 197.
10. Joshi 2002, 64–66.
11. Joshi, 2002, 70–1.
12. Nicholas Dirks, ed. *Colonialism and Culture* (Ann Arbor: University of Michigan Press, 1992): 3.
13. *Friend of India*, 27 October 1836, as quoted in C. A. Bayly, *Empire and Information: Intelligence Gathering and Social Communication in India, 1780–1870* (Cambridge University Press, 1996): 218.
14. Quoted in Joshi, 1998, 199.

15. Laurence Henry Forster Irving, *Henry Irving: The Actor and his World* (London: Columbus Books, 1989, originally published by Faber and Faber, 1951): 49.
16. Evan Cotton, 'A Famous Calcutta Firm: The History of Thacker Spink and Co.', *Bengal Past and Present*. 109.1/2 (1990): 166.
17. Leslie Howsam, *Kegan Paul – A Victorian Imprint: Publishers, Books and Cultural History* (London and Toronto: Kegan Paul International and University of Toronto Press, 1998): 19.
18. Quoted in Joshi 2002, 93.
19. Nirad C. Chaudhuri, *Autobiography of an Unknown Indian* (London: Hogarth, 1987): 130, 190.
20. See Thomas Pinney and David Alan Richards eds., *Kipling and His First Publisher: Correspondence of Rudyard Kipling with Thacker, Spink and Co., 1886–1890* (High Wycombe, Bucks: Rivendale Press, 2001).
21. Arthur Quiller-Couch, 'Fifty Years – Books and Other Friends.' *The Times*. 46053 (10 Feb 1932): 13.
22. Anon. 'W. Thacker and Co.'s Failure'. *The Times*. 46150 (3 June 1932): 4.
23. H. J. Jackson, *Marginalia: Readers Writing in Books*. (New Haven and London: Yale University Press, 2001); H. J. Jackson, *Romantic Readers: The Evidence of Marginalia* (New Haven and London: Yale University Press, 2005); David F. Norton and Mary J. *David Hume's Library* (Edinburgh: National Library of Scotland, 1996).
24. Stanley Fish, 'Is There a Text in This Class?' *Critical Enquiry* 2, 3 (1976): 465–86. Rpt. in David Finkelstein and Alistair McCleery (eds) *The Book History Reader* (London: Routledge, 2001): 350–8.
25. James L. Machor ed., *Readers in History: Nineteenth-Century American Literature and the Contexts of Response* (Baltimore: Johns Hopkins University Press, 1993): x.
26. See, for example, Douglas Mark Peers, 'The Raj's Other Great Game: Policing the Sexual Frontiers of the Indian Army in the First Half of the Nineteenth-Century' in Anupama Rao and Stephen Pierce (eds) *Discipline and the Other Body: Correction, Corporeality, Colonialism,* (Durham, NC: Duke University Press, 2006): 115–50; Robert Young, *Colonial Desire: Hybridity in Theory, Culture and Race* (London: Routledge, 1995).

7
Thacker, Spink and Company: Bookselling and Publishing in Mid-Nineteenth-Century Calcutta

Victoria Condie

Sydney Shep's chapter on 'The Transnational Turn in Book History', with which the first volume of the collection *Books Without Borders* opens, sets out to argue that prevailing frames of reference need to be re-thought to enable book history as a discipline to move forward. One way of achieving this goal might be to deconstruct and then expand national book histories so as to arrive at 'the essential nature of our object of study: books without borders'.[1] In the present volume both David Finkelstein and Robert Fraser demonstrate, in their respective chapters on book consumption and publishing in British India (Chapters 6 and 9), how the imperial commercial nexus supplied in itself a convincing illustration of Shep's cross-national paradigm. India was manifestly part of the Empire, and yet the kinds of books imported into the sub-continent from Britain, or else published in India itself, crossed every sort of frontier, and not just geographical ones. The activities of a British-Indian firm such as Thacker, Spink and Company shed light on this facet of book production, distribution and reception. They also provide a commentary on, and manifold insights into, the nature of British rule.

'Everybody in India knows Thacker, Spink and Company', so wrote 'Septimus' in a reminiscence entitles 'Rudyard Kipling's English Debut' for the 1917 edition of *Indian Ink*, a magazine published by Thacker, Spink and Company in aid of the Imperial War Fund. 'Septimus's' exaggerated claim, made doubtless for effect, nevertheless contains an element of truth. The official *Directories*, Indian law books, sports and horsemanship titles, guide books, and general literature caused the firm to become part of the British-Indian cultural landscape for most of the nineteenth and early twentieth centuries. Put very broadly, the period between the firm's founder, William Thacker's arrival in Calcutta and the liquidation of the firm in the early 1930s covers almost all stages through which British India passed: the closing years of the East India Company, the loss of its charter and metamorphosis into the Indian Civil Service, full Imperial rule after 1857, and the inevitable move towards the end of that rule.

The history and activities of Thacker, Spink and Company and the firm's contribution to the book trade in India have never been fully documented. The only study to recount the firm's history is an article written by Evan Cotton in 1931 entitled 'A Famous Calcutta Firm: The History of Thacker, Spink and Company'.[2] In his article, Cotton outlines the history of the firm with reference to its various locations in Calcutta and London, the partnership between William Thacker and his nephew William Spink, and the offices held by Spink and his descendants in the non-official British community in Calcutta, and the publication of the first issue of Thacker's *Post Office Directory* in 1863. He also makes brief mention of the firm's association with Rudyard Kipling and includes much anecdotal material. More recently, Rimi Chatterjee refers to Thacker, Spink and Company's association with Macmillan and Company in London and Calcutta;[3] and Thomas Pinney and David Allan Richards have written about the firm, but only in the context of its association with Kipling.[4] The firm continued in Calcutta until 1933, when it is listed as being in liquidation. After this it ceased to exist as Thacker, Spink and Company and traded as Thacker's Press and Directories Ltd. It was later taken over by a succession of Indian entrepreneurs. As Chatterjee states, no archive has yet been traced nor is it known whether any exists. Consequently any account of Thacker, Spink and Company must be constructed mainly from secondary material, bearing in mind the arbitrary nature of some of the sources.

This chapter presents the first stages of my ongoing research into the history and activities of Thacker, Spink and Company. It outlines chronologically the establishment of the firm and considers its activities in the non-official British community in Calcutta and in bookselling and publishing from its founding in 1819, until its first association with Kipling, which has been the subject of Pinney's and Richards' book and which marks the high point of the firm's activities. The principal sources used to construct the study thus far include Minutes referring to the firm located in the Bengal Despatches of the East India Company between 1818 and 1857; the Directories and Registers published for the Bengal Presidency in the 1820s and 1830s; and the Directories which Thacker, Spink and Company produced annually from 1863 and which contain commercial and trade lists, advertisements for products and services offered by the firm, and lists of their current and forthcoming publications. References to Thacker and Company denote the firm before 1851; Thacker, Spink and Company to the post-1851 partnership.

In Volume 3 of *Scenes and Characteristics of Hindustan with Sketches of Anglo-Indian Society* published in 1835, Emma Roberts wrote:

> Next to the jewellers' shops the most magnificent establishment in the city is that of the principal bookseller, Thacker and Company; there are others of inferior note, which have circulating libraries attached to them; but the splendid scale of this literary emporium, and the elegance of its arrangements, place it far and above all its competitors.[5]

By 1835, Thacker and Company had been established in Calcutta for 16 years, but according to Emma Roberts' account had risen to a position of pre-eminence. William Thacker's connections with Calcutta had begun in 1819 when he received a licence from the East India Company. The Court Minute for 30 December 1818 records:

> Mr William Thacker has also our permission to proceed to your Presidency for the purposes of deposing of the consignments of Messers Black, Kingsbury, Parbury and Company and of recovering considerable sums held to be due to them upon the usual terms and conditions.[6]

The firm of Black, Kingsbury and Allen was bookseller to the East India Company. Evan Cotton claims that William Thacker 'had made four voyages to the East as surgeon of an Indiaman before receiving permission to reside in the Presidency in 1819';[7] and a similar claim is made by Donald McDonald in his account of the Indian Medical Service, in which he states: 'It is interesting that the well-known firm of publishers, Thacker and Spink of Calcutta was founded in 1819 by William Thacker, who had been surgeon of the "Earl of St Vincent" from 1810–11.'[8] No record, however, appears to exist of a William Thacker as surgeon in the Register of East India Company ships with particular reference to the voyages of the 'Earl of St Vincent' in 1810–11. Although it would not have been uncommon for an individual engaged in the book trade in the early nineteenth century also to have worked as a surgeon, for the purposes of this study it will be assumed that the first documented reference to William Thacker's association with India occurs in the Minute of 30 December 1818.

The next mention of William Thacker in Calcutta appears in the *East India Register and Directory* for 1821, where he is listed among the European inhabitants of Bengal as 'Thacker, William, surgeon and agent for Black and Parry, booksellers'.[9] In the same year he appears in the *Calcutta Kalendar and Post Office Directory* (printed by and for S. Greenway and Company) as 'Thacker, William, Agent for Black and Parry, booksellers, Loll Bazaar'.[10] The 1824 plan of Calcutta drawn by J. A. Schalch shows Loll Bazaar, a street rather than an area, at right angles to Tank Square. In the north-east corner of the square the Church of St Andrews had been newly built, and opposite this was St Andrews Library, where Thacker and Company was first established. J. P. Losty notes the proximity of the Oriental Library founded by Harry Colesworthy, but points out that both were booksellers rather than libraries.[11]

The *Bengal Almanac and Annual Directory* for 1822 and 1823 include Mr William Thacker as an annual subscriber and list him under British and Foreign subjects together with profession (in this case surgeon and bookseller) and year of arrival in India (1818).[12] The reference to his tandem careers would appear to corroborate the information provided by Cotton and McDonald, and the Minute and *Directory* entry can therefore provide the *terminus post quem* of William Thacker's Indian career. He is last referred to as 'surgeon' in *The New Annual Bengal Directory and General Register* for 1824.[13] On its title page, W. Thacker and Company is referred to as seller of the Directory in Calcutta. By 1824 other firms involved in bookselling in the city, besides Samuel Smith and Thacker and Company, include R. Alexander, J. J. Fleury, Grigg and Company, and Pengelly and Company.

Recorded references to Thacker and Company throughout the 1830s are also scarce. *The Bengal Directory and General Register* records for the period 1834 to 1839 include 'William Thacker and Company' in the Trade Lists, and the firm's premises by 1835 as being located at 1 Old Court House.[14] William Thacker appears in the List of Residents only until 1837, and Evan Cotton records that Thacker died in London in 1872.[15] As the first agency in London was established, again according to Cotton, in 1839 at New Broad Street,[16] this would suggest that Thacker left Calcutta finally in 1837. By 1841 Thacker and Company had transferred its premises to 4 Government Place, where it remained until 1869, then moving to 5 Government Place until 1877, and subsequently occupying 5 and 6 Government Place until 1916.

As a consequence of the growth of the non-official European community in the Bengal Presidency, commercial associations began to be established. The non-official community appears to have had a rather marginal existence under both the East India Company and the *Raj*. In the divisions of Thacker's *Directories* and those which came before, the 'Commercial' and 'Trade' sections (in that order) came near the end, only before conveyancing, postal and street directory information. Raymond K. Renford, who has written extensively on this subject, points out that from early on the East India Company had had trouble from 'interlopers'; that is, individuals who were not in the civil, military or naval employ of the Company or British Government.[17] Of the three Presidencies, Calcutta provided the most fertile ground for these so-called 'commercial speculators'. Any individual not a member of the Company who wished to travel to India to engage in trade had to apply to the Court (as seen above in the case of William Thacker) for permission which, if granted, was done so jealously as it was thought that too wide an opening would result in an indiscriminate flood of Europeans threatening the Company's interests. However, between 1814 and 1831, 1,253 licence applications were agreed to, the majority being to partners and assistants in mercantile establishments.

With the growth of the non-official community a number of associations developed to meet the needs of smaller firms that were all too often looked down on by the civil and military establishments. However, these Trades' Associations possessed their own hierarchies. Chambers of Commerce, for instance, carried much more weight than Trades' Associations, even if the latter included large retail establishments and, as in the case of the Calcutta Trade Association, were close to Government. The members of the Trades' Associations and Chambers of Commerce came to reflect the more reactionary attitudes of British India in the late nineteenth century and as a result became less influential. In Calcutta and Bombay, members of both the Chambers of Commerce and Trades' Associations violently denounced the Ilbert Bill of 1883.

In July 1830, the Calcutta Trade Association was formed. It was the oldest public body in the country, the Trades' Association of Bombay not being established until 1868. In 1852 a compression of an account of the transactions of the Calcutta Trade Association between 1830 and 1850 was printed and presented to its members by the committee.[18] It begins with an address written by William Spink, the current Master of the Trade Association, in which he states the reasons for setting up the association; namely, to encourage the system of ready money payment given that indiscriminate credit is ruinous to tradesmen, to define limits of credit where it is allowed, and to encourage communication amongst those engaged in business in Calcutta.[19] The *Report* lists the names of those tradesmen present at the first public meeting on 12 June 1830.

Twenty-six tradesmen were present representing professions such as coach making, cabinet making, boot making, general shop keeping, commission agencies, auctioneers, and bookselling. Among the booksellers were T. Ostell (representing T. Ostell and Company) and George Parbury (representing Thacker and Company).[20] Parbury remained a member of the Calcutta Trade Association until 10 September 1831 but was never appointed to any position within the Association.[21] His name appears in the transactions of a committee set up to consider whether the Association should extend beyond the protection of property and interests of its members to provide support for the widows and children of deceased tradesmen.[22] William Thacker also remained a member until September 1831 but like Parbury was never appointed to any position. William Spink became a member in 1846.[23]

As far as Thacker, Spink and Company's activities in publishing and bookselling are concerned, there is little evidence to be gleaned about these in the 1820s and 1830s. In 1823 the firm published *The Oriental Magazine and Calcutta Review*, which at the close of its first year of publication was converted into *The Quarterly Oriental Magazine and Review and Register*. It was first printed at the Baptist Mission Press but by 1827 was being printed at the Hindoostanee Press by Samuel Smith and Company.[24] In 1831 *The Bengal Annual Register and Directory* records Thacker and Company as being responsible for the monthly publication *Gleanings of Science*.[25] A year later the firm published a monthly periodical, *The Calcutta Christian Observer*, printed at the Baptist Mission Press and intended to be the mouthpiece of the missionary body. In 1833, however, the charge of publishing and circulating the work was transferred from Thacker and Company to Mr G. C. Hay at the Depository of the Calcutta Christian Tract and Book Society with the explanation that:

> the Proprietors need to economise has necessitated the transference of the charge of publishing and circulation from Thackers to Hay and Company.[26]

In 1835, Thacker and Company is listed in *The Bengal Directory and General Register* as publishing monthly *The Journal of the Asiatic Society* and *The Christian Observer*.[27] The latter continued to be published until 1847. In 1836 the firm published monthly *The Indian Journal of Medical Science*, which continued until 1839, when no further mention is made.[28]

As well as the publication of journals that did not have a very long life span, Thacker and Company was also becoming involved in official publishing. Minutes recorded in the Despatches of the East India Company for 1842 refer to the Company's acceptance of

> Messers Thacker's offer to undertake the publication of the Topographical Report on Ajmere, on Government purchasing 200 copies for 580 rupees.[29]

In 1843, three Minutes refer to payment made to Thacker and Company for Sevestre's Reports of cases decided by the Sudder Courts (Court of Appeal) in Calcutta.[30] The provision of legal works and editions of Acts by Thacker and Company for the Governments of the Bengal and Bombay Presidencies continued into the 1850s. A Minute of 1849 also refers to the preparation of 1000 copies of Account Books for soldiers by Thacker and Company at 8 annas *per* copy. The remark appended to this Minute states:

> The cost of these Account Books here including the binding, is 4 and ¼ pence. It is therefore unadvisable to procure them hereafter in India at the cost of 8 annas or 1 shilling.[31]

This suggests that the costs involved in book production and the profits possibly made were not infinitesimal, and a number of remarks appended to Minutes recording payment to Thacker and Company for books enforce this; for example, in response to the payment to the firm of 2,250 rupees for 250 copies of the Acts of 1849, it is remarked:

> We have to observe that the charge of 9 rupees for a volume containing so little letter press seems high.[32]

This involvement with official publishing in the 1840s did not preclude, however, the publication of what might be termed works of general literature; such as *Miscellaneous Writings in Prose and Verse Comprising Dramatic Characters, Poems, Songs, Tales, Translations, Travels* by Captain A. H. E. Boileau of the Bengal Engineers. Published by Thacker and Company and Ostell and Lepage in 1845, it illustrates Thacker's consistent, albeit small, involvement with general works written by men and women resident in India.

The most significant commercial venture undertaken by Thacker, Spink and Company was the publication of the annual Directories, which began with *Thacker's Post Office Directory* in 1863. The firm was not the first to produce Directories for the Bengal Presidency, and a number of those earlier compilations have already been referred to.

In addition to these, the Presidency saw in the 1840s *Scott and Company's Bengal Directory* printed and published in Calcutta by Scott and Company, and then in the 1850s A. G. Roussac's *New Calcutta Directory* that first appeared in 1856 and was printed at the Military Orphan Press. The title page of *The New Calcutta Directory* lists the following firms as sellers of the work: R. C. Lepage and Company; Thacker, Spink and Company; P. S. D'Rozario and Company; G. C. Hay and Company; and W. Newman. The price is not indicated on the title page of the 1856 Directory but by 1860 is advertised as 12 rupees for subscribers, 16 rupees for non-subscribers, and for Mofussil subscribers an additional charge of 1 rupee was added for postage. Roussac's Directory is divided into ten parts: Almanac; Ecclesiastical; Civil; Military; Marine; Societies including Schools and Hospitals; Commercial; Street Directory and List of Inhabitants; Mofussil; and an Appendix listing the shipping arrivals and departures, and births, deaths, and marriages. In the Commercial section under the alphabetical list of Professions and Trades, Thacker, Spink and Company is referred to as booksellers, publishers, stationers, army, and general agents.[33] The firm consisted at this time of two partners, William Thacker (now back in London) and William Spink, and five assistants. Its branches are listed as W. Thacker and Company, 87 Newgate Street, London; Thacker, Spink and Company, 4 Government Place, Calcutta; and Thacker and Company, Forbes Street, Bombay. According to the evidence of the *Bombay Almanac and Book of Direction*,[34] the branch was established in Bombay in 1852 under the agency of Mr Frederick Vining. It became Thacker, Vining and Company in 1861.

Thacker, Spink and Company must have glimpsed an opportunity when they published their own Directory in 1863, printed at the Military Orphan Press. No price is listed in the 1863 Directory, nor is it in subsequent ones until 1869, when it appears as 14 rupees. *Thacker's Post Office Directory* follows Roussac's orderings and is set out in 17 parts: Almanac; Civil; Military; Uncovenanted Civil Service; Law; Marine; Clerical; Educational; Commercial; Trade; Conveyance; Banking; Assurance; Postal; Miscellaneous; Street Directory; and the Mofussil. This order remained essentially unchanged in subsequent Directories. This first Directory also contains a page-long 'Preface' consisting of a disclaimer, an oblique reference to Roussac's Directory, an acknowledgement, and a statement of intent concerning future Directories. The reference to Roussac's Directory is couched thus:

> In the forthcoming volume for 1864, much of the difficulty will be conquerable; but it will be readily imagined that a rival to the Work

already existing would naturally meet with no small opposition and that such opposition could not but throw preliminary, insuperable obstacles in the way of success.

Roussac had taken out an action against Thacker, Spink and Company as he regarded publication of Thacker's Directory as an infringement of his rights. According to Cotton the matter was settled,[35] but this does not seem to have stopped the Projectors, as the publishers referred to themselves in the 'Preface', claiming:

> The repeated failures to produce all other Directories in sufficient time, as well as their high price and unwieldy size, have led to the limit of this work, by more skilful typographical arrangement, to its present size, hereby enabling a reduction of price to be effected, with the desideratum of a really usable Book (containing every possible information) produced at the time it is needed.

Thacker's 1863 Directory is 108 pages long whereas Roussac's 1863 Directory runs to 1,107 pages. Roussac ceased producing his Directory after 1863.

Although the evidence contained in the Directories for the 1860s appears limited, it can provide the following information about the activities of Thacker, Spink and Company. The firm was sufficiently well-established in Calcutta by 1863 to publish a Directory in direct competition to A. G. Roussac. Thacker's Directories were to be conceived along different lines from all predecessors and competitors (at least according to the firm) in that they would be reasonably priced and contain information useful to the conduct of daily business. By 1865, the title of the Directory became *Thacker's Directory*, suggesting that the firm was confident of being accepted as the publishers of the pre-eminent Directory for Bengal. Thacker, Spink and Company by now was also running its own press, located close to their premises in Government Place at 1 Fancy Lane, and, according to the evidence of the Directories, had become publishers and booksellers to the Calcutta University.

The impression from the Directories of Thacker, Spink and Company as a business is one of variety, but their activities as listed in the Trade Lists do not differ remarkably from other similar firms in Calcutta. Like Thacker, Spink and Company, Barham Hill, W. Newman, Wyman and Company, G. C. Hay and Company, and P. S. D'Rozario are all listed as account-book sellers, booksellers, stationers, bookbinders, mathematical instrument importers, photographic apparatus sellers, print sellers, picture galleries, scientific instrument importers, and depots of European goods. The Directories for the 1860s contain very little extant advertising material: where it does occur with reference to Thacker, Spink and Company it is for consignments of law books from specialist London legal publishers such as William Maxwell, or for camp equipment, or services such as printing and lithography. Although there are references to the 'many books' printed at the press, extant lists of these do not appear in the Directories until 1872. The publication of the yearly Directories and works such as the *Bengal Law Reports* remains constant, reflecting the fact that the firm was official publishers. The publication of periodicals, however, fluctuates: *Sutherland's Weekly Reporter* (a legal periodical) is listed between 1865 and 1870, after which it was taken up by the Bengal Printing Company's press; the bimonthly *Literary Register and General Advertiser* and the monthly *Indian Society* appear between 1866 and 1869, after which there is no further mention of them.

During the 1870s and 1880s, Thacker, Spink and Company appears to begin to use the Directories to project itself as an expanding business. The Directories were renamed *The Bengal Directory* and by 1877 the price had increased to 16 rupees (or 14 rupees for prompt cash payment). Advertisements become more plentiful with the end pages of the Directories being given over to those predominantly for the firm's own goods and services. As far as goods other than books are concerned, Thacker, Spink and Company could supply the Bengal Presidency with 176 different items ranging from stationery to indoor and outdoor games equipment, mathematical and surveying instruments, and theatrical appurtenances.

The sort of books published and sold by Thacker, Spink and Company divide into categories in the 1870s and 1880s: standard Indian law works; works on Indian languages, history, biography, and politics; travel books; the natural sciences; finance and produce of India; military works; gardening; medicine; surveying; theology; literature and poetry; examination manuals; telegraphic codes and ready reckoners; educational works advertised in the 1877 Directory as including Macmillan and Company's English Series of Textbooks for Indian Schools, witness to the fact that the firm was the agent for Macmillan; publications of the Secretary of State for India in Council; and maps of India and adjacent countries. In the 1883 Directory, the list of works published and sold by Thacker, Spink and Company runs to 60 pages.

Despite the apparent range of material, Thacker, Spink and Company remained, essentially, official publishers. As Pinney and Richards argue, the firm did not need an extensive, speculative line in general literature, as the buyers of new books did not form a very large proportion of the British population in India in the nineteenth century.[36] Although a number of books written by Indians appear in the lists (especially as far as standard Indian law books are concerned), it would seem the emporium was frequented mainly by Europeans. Remembering the early 1920s, Nirad Chaudhuri wrote about the envy of his friends

> who saw books and periodicals coming to me from Thacker, Spink and Company, the English booksellers of Calcutta, into whose shop they dared not enter.[37]

From the Directories of the late 1880s, and from catalogues (sometimes illustrated) appended to, for example, editions of Rudyard Kipling's *Departmental Ditties* from 1886 onwards, there is a sense of the firm settling back on the works which were obviously popular with the British in India. One such catalogue, appearing in the third edition of *Departmental Ditties* of 1888, includes books about horsemanship, such as *Riding on the Flat and Across Country* (in its second edition, revised and enlarged) by the prolific Captain M. H. Hayes; E. H. A's book of natural history essays *The Tribes on My Frontier* (in its third edition); and the comic *Lays of Ind* by 'Aliph Cheem' (Major Yeldham) in its eighth edition. Other authors and titles recur, such as R. A. Sterndale's *Denizens of the Jungle; The Management and Medical Treatment of Children in India; Sir H. C. Thuillier's *A Manual of Surveying for India*; and Colonel R. H. Beddome's *A Popular Handbook of Indian Ferns*. In the Directories, lists of guide books such as *A Guide for Visitors to Delhi and Its Neighbourhood* and *A Guide to Masuri, Landaur, Dehra Dun and the Hills North of Dehra* also appear, thus widening the range but continuing to appeal to a market more open to factual books than to fiction.

In conclusion, the apparent lack of archival material proves a disadvantage to any study of Thacker, Spink and Company, but there is still much valuable information to be gleaned from the Directories themselves, the publisher's catalogues appended to surviving Thacker, Spink books, and also publishers' archives of firms who dealt with the company. Thacker, Spink and Company's books could not have been published or found a readership anywhere except in imperial India. The firm may not have moved beyond the confines of the British community, but the books produced for this community were almost all about the country in which it was established. A study of this firm, a micro-history, therefore has the potential to provide an insight into publishing, bookselling and the reception of books; into the roles played by the small to medium-sized trading firms active in the nineteenth and early twentieth centuries; and into the colonial culture of British India.

Notes

The Oriental and India Office Collections (abbreviated hereafter as OIOC) held in the British Library have been the source for the Minutes, recorded in the Despatches of the East India Company, quoted in this chapter.

1. Robert Fraser and Mary Hammond, eds, *Books Without Borders, Volume 1: The Cross-National Dimension in Print Culture* (Basingstoke: Palgrave, 2008), p. 32.
2. *Bengal Past and Present*, vol. 109, pts 1–2, nos 208–208 (1990), pp. 164–69.
3. 'A History of the Trade to South Asia of Macmillan and Company and Oxford University Press 1875–1900' (D.Phil. thesis, University of Oxford, 1997).
4. *Kipling and His First Publisher: Correspondence of Rudyard Kipling with Thacker, Spink and Company 1886–1890* (High Wycombe: Rivendale Press, 2001).
5. London: W. H. Allen and Co., pp. 8–9.
6. E/4/695, vol. LXXX, p. 319, OIOC.
7. Cotton, p. 165.
8. *Surgeons Twoe and a Barber: Being Some Account of the Life and Work of the Indian Medical Service (1600–1947)* (London: Heinemann Medical Books, 1950), p. 131.
9. London: printed by Cox and Baylis, Great Queen Street, p. 168.
10. Calcutta: printed for S. Greenway and Company, p. xxxii.
11. *Calcutta: City of Palaces* (London: The British Library, 1990), p. 86.
12. Calcutta: printed at the Mirror Press by P. Crichton.
13. Calcutta: printed by Samuel Smith and Company at the Hurkaru Press, Pt VI, p. 452.
14. Calcutta: printed and published by Samuel Smith and Company.
15. Cotton, p. 167.
16. Cotton, p. 166. David Finkelstein refers in his essay to the various London premises occupied by Thacker and Company.
17. *The Non-official British in India to 1920* (Delhi: Oxford University Press, 1987), p. 10.
18. *Report of the Proceedings of the Calcutta Trade Association: From Its Foundation in 1830 to December 1850* (Calcutta: printed for the Association by P. S. D'Rozario and Company).
19. *Report*, pp. 5–9.
20. *Report*, p. 218.
21. *Report*, Appendix DD.
22. *Report*, p. 8.
23. *Report*, Appendix DD.
24. Mrinal Kanti Chanda, *A History of the English Press in Bengal 1780–1857* (Calcutta and New Delhi: K. P. Bagchi and Company, 1987), p. 130.
25. Calcutta: printed and published at the Hindoostanee Press, pp. 218–19.
26. 'The Calcutta Christian Observer', the Editor's Preface, vol. for 1838, p. 7.
27. *The Bengal Directory and General Observer* (1835), p. 337.

28. *The Bengal Directory and General Register*, p. 335.
29. E/4/772, vol. XXXIII, p. 46, OIOC.
30. E/4/796, vol. LVII, p. 659, OIOC.
31. E/4/800, vol. LXI, p. 643, OIOC.
32. E/4/810, vol. LXXI, p. 670, OIOC.
33. *New Calcutta Directory* (1856), p. 173.
34. Bombay: printed and sold at the 'Bombay Gazette' Press.
35. Cotton, p. 166.
36. *Kipling and His First Publisher*, p. 7.
37. *Thy Hand, Great Anarch, India 1921–1952* (London: The Hogarth Press, 1990), p. 85.

8
Two Paradigms of Literary Production: The Production, Circulation and Legal Status of Rudyard Kipling's *Departmental Ditties* and Indian Railway Library Texts

Shafquat Towheed

Rudyard Kipling, one of several authors commissioned by the Canadian editor Robert Barr to help launch his new magazine *The Idler*, gives us his account of how he came to produce his first piece of published writing in 'My First Book':

> So there was built a sort of book, a lean oblong docket, wire-stitched, to imitate a D. O. Government envelope, printed on one side only, bound in brown paper, and secured with red tape. It was addressed to all heads of departments and all Government officials, and among a pile of papers would have deceived a clerk of twenty years' service. Of these 'books' we made some hundreds, and as there was no necessity for advertising, my public being close to my hand, I took reply-postcards, printed the news of the birth of the book on one side, the blank order-form on the other, and posted them up and down the Empire from Aden to Singapore, and from Quetta to Colombo. There was no trade discount, no reckoning twelves as thirteens, no commission, and no credit of any kind whatever. The money came back in poor but honest rupees, and was transferred from the publisher, the left-hand pocket, direct to the author, the right-hand pocket. Every copy sold in a few weeks, and the ratio of expenses to profits, as I remember it, has since prevented my injuring my health by sympathising with publishers who talk of their risks and advertisements. The down country papers complained of the form of the thing. The wire binding cut the pages, and the red tape tore the covers. This was

not intentional, but Heaven helps those who help themselves. Consequently there arose a demand for a new edition, and this time I exchanged the pleasure of taking money over the counter for that of seeing a real publisher's imprint on the title page. More verses were taken out and put in, and some of that edition travelled as far as Hong Kong on the map, and each edition grew a little fatter, and at last, the book came to London with a gilt top and a stiff back, and was advertised in the publishers' poetry department. But I loved it best when it was a little brown baby with a pink string round its stomach; a child's child, ignorant that it was afflicted with all the most modern ailments; and before people had learned, beyond doubt, how its author lay awake of nights in India, plotting and scheming to write something that should 'take' with the English public.[1]

Like all creation stories, Kipling's account of how he became an author is a carefully crafted narrative, written retrospectively and idealising a state of almost childlike innocence about the realities of literary production in the late nineteenth century. The production of 'books' – for that is literally what Kipling's venture here is – is seen as an autonomous craft, an exercise in small-scale manufacture with an almost Calvinist self-justification ('Heaven helps those who help themselves'), independent of the need for literary promotion ('there was no necessity for advertising') and untouched by the realities of the marketplace ('there was no trade discount, no commission, and no credit of any kind'). As pure as any immaculate conception, Kipling's curiously manufactured and curiously culturally hybridised text starts life as a 'little brown baby' complete with a 'pink string round its stomach' to ward off the evil eye, and grows up to become a published and respectable London volume with a 'gilt top and a stiff back'.

The actual publication history of *Departmental Ditties* from its birth as a 'little brown baby' to its final arrival in London with a 'gilt top and stiff back' suggests the trace of a complex itinerary from autarchy to capitalism, from coterie publication to mass production, from a specific Anglo-Indian readership to a multifarious one, and from literary periphery to cultural core. Most of the poems in 'Departmental Ditties' had first appeared in Kipling's own beloved *Civil and Military Gazette* (CMG), a Lahore based daily newspaper founded in 1876, between February and April of 1886, and several of the 'Other Verses' had previously appeared in the *CMG*, the *Pioneer* of Allahabad and the *Pioneer Mail*. The book was presented to its gazetted readership as an official departmental envelope, with the impression of the printer, 'Lahore: Civil and Military Gazette', where the red wax seal would have been. This small narrow folio, measuring 4½ × 10½ inches, featured 25 poems, each on one page, and printed on one side only, making a total of 29 leaves. There were no headlines, no page numbers, no title page (the title was on the recto of the front cover only), and apart from the *CMG*'s seal, no attempt to present it as a conventional text. Kipling's presentation of the collection of verse as an 'official document' itself presents potential problems. For example, the 1867 Press and Registration of Books Act, Imperial India's first law requiring the deposition of all published texts for posterity (and of course, a means of state surveillance and censorship), required the registration and deposition of all published texts, except for 'books meant for official use only' with a penalty of a two year jail sentence and a five-thousand-rupee fine for offenders; these stipulations alone beg the question of whether Kipling was aware of what he was risking in the presentation of his text.[2] Kipling's first, home produced, envelope wrapped and wire stitched edition appeared on 18 June 1886, and the production run for this cottage industry was no less that 1,500 copies. Books were distributed through ICS offices and advertised in the *CMG*, presenting an explicitly closed communications circuit (producers, distributors, and consumers were all contained within the specific self-selecting Anglo-Indian gazetted community) and despite the fact that the book was typeset and manually printed by Indian labour, it explicitly precluded the possibility of Indian readers; *Departmental Ditties* proudly proclaimed that it was addressed to all 'heads of Depts. and all Anglo-Indians'.[3] The popularity of Kipling's first venture gained him cultural capital amongst his own community; but it did could not achieve the wider sales and earnings to which he already aspired.

Kipling had engaged his first commercial publisher, Thacker, Spink and Co. (see Chapters 6 and 7 of this volume) in an enlarged edition of *Departmental Ditties* as well as his first collection of short stories, *Plain Tales from the Hills*, but the relationship between author and commercial publisher, never good at the best times, broke down in acrimony during the course of 1888, with Kipling accusing the Calcutta firm of deducting commissions to which he had not agreed. Nor were Thacker's contractual payments particularly generous. Eager to establish himself as a fulltime professional writer, Kipling needed a publisher that could secure larger sales and better contractual terms.

Designed to meet a rapidly increasing market for railway fiction, Émile Moreau, the senior partner at A. H. Wheeler & Co., had commissioned

Kipling early in 1888 to write six short paper bound books, to be retailed at 1 Rupee, for distribution and retail through Wheeler's monopoly of railway bookstalls. The Indian Railway Library series comprised at least twenty-four titles, with books by Ivan O'Beirne, James Murdoch and 'Beatrice Grange' (the pseudonym of Kipling's sister Trix) as well as by Rudyard Kipling; but Kipling was commissioned to start the list.[4] Four of Kipling's Railway Library books (numbers 2, 3, 4 and 5 in the series) were displayed in the November 2005 exhibition 'Reaching the Margins: The Colonial and Postcolonial Lives of the Book, 1765–2005' in Senate House Library in the University of London, all in their original paper covers lovingly illustrated by Rudyard's father John Lockwood Kipling, suggesting that Wheeler's list was very much a Kipling family affair.[5]

Much work remains to be done with A. H. Wheeler's Indian Railway Library list, particularly in terms of both the distribution and consumption of these popular and cheap paperback books. One thing is very evident however: the stark difference between the scope and ambition of Wheeler's Railway Library and the closed circulation of *Departmental Ditties*. The intended reader of Wheeler's list was miscellaneous, mobile, perhaps even spontaneous, and not necessarily exclusively Anglo-Indian; in fact, it was anyone literate in English with a rupee to spare at one of Wheeler's railway bookstalls dotted across the fast expanding Indian Railway network, which by 1888, was carrying some ten million passengers annually.[6] The books were also produced in substantial print runs. The fourth edition of *Soldiers Three* and the third editions of *In Black and White*, *The Phantom 'Rickshaw* and *Wee Willie Winkie* for example, had print runs of 3,000 copies for the India market, so the cumulative production from Wheeler's Allahabad print shop must have been considerable.[7] The rapid dissemination of Kipling's works courtesy of Indian Railways brought with it new challenges as well as new readers. Britain's signing of the Berne Convention on International Copyright on behalf of its colonies and self-governing dominions in 1886 insured that for the first time, works first published in India received copyright protection in all signatory countries, but this did not of course include the United States of America.[8] The Indian Railway Library books did more to introduce him to a mass readership than anything that he had published so far; but they also enabled the first unauthorised publications of his work for the American market. On one hand they created and sustained a new royalty yielding British and Colonial readership; on the other, they facilitated the easy piracy of Kipling's writings for his new, royalty exempt readers in America.

Departmental Ditties, Kipling's 'little brown baby' limned a unique moment in Indian history, politics and literature upon its publication in 1886. Maurice Macmillan's productive honeymoon tour of India in 1884–5 had led to the founding of Macmillan's immensely profitable Colonial Library immediately after the signing of the Berne Convention in 1886, both responding to and feeding off the palpable, commercially viable and legally enforceable book hunger of a rapidly increasing Indian readership.[9] As if to underscore this move towards an enlarged 'reading (and purchasing) nation', Thacker, Spink and Co.'s *vade mecum* to all things Indian, *The Bengal Directory*, officially changed its name (and scope) in 1885 to *Thacker's Indian Directory*:

> The Directory is now called 'THE INDIAN DIRECTORY' in order to make its title more nearly correspond with the enlarged scope of its contents. For twenty-two years this Directory has been known as 'The Bengal Directory', embracing only the provinces more immediately under the direct control of the Governor-General of India. With the last issue some expansion was attempted by adding to the Mofussil Section every district under the Madras and Bombay Governments. THE INDIAN DIRECTORY now includes in the Mofussil Directory, every district and principal town in British and Foreign India, every Native State, and forms a complete guide to India as a whole.[10]

As Thacker's glancing recognition suggests, the centripetal pull of *Mofussil* periphery on the Imperial core of Calcutta was increasingly shaping Indian book production, distribution, advertising and consumption; and yet, despite their profitable recognition of the 'enlarged scope' for literary consumption in the newly incorporated *Mofussil* territories, the guide maintained a separate entry for the seat of Imperial power, Calcutta. As a new territory for literature, the Indian hinterland needed to be claimed for expansionist (and monopolist) comprador capitalism, and the need identified by Thacker was exactly what A. H. Wheeler's Indian Library would be designed to meet. Cheaply bound paperback fiction, sold for 1 Rupee and distributed through their monopoly of the railway station bookstalls, the Indian Railway Library series, more than anything else, offered Kipling his first mass readership, a reading community limned by the every expanding network of Indian railways, and serviced through specific forms of retail (such as hawking).

On the political front, 1885 had seen the founding of the Indian National Congress, in large measure stimulated by Lord Lytton's suppression of the burgeoning Indian press through the Vernacular Press

Act of 1878, an unenforceable piece of legislation that was repealed in 1880. But the new communities of literate Indians were not just consumers of the written word, as Thacker eagerly anticipated, or even simply readers subject to the complicated vigilance and control of *Pax Britannica* by means of the 1867 Registration Act, a transaction whose implications Robert Darnton has so eloquently demonstrated; they were also enthusiastic and prolific producers of print matter. Surveying the state of printing in 1883 for the *Punjab Gazetteer of the Lahore District*, Rudyard's father John Lockwood Kipling captured the enthusiasm and the aptitude of Indians for the world of print beyond the Imperial centre of Calcutta:

> There is perhaps no one of the arts imported from England that has been accepted with more cordiality and aptitude than that of printing. Though capable of being treated so as almost to reach the dignity of a fine art, the business itself is not very difficult to learn. There are several native printing-presses where excellent work is produced. These are all hand-driven. It is a curious fact that a large daily newspaper like the *Pioneer* finds hand labour cheaper and more trustworthy than the steam engine. Here similar conditions obtain, and it will probably be long before it is worthwhile to print by steam. Lithography, though much used for the vernacular papers, &c., is in a poor way. Chromo and chalk lithography have not been attempted; indeed the only pictures produced are rude illustrations in outline to the many cheap books of legends and poetry which are sold at fairs and gatherings as well as at small shops in the city. Book binding has been learnt by men employed at the Railway, Jail, Government and Mission presses; but it seems to be invariably lacking in finish, and has not been taken up as might have been expected.[11]

Kipling senior was himself an active supporter of Indian printing; the *Punjab Gazetteer of the Lahore District, 1893–4* noted that the only good lithographic work in Lahore was done by a Bengali under the supervision of the principal of the Mayo College of Art. J. L. Kipling's views (which incidentally, gloss an indigenous and often overlooked form of book retail and distribution – the itinerant hawker) were echoed by the prominent philologist George Grierson, who observed in 1889 that 'there is now scarcely a town of importance which does not possess its printing-press or two. Every scribbler can now see his writings in type or lithographed for a few rupees, and too often he avails himself of the power and the opportunity'.[12] C.A. Bayly has shown the link between the post 1857 expansion in small scale Indian printing and the increasing difficulty faced by the British in maintaining surveillance over their subjects; Robert Darnton has linked the proliferation of the printing press in Bengal to the increasing inefficacy of laws stipulating the registration of vernacular books, while Philip Altbach has demonstrated the extent to which small printing presses (and small print runs) remained a distinct feature of Indian publishing well into the twentieth century.[13] In the decade from 1883 to 1893, the explosion of printing in Kipling's literary cradle, the city of Lahore was recorded by its official organ, the *Punjab Gazetteer of the Lahore District*, and the concomitant rise in book retailing glossed by the official Licence Tax reports for the state (summarised in Tables 8.1 and 8.2).

There are discrepancies between these two sets of figures, and I would suggest that the *Gazetteer*'s assessment is more accurate, as it names proprietors of individual presses, some of which may have been exempt from licence taxes; the 1893–4 Gazetteer also lists all the titles of newspapers

Table 8.1 Punjab Licence Tax Report for the years 1880–6 (Lahore: The 'Civil and Military Gazette' Press, 1884), BL OIOC IOR/V/24/2631

	1880–1	1881–2	1882–3	1883–4	1884–5	1885–6
Books and stationery, number of licences	6	7	18	37	12	58
Books and stationery, tax revenue (Rs)	75	160	295	385	120	725
Printing presses, number of licences	20	18	18	21	17	9
Printing presses, tax revenue (Rs)	420	450	520	605	520	300
Overall tax collected for the state of Punjab (Rs)	450,956	429,648	432,980	460,473	457,809	457,777

Table 8.2 Overview of printing in Lahore, from the *Punjab Gazetteer of the Lahore District, 1883–4* (Calcutta: Calcutta Central Press Company, 1884) and the *Punjab Gazetteer of the Lahore District, 1893–4* (Lahore: The 'Civil and Military Gazette' Press, 1894).

Licenced Printing Presses	1883–4	1893–4
English owned	6	5
Indian owned	26	54
Total	32	59

of periodicals printed in Lahore, together with circulation figures for most of them. By 1894, there were five English language newspapers: the *Civil and Military Gazette* (the only British owned English-language daily in town) the *Punjab Patriot* (Weekly) the *Tribune* (Twice weekly) the *Arya Patreka* (Fortnightly) and the *People's Journal* (Weekly). W. Ball's *Punjab Trading Company's Press* that appeared in the first Gazetteer in 1883–4 seems to have gone under; as David Finkelstein has shown, newspaper publication in India in this period was rarely profitable over a sustained period, and this situation was particularly acute for Anglo-Indian newspapers.[14]

At the same time, there were no fewer than 19 publications in vernacular languages, including the newspaper with the largest readership of all, the Urdu language *Paisa Akhbar*, with a circulation of 5,100 copies; unfortunately there are no figures for the *CMG* to compare this with, but it is safe to assume that this vernacular weekly already surpassed the English-language daily by a considerable margin, offering us yet another reason for Kipling's visceral contempt for the Indian vernacular press. Indeed, the Indian owned English language *Tribune* was already achieving circulation figures of 1,400 per week (Kipling's first book had a total print run of 1,500 copies), suggesting that a substantial minority, and perhaps even the majority of Anglophone readers in Lahore at the time were Indian rather than British. Clearly, thousands of new Indian readers were entering the culture of print every year; it was not a readership that Kipling could afford to ignore forever.

Kipling's own exercise in privately printing *Departmental Ditties* on the press of the *CMG* fits comfortably with the wider context of the rise in Indian English and vernacular printing in Lahore at the time; indeed, if anything, there were Indian printing presses in the city that were already in the process of fashioning larger readerships. As with the Indian small presses, Kipling had borne the risk of the publication of his collection of verse, and similar to so many Indian-owned periodicals, he had utilised the subscription model of the *CMG* to advertise his book; the *CMG* had urged its readers on 2 June 1886, to place their orders for the volume, ready and available at the cost of 'Re 1'. It is still a matter of debate whether Kipling's Indian Railway Library books were peddled by itinerant hawkers, but if they were, then we can surmise an even larger potential Indian readership; C.W. Bolton in Calcutta had observed in 1878 that dozens of unregistered titles in a variety of languages could be 'procured from itinerant hawkers on the roads', evading both the official scrutiny of censorship and the official records of the book trade.[15]

And yet Kipling's homemade text had explicitly defined a segregated readership ('To all heads of departments and all Anglo-Indians') and a private mode of circulation (departmental correspondence and the *CMG*) which seemed to ignore the growth in the Indian production, consumption and distribution of printed matter, and which many commentators have accepted as normative. Thomas Pinney and David Alan Richards in their otherwise excellent edition of Kipling's correspondence with Thacker, Spink and Co., for example – while noting that there were only two Englishmen on the entire staff of the *CMG*, and that all the compositors were Indians who apparently 'did not known English' – fail to place the production or consumption of *Departmental Ditties* within the wider context of the burgeoning small scale activity of Indian presses in this period.[16]

Nor of course, do they accept the premise that Kipling's transition from small producer and coterie writer to becoming one of the stalwarts of Wheeler's new Indian Railway Library entailed any acceptance of the increasing and palpable appetite of Indian readers. Priya Joshi has rightly complained of the lack of representation of the Indian as a reader of fiction in the literature of the period, observing that 'Indians in the British Empire never seemed to read at all'; this lack of representation is even more reprehensible from those, such as Kipling, that ought to have known better.[17] In January 1888, at the same time as the appearance of the first Indian Railway Library books pitched at an inclusive, miscellaneous and increasingly 'national' readership, he mounted a transparent attack on Indian reading habits (too literary for their own good, he concluded) in 'A Little Morality' in the *Pioneer*. As part of his work for the *CMG*, Kipling presented himself as a reader of Indian journalism, observing in a letter to the Rev. Willes that 'some thirty papers go through my hands daily – Hindu papers, scurrilous and abusive beyond everything, local scandal weeklies, philosophical and literary journals written by Babus in the style of Addison', but he could never bring himself to represent Indians in any meaningful sense as readers, despite the physical evidence of the burgeoning number of publications passing through his fingers.[18] Yet again, Kipling was self-consciously refuting the demands of new Indian readers whose appetites had been whetted by the Railway Library books.

What is certain is that both the modes of production, circulation and consumption that I have outlined co-existed in different forms in late nineteenth-century India, and that both involved different degrees of intellectual and financial negotiation with an increasingly demanding

Indian reading community. In circulating texts without the benefit of a comprehensive International Copyright Law, Kipling was endangering his literary property, and at the same time, making it available to unexpected and unintended readers. This creative and pecuniary tension would shape the rest of Kipling's life as a writer.

Poised between *mofussil* and core, between the typical small-scale manufacture of the Indian regional press (such as the *CMG*) and the mass manufacture and distribution of Wheeler's Railway Library, and between the localised print culture and uncertain legal status of his Indian literary apprenticeship and the complex legal and textual predicament of his Anglo-American maturity, Kipling's first innocuous volume of verse glosses the multiple, centripetal forces that shaped his literary career. Unprotected by any enforceable international copyright law, both Kipling's hand-made, wire-stitched privately distributed 'official document' and his widely hawked and disseminated 1 Rupee Railway Library texts mapped out many new readers, as well as new risks. In a literary life divided between the world's three largest English speaking nations, both the extraordinary circulation and textual vulnerability of Kipling's writings bear potent testimony to the recursive, multiple, haunting colonial lives of the book.

Notes

1. Rudyard Kipling, 'My First Book', *The Idler*, 2 December 1892, pp. 475–82. *Departmental Ditties* was not of course, Kipling's first book; that honour goes to *Echoes: By Two Writers* (Lahore: The 'Civil and Military Gazette' Press, 1884), a collection of verse written with his sister 'Trix', Alice Macdonald Kipling (1868–1948). I am grateful to Lionel Bently and Priya Joshi for their insightful comments.

2. 'An Act for the regulation of printing presses and newspapers, for the preservation of copies of books printed in British India, and for the registration of such books', Act Number XXV of 1867 in *A Collection of the Acts Passed by the Governor General of India in Council in the Year 1867* (Calcutta, 1868), BL OIOC V/8/40. See also Robert Darnton, 'Literary Surveillance in the British Raj: The Contradictions of Liberal Imperialism', *Book History* 4 (2001), pp. 133–76. It needs to be said that enforcement of the act was patchy, evidenced by the dropping of the Rs 2 registration charge in 1890.

3. Rudyard Kipling, *Departmental Ditties and Other Verses* (Lahore: The 'Civil and Military Gazette' Press, 1886), B. L. Ashley 4879. This edition was not registered in the *Catalogue of Books Printed in the Bengal Presidency* (Calcutta: Government Printing Press, 1886) and therefore evaded the enforcement of the 1867 Act. The second edition printed by Thacker, Spink & Co. in Calcutta was duly recorded with Imperial oversight; see *Catalogue of Books ... for*

the Fourth Quarter Ending 31 December 1886 (Calcutta: Government Printing Press, 1886), OIOC SV.412, f. 352, entry 1254.

4. Ivan O'Beirne, *The Colonel's Crime, a story of to-day, and Jim's Wife* (Allahabad: A. H. Wheeler & Co., 1889), Indian Railway Library no. 7 and *Major Craik's Craze* (Allahabad: A. H. Wheeler & Co., 1892), no. 17; James Murdoch, *A Yoshiwara Episode & Fred Wilson's Fate* (Allahabad: A. H. Wheeler & Co., 1894), no. 22; and 'Beatrice Grange' pseud. Alice Kipling, *The Heart of a Maid* (Allahabad: A. H. Wheeler & Co., 1890), no. 8.

5. *The Story of the Gadsbys: A Tale without a Plot* (Allahabad: A. H. Wheeler & Co., 1890), *In Black and White* (Allahabad: A. H. Wheeler & Co., 1888), *Under the Deodars* (Allahabad: A. H. Wheeler & Co., 1889), and *The Phantom 'rickshaw, and Other Tales* (Allahabad: A. H. Wheeler & Co., 1888); see Robert Fraser, John Spiers and Shafquat Towheed, *'Reaching the Margins': The Colonial and Postcolonial History of the Book 1765–2005 Exhibition Catalogue* (London: Senate House Library, 2005), pp. 19–22 (http://www.ull.ac.uk/exhibitions/colonial/shtml).

6. See K. R. Vaidyanathan, *150 Glorious Years of Indian Railways* (Mumbai: English Edition, 2004), p. 151. The first passenger train on 16 April 1853 carried 400 passengers.

7. Exact numbers for all of the print runs for each book have yet to be established, but it is clear from the size of print runs for editions for which we have data that the cumulative total was in excess of 10,000 copies of each of Kipling's books; see James McG. Stewart, *Rudyard Kipling: A Bibliographical Catalogue* (Toronto: Dalhousie University Press, 1959).

8. See Lionel Bently and Brad Sherman, 'Great Britain and the signing of the Berne Convention in 1886', *Journal of the Copyright Society of the USA* 48:3 (2001), pp. 311–40.

9. Charles Morgan, *The House of Macmillan 1843–1943* (London: Macmillan, 1944), pp. 187–9.

10. Foreword, *Thacker's Indian Directory* (Calcutta: Thacker, Spink & Co., 1885).

11. J. L. Kipling, *Punjab Gazetteer of the Lahore District, 1883–4* (Calcutta: Calcutta Central Press Company, 1884), p. 100. The 1885 *Thacker's Indian Directory* listed J. L. Kipling as one of nine 'ungraded' officers (six of whom were Indian) employed by the Mayo School of Art; his Rs 1,000 pcm salary was twice that of the next 'ungraded' officer.

12. George Grierson, *The Modern Vernacular Literature of Hindustan* (Calcutta: 1889), p. 145.

13. See C.A. Bayly, *Empire and Information: Intelligence Gathering and Social Communication in India, 1780–1870* (Cambridge: CUP, 1996); Robert Darnton, 'Literary Surveillance in the British Raj: The Contradictions of Liberal Imperialism', *Book History* 4 (2001), and Philip Altbach, *Publishing in India: An Analysis* (Delhi: Oxford University Press, 1975).

14. David Finkelstein and Douglas M. Peers (eds), *Negotiating India in the Nineteenth-Century Media* (Basingstoke: Macmillan, 2000), pp. 11–13.

15. C.W. Bolton, 'Reports on Publications Issued and Registered in the several Provinces of British India during the year 1878', *Selections from the Government of India*, Home Revenue and Agricultural Department No. LIX (Calcutta: Government Printing Press, 1879).

16. Thomas Pinney and David Alan Richards (eds) *Kipling and his First Publisher: Correspondence of Rudyard Kipling with Thacker, Spink and Co.* (High Wycombe: Rivendale Press, 2001).
17. Priya Joshi, *In Another Country: Colonialism, Culture and the English Novel in India* (New York: Columbia UP, 2002), p. 35.
18. Rudyard Kipling to Rev. G. Willes, 17 November 1882: MS Dalhousie University, cited in Thomas Pinney (ed.), *Kipling's India: Uncollected Sketches 1884–88* (New York: Schocken Books, 1986), pp. 3–4.

9
War and the Colonial Book Trade: The Case of OUP India

Robert Fraser

On the night of 10 October 1943, under pressure from heavy Monsoon rains, the two rivers in Madras – the Cooum and Adyar – burst their banks. Floods 'as bad', reckoned the *Madras Mail*, 'as any known in living memory', swilled across the city, soon reaching the business district where overseas publishers had their offices and *godowns*, or warehouses. Water, as one harassed editor reported, was 'lapping at the gates of Longmans' and it rapidly inundated the bottom storey of the Kardyl Building in Mount Road, which housed the *godown* of the Oxford University Press (OUP). Much of the stock – bound books and loose quires – was ruined. From the relative safety of Head Office in Nicol Road, Bombay, R. E. Hawkins – overall Manager of the Indian Branch – relayed the plight of one of his hapless authors back to Oxford. 'Roused from sleep by the rising waters,' he said, 'she waited for rescue on the roof of her house, repelling the rats and snakes that also sought sanctuary.'[1] The following evening, safely down again, she heard wailing over the stricken city what under the circumstances seemed almost a homely sound. It was an air raid siren, keening the arrival of yet another consignment of Japanese bombs.

Thus concluded an episode that seems to belong in a novel – one of Paul Scott's say – evoking the balance between inner and outer threat characterising the last few years of British political and commercial ascendancy in India. But the scene was real enough, several of the Madras populace were drowned, and the damage at Mount Road was assessed at 5,500 rupees.[2] The remaining stock had to be dried out, no easy task in the wet season when, as Hawkins now lamented, 'leather sprouts fungus'. It was, for Oxford and India, one of the lowest points of the war. With the Japanese at the gates of Bengal, a quarter of the working population of Calcutta had fled. The once lucrative Burmese market had collapsed. John Brown, OUP's office manager in Bombay, an early conscript, had been captured by the Japanese.[3] Nobody knew where he was, though he was later to be identified as a Prisoner of War on Taiwan.[4] Deadlock subsisted between the British government, the Hindu-dominated Congress Party and the Muslim League over the political future of the sub-continent. Resentments still seethed, and in Calcutta the expatriate wife of the Principal of St Paul's College was stabbed in the open street. Hawkins was negotiating over the rights to what he hoped might be a bestseller: *The Mind of Mahatma Gandhi*. But the subject was *incommunicado*, and rights difficult to obtain. There was, moreover – as his employer and regular correspondent, Sir Humphey Milford, 'Publisher to the University of Oxford', brutally informed him – little demand for such a title in England, where indifference to the long-term fate of the colonies seemed, for the time being at least, to be almost total.[5]

And yet the correspondence itself, with its plethora of detail, tells a complementary and countervailing story. Roy Hawkins was 36. Senior among three British OUP officers in India, including the absent Brown, he had overall responsibility for operations there on a salary of 1,100 rupees a month, though his standard 33-month contract had actually expired in 1940, and he had enjoyed neither home leave nor increment since the outbreak of war.[6] Milford, who was approaching retirement, was one of Oxford's grandees. Since 1913 he had held the key post of Publisher, taking a personal interest in the development of the India branch, which had largely been formed on his initiative. It was to Milford that E. V. Rieu, first manager of the branch in Bombay, had reported on his arrival there in 1912, and his constant, solicitous interest in the Indian connection is warmly attested to by his letter books of the period.[7] India at this time was, after all, very much the jewel in Oxford's crown. It was, moreover, where promising recruits to the Press were frequently sent to be trained. Two of the firm's senior home-based officials, Geoffrey ('Jock') Cumberlege, who in 1945 would succeed Milford as Publisher,[8] and Raymond Goffin, presently a private in the Royal Berkshire Regiment,[9] had begun their careers in Bombay, and both had written textbooks for the Indian market.[10] So when Hawkins had taken up his post in 1937, it is no surprise to find Milford requesting quarterly updates from him. They run from 1937 until 1944, and afford a valuable impression of a distinguished colonial publishing venture *in extremis*.

Hawkins, who was to devote his whole career to India, was a meticulous man, so the local set-up emerges clearly from these letters. The

Indian branch, as it was invariably known, had for some years been expanding. By 1938 it employed 105 people between its three offices – 44 in Bombay, 37 in Calcutta, 24 in Madras – as compared to 80 in 1934.[11] (At home the essential status distinction was between those paid weekly in cash, and those paid monthly by cheque; here it was between those earning less than 150 rupees per month, who were entitled to a regular grain allowance, and those above that threshold who were not). Markets too were growing and diversifying, as Milford encouraged the boys on the ground to explore new worlds of readers in Persia, where the language of school instruction had changed from French to English in 1934, and East Africa with its thrusting Asian population.[12] The network of technical support is also apparent from these reports. Paper came from two mills: the Tishaghur Mills in Park Street, Calcutta and the Mysore Mills in Bangalore (both of which were still to be in business in 2005). The branch used one bindery, also in Calcutta. Some of these facilities were shared with other companies, friendly rivals such as Macmillan, Nelson and Longman, with whom the Oxford people were obliged constantly to consult, especially in times of crisis. Indeed, one of the heartening aspects of this correspondence is the impression it conveys of a more or less congenial expatriate publishing community, in marked contrast to the naked competition that often characterised the book trade in Britain.

Most importantly, these reports have a lot to tell us about just what books Oxford was marketing in India at the time, where they originated, who wrote and printed them, and at whom they were aimed. They fall into four categories: Clarendon Press books (academic monographs imported from Oxford); London books, that is general trade items – principally Bibles and technical manuals – produced by the firm's commercial arm at Amen House in Warwick Square off Ludgate Hill; branch books, that is to say volumes produced locally; and the merchandise of other firms – Harraps and Constables for example – handled under licence.[13] It is the third of these divisions that is of interest in the unfolding scenario of war.

What happened in September 1939 was that the commercial and intellectual mix constituting the branch books was shaken and not so gently stirred. Habitually the cocktail consisted of three ingredients: so-called India Branch production (books commissioned, written and man-ufactured on the spot), India Branch London Branch quires (that is, books made up in India from sheets imported from Amen House); and Indian Branch Clarendon Press quires (that is, books made up in India from sheets imported from Oxford). After 1939 this recipe officially served as before; in practice Neville Chamberlain's speech on September 3rd changed a great deal. With Europe at war, and Asia as yet free of it, Bombay could no longer carry on as it had done previously; it was also freed from outside supervision in several significant and rewarding respects. Inevitably attention in England was being directed elsewhere. At the declaration of hostilities, the London branch had evacuated its entire staff – including famously the Anglo-Catholic novelist and playwright Charles Williams, who edited the firm's newsletter – to Southfield House, Hill Top Road, just outside Oxford.[14] The focus of effort had also changed, since the Press soon landed a highly advantageous, though strictly confidential, government and Admiralty contract to produce maps, codebooks and cipher books. As Atalanta Myerson has effectively shown, this imperative commission pre-occupied the Press domestically for the duration of hostilities, absorbing much editorial time and mountains of paper.[15]

So it is hardly surprising if India faded a little from view. To begin with, in any case, South Asia appeared to be 'far from the seat of conflict'. War conditions also made the place less accessible from England since, though air letters continued to arrive, as far as bulk freight was concerned Indian ports were now much more difficult to reach. In May 1940, fearful of an Italian assault on Egypt, Churchill instructed the Admiralty to thin out shipping in the Eastern Mediterranean.[16] Henceforth, for the first time since the opening of the Suez Canal three quarters of a century previously, traffic to Asia was sent round the Cape. The result initially was to slow down shipments to pre-1869 levels. By July, Hawkins is observing: 'since shipping was diverted round the Cape, we have had little stock from England'.[17] This is phrased as a complaint, but all the signs are that Hawkins treated it as an opportunity, even when supplies began to trickle through. After all, Asian markets were still wide open, the Indian government was yet to ration paper, and the pressures of nationalism and educational aspiration continued unabated. Hawkins had read between the lines of Milford's replies; Oxford was clearly tied up in some kind of official war work, though unable for legal reasons to say what it was. Paper rationing in Britain, in any case, was no secret, even if Oxford manufactured its own. The upshot was an unusual offer from an overseas branch: Hawkins proposed that, if Oxford found herself overstretched, Bombay was prepared to assist with her printing.

There is no sign that the offer was taken up. The confidence behind the suggestion, however, bore fruit in other ways, since, despite the lack of overseas supplies, local business flourished. Before the war sales had already been rising; for the first time in 1938–9 they had exceeded a million rupees. In November 1939 Hawkins was able to report that: 'up the present the war has made little difference to our business'. In January of the following year, in the midst of Europe's co-called 'phoney war', his tone is even breezier:

> The effects of the war on India, provided we do not start fighting here too, will be beneficial. We are already getting better prices for our exports, and many new manufacturing industries are being started up to supply those goods which are now too rare or too expensive to bring from abroad. Politically too I think – perhaps because of this economic situation – we shall settle down without dislocation of civil life. So that the war is not likely to mean any diminution of our business in educational and general books, but if anything will stimulate it. And if there is a general rise in prices, a rise in the cost of books will have no special effect. I conclude that our policy should be to increase our income rather than decrease our expenditure.[18]

So Hawkins' policy – accepted perforce by officials in Oxford who had little time or energy to argue otherwise – was to expand. There were, of course, challenges to be met, since indirect price inflation was unavoidable. Owing to food imports the cost of living index was creeping up, and salaries had to rise to keep pace. The price of Indian printing paper went up by 30 per cent over four months, and that of cover paper and cloth rose by 50 per cent.[19] When a surcharge on insurance premiums was imposed on all firms, Macmillan took the lead by reducing discounts by a uniform 5 per cent. Oxford followed suit immediately, but the small resulting drop in demand was more than compensated for by the increase in revenue. Already that January Hawkins is boasting: 'The present position is very satisfactory in so far as the sales are only Rs. 10,000 below last years' record ones: as you know, Calcutta sales have shown a steady increase every year since 1932, during which period they have nearly doubled.' By November this has become 'all branches are still selling as well, or better, than ever'.[20] This is English understatement: as the figures demonstrate, they were actually performing very impressively.

However, it is not simply the volume, but the kind, of new business that is striking. The increase, as you would expect, is principally accounted for by branch production. But, even within this band, there is an interesting shift in the privileged language medium. Again, Hawkins had foreseen this development, writing to Milford shortly after his appointment in 1937; 'The new Ministries, particularly the Congress ones, are showing a lively interest in education, and many schemes for reshaping syllabuses are being discussed. The general idea is to extend and cheapen a form of primary education that will be of more practical use to the villager: it will be given through the mother-tongue ... The Secondary school syllabuses are sure to be modified too, and we are likely to have a busy time remaking our own list.'[21] The impact of these new directives is soon visible. In 1938, the year before hostilities, the Indian branch had issued 46 new titles in English and 93 reprints, compared to 15 new publications in all of the Indian vernaculars, with 7 reprints (Table 9.1 and 9.2). In 1939, the gap narrowed, with 33 new English-medium titles and 132 reprints, compared to 16 new titles in the vernaculars, with 18 reprints. By the end of 1940, the year of Hawkins' buoyant letter, new Indian language publication has edged ahead for the first time: 36 new titles, as opposed to 30 in English. Throughout that year, the lion's share of English language production consisted of reprints: 122 in all. This momentum was not evenly maintained, and by the end of 1943 the pattern has almost reverted. Nonetheless (Table 9.3), the short-term redressing of the balance in favour of Indian-language books suggests just where, in the period between say Dunkirk and the Japanese attack on Pearl Harbour, the commercial advantage – and much of the activity – lay.[22]

Table 9.1   New publications by OUP India Branch, 1938–43: arranged by language group

Year	In English	In Indian Languages
1938	46	15
1939	33	16
1940	30	36
1941	29	38
1942	57	50
1943	42	12

Table 9.2   Books reprinted by OUP India Branch, 1938–43: arranged by language group

Year	In English	In Indian Languages
1938	93	7
1939	132	18
1940	122	18
1941	83	27
1942	106	26
1943	149	24

Table 9.3 Books published by OUP India Branch, 1938–43: percentage of new titles to total output

Year	In English (%)	In Indian Languages (%)
1938	49	214
1939	25	89
1940	25	200
1941	35	141
1942	54	192
1943	28	50

Pearl Harbour, of course, marked a watershed. Hawkins' report of January 1940 had contained the all-important proviso 'provided we do not start fighting here too'. Following the American declaration of war in December 1941 and the opening up of the Eastern theatre, British India, if not exactly fighting, was on heavy war alert, and the business community, of which publishing formed a minor part, faced challenges of an altogether different order. Whole markets disappeared: in Singapore, Malaya and most drastically and worryingly close-at-hand, in Burma, previously responsible for about 15 per cent of OUP's Calcutta sales. In Rangoon £1,000 worth of stock was lost.[23]

In neighbouring Bengal the effect was immediate. By February 1942 Calcutta University had postponed its exams, only one in four students was attending college and all girls' schools had closed. Within a few months these disruptions had spread down the Eastern seaboard of India. Early in April 1942 a state of emergency was declared in Madras, and a large part of the population quitted the city 'headed by the government'. Two-thirds of the school population absconded. Apart from the ever-present fear of invasion, Hawkins was concerned by a lingering threat of civil disobedience from the ongoing Quit India movement. The Burma rice harvest having failed, Bengal was now in the grips of the severest famine it was to endure during the entire twentieth century. In Calcutta, where the office was under the management of an enterprising Bengali – Ranga Lal Sen – starving people were 'a common sight'.[24] The manager of the Madras branch, 32-year-old P. J. Chester, was being threatened with conscription; his future remained uncertain, and, in the meantime, his wife was deputizing for him. Within a few weeks she too had left the town by special train.[25] In November the Government of India at last got round to rationing paper, reserving 90 per cent for official purposes. Shipments remained extremely irregular. In the first quarter of the year the branch received only six, and two had been lost at sea aboard a boat bound for Calcutta and Madras.[26]

In the circumstances there was little publishing firms could do but raise prices. This time it was Longmans who took the initiative, but again Oxford soon followed suit. Faced with a choice between reducing discounts again – thus penalising hard-pressed local booksellers – and hitching prices by 12 per cent all round, they took the second and riskier path. For the first time a note of despondency enters the correspondence. Nonetheless, by May, Hawkins is reporting that the loss of sales to schools is being offset by the embarkation of British and American troops at the port of Bombay.[27] Ever alert to the main chance, he has rushed through the press a guidebook, Moraes' and Stimpson's *Introduction to India*, to help them find their feet.[28] He anticipates ready pickings. Partly as a result, whilst sales from the Calcutta office have dropped by 10 per cent, in Bombay the fall is less than 1 per cent. Elsewhere sales have actually risen, and with them, Hawkins' mood.

The fact is the business community was adapting its ways of working, and those enterprises that remained in operation were soon flourishing. This was as true of publishing as of every other commercial sector. Indeed, as Hawkins was later to report, 'There has been ... a mushroom growth of general publishing firms in the last few years, favoured by the lack of competition, the increased market and the chance of quick profits.'[29] With the gradual reopening of colleges after the panic of early 1942–3, the educational market once again took off. There were 'unusually large profits' that year, and in the following 12 months, with Europe still embroiled in the Normandy campaign, sales at the India branch again broke all existing records.[30] The fruits of this staggered growth were shared by the office staff too, as the figures for the commissions on sales earned by the four office managers over this period well show.

Indeed, far from looking back – and despite discouraging episodes like the floods in Madras – Hawkins is soon making plans for the post-war period. The creation of a Muslim-dominated state in Pakistan seemed increasingly likely. Is it not wise, he asks, to consider opening an office

Table 9.4 Commissions on profits earned by office managers, OUP India Branch, 1939–43, expressed in sterling

	Hawkins (Bombay)	Chester (Madras)	Sen (Calcutta)
1939	£202.13s.6d	£101.6s.9d	£101.6s.9d
1940	£353.13s.2d	£176.16s.7d	£176.16s.7d
1941	£370.17s.0d	£185.8s.6d	£185.8s.6d
1942	£350.5s.10d	£175.2s.10d	£175.2s.10d
1943	£319.13s.1d	£159.16s.7d	£159.16s.7d

there eventually, bringing out a fourth member of the expatriate staff to run it? 'If the Indian Branch can be of any help in getting trade started again in Malaya, you will doubtless let us know.' If an opportunity occurs of investigating trade links with China, Hawkins would, he gamely insists, much appreciate being considered for the job.[31] Almost two years before VJ day, he is even enthusing about possibilities for English-language textbooks in Japan. Language teaching in any case, will evidently form a large share of overseas business. Already Churchill had caused discomfort by rising to his feet in the House of Commons to announce government backing for Basic English, C. K. Ogden's scheme for a substitute language for non-native speakers employing a vocabulary of 600 words. If it takes off, many of the existing textbooks will have to be rewritten. Predictably Longman is rubbing their hands at this prospect, as is the now ten-year-old British Council, but Oxford mandarins on both continents are horrified. The chimera fades as Basic goes out of fashion, but Hawkins knows where his bread and butter lies. The language teaching market is ripe for the picking, and he is determined to seize it.[32]

In Oxford, these initiatives found a ready ear. Milford was not due to retire until September 1945, but, as in 1912–3, there was a handover period of about year before his successor, Jock Cumberlege, took over as Publisher. Cumberlege had worked at the Bombay Head Office for four years in the early 1920's. He had experienced the curb of overseas supervision first-hand and was keen to give Bombay its head. In May 1944 Hawkins is briskly informed that reports on routine India branch business are no longer required in Oxford, whereupon – frustratingly for us – the quarterly reports abruptly cease.[33] With them, Milford's paternalistic regime draws to a close. From the continuing, though now occasional, communications between Bombay and London, however, it is abundantly clear just how radically the atmosphere has changed. Hawkins for one is enthusiastic to democratise the market. There are, he remarks, 50 bookshops in the city of Bombay carrying general books; in addition, and ignored by most overseas firms, there are hundreds of one-man booths flogging books to passers-by in the street. Soon Hawkins is reminding Cumberlege of this fact of local life: 'I merely want to indicate that there is all the machinery for a market here if we wish to use it.' As far as Oxford is concerned, however, the priorities are now clear. Henceforth the main emphasis is to be on inter-branch trade, much of which Bombay will be expected to initiate by itself.[34] They are to build up and export their own lists, liase directly with New York and other branches, and to consolidate the liaison with East Africa that has been interrupted by the war. They are, in other words, to make their own paradise. There are still a few wartime commissions to be tidied up, of course. The order for a Service of Thanksgiving for the Armistice is printed in Oxford and sent out under conditions of strict secrecy to India, where a specially adapted programme for the event will include the hymn 'Praise my Soul, the King of Heaven', by a former Director of the East India Company, Robert Grant.[35]

Already the gesture seems a little dated. With a Labour government in control, and the Congress Party posed to take over two years later, the metropolitan network is loosening fast. In May 1946, Cumberlege spells out where Hawkins must look to now, not that he needs much encouragement: to Persia, East Africa and Iraq; to Aden, China and Egypt.[36] In August 1947 the long-promised Independence dawns, both for India and Pakistan. Import controls are imposed in India; in Bombay, a few streets away from Hawkins' Head Office, an infant called Salman Rushdie lets out his first yelp.

And so to a tentative conclusion: Commercial publishing in India during the war years was the product of an elaborate nexus of conditions, some of them sub-continental, most of them global. The Second Word War, even more so than the first, was the ultimate cross-national event. It disturbed patterns of trade and avenues of transit, causing shortages in unexpected places, and opening up unlooked for opportunities in others. In certain respects it induced India into unprecedented modes of collaboration or cooperation (several Bengalis, for example, fought for the Japanese). In other ways it isolated a colony whose destiny, for better or for worse, had been caught up for some 180 years in an unequal relationship where many, but not all, of the shots were called elsewhere: from the plush plum-coloured armchairs of the directors of the East India Company in the City of London, then from the corridors of the India Office in Whitehall. Since 1912, when Emile Rieu had set up the India Branch of OUP, its affairs had been directed magisterially from Oxford or London. From the outset of hostilities in 1939, however, Bombay had increasingly to go it alone. In doing so, it began to carve out its own future, and in the process to diversify its local markets and to lay the ground for a commercial collaboration with its patent company that was eventually to be established on fairer, more equal terms. The end result was to be fortunate, not simply for the branch itself, but for OUP worldwide. In Chapter 5 in Volume 1 of *Books Without Borders*, I illustrated how unimaginative overall planning during much the same period, together with rigidities in organization and a general indifference to the market, caused Thomas Nelson and Sons, one of Oxford's principal rivals in the imperial textbook trade, to founder in the post-war years, and eventually to cease business altogether. Nelsons had never properly confronted the challenges and opportunities posed by its various branches in France, Canada and elsewhere. Learning from its wartime experiences, and cushioned to some extent by its status as a university department, Oxford by contrast used the post-war decades gradually to renegotiate its relationship with all of its offices overseas. As a result it flourished, as Nelsons did not.

That the war should have initiated this beneficial process of renewal is not in the least surprising. A disaster in so many respects, international conflicts on this scale sometimes have the compensatory effect of freeing up a variety of social and economic constraints. In the Second World War several communities had felt such beneficial effects. On the home front in Britain, women signed up in the factories to mass-produce munitions to the strains of the BBC's entertainment programme *Music While You Work*. The liberation was to be temporary since after the armistice most returned to the home. Yet the opportunities – and the new patterns of life – the war had opened up could not be withdrawn permanently. In Britain greater gender equality at work – to this day incomplete – was to be one long-range result of the conflict. Throughout the empire too, soldiers from the colonies either volunteered for, or were conscripted into, the armed forces, disclosing to them vistas of experience – and political ideals – which were eventually to transform whole swathes of the world, especially in sub-Saharan Africa.

The effects on business are less well documented though just as dramatic, and publishing was no exception. In India, where in 1939 political independence was already on the cards, the effects are clear to see. Though the fortunes of OUP's India branch, between 1939 and 1945, reflect the shifting face of the global conflict, the triggering of successive military zones and the impact of distant regulations, the overwhelming evidence is that the war became the branch's Open Sesame. It closed down certain markets, of course, and put an unprecedented strain on resources: on paper, distribution and the like. However, it also relieved local management temporarily of Oxford's controlling hand. The correspondence between Hawkins and Milford had originated as a sort of monitoring device to provide supervision for a younger member of staff working in an infant branch in a distant location. Ironically what it reveals is an emancipation of employee and branch well beyond practicable direction from abroad. Inevitably, just as in England, there was a time lag before these re-ordered priorities were to become permanent. Indeed, as the records suggest, and OUP India's official historian Rimi Chatterjee confirms, some of the momentum of the war years was inevitably lost during the later 1940s and the 1950s. Hawkins himself would remain in post until 1970, and he grew more cautious with the years. As Chatterjee puts it with generous understanding 'He was still a consummate publisher, but with all his interest in India, his heart was still at the Clarendon Press.'[37] He was also slower to grasp the implications of nationalism for OUP's local hiring policy than he might have been. By 1944, for example, the branch was short of managers, yet Hawkins' solution to this temporary difficulty had been to request that three junior members of the Press's British-based staff be sent out for expatriate training. Such policies seem timid now, and after independence they were in practice bound slowly to abate. Indeed indigenisation was already under way, even if in the eyes of some it was to advance far too slowly. Early in the war, the ever-efficient Ranga Lal Sen was offered what, in the contractual terminology of the time, was known as 'home leave' in England. He politely declined, since his home he said was in Calcutta.[38] To his personal disappointment, Sen was never to be promoted, but by 1970 the managers of the Calcutta and Bombay offices would both be Indian citizens.

In other important respects the Indian Branch was now more autonomous and flourishing than ever before. In the immediate post-war years, two of its home-commissioned titles, Minoo Masani's *Our India* and Jim Corbett's *Man-Eaters of Kumaon*, became international bestsellers, with hefty sales in America.[39] The latter was adopted by the parent firm as a mainstream World's Classic. Even so in 1944 Hawkins, playing his options in uncharted waters, was still planning to adjust local discounts so as to encourage again direct sales from England. The imposition of import duties on books by the Congress Party government in 1947 put paid to these suggestions; it also ensured that local publishers and booksellers had from now on to make their own, independent arrangements. Indeed it could be argued that the charter of OUP India Branch's independence, so energetically prepared in wartime, was not fully to be realised until 1971, when the headquarters of the branch moved to Ansari Road in Darya Ganj in Delhi, a change consolidated five years later when Ravi Dayal took over as general manager. The liberation was accelerated by the economic conditions of the 1980s when the sliding value of the rupee, another hiccup of which the firm took full advantage, obliged the firm to concentrate its activities locally to an extent never before attempted. Its spectacular success is amply attested by the range of Delhi-published Oxford titles cited in several of the essays in the present volume.

In November 1937 the young Indian writer Raja Rao had written in the 'Foreword' to his revolutionary first novel *Kanthapura*, 'We cannot write as the English. We should not.' For all that, Rao's seminal book was published the following year by George Allen and Unwin in London. Ten years later he might as well have extended his claim to read: 'We cannot publish as the English. We should not.' *Kanthapura* is a now a modern Indian classic, several times reissued by local firms such as Orient Paperbacks, whose Hind edition with a cover design by Narayan Barodia is printed by the Shiksha Bharati Press in New Delhi. The most widely prescribed critical edition, expertly typeset by Rashtriya Printers, appeared in 1989 from the OUP's Delhi offices in the nearby YMCA library building, followed by a second edition in 2000. The resonance of these facts is another of the long-term fruits of war.

Notes

Unless otherwise stated, the typescript documents referred to in this essay are held in the OUP archive in Oxford.

1. R. E. Hawkins to Humphrey Milford, 22 November 1943. From the useful file headed BOMBAY 1937–44. OUP/PUB12/3.
2. R. E. Hawkins to Humphrey Milford, 22 February 1944. OUP/PUB12/3
3. R. E. Hawkins to Humphrey Milford, 17 August 1942. OUP/PUB12/3.
4. R. E. Hawkins to Humphrey Milford, 17 August 1943. OUP/PUB12/3.
5. Humphrey Milford to R. E. Hawkins, 24 September 1943. OUP/PUB12/3. The book's editors were R. K. Prabhu and E. R. Rao. In fact, when published by the India branch in 1945, this compilation proved fairly successful, with large sales outside India. It went to a second edition the following year, and remained in print until the 1960s.
6. R. E. Hawkins to Humphrey Milford, 22 November 1943. OUP/PUB12/3. In 1940 the rupee averaged 13.23 per pound sterling, giving Hawkins an annual salary of just short of £1,000, or £30,000 in 2005 values. There was an additional commission on profits. See Table 9.4. As for home leave, a forlorn telegram to Milford on 19 June 1940 reads 'IMPOSSIBLE FLY ENGLAND RETURNED BOMBAY = HAWKINS.'
7. Peter Sutcliffe, *The Oxford University Press: An Informal History* (Oxford: Clarendon, 1978), 200–1.
8. Sutcliffe, 200–2.
9. E. C. Parnwell to R. E. Hawkins, 7 September 1939, OUP/PUB12/3. Parnwell, who had joined the press in 1915, had in 1928 been entrusted my Milford with general responsibility for 'education overseas'. Travelling widely, he was the first OUP employee to discern the vast potential of the educational market in Africa, overseeing the highly successful Oxford English Readers for Africa (Sutcliffe, 213–6).
10. G. F. L Cumberlege ed., *Several Essays*, and R. C. Goffin ed., *Some Representative Verse and Prose*. India Branch Books File at Amen House, 10 March 1933. OUP/PUB12/3. A third member of the home staff who had done time in India was A. L. P. Norrington, later to be appointed Secretary to the Delegates.
11. R. E. Hawkins to Humphrey Milford, 1 March 1938. OUP/PUB12/3.

12. Parnwell had visited Persia in 1933 to investigate the possibilities there. See E. C. Parnwell to Humphrey Milford, 11 March 1933. From the file headed 'General India Branch Correspondence with London, 1928–48'. IB/00000029. In late 1936 Hawkins himself had made an exploratory trip to Iraq, Persia and Palestine.

13. L. Brander of Amen House to R. E. Hawkins, 14 November 1946. IB/00000029.

14. Sutcliffe, 248.

15. Atalanta Myerson, 'Top Secret Books: The Oxford University Press in World War Two', *Gutenberg Jahrbuch* 2004, 269–74.

16. Winston Churchill, *The Second World War*, 3rd edition, (London: Cassell, 1951), ii (*Their Finest Hour*) 40, 112, 370, 373.

17. R. E. Hawkins to Humphrey Milford, 29 July 1940. OUP/PUB12/3.

18. R. E. Hawkins to Humphrey Milford, 22 January 1940. OUP/PUB12/3.

19. R. E. Hawkins to Humphrey Milford, 22 January 1940. OUP/PUB12/3.

20. R. E. Hawkins to Humphrey Milford, 16 November 1940. OUP/PUB12/3.

21. R. E. Hawkins to Humphrey Milford, 10 October 1937. OUP/PUB12/3.

22. R. E. Hawkins to Humphrey Milford, 22 February 1944. OUP/PUB12/3. The comparative figures are set out in Table 9.1.

23. R. E. Hawkins to Humphrey Milford, 4 May 1942. OUP/PUB12/3. The stock had been on sale at the American Baptist Mission Press.

24. R. E. Hawkins to Humphrey Milford, 22 November 1943. OUP/PUB12/3

25. R. E. Hawkins to Humphrey Milford, 31 October 1942. OUP/PUB12/3.

26. R. E. Hawkins to Humphrey Milford, 4 May 1942. OUP/PUB12/3.

27. R. E Hawkins to Humphrey Milford, 4 May 1942. OUP/PUB12/3.

28. R. E. Hawkins to Humphrey Milford, 31 October 1942. OUP/PUB12/3. Illustrated by the artist G. H. C. Moorhouse, the book proved a runaway success. After its first edition in 1943, two more were required within the year. After the war it enjoyed a substantial international sale during the lead-up to Indian independence. The fourth edition of 1944, though printed in India, was issued by OUP jointly in Bombay and New York.

29. R. E. Hawkins to Humphrey Milford, 22 February 1944. OUP/PUB12/3.

30. A useful indication of the growth in trade during the first five years of the war is given by the commissions on profits paid to the three branch managers during the years in question. See Table 9.4. Source: Memo from OUP's London warehouse in Neasden Lane, London NW10, 14 April 1944. OUP/PUB12/3. The Neasden warehouse remained open throughout the war.

31. R. E. Hawkins to Humphrey Milford, 22 November 1943. OUP/PUB12/3.

32. The crisis over Basic, and the whole vexed issue of competing language teaching methods during this period, is usefully covered in a later Oxford book: A. P. R. Howatt, *A History of English Language Teaching* (OUP, 1984).

33. E. C. Parnwell to R. E. Hawkins, 21 February 1945. IB/00000029.

34. Geoffrey Cumberlege to India Branch, 17 October 1945. IB/00000029.

35. Oxford to India Branch, 21 February 1945. Headed 'STRICTLY CONFIDENTIAL'. IB/00000029.

36. Geoffrey Cumberlege to R. E. Hawkins, 24 March 1945. IB/00000029.

37. Rimi B. Chatterjee, *Empires of the Mind: A History of the Oxford University Press Under the Raj* (New Delhi: Oxford University Press, 2006).

38. R. E. Hawkins to Humphrey Milford, 22 January 1940. OUP/PUB12/3.

39. Sutcliffe, 268.

10
Between Bloomsbury and Gandhi? The Background to the Publication and Reception of Mulk Raj Anand's *Untouchable*

Susheila Nasta

Untouchable, Mulk Raj Anand's first and perhaps best-known novel, was published in 1935 by the small left wing British publisher, Wishart Books Ltd. Now a prestigious Penguin Modern Classic, it is frequently heralded as one of the most significant milestones in the history of modern Indian writing in English, and has been republished and translated several times since its first appearance. The novel's route to publication, however, was not an easy one; even though Anand at the time was well connected both in Britain (amongst the Bloomsbury group), and the subcontinent (as a Founder of the Indian Progressive Writer's Association). Following rejections from nineteen publishers, Anand was grateful in the end for the patronage of his friend and fellow-novelist, E. M. Forster, who, in writing an influential preface to the first edition, provided some much-needed early legitimization for the book among a sceptical British reading public. To many, the central focus of this novel, concerning a day in the life of Bakha, one of India's untouchables (a sweeper and latrine cleaner) seemed to be too 'vulgar', even too 'dirty'; too inappropriate a subject to be admitted easily into the 'supposedly' respectable world of 1930s' British fiction. In colonial India furthermore, the book's reception and circulation was thwarted soon after publication, though for different reasons. There Anand's attempt to write the story of Bakha, a voiceless subaltern, into Indian history was seen by the then colonial government as potentially explosive: not only because of the novel's explicit political agenda – which castigated the iniquities of the ancient Hindu caste system and manifestly sought parallels with the plight of the colonized under British rule – but also because an early draft had been directly influenced by the interventions of Mahatma Gandhi, whom Anand visited at his *ashram* in Ahmedabad in the late 1920s.[1] Perhaps not surprisingly, soon after publication the novel was placed on the list of proscribed books, and banned as an import by the colonial government, along with Anand's following two novels, *Coolie* (1936) and *Two Leaves and a Bud* (1937).[2] Despite the chequered nature of its early history, *Untouchable* was to receive many accolades following Independence in 1947; especially from nationalist critics keen to establish Anand's reputation as a 'founding-father' of the Indo-Anglian novel, one who – alongside his now distinguished contemporaries, R. K. Narayan and Raja Rao – was regarded as having been essential to the establishment of a uniquely Indian vision of modernity. Thus *Untouchable* is frequently claimed as *belonging* to the *national* tradition of Indian writing in English; indeed as one of the texts marking its inauguration. Yet when one examines the actual circumstances of the novel's composition, as well as the history of its subsequent journey into print, a slightly different trajectory presents itself – one, which might more accurately locate the book as deriving from a cross-cultural literary geography situated somewhere *between* Gandhi and Bloomsbury. Without doubt, *Untouchable* was a first novel of its kind in the history of Indian writing in English. Anand's passionate desire to portray 'the human condition of an Indian in the lower depths', combined with his attack on the structures of colonial power, served a recognizable political agenda linking him with the nationalist movement of the 1930s.[3] Yet the novel also emerged out of an eclectic range of far broader international influences. In this way it was to lay the ground for a new cultural landscape not only anticipating the hybridity of the Indian novel in English today but also creating an important conduit, or in Anand's own metaphor a symbolic 'bridge', between the 'the Ganga and the Thames'.[4]

This chapter locates the background to the publication and reception of Anand's groundbreaking novel stemming in a series of rich transnational connections – literary, historical, political – between several cultural worlds. Straddling (amongst several others) the world of Bloomsbury and the run up to Independence of Gandhi's India, the genesis and reception of the book (both at its publication and subsequently), provide us with a case study of the impact of national and cultural politics, often determined by narrowly conceived notions of 'taste', 'tradition' or 'genre', on aesthetic and literary judgments. In a broader sense this very background served to highlight the danger of falsely institutionalizing or compartmentalizing such texts as have arisen from sometimes contradictory colonial histories split by their very nature across national boundaries and sitting uncomfortably within established 'academic orthodoxies'.[5] The hasty imposition of fashionable critical/theoretical discourses onto texts existing outside the boundaries of fixed national traditions can sometimes stultify reading practices; ultimately it can also frustrate the free passage and circulation of such works across what are still, regrettably, fiercely guarded canonical borders. In this context it is worth bearing in mind a recent observation of Sydney Shep, noting that whilst the academic discipline of Book History has traditionally conformed to nationalist models of print culture, it now needs to step *outside* such fixed paradigms to investigate the shifting contours of its own frontiers. Conscious of the pressing need to widen the angle of vision, she stresses that we must now focus on rearranging 'book history's furniture' the better to contemplate 'the physical, intellectual and spiritual mobilities ... of those material objects we call books'.[6]

Before examining the fascinating background to the genesis and publishing history of *Untouchable*, it might be worth pausing for a moment to consider the surprisingly narrow and often polarized critical landscape surrounding evaluations of Anand's fiction, since the evolution of the related critical nomenclatures often proves revealing of the formation of national canons and literary judgments. Most commonly – despite several positive reviews early in his career and connections with several major writers in 1930s Britain, Anand has been all but invisible in British literary histories.[7] If accorded any serious mention – at least until very recently – his work has most often been noted either in the context of anti-colonial resistance or occasionally in relation to controversies sparked by E. M. Forster's well-intentioned 1935 preface to *Untouchable*. In such accounts Anand is seldom described as a dynamic activist, or as a key contributor to the refashioning of Britain as a crucible for international modernity, but as a colonial outsider 'lifted up' by the patronage of Forster's liberal humanist cosmopolitanism.[8] Frequently portrayed through a series of predictable and myopic critical caricatures, Anand thus makes an occasional appearance as a kind of collaborative mimic or colonial 'babu' writing back to Empire; or, alternatively, as an overly noisy and dogmatic Marxist situated on the fringes of a Euro-American modernity, alienating the majority of his Bloomsbury friends by his anti-imperialist politics and his residual commitment to an increasingly unpopular Stalinism after the outbreak of war. As V. S. Pritchett comments, reflecting on Anand's sudden return to India following the end of hostilities in 1945:

> He vanished ... and there seems to be a long silence – no doubt the war was responsible.[9]

In fact Pritchett was one of Anand's more sympathetic readers and reviewers at the time. However his comment on Anand's so-called 'disappearance' from London literary life is interesting, not least because its implies an *absence from* and *invisibility in* British literary history. Such inconspicuousness was to remain even *after* the dawn of New Historicist reclamation in the era of postcolonial literary studies. A particularly graphic example occurs in the context of an essay for the new millenium published in the *Times Literary Supplement* (*TLS*) in October 2000 and dedicated to reviewing the new Modernist volume of the *Cambridge History of Literary Criticism*. Oddly enough, given the predictability of the exclusive Euro-American focus of the review – ironically entitled 'How the Critic came to be King' – it was illustrated by a now celebrated photograph, taken on behalf of the BBC Eastern Service's radio magazine programme *Voice* in 1942 (Figure 10.1).[10] *Voice* was broadcast monthly and was a regular feature to which Anand and several other prominent Indian writers and journalists of his generation were invited to contribute.[11]

The original version of this image, now held in the BBC picture archives, lists the names of ten writers and critics: they include Una Marson (Caribbean poet and presenter), Venu Chitale (assistant producer), J. M. Tambimuttu (major poet and editor of *Poetry London*), Mulk Raj Anand, Narayana Menon (writer and broadcaster), T. S. Eliot (poet and critic) William Empson (poet and critic) and George Orwell (novelist and essayist). But the caption running beneath the photo as reproduced in the *TLS* wipes out the names of all the non-Euro-American participants,

Figure 10.1 Line-up for *VOICE*, a monthly radio magazine programme in the Eastern Service of the BBC, December 1, 1942: (Left to right, sitting) Venu Chitale, J. M. Tambimuttu, T. S. Eliot, Una Marson, Mulk Raj Anand, C. Pemberton, Narayana Menon; (standing) George Orwell, Nancy Barratt, William Empson. BBC Copyright

and in so doing perpetuates the deletion of the cross-cultural relationships existing between these writers so interestingly grouped together.
The *TLS* caption simply read: 'among others – T. S. Eliot, George Orwell
and William Empson.[12] As I have argued at length elsewhere, the
occlusion of these major colonial writers not only pinpoints an ongoing critical failure to acknowledge the role writers such as Anand played
in the reinvention of Britain as a transnational locale for the growth
of a global modernity, but comfortably relegates these supposed 'others'
to yet another containable location on the margins of mainstream literary studies: namely that of the 'colonial' or the 'postcolonial', placed
outside and conveniently separated *from* the key tenets of the body of
European modernity.

Interestingly, as I intimated at the outset, certain readings of Anand's
work by a generation of sub-continental scholars have inadvertently
reproduced similar acts of narrow critical reading. Despite the unani-
mous celebration of Anand's stature as 'founding-father' of the tradition
of Indo-Anglian literature, his work is often entrapped by its categoriza-
tion as 'nationalist', worthy 'social realist', or in the case of *Untouchable*
as providing the first proletarian Indian-Anglian novel. True, a number
of recent studies in South Asia have begun to view Anand's contribution
through a more wide-angled and global lens. Vinay Dharwardker, for
example, praises Anand for his global vision of a 'pro-subaltern cosmopolitanism', and Harish Trivedi compares Anand's early experience
of 1920s Britain with the experiences of some later diasporic writers
such as Salman Rushdie. The majority of critics, however, persist in
taking Anand's agenda of social and political protest as their prime
point of departure.[13] Surprisingly, this kind of approach surfaces again
in Priya Joshi's recent monograph *In Another Country: Colonialism,
Culture and the Indian Novel in India* (2005), which sets out to explore
the global markets surrounding colonial publishing in India and in
the process to overturn the rigid binaries of nationalist models of book
history. Whilst Joshi (following Edward Said) views the interrelationships
between the imperial and post-imperial worlds as a zone that is 'intel-
lectually and culturally integrated', she fails to comment on Anand's
work in this light, noting instead and rather reductively that Anand as
social realist is 'somewhat mechanical rather than literary or innovative'.[14] Social realism of course does not sit easily with some fashionable
theoretical paradigms. Anand has suffered particularly from postcolonial critics in this respect. Either his so-called revolutionary political
radicalism has been seen in the end as essentially conservative and
complicit, or he not been regarded as sufficiently experimental – unlike

say G. V. Desani, whose *All About H. Hatterr* (1948) is regularly cited as literary precursor to the inauguration of the cosmopolitan tradition of migrant writing marked by the publication of Salman Rushdie's *Midnight's Children* in 1981.[15] Of course this question of 'experimentalism' versus 'engagement' is an old chestnut in debates concerning the development and evolution of early twentieth century modernism. The opposition between these two ideals has been shown to be fallacious by many, including Jean Paul Sartre, who makes the useful observation that 'art loses nothing in engagement. On the contrary ... the always new requirements of the social and metaphysical engage the artist in finding a new language and new techniques'.[16] Although Anand embarked on a long career as social activist and follower of Gandhi, he still remained influenced during the period when he was first drafting *Untouchable* by the 'experimental' prose of the literary world he encountered in 1930s Bloomsbury. The fact, however, that works by writers such as Virginia Woolf, E. M. Forster and James Joyce were to impact significantly on the genesis of *Untouchable* does not point simply (as some have argued) to colonial mimicry, or conservative collaboration but instead, to Anand's desire to explore the potentiality for the creation of a revolutionary, new form. As Jessica Berman suggests in an illuminating article, interpreting Anand's early novels as constitutive of, rather than an appendage to, the body of a newly developing global modernity, the now well-known impact of Joyce's banned novel *Ulysses* on *Untouchable* was not 'simply a unilateral matter of influence, influence though it certainly was'. Rather, such intimate intertextual and inter-political relations highlight 'the multidirectional flow of global literature ... where streams of discourse move not just from metropolis to colony, or even back from colony to metropolis, but ... from colony [Ireland] to metropolis to another colony [India] and back again'.[17] Or, as Anand was to put it in 'Why I Write', a piece which both details the autobiographical background to the drafting of *Untouchable* and signals his awareness of the need to move beyond the prescriptions of any one orthodoxy, any one tradition:

> I have the conviction that if man's fate could be revealed ... beyond the mere subjectivism of literary coteries, which ends in blind alleys, in the newly freed countries of the world, the freedoms, beyond political freedom, may be ushered.[18]

The reasons for this are perhaps obvious. Written breathlessly over one weekend, but redrafted and edited several times between 1928 and

1934, the book was initially composed during a period when Anand was resident in London as a student and would-be writer, frequenting the Georgian drawing rooms of Bloomsbury and the reading rooms of the British Library. However, he was also fired, like so many other young Indian radicals of his generation, by the intensification of Gandhi's *swadeshi* campaign, the Indian Freedom movement and a commitment to international socialism. Initially inspired by the memory of a childhood playmate, who, despite the absence of a formal education could recite several cantos from the Punjabi epic poem, *Heer Ranja*,[19] Anand's desire to write Bakha into existence crystallized during a period when he himself, as a recently arrived migrant in London and pupil of the modernist Islamic poet Iqbal, was being subjected to a number of powerful but often competing cultural influences. *Conversations in Bloomsbury* is a series of witty autobiographical essays written with hindsight and recounting his early days as a student as he attempted to navigate between the houses of European modernism and his burgeoning political radicalism. The opening lines of its Preface in some senses set the scene for the genesis and reception of *Untouchable*:

> I arrived in London after a brief jail-going in the Gandhi movement in the early twenties and found myself removed suddenly from the realities of the freedom struggle into the world of Bloomsbury where the pleasures of literature and art were considered ends in themselves.[20]

Moreover, Anand's preface to these *Conversations* – literary and political dialogues which in a sense he continued to have throughout his life *with* Bloomsbury as an icon of Western modernity – suggest the difficulties of his contradictory position in 1925 as an Indian colonial writer and radical socialist attempting to forge a global, transnational vision. They are also suggestive of the polarities of art, politics and national culture which later came to predetermine the book's location and publishing history. For like many other colonial and postcolonial writers who followed him, Anand was caught both within and outside the frame of a British canon that sought both to define and to exclude him.

I am signalling 'Gandhi' and 'Bloomsbury' here both as literal influences on Anand in the actual writing of the book, and as complementary elements in the book's publishing history: for both were crucial to the material emergence of *Untouchable* into print. They were also to function as signifiers of the cultural geographies lying between Anand's composition of the work and the contexts determining its reception. It might be worth elaborating briefly on the notion of Gandhi and Bloomsbury. A shorthand way to read them, and in many ways a predictably polarized one, would be to equate 'Gandhi' with Anand's anti-colonial political activism and, 'Bloomsbury' with Anand's formative encounter in the 1930s with the elitist literary salons of high modernism. However, if examined them more closely, these can now be re-interpreted and realigned. Gandhi himself, like Anand, was a classic instance of an early cross-cultural and cosmopolitan traveller, a man whose life and works not only straddled several worlds, but also, like many other young Indian lawyers of his generation, lived for a while in several of them.[21] Similarly the notion of 'Bloomsbury', as easy password for an elitist cultural movement has recently come under scrutiny from contemporary urban geographers, keen to expand the limited parameters of its aesthetic jurisdiction. As such it has come to be seen less as a rarefied literary *space,* dominated by the likes say of Virginia and Leonard Woolf, T. S. Eliot, D. H. Lawrence, Edith Sitwell or E. M. Forster but rather as a real and multicultural *place,* a dynamic and polyphonic 'contact zone' where notably, several languages were spoken on the streets and where many so-called 'foreigners' and colonials resided whilst studying at the British Museum, or pursuing courses at nearby University College, London. The 'geographical heart of Bloomsbury' – the area from Euston Road to Holborn, Woburn Place, Tavistock Place and the edges of Russell Square – was as Sara Blair notes, totally 'cosmopolitan'.[22] Significantly too, Anand's connections with British writers during his time in London extended well beyond the elitist parameters of the so-called 'Bloomsbury' modernists to more socially-committed figures such as Dylan Thomas, George Orwell, Stephen Spender, Aldous Huxley, Louis MacNeice, Naomi Mitchinson and Stevie Smith.

Books, like the ideas of writers themselves, have always travelled and *Untouchable* is a particularly apposite example of the ways in which the lives of books often straddle and open up the borders of several worlds. Anand's italicized authorial signature at the close of *Untouchable* – 'SIMLA – SS. *Viceroy of India* – BLOOMSBURY' – playfully draws the reader's attention to some of the different physical and cultural contexts of its gestation – India, shipboard and London – locations which deliberately mark the liminality of the novel's composition and subsequent rite of passage. As readers familiar with Anand's work will no doubt be aware, there are several slightly different versions in circulation of the story of how *Untouchable* came to be written and published. It is well known, for example, that in his early drafts Anand drew on a wide range of autobiographical and cultural influences including his own immersion (as a fluent Panjabi and Urdu speaker) in the vernacular traditions of Indian literature, his readings of Russian writers – Tolstoy and Gorky – as well as works by Bloomsbury members such as E. M. Forster, Virginia and Leonard Woolf and T. S. Eliot. However, it was the electrifying fusion of art and politics he was to encounter through his first reading of James Joyce's novel *Ulysses*, combined with Gorky's fictional portraits of the 'lowest dregs of humanity'[23] that were to have the most resounding influence. Recognizing that 'in the face of India's poor, I might have to go beyond literature as defined in Bloomsbury' and create 'new writings from vital experience', Anand was to come across a short piece written by Gandhi, entitled 'Uka', and published in his magazine, *Young India*. Still at the time a student at University College and very much a Bloomsbury 'groupie', Anand was inspired by the simplicity and stark austerity of Gandhi's essay – which, fascinatingly, was on the subject of a sweeper boy he later adopted and took into his ashram:

> The narrative was plain, direct and without all those circumlocutions about Bakha, which I had attempted, in imitation of Joyce's 'language of the night'. I now saw the mocking bird in myself and was ashamed of my impressionableness.[24]

In what is an oft-cited, and possibly apocryphal story in the history of modern Indian literature, we are told that Anand (clutching his half-finished manuscript under his arm) secured a personal invitation to visit Gandhi at his *sabarmati ashram* near Ahmadebad. Gandhi was not a habitual reader of novels. He swiftly instructed Anand to get out of his corduroy costume, don a *kurta-pyjama*, learn to stop drinking alcohol and clean the latrines once a week. Some weeks later, having read the first draft of Anand's book, he returned with the harsh verdict that the novel did not convince: mainly, because Anand's anti-hero Bakha, spoke far too many long words for an untouchable and was too much of 'a Bloomsbury intellectual'. Advised to cut out at least 'a hundred or more pages and rewrite the whole', Anand was to industriously revise his manuscript for a further three months before returning to London to begin the quest for a publisher.[25] Although, as Berman notes, there is no hard evidence for Gandhi's editorial interventions (other than recycled versions of this story), and no 'extant manuscript', this tale has come to determine the ways in which the politics of

Anand's early literary career have been interpreted. Most importantly perhaps, it has continued to feed the assumptions behind critical readings keen to draw attention solely to Anand's credentials as an authentic 'social realist' and literary icon of Indian nationalism.[26]

A lesser-known but perhaps equally telling story behind the composition of *Untouchable* appears in *Conversations in Bloomsbury*, where Anand recalls an important discussion with E. M. Forster about the ending to *A Passage to India* (1924). It is important to note that whilst Anand's recollection of this episode refers to a meeting between himself and Forster in 1925 – several years before *Untouchable* was conceived and well before Forster came to write his famous preface of 1934 – Anand's written narrative of this symbolic encounter was only made available in print in 1981 when his Bloomsbury memoir was published. Despite this gap in time, Anand's account is revealing, especially given the political direction his first novel was to take and Forster's pivotal role in facilitating its publication. Having already devoured *Passage to India* shortly after his arrival in Britain, and reclining (so we are told with E. M. Forster and Leonard Woolf) under a tree in Bloomsbury, Anand asked Forster an incisive question about its ending:

> 'Mr Forster, Sir,' I began, trying to be tentative, 'you make Aziz and Professor Fielding go apart – even their horses go in different directions [...] Do you think they will [only] come together when India becomes free?[27]

Forster's evasive retort as reported by Anand that 'I am Morgan to all my friends. Not "Mr Forster, Sir"', clearly constituted a veiled rejoinder. Yet he does not in Anand's retelling engage either with the political implications of the question or with the deliberate irresolution of the novel's famous ending in which the two friends, one Indian and one English, are unable to connect, swerving apart surrounded by a chorus of voices echoing, 'No, not yet.[...] No, not there'.[28] Later in his account of this dialogue, Anand makes it abundantly clear that he identifies not only with Aziz's incipient nationalism but also with what he calls Aziz's inability to express the truly 'revolutionary potential' of his 'desire for revenge'. Clearly equating Aziz's situation more broadly with the predicament of the powerless in colonial India, Anand, much to Forster and Leonard Woolf's uncomfortable amusement, continues by making further parallels: between his own predicament and that of Aziz, Caliban as rebel in Shakespeare's *The Tempest*, and later with

Gandhi.[29] Whilst it is difficult to know whether or not Anand's account of this conversation is to be believed, it does invite us to reflect on a number of issues concerning the interrelationship between *A Passage to India* and *Untouchable*. It has often been suggested that Anand's novel ends with a positive vision signalling the 'possibility for future reform and progress towards freedom for both Bakha and India'. As Ralph Crane notes, *Untouchable* thus overturns the pessimism at the close of Forster's novel, which offers little hope for any 'meaningful interaction' between the Indians and the British.[30] It is clear, as we have seen from Anand's recollections of his 'conversations' with Forster that he was keen to interrogate and move beyond the questions raised at the close of *A Passage to India*, and to find a new point of departure: to develop, in other words, a productive dialogue with the political and cultural issues implicit in Forster's text but not fully realized within it. Interestingly, we are given a hint of the possibility for an alternative vision of modernity from Forster himself in the 'Temple' section of *A Passage to India* when Aziz, living as a self-exiled Muslim doctor in a Hindu state, asks Professor Godbole for advice on his newly written poetry. As Godbole comments – perhaps prophetically – the promise of Aziz's future will be fulfilled not by a simple rejection of his embryonic nationalist concerns, or by abandoning his local allegiances to Urdu and Islam – but by embracing a more cosmopolitan vision of 'internationality'. For it is 'India', as Godbole is quick to note, seeming as it might to the British 'not to move', that will in fact 'go straight there' and create a new space for cultural expression, 'while … other nations waste their time'.[31] There is no doubt that, when Forster first drafted his short preface to *Untouchable* in 1934, he was already aware that Anand was extending his reach well beyond a simple recounting of a day in the life of his untouchable anti-hero, Bakha. Pointing perhaps to the possibility of resolution not realizable at the time he penned his own novel, he comments at its close: 'The Indian day is over and the next day will be like it, but on the surface of the earth if not in the depths of the sky, a change is at hand'.[32]

E. M. Forster completed his preface to *Untouchable* in 1934, a couple of years after Anand's return from his spell at Gandhi's ashram and following the book's unsuccessful submission to 19 British publishers between 1932 and 1934. These included major houses such as Macmillan (Anand's first choice), Jonathan Cape, Hutchinson, Unwin, Kegan Paul and Chatto. Various accounts have circulated over time regarding the trials and tribulations Anand experienced in getting *Untouchable* into print.

As Saros Cowasjee, Anand's literary biographer states, whilst the almost suicidal author collected rejection slips, several of his English literary acquaintances attempted to reassure him. On reading the manuscript Naomi Mitchinson, for example, described the book as both 'fascinating and horrible', and suggested to Anand that 'a good many people just won't read it' simply because of 'the dirt and cruelty ... conveyed in it'. However, she also praised Anand's ability in conveying that 'dirt' with a candid vision that avoided unnecessary romanticization. And Bonamy Dobrée (one of Anand's closest friends), recommended the book to Jonathan Cape with the strong affirmation that although the novel addresses, 'things we don't know', it is confidently 'written by somebody who ... does'. When Anand eventually came to submit the now well-travelled manuscript to Chatto and Windus – one of his last attempts – it was accompanied by a letter that Anand had received from his friend E. M. Forster dated 5 May 1934. Forster writes:

> Dear Mr Anand,
> I am just going abroad, and have only had time to read hastily through your Ms., but I found it extremely interesting. It recalled to me very vividly the occasion I have walked the 'wrong way' in an Indian city, and it is a way down which no novelist has yet taken us ... you present it all very convincingly. You make your sweeper sympathetic yet avoid making him a hero or a martyr, and by the appearance of Gandhi and the conversation about machinery at the end, you give the book a coherence and shape which it would otherwise have lacked. ... The objection against the Ms from the practical point of view seems ... not ... its length but its 'squalor'. I put this word in inverted commas as indicating that it doesn't convey my personal opinion, but it may well represent the opinion of the public, which the publishers are bound to consider when making their decision.[33]

Anand had been reluctant to approach Forster earlier in his search for a publisher for fear of being seen to be a 'typical Indian Babu', begging 'a letter of recommendation'.[34] Yet when the manuscript was eventually dispatched (following the advice of the poet Oswell Blakeston), to Edgell Rickward, Editor of Wishart Books Ltd, former editor of *The Calendar of Modern Letters* and an avowed Marxist, Anand received his first positive reply, a reply that was accompanied by a small advance of £35 and the proviso that Forster should ease the book's reception by prefacing it with an introduction. Forster readily agreed and the book was finally published on 1 May 1935. Rickward clearly admired Forster's introduction and wrote the following reply to Anand on the 30 November 1934:

> I am glad to get your letter, and to find that you admired Forster's introduction as much as I do. I think from every point of view it was just what we wanted. It is a little masterpiece of suggestion and understanding, and will be the book's *passport* through the latent hostility of the ordinary reviewer.[35]

Although Rickward praised Anand's manuscript for it's 'sincerity' and 'skill', he was clearly nervous about the book's potential sales, fearing that the firm would find it hard to 'dispose of more than one thousand copies'. He was also quick to point out that the 'prospect of good sales in India must largely affect our decision'.[36] Rickward's original aim to market *Untouchable* as widely as possible in order to reach an Indian audience is ironic in the light of the book's later proscription, though Anand did attempt in 1939 to get Wishart Books to transfer the publishing rights to The Socialist Book Club in Allahabad, along with some of his later novels and works by other leftist friends, such as John Strachey's *Theory and Practice*.[37] It is not clear how far this arrangement progressed as the correspondence from the archive is incomplete but there was clearly a concerted move to provide reciprocal rights with Wishart Books on a number of left wing titles, even though Wishart turned out later to be one of the first British publishers to be banned export rights in India. Interestingly, despite the fact that the book has been published in several editions over the years, E. M. Forster's original preface has not only always remained with it but is most often (as in the current Penguin edition), featured on the front cover.

Unsurprisingly the preface begins in a fairly self-referential manner with a reference to Forster's own novel, *A Passage to India*. Whilst this blurring of the line between the two books has been viewed as 'absorptive rather than equalising',[38] Forster's opening anecdote is a powerful one. And it finally made it clear to Anand exactly why so many puritanical British publishers had turned down his so-called 'dirty' novel. As Forster begins:

> Some years ago I came across a book by myself, *A Passage to India* which had apparently been read by an indignant Colonel. He had not concealed his emotions. On the front page, he had written 'burn when done' and lower down, 'has a dirty mind, see page 215'. I turned to page 215 with pardonable haste. There I found the words: 'The sweeper

of Chandrapur had just struck, and half the commodes remained desolate in consequence'. This lighthearted remark has excluded me from military society ever since.[39]

Only one edition of *Untouchable* to my knowledge does not conform to the pattern of retaining Forster's canonical preface without comment and that is the Bodley Head edition, published in 1970, which adds a revealing 'Afterword' by Saros Cowasjee, one of Anand's most perceptive critics and biographers, providing details of the novel's troubled publication history. Notably too the Bodley Head edition carries a slightly amended dedication. Whereas the first edition of the book is dedicated to the writer Edith Young, in the 1970 edition Anand adds the names of M. K. Gandhi and K. S. Shelvankar as inspirations for the novel. Later editions, such as the Penguin Modern Classic currently in print, revert to the original dedication.

The question of prefaces written to introduce colonial texts by canonical British figures has long been a controversial one for the politics of prefaces in general but also for the after-lives of the texts themselves. Often, as Amardeep Singh has pointed out, the split between preface and text merely heightens a sense of colonial alterity as the canonical 'preface-writer assumes a European readership, and poses the non-European writer's culture as remote and unrecognizable'. Yet, as Singh suggestively continues, such prefaces can also challenge 'European modernism's temporal and spatial universalism' precisely because of their 'visible textual proximity', and the fact that preface and text (as in the case of Forster and Anand) have continued to appear alongside each other for years. On the one hand such material proximity may arguably delimit the future promise of the colonial author so framed by reinforcing old binaries of centre and margin; on the other, such prefaces can also serve to highlight 'a scene of exchange' that existed 'between European and non-European writing', an interrelationship which helps to 'push' the frontiers of European 'modernism *outside of itself*'.[40] In this sense, Forster's preface to *Untouchable*, a frame which has appeared with every published edition of the book, not only registers an already existing and continuing dialogue between the two authors but is also suggestive of a realignment that can extend the borders of European modernism into the global histories of colonial and post-colonial space.

At the time of course, Forster's preface served the primary purpose of creating a 'passport' (as one reviewer in the London Mercury noted) for 'an author whose work might easily have escaped attention'. In this role

Forster was simply an important 'intermediary, legitimating Anand as a writer to be taken seriously and providing some much-needed recognition that was crucial to the book's later survival. In addition, by praising the 'purity' of Anand's intentions, Forster not only deliberately dissolved some of the assumed boundaries between himself and Anand but directed much of the adverse criticism of the book's 'dirt' against himself, making it clear that 'material that lends itself to propaganda' can also 'be so treated as to produce the pure effect of art'.[41] As Cowasjee tells us:

> Though *The Times, London Mercury* and *Punch* agreed with Forster's appraisal, the *Left Review, News Chronicle, Observer, Star, Sunday Referee* and *The Manchester Guardian Weekly* took up issue with him. Much of the argument centred on whether the book was 'dirty', or 'indescribably clean' as Forster made it out to be.[42]

Interestingly too, it was in the heart of the salons of upper class 'Bloomsbury' that Anand met with some of the harshest criticism, a reaction which served to distance him from his acquaintances there, and spurred him on to publish his ensuing, and politically more explicit novels *Coolie, Two Leaves in a Bud* and *Across the Black Waters* (1940). *Across the Black Waters* not only exposes Britain's exploitative enlisting of Indian *sepoys* to cross to *Villayet* (England) as cannon-fodder during the First World War but, as I have argued elsewhere, it also demonstrates how so-called 'barbarism', was generated from 'within as much as without, the inevitable product of Western modernity that had led to global atrocities worldwide'.[43] Several controversial non-fictional pieces also appeared around this time, such as the starkly political *Letters on India* (1942) and the more autobiographical essays in *Apology to Heroism* (1946). Edward Sackville-West's response to *Untouchable's* use of the outcast(e) Bakha as the main protagonist in the novel, is perhaps indicative of the mood of many diehard *Bloomsburyites*. For as he is reputed to have said: 'You can't do a novel about that kind of person ... one only laughs at Cockneys, like Dickens does'.[44] Or, as Cyril Connolly, one of the first metropolitan reviewers of the novel was to observe, the 'untouchable' of the title was perhaps simultaneously a vehicle to represent Anand's sense, not of 'exile' as an Indian writer living in the imperial metropolis, but of alienation in a fundamentally racist climate where all 'WOGS' (Western Oriental Gentlemen as Anand later describes them in *The Bubble* [1984]), were still seen as 'untouchables' themselves.[45]

I would like to draw this discussion to a close with a brief postscript. Despite the difficult odds *Untouchable*, survived the mixed reception it received in the 1930s and won praise even from conservatives such as Eliot, with whom Anand worked briefly at *The Criterion* between 1932 and 1934. Yet by the early 1940s, despite regular appearances with notable figures such as George Orwell and William Empson on the BBC Eastern Service, Anand's reputation in Britain had seriously begun to decline. Anand's prolific publication of a series of explicitly political and anti-British works did not of course aid the situation. He was also sternly criticized by many of his former friends for taking up arms in Spain and stubbornly refusing to drop his communist commitment to Stalin after the outbreak of war in 1939. In fact, by the time Leonard Woolf was to publish his less complimentary and less renowned preface to Anand's utterly unambivalent anti-imperialist *Letters on India* in 1942, the attitude in 'Bloomsbury' circles towards the once much fêted Indian intellectual had decisively changed. Woolf, once a close associate, begins affectionately, but soon makes clear his reasons for departing from the expected convention of a supportive introductory note:

> It will not be the usual kind of introduction, which seems to me nearly always impertinent, in both senses of the word, for in it a distinguished or undistinguished person irrelevantly pats the author on the back. Even if I wanted to – which I do not – I would not dare to pat you or any other member of the Indian National Congress Party on the back. ... The British record in India is not as black as you make out, black though it might be.[46]

The scathing tone evident in Woolf's preface was perhaps to signal the mood of things to come. It certainly marked a significant shift in the British reception of Anand's work that persisted well into the mid 1940s and was perhaps to determine Anand's so-called 'disappearance' back to India after the war. And even though Anand was to continue to make several contributions to BBC radio programmes, he was reluctant to be 'co-opted', as was the Sri Lankan poet Meary James Tambimuttu, to reinforce what he regarded to be 'the ascendant ideologies of Britain and North America' especially 'the propaganda movements against fascism and communism'.[47] One wonders, with hindsight, whether Anand's strange 'absence' from the narratives of British literary histories of the 1930s and 1940s can simply be attributed to his colonial background and the apparently 'nationalist' Indian subject-matter of so many of his works or whether his passionate political agenda and increasing radicalism after the outbreak of the Second World War alienated precisely those in literary power who had originally supported him. For whilst Anand was often to declare a utopian affirmation of Western modernity during his period as a young colonial student in Bloomsbury, his relationship with European enlightenment thinking had always been problematic. It is perhaps owing to the complexity of such contradictions that his work can now be seen to have laid the ground for a split and transnational vision of modernity, a modernity that could straddle the words and worlds of both 'Bloomsbury' and 'Gandhi'. That, however, is a subject for another essay.

Notes

1. There is some disagreement about when precisely Anand did visit Gandhi at his ashram. Anand says he made this visit in the Spring of 1929; see: Mulk Raj Anand, 'Why I Write' in K. K. Sharma, ed., *Indo-English Literature*, (Vimal Prakashan, Ghaziabad, 1977), p. 14 'and Saros Cowasjee notes the date as 1932 in several of his essays. See: 'Mulk Raj Anand: The Early Struggles of a Novelist', *Journal of Commonwealth Literature*, 7, 1, 1972, p. 53; also, 'Afterword' to *Untouchable* (Bodley Head, London, 1970), p. 180.

2. According to Srinivasa, Iyengar, *Indian Writing in English* (Asia Publishing House: New York, 1962), p. 335. All three novels were banned in India and *Two Leaves in a Bud*; as Iyengar notes, was 'withdrawn from circulation in England on the threat of prosecution as an obscene book'. Further details appear in Norman G. Barrier, *Banned: Controversial Literature and Political Control in British India, 1907–1947* (Columbia, MO: University of Missouri Press, 1974). As Barrier notes (p. 126): 'Of the 175 titles seized whilst entering India between 1932 and 1934, at least 150 titles were Communist or by known sympathisers', p. 137. He adds that 'Between 1935 and 1938 customs seized 450 titles, most of which were communist-linked. John Strachey, Mulk Raj Anand, Agnes Smedley and P. R. Dutt fell snare either to customs or postal centres dotting India'. Customs officers, postal authorities etc. were not required to read or comment on any of these books. They were however issued with a crude list identifying obvious links: anything with Gandhi in the title (Barrier, p. 116), anything from Wishart, and proceeded on that basis. It was therefore most likely guilt by association. I am grateful to Robert Fraser, editor of this volume, for this insight.

3. Mulk Raj Anand, 'The Making of an Indian-English Novel: *Untouchable*', Maggie Butcher, ed., *The Eye of the Beholder* (Commonwealth Institute: London, 1983), p. 35.

4. Mulk Raj Anand, *Roots and Flowers: Two Lectures on the Metamorphosis of Technique and Content in the Indian-English Novel* (Karnataka University Press: Dharwar, 1972), p. 16.

5. Bryan Cheyette, 'Venetian Spaces: Old-New Literatures and the Ambivalent Uses of Jewish History, Susheila Nasta, ed., *Reading the 'New' Literatures in a Post-colonial Era* (D.S. Brewer: Cambridge, 2000), p. 57.

6. Sydney Shep, 'Books Without Borders: The Transnational Turn in Book History' in Robert Fraser and Mary Hammond eds, *Books Without Borders, Volume 1: The Cross-National Dimension in Print Culture* (Palgrave Macmillan: Basingstoke, 2008), pp. 13–37.

7. See Mulk Raj Anand, *Conversations in Bloomsbury* (Arnold-Heinemann: New Delhi, 1981); also Kirstin Bluemel, *George Orwell and the Radical Eccentrics: Intermodernism in Literary London* (Palgrave Macmillan: Basingstoke, 2004), pp. 69–92; also, Susheila Nasta, *Home Truths: Fictions of the South Asian Diaspora in Britain* (Palgrave Macmillan: Basingstoke, 2002), pp. 25–34.

8. Amardeep Singh, 'The Lifting and the Lifted: Prefaces to Colonial Modernist Texts', *Wasafiri*, Vol. 21, 1, March 2006, pp. 1–3; hereafter referred to as Singh.

9. Letter to Saros Cowasjee dated 4 October 1968; cited in Cowasjee, 'The Early Struggles of a Novelist', p. 49.

10. Stephen Collini, 'How the Critic Came to be Kind', *TLS*, 8 October 2000, p. 19.

11. See Ruvani Ranasinha, *South Asian Writers in Twentieth-Century Britain: Culture in Translation* (Oxford University Press: Oxford, 2007) for a full discusson of this.

12. Collini, p. 19.

13. Vinay Dharwardker, 'The Historical Formation of Indian-English Literature', in Sheldon Pollock, ed., *Literary Cultures in History: Reconstructions from South Asia* (University of Calafornia Press: Berkeley, 2003), p. 250 and Ricard Allen and Harish Trivdei, eds, *Literature & Nation: Britain and India 1800–1990* (Routledge: London, 2000), pp. 109–10, 162.

14. Priya Joshi, *In Another Country: Colonialism, Culture and the Indian Novel in India* (Columbia University Press: New York, 2002), p. 210.

15. Jessica Berman's insightful essay, 'Comparative Colonialisms: Joyce, Anand and the Question of Engagement', in *Modernism/Modernity*, Vol. 13, 3, 2006, pp. 465–86, develops this argument further as does Arun Mukherjee, 'The Exclusions of Postcolonial Theory and Mulk Raj Anand's "*Untouchable*": A Case Study', *Ariel*, 22, 3, pp. 27–48. It is also key to Bluemel's description of Anand in her monograph (cited earlier) as an 'intermodernist'.

16. Cited by Berman, p. 466.

17. Berman, p. 466.

18. Mulk Raj Anand, 'Why I Write', p. 16.

19. Mulk Raj Anand, 'The Making of an Indian Novel: *Untouchable*', p. 35; also Saros Cowasjee, 'Mulk Raj Anand: The Early Struggles of a Novelist', p. 53.

20. See 'Preface' to *Conversations in Bloomsbury*, p. 5.

21. An interesting discussion of this can be found in V. S. Naipaul's tribute to Gandhi's partially nomadic life as an influence on his early work. See: 'VS Naipaul with Alastair Niven' in Susheila Nasta, ed., *Writing Across Worlds: Contemporary Writers Talk* (Routledge: London, 2004), pp. 109–111. See also Javed Majeed, *Autobiography, Travel and Postnational Identity: Gandhi, Nehru and Iqbal* (Palgrave Macmillan: Basingstoke, 2007), pp. 239–69.

22. Sara Blair, 'Local Modernity, Global Modernism: Bloomsbury and the Places of the Literary', *ELH*, 71–3, 2004, p. 821–25.

23. Cowasjee, 'Mulk Raj Anand: The Early Struggles of a Novelist', p. 53.

24. Mulk Raj Anand, 'The Making of an Indian Novel', pp. 35–7.

25. Mulk Raj Anand, 'Why I Write', p. 14. See also his account of this episode in Mulk Raj Anand with Jane Williams, 'Talking of Tambi: The Dilemna of the Asian Intellectual' in *Tambimuttu: Bridge Between Two Words* (London: Peter Owen, 1989), 191–201.
26. I am following Berman's argument here.
27. E. M. Forster, *A Passage to India* ([1924]; Penguin: Harmondsworth, 1978); p. 316; all future references are to this edition.
28. Mulk Raj Anand, *Conversations in Bloomsbury,* pp. 22, 69, 74.
29. *Conversations in Bloomsbury*, p. 74.
30. Ralph Crane, *'Untouchable'*, *Literature Online*, http://lion.chadwyck.co.uk, p. 2.
31. *A Passage to India*, pp. 273–4, also p. 290.
32. E. M. Forster, 'Preface' to *Untouchable* ([1935]; Penguin: Harmondsworth, 1986), p. viii; all future references are to the 1986 Penguin edition.
33. Saros Cowasjee details this history in his 'Afterword' to *Untouchable* (Bodley Head: London, 1970), pp. 179–185. Forster's letter to Anand is also published in Syed Hamid Husain, ed., *Only Connect: Letters to Indian Friends; E.M. Forster* (Arnold-Heinemann: New Delhi, 1979), p. 73.
34. Mulk Raj Anand, 'The Making of an Indian Novel', p. 40.
35. Saros Cowasjee, 'Afterword', p. 184.
36. Saros Cowasjee, 'Mulk Raj Anand's *Untouchable*: An Appraisal', K.Sharma, ed., *Indo-English Literature: A Collection of Critical Essays* (Vimal Prakashan: Ghaziabad, 1977), pp. 88–9.
37. Letter dated 28 July 1939 addressed to Anand from Z. H. Ahmad of the Socialist Book Club, Allahabad; held in Beinecke Rare Book and Manuscript Library, Yale University (Ref: 3006/S-3), p. 1–3.
38. Amardeep Singh, 'The Lifting and the Lifted: Prefaces to Colonial Modernist Texts; p. 3.
39. 'The Making of an Indian Novel', p. 40. Note here that Anand slightly misquotes Forster's actual preface in this essay. I have used the version of the preface published in the Penguin edition.
40. Amardeep Singh, pp. 1–3.
41. *London Mercury*, XXXII (May 1935), p. 89
42. Saros Cowasjee, 'Afterword', p. 184.
43. Susheila Nasta, *Home Truths: Fictions of the South Asian Diaspora in Britain*, p. 28.
44. Anand quotes this comment in 'The Story of My Experiment with a White Lie', *Critical Essays on Indian Writing in English* (Macmillan: Bombay, 1972), pp. 2–18.
45. Mulk Raj Anand, 'The Story of My Experiment with a White Lie', p. 16.
46. Leonard Woolf, 'Introduction' to Mulk Raj Anand, *Letters on India* (Special edition of Labour Book Service: London, 1942), pp. vii–viii.
47. See Chapter 11, Ruvani Ranasinha, 'Talking to India: The literary production and consumption of selected South Asian Anglophone writers in Britain and the USA (1940s–1950s)', pp. 170–180.

11

Talking to India: The Literary Production and Consumption of Selected South Asian Anglophone Writers in Britain and the USA (1940s–1950s)

Ruvani Ranasinha

In response to Susheila Nasta's essay on Mulk Raj Anand, a number of irresistible questions arise concerning the effects of the participation of a range of South Asian literary figures in the cultural nexus of late British imperialism. This chapter in consequence traces some of the shifting political agendas in Britain and North America that influenced the selection and consumption of certain South Asian Anglophone texts during the 1940s and 1950s. Already, by that time, with the advocacy and backing of established English authors and publishers, South Asian authors such as Raja Rao (1908–2006) and Anand had created the taste they were judged by. They had broken into the literary scene and compelled new ways of reading, playing an extremely influential role in shaping the content of South Asian Anglophone writing published in Britain during the pre-Second World War period, during the war itself and its immediate aftermath.

The focus of this particular chapter, however, will be on the way writers of a slightly later generation, particularly the Indian prose writer Nirad C. Chaudhuri (1897–1999) and the Sri Lankan poet and publisher Meary James Thurairajah Tambimuttu (1915–83) were co-opted to reinforce the ascendant ideologies of Britain and North America, particularly the propaganda movements against fascism and communism during the 1940s and 1950s respectively.

On his arrival in Britain in 1938, the Sri Lankan poet Tambimuttu soon established himself in the literary and artistic circles of London's Soho and Fitzrovia that included the poets T. S. Eliot, Dylan Thomas, George Barker, David Gascoyne (Figure 11.1), William Empson and Gavin Ewart. Within a year, at the age of 23, he founded the influential *Poetry*

London magazine, which he continued to edit until 1950. During this time he also worked as a freelance contributor to the BBC's Eastern Service, including its arts magazine, *The Voice*. Figure 10.1 on p. 154 – a group photograph taken in December 1942 of some leading personalities involved in that programme, many of them prominent writers – portrays him sitting, eyes lowered, alongside Eliot and Anand, and just in front of George Orwell's right arm. This is only proper since Tambimuttu was at this time Orwell's right hand man in a radio series aimed at India's English speakers, 'Talking to India', broadcast throughout the war. This was a series designed to impart propaganda to Anglophone South Asians to encourage support for Britain's war effort.

Figure 11.1   J. M. Tambimuttu with the poet David Gascoyne in 1943, shortly before Poetry London Editions issued Gascoyne's *Poems 1937–1942*, with illustrations by Graham Sutherland

Orwell aimed at India's opinion-forming intelligentsia in the hope of maintaining the conditional allegiance of the nationalists, especially the two million soldiers, in the fraught context of the Quit India Movement of the early 1940s, and in order to counter the Axis propaganda offensive launched by Subhas Chandra Bose's Radio Azad Hind (Free India Radio). The easy successes Japan and Germany achieved between 1939 and 1943, above all the fall of Singapore in 1942, which resulted in the formation of an Indian National Liberation Army, compounded the need for propaganda. Thus during his stay in Britain, Tambimuttu's observations were not directed exclusively to his new home. In translating and refracting particular versions or aspects of British culture to sub-continental audiences, his contributions were incorporated into British political agendas.

The Eastern service comprised news bulletins written by Orwell, and read aloud by Asian speakers, alongside some cultural broadcasts written by the Asian contributors. A memorandum by the head of the Overseas Service in 1942 describes the primary purpose of news commentaries to the subcontinent as 'propaganda': 'They make it possible to put across the British view of the news without sacrificing the reputation that has carefully been built up for veracity and objectivity'. The memo defines the role of 'Dominion speakers' as cultural mediators: 'The use of Dominion speakers increases the confidence felt by the audience; particularly in times of difficulty or strained relations, there is thought to be great merit in leaving *the right type of Dominion speaker* free to reflect criticism and in other ways to build up confidence in himself as much as a representative of the Dominion audience as a British spokesman.'[1]

These news bulletins were distinct from the educational, cultural broadcasts, written by Tambimuttu amongst other South Asian writers that served to disseminate propaganda in different ways. Orwell describes the purported aims of one such programme, entitled 'Through Eastern Eyes':

> The general idea is to interpret the West, and in particular Great Britain, to India, through the eyes of people who are more or less strangers. An Indian, or a Chinese perhaps, comes to this country, and because everything is more or less new to him he notices a great deal which an Englishmen or even an American would take for granted.[2]

Keeping in mind his instruction from Orwell that his talks should 'have a direct bearing' on his sub-continental audience, in Tambimuttu's talk on London Traffic broadcast in 1941, Tambimuttu likens the 'immense London bus' 'to a Ceylon tea-factory on wheels'. As anticipated, his cultural mediation connects distant, distinct cultures and populations (and implicitly their political destinies) through simple, visual images.

The cultural broadcasts were clearly intended to offer more than fresh perspectives on aspects of everyday British life and culture. Orwell implicitly encouraged one contributor to make observations that would incite Indian listeners' sympathy for Britain's war effort. Orwell suggested to Damayanthi Sahni that in her talk about London theatre she 'might mention the damage that London theatres have suffered in the air raids, the courageous struggle by which the dramatic profession have carried on. These are only suggestions'.[3] Tambimuttu needed less prompting. In his talk 'The man in the Street' (broadcast in 1941), he describes London's wartime pub culture during the blackouts and air raids, where London streets were rendered 'unreal and intangible' by the 'dim blue lighting'. Situating the pub as a site of social transformation where the 'BBC news, newspapers, and personal opinions' were 'digested to form British public opinion', Tambimuttu presents a sympathetic portrait of the Englishmen who feel this war 'keenly' and discuss it with 'judicial patience'.[4]

These cultural broadcasts concerning symptomatic aspects of British culture (particularly the series on how British institutions work) feed into the overarching promotion of a critical liberal humanist tradition in opposition to political orthodoxy. This belief is endorsed in Tambimuttu's talk 'How it works – The British Press' of 1941 where he posits a 'free' press, in contrast to a controlled Marxist press:

> English journalism is, in my view, of a higher standard than the journalism in America and the continent. ... English journalism is generally sober and pries into other people's lives as little as possible. English journalists are mostly chosen for their ability to write well and accurately about facts and events.[5]

Similarly his talk 'Open Letter to a Marxist' of 1942 he gives a predictable critique of Marxism:

> the danger of Marxism, as I see it, lies in its ecclesiastical dogmatism, which is steadily growing on its disciples. Many who have accepted the doctrines of Marxism ... have transformed the economic interpretation of history into a metaphysical dogma of deterministic

materialism ... [it is a] theory that ignores the individual element in history and reduces it to an automatic repetition of abstract formulae.[6]

Other contributors such as Anand were less open to 'suggestions' and many of his contributions were censored.

A decade later in a post-war, post-empire context (Figure 11.2), Nirad C. Chaudhuri's literary reception in Britain in 1951 reveals a distinct agenda amongst his different, more conservative readerships. Chaudhuri published his memoirs, *The Autobiography of an Unknown Indian*, with Macmillan in Britain in 1951 while he was living in Delhi. His best-known and finest achievement evokes in loving, intense detail 'the conditions in which an Indian grew to manhood in the early decades of the twentieth century'.[7] Chaudhuri devotes a chapter to each of the four environments that had the greatest influence on him: his birthplace, his ancestral village, his mother's village and his 'imagined' England. The *Autobiography* concludes with Chaudhuri's critique of the early Indian

Figure 11.2   Nirad C. Chaudhuri in the early 1950s

nationalist movement, and contrasts his experience of the arrogance of colonial Englishmen with his idealised conceptions of English civilisation, for him 'the greatest civilisation on earth'.[8]

Chaudhuri's description of the atavisation of the Indian nationalist movement and his lament at the withdrawal of British imperialism, emerging at a time when Britain was trying to come to terms with the loss of the Indian empire, boosted the initial success of his *Autobiography* in Britain, although unsurprisingly it won him few admirers in India. My analysis of the contemporary British reception of Chaudhuri's *Autobiography* will show how his views were employed to promote British neo-imperialism.

It was the extremely influential J. C. Squire (1884–1958) – of the *London Mercury*, chief literary critic of the *Observer* and reader for Macmillan, who recommended Chaudhuri's *Autobiography* for publication. Squire's subsequently reviewed Chaudhuri's first book in *The Illustrated London News*. His review illustrates the text's appeal to certain readerships. Squire's 'appreciation' derives from the way in which Chaudhuri's laudatory account of British rule, reinforces Squire's own views. Squire believed:

> we had justified ourselves in India by our policemanship, our care for the forestry, our irrigation works, our precautions against plague and famine, Lord William Bentinck's measures against suttee and child marriage, our keeping the peace between Moslems and Hindus, our co-operation with the enlightened Princes and our surveillance of the less enlightened'. He goes on to argue '… Kipling's "poor little street-bred people" were led astray by the more cunning of their kind; and India went, to the great detriment of both parties'. Squire praises the fact that 'all this kind of question' is 'surveyed in Mr. Chaudhuri's book'.[9]

Similarly *The Sunday Times* reviewer describes Chaudhuri as exasperated by just those Indian qualities which so 'regrettably [here we can read perhaps 'but understandably'] antagonised the British in India'.[10]

In his review Squire employs Chaudhuri's views to promote British neo-imperialism. Squire quotes Chaudhuri who claims that: 'as long as the English remained strong they had nothing to fear from Indian nationalism, but everything as soon as they grew weak'. Squire makes use of Chaudhuri's argument as a warning, to justify further British neo-imperial intervention when he adds 'the same thing … might be said about Burmese … Malayan … Persian … Egyptian … and even Russian nationalism'.[11] This review is written in the context of the Persian crisis in 1951 when Teheran wanted to nationalise the Anglo-Iranian oil company and gave Britain 15 days to leave. The degree to which Chaudhuri's position cohere with the right-wing views of the British Conservative party can be seen in Churchill's observations on the crisis in 1951: 'if a strong Conservative government had been in power the Persian crisis would never have arisen in this way. It is only when the British Government is known to be weak and hesitant that these outrages are inflicted upon us'.[12]

It is not only Chaudhuri's negative views of post-independent India in his *Autobiography* that found favour amongst his conservative publishers, journalists and readers in Britain. Anglicised Asian writers' familiarity with Western culture proved a particular source of incredulous fascination and gratification for some British consumers; as Squire's report of Chaudhuri's next book impressionistic travelogue of his first visit to Britain in 1955 entitled *A Passage to England* suggests: 'There are passages showing a greater awareness of the English character and the English past, as well as the English landscape, than I have ever encountered in any book by any foreigner, let alone an Asiatic.'[13] Chaudhuri's effusive praise and intense delight at the continued existence of 'Timeless England' in *A Passage to England* (1955) played an important role in his initial acclaim in Britain. A report on *A Passage to England* describes the 'extraordinary story' of Chaudhuri's BBC sponsored visit in 1955, 'where he found what had been absorbing for half a century was a reality. This visit enabled Chaudhuri to overcome his doubt that we had really weathered the storms of the last generation and were still capable of enough national energy to continue developing in the present the brilliant civilisation which he admitted in our past'.[14] A letter Chaudhuri received from his English hosts after his visit in 1955 also suggests that his Anglicisation and desire to assimilate made him popular and non-threatening, and reveals his particular circle's attitudes towards foreigners during this era. The letter reads: 'Everyone was pleased to have met you, especially as you fell in with all our habits and customs as if you had lived among us for years.'[15]

During the 1950s both Chaudhuri and Tambimuttu, alongside other South Asian Anglophone writers, published articles in leading North American journals. These articles further underline how these writers were co-opted to reinforce the shifting ideologies of the dominant metropolitan countries. Reading their contributions particularly those expressing fears of the dangers of communism, shows how US literary editors had a different agenda than British ones, in publishing the work of certain South Asian intellectuals, in the context of the military, political and ideological rivalry between communist and capitalist systems during the Cold War. While certain British publishers such as Macmillan and Chatto and Windus, were more concerned with the legacy of the Indian empire, by contrast in accordance with the dominant political consensus of the time, North American journals such as *the Atlantic Monthly* like the *Encounter* magazine aimed to produce a counter-intellectual movement to communism.[16]

In this vein, Chaudhuri warns in an article in *The Atlantic Monthly* in 1954:

> Indians with Western leanings are prone to overlook the danger from Communism, because from their standpoint Communism is as Western as the liberal civilization of Western Europe, and also because they feel that the spread of Communism will ... promote the sole form of Westernization they are now capable of understanding – namely, Westernization in material things. Thus many upper class Indians are flirting with Communistic ideas in the same manner as the French nobility, blissfully unconscious of their march towards guillotine, flirted with the ideas of Voltaire and Rousseau.

Chaudhuri's cautiously optimistic conclusion clearly invites and justifies Western interference and intervention:

> The only ... rival for retrograde Hinduism [Hindu nationalism] ... is Communism. ... there is bound to be a conflict for power between Hindu nationalism and Communism.
>
> It is my personal belief that in this struggle, unless there is active intervention by the Soviet Union, combined with complete inaction on the part of the West, Communism will *not* win. ... It may make a world of difference if the true West shows itself capable of revivifying and renovating its faith and values, and preaching them to Asia ... something can still be done to create a militant Western faith which will be an adequate substitute for Communism and a dissolvent of retrograde Hinduism.[17]

Also writing for the *Atlantic Monthly* Tambimuttu's article on 'Indian Poetry' appeared alongside essays and stories by Narayan, Anand, Rao, Sahgal and Vijaya Lakshmi Pandit in a supplement entitled 'Perspectives of India' in October 1953. This was shortly after the end of the Korean War, when the US was particularly paranoid about communist propaganda. The supplement purported to showcase 'the writing and contemporary culture of countries whose achievements are little known in the USA, and to further a sense of intellectual community with these countries'. But like *Encounter*, the magazine's real agenda was to maintain contact with Indian intellectuals to pre-empt 'leanings' to communism, as the editorial by Harvey Breit makes clear:

> While in many instances the [Indian] writer is oriented towards the West, especially if he has had a British education, he may also be one who feels a magnetic pull toward Moscow or Mao. He is often an Indian democrat who, like some of his political leaders, identifies the West with imperialism and therefore views it with distrust.
>
> Who can blame him? ... In India ... where illiteracy is a basic problem, the intellectual plays a weighty role in his country's life. Far more than we can imagine, he helps create the climate of opinion. We ought not to neglect him. It remains for us to exchange our ideas with those of the Indian reader, and to show him that we are not indifferent to the creative process wherever we find it.[18]

At this juncture the USA presented its anti-communism as anti-imperialistic. As Gayatri Spivak has observed native informants from formerly colonised countries 'gave support to the American self-representation as the custodian of decolonization' during the Cold War years.[19]

So to conclude, I would broadly agree with arguments such as Sukdhev Sandhu's in his excellent study *London Calling* that, in contrast to customary representations, 'metropolitan individuals and institutions have traditionally been very keen to encourage marginal voices'. I would, however, enter an important caveat by arguing that such support is frequently offered on specific terms and conditions, principally those of reinforcing agenda prevailing in the metropolis itself at any given moment. Sandhu's account of black and Asian migrants' encounters with literary London imbues their interaction with the dominant host culture with a certain neutrality, ignoring in the process the degree to which minority discourse is often shaped by the complex demands of various sections of the mainstream. He writes:

> They found in this old, old city a chance to become new, to slough off their pasts ... London gave them the necessary liberty. It asked for very little in return. Certainly not loyalty ... they had free congress. They were emotionally and intellectually unshackled.[20]

While it is certainly true that many writers found moving to Britain a liberating experience,[21] some of the important shifts in migrant writing reflect the pressures brought to bear by reader responses in the 'host' societies, and sometimes in the 'home' countries as well. These expectations vary over time, according to changing social and political factors.

Furthermore, Chaudhuri and Tambimuttu's contrasting literary receptions amongst the rightwing and counter-cultural readerships they respectively gravitated towards, reveal the centre and periphery as internally variegated rather than monolithic, stable and undifferentiated categories. As we have seen what happens at the centre changes at different historical junctures, and this undermines totalising, transhistorical theorisations of the relation between the centre and the periphery. Nor is there a straightforward opposition or relationship between the centre and a 'revolutionary' margin.

Notes

1. R. A. Rendall, Memo, 9 February 1942, in Davison, ed., *All Propaganda is Lies*, 88–9, emphasis mine.
2. Orwell, Memo, 1 February 1942, in Peter Davison, ed., *The Complete Works of George Orwell: All Propaganda is Lies* (London: Secker and Warburg, 2001), 163. The format of a series of talks addressed to a group unfamiliar with British culture, may owe something to Duse Mohammed Ali's articles published between 1909 and 1911 in the *New Age*, edited by Orage and supported by Shaw and Pound. As Innes has argued, Ali adopts the persona of an un-anglicised Egyptian for whom all things British are something new and strange that may have been influenced by Malabari's criticisms of English culture in his 'An Indian Eye of English Life' (1893).
3. Orwell to Sahni, 3 October 1941, in Peter Davison, ed., *The Complete Works of George Orwell:* (London: Secker and Warburg, 2001), vol. 13, 53.
4. Tambimuttu, 'The Man in the Street', broadcast 17 October 1941, Contributors Talks File 1 (1941–62), transcript, 4.
5. Tambimuttu, 'How it works: The British Press', broadcast 21 December 1941, BBC Contributors Talks File 1 (1941–62), transcript, 5.
6. Tambimuttu, 'Open Letter to a Marxist', broadcast 20 September 1942, Contributors Talks File 1 (1941–62), transcript, 4.
7. Nirad C. Chaudhuri, *The Autobiography of an Unknown Indian* [1951] (Bombay: Jaico Publishing House, 1997), 'Preface'. Hereafter *Autobiography* pagination will appear in the text.
8. Nirad C. Chaudhuri, Interview, *Everyman*, BBC1, BBC Written Archives Centre, Reading, 26 June 1983, transcript, 7.
9. John Squire, 'A Bridge between England and India', *Illustrated London News*, 3 November 1951: 706.
10. Raymond Mortimer, 'The Square Peg', *Sunday Times*, 9 September 1951: 3.
11. Squire, 'A Bridge between England and India', 706.
12. Anonymous, 'Editorial', *Sunday Times*, 7 October 1951: 1.

13. Reader's Report on *A Passage to India*, undated.

14. Reader's report on *A Passage to England*, undated.

15. Cited in Nirad C. Chaudhuri, *A Passage to England* [1959] (Delhi: Orient Paperbacks, 1971), 119.

16. *Encounter* was an anti-communist literary and political monthly initially secretly funded by the US Central Intelligence Agency. See Ian Hamilton, *Oxford Companion to Twentieth Century Poetry in English* (Oxford: Oxford University Press, 1994), 512.

17. Nirad C. Chaudhuri, 'The Western Influence in India', *Atlantic Monthly* 193.3 (1954): 73, 74.

18. Harvey Breit, 'Editorial', *Atlantic Monthly* 192.4 (1953): 3. Later Breit supported other Indian authors, writing a preface for Tamil writer M. Anantarayanan's (1907–1963) *The Silver Pilgrimage* originally published by Criterion Press in New York in 1961.

19. Gayatri Chakravorty Spivak, *A Critique of Postcolonial Reason: Towards a History of the Vanishing Present* (Cambridge, Mass.: Harvard University Press, 1999), 360.

20. Sukhdev Sandhu, *London Calling: How Black and Asian Writers Imagined A City* (London: Harper Collins, 2003), xxxii, xxvi.

21. Markandaya, Hosain and Wynter among others have expressed that they would not have been able to become writers if they had not migrated to Britain. Firdaus Kanga and Suniti Namjoshi are examples of South Asian writers who felt freer to write about and live alternative lifestyles in the West.

12
Salman Rushdie and Zulfikar Ghose in the Literary Marketplace

Sarah Brouillette

The transnational circulation of contemporary literary fiction depends upon a multifaceted set of organizational developments which implicate publishing in global trends in capital and media concentration and in market expansion in the content and trademark industries. It also entails a series of value-regulating mechanisms that shape our ways of reckoning with the products available to us within this complex and shifting system. James F. English and John Frow group such mechanisms within the 'the literary-value industry', defined as 'the whole set of individuals and groups and institutions involved not in producing contemporary fiction as such but in producing the reputations and status positions of contemporary works and authors, situating them on various scales of worth'.[1] Agents involved in this process include prize adjudicators, syllabus-makers and list-makers, book-club participants, librarians, theorists, and journalists. In what follows, I draw attention to some of the features of value regulation within the field of postcolonial literary production as I see it. My specific interest is in thinking about how the mechanisms of evaluation at work within this system influence writers' self-understandings, so that it becomes increasingly problematic to separate out and distinguish among their literature's content, its availability for transnational product circulation, and its relative consecration as a valued work.[2]

Several things characterize the postcolonial literature that typically achieves significant success in the current industry: it is English-language fiction; it is relatively 'sophisticated' or 'complex' and often anti-realist; it is politically liberal and suspicious of nationalism; it uses a language of exile, hybridity, and 'mongrel' subjectivity; and it is marketed, assessed, and consecrated in a way that emphasizes the relationship between the text and the writer's biographical connection to some specific location.[3]

Producing much material with these broad traits, writers from South Asia have come to play a constitutive role in defining value within the wider industry. Here I consider how two contrasting figures negotiate the positions they occupy. My argument is that they each experience the market function of signatured biographical authorship as a burden, and they work out some separation between themselves and what they construct as attributable to their South Asian 'origins' as a response. The differences in how they arrive at their careful self-constructions have to do with divergent career trajectories.

I. Salman Rushdie and complicity

There are a variety of reasons why English-language writers from South Asia have produced an ideally cosmopolitan writing. Recent immigration patterns have been characterized by the metropolitan movements of a relatively prosperous middle class of educated professionals who are thought to be fairly happily deterritorialized. Authors emerging from this matrix have been said to combine social privilege with subversion. Writing in English, they are available for consecration as embodying a national or supranational voice, unmoored from the more 'minor' perspectives identified with vernacular regional writing.[4] They are also ostensibly willing to separate politics and aesthetics in the usual manner, to act as interpreters of the lands they have left behind, and to deploy a 'semantics of subalternity' attractive to Anglo-American readers.[5] It is in this spirit that Leela Gandhi claims that 'the figure of the new/postcolonial Indian English novelist is in a deliciously "win-win" situation', speaking from 'an enviable position' of simultaneous privilege and dissent, articulating a special kind of subversion that comes with social status.[6]

It is Salman Rushdie who normally stands as the paradigmatic figure of this privilege. Initially operating primarily within the London literary milieu, he has gradually moved into a more global position, his career emerging as an analogue to a literary marketplace increasingly defined by transnational corporate concentration. A battery of ethical qualms has accompanied this process. Ajijaz Ahmad's influential understanding of the category of Third World literature – one within which Rushdie features prominently – insists on its definition by the 'grids of accumulation, interpretation and relocation which are governed from the metropolitan countries', where is it 'available to the metropolitan university to examine, explicate, categorize, classify, and judge as to its worthiness for inclusion within its curriculum and canon'.[7] It is only after facing the mechanisms of consecration that a given title is 'first designated a Third World text, levelled into an archive of other such texts, and then globally redistributed with that aura attached to it'.[8] Third World literature simply *is* that work that has managed making it beyond some more specific locality, while still having attached to it, always, the aura of its transcended origin. This literature's lack of autonomous circulation is countered by 'other kinds of cultural productivities', though. These are the 'entire linguistic complexes as yet unassimilated into grids of print and translation'. They are necessarily difficult to identify, but they are at least 'not archival [but] local and tentative', and they arise from histories that are 'more variegated and prolix, more complexly and viscerally felt'.[9]

It is in these terms that Ahmad associates successful writers with the negative characteristics of the 'unmoored' global literary marketplace, while more local vernacular figures maintain positions of prestige dependent on their lack of access to the same sphere. I cite his remarks because they show that while the romantic author-figure has been discredited within the general literary field, he has managed to retain some continued life for certain postcolonial audiences. This romantic residue is significant to Rushdie's reception. Amit Chaudhuri claims that Rushdie's example has become 'a key to the way Indian writing is supposed to be read and produced [...] Rushdie both being the godhead from which Indian writing in English has reportedly sprung, revivified, and a convenient shorthand for that writing'.[10] Characterized by its abundance, its non-linearity, its incorporation of magical elements, and its references to an Indian epic tradition, Rushdie's style has come to seem 'emblematic of a non-Western mode of discourse,' at once postcolonial and 'inescapably Indian'.[11] In turn his name has become ubiquitous in debates about the special status of Indian Writing in English (IWE) within global markets, a status thought to perpetuate and justify a relative lack of attention to South Asia's abundant vernacular writings. In fact he can seem sometimes to stand in for the total position of IWE more generally, as it has been globally consecrated in, for example, Arundhuti Roy's 1997 Booker Prize (the first for a writer still resident in India), V. S. Naipaul's 2001 Nobel Prize, and the celebratory International Festival of Indian Literature held in Delhi in 2002.

It is precisely on the grounds of his responsibility as one 'godhead' of IWE that Rushdie faces scrutiny. Does he belie the realities of the migrant condition with his metaphorical terminology of 'border crossing' and exile, a language he willingly deploys despite his thoroughly privileged life in the Anglo-American metropoles? Revathi Krishnaswamy states that his works have been key to the way 'words such as "diaspora" and "exile" are being emptied of their histories of pain and suffering and are being deployed promiscuously to designate a wide array of cross-cultural phenomena'.[12] This gesture, distinguishing Rushdie's brand of 'voluntary self-exile' from a more legitimate 'forced' version[13] – establishing what Rob Nixon has called 'the ratio of violence to choice in the prompting of [a writer's] departure'[14] – is common to those who challenge his special celebrity.

Far from indifferently ignoring the politicization of IWE, or of his own work as the obvious (and obviously marketed) exemplar of that writing, Rushdie has mounted a full-scale attack against the sources, nature, and implications of these and like claims. His anxious self-positioning is most apparent in his opposition to what he blithely calls 'the East' – a highly expedient category with an expansive set of features encompassing all those audiences who have rejected his status and output.[15]

One example is his response to the Indian authorities' refusal of his requests for locations to shoot the film version of *Midnight's Children*. Rushdie adds their denials to a long history of discord, claiming he had never recovered from the 'terrible blow' of India's opposition or indifference to his work. His language is interesting: 'That *Midnight's Children* should have been rejected so arbitrarily, with such utter indifference, by the land about which it had been written with all my love and skill, was a terrible blow.'[16] Whereas he has only love for the land of the novel's setting, a land to which he claims further connection in having written *Midnight's Children* as a way of representing and memorializing his own childhood in Bombay, that beloved 'land' rejects his work at once entirely and 'arbitrarily'. In doing so it rejects the author's love. Such posturing establishes a stark opposition between Rushdie and the entirety of South Asia, affirmed in his statement that 'the rejection of *Midnight's Children* changes something profound in my relationship with the East. Something broke, and I'm not sure it can be mended'.[17]

A further case is by his now infamous article on the state of literature in India, appearing in a 1997 *New Yorker* issue dedicated to celebrating the bicentenary of the country's independence. In it Rushdie announced that Indian prose writing in English

> is proving to be a stronger and more important body of work than most of what has been produced in the eighteen 'recognized' languages of India, the so-called 'vernacular languages' [...] this new,

and still burgeoning 'Indo-Anglian' literature represents perhaps the most valuable contribution India has yet made to the world of books.[18]

This is a remarkably self-congratulatory statement, and it appears near the beginning of a piece that is rife with both outright and guarded forms of self-justification. He states that '[f]or some Indian critics, English-language Indian writing will never be more than a postcolonial anomaly – the bastard child of Empire, sired in Indian by the departing British.'[19] He claims that criticism levied at Indo-Anglian literature comes solely from Indians – though often ones 'who are themselves members of the college-educated, English-speaking élite' – and then carefully notes all of the characteristics attributed to this writing by those 'Indian critical assaults':

> Its practitioners are denigrated for being too upper-middle-class; for lacking diversity in their choices of themes and techniques; for being less popular in India than outside India; for possessing inflated reputations on account of the international power of the English language, and of the ability of Western critics and publishers to impose their cultural standards of the East; for living, in many cases, outside India; for being deracinated to the point where their work lacks the spiritual dimension essential for a 'true' under-standing of the soul of India; for being insufficiently grounded in the ancient literary traditions of India; for being the literary equiva-lent of MTV culture, or of globalizing Coca-Colonization; even, I'm sorry to report, for suffering from a condition that one sprightly recent commentator [...] calls 'Rushdie-itis ... a condition that has claimed Rushdie himself in his later works.'

No specific critique of Rushdie's prominence or success can match his own self-conscious list of objections to such work. Rather than answer-ing any of these criticisms, though, his form of rejection of such attacks is to lament a 'cheapening of artistic response', as well as the fact that 'so few of these criticisms are literary [...] they do not deal with lan-guage, voice, psychological or social insight, imagination, or talent [...] they have to do with class, power, and belief'.[20] Indeed this piece on the merits of Indian writing since independence focuses significantly more attention on the hostile *reception* of Indo-Anglian writing than it does on the sort of aesthetic evaluation Rushdie claims to want to trumpet instead. It also clearly separates Rushdie from what he identifies as an

Indian or South Asian – hence 'regional' or 'minor' – critical tendency. To use Pascale Casanova's terms, he rejects a 'heteronymous' national or regional tradition aligned with the land of his birth, appealing instead to a specifically autonomous aesthetic lineage[21] apparently distinct from 'class, power, and belief'. This seems to me Rushdie's exemplary gesture of authorial self-construction: namely, his claim to want to turn his back on those varied approaches to literary production that are interested in anything other than the somewhat mystified artistry and 'talent' at play in the work itself.

His 2001 novel *Fury* is revealing in this light.[22] It tells the quasi-autobiographical story of Malik Soyinka, a lapsed English academic turned New York-based culture industries worker, and combines it with an account of a national liberation struggle based on the real political turmoil taking place in Fiji in 1999–2000. After falling in love with a woman who has a personal connection to the region, Malik uses the crisis as material for his work, and the region's combatants take up Malik's stories as iconic political totems in turn. *Fury*'s interest in the circulation of political narratives is a paranoid one. The novel articulates a fear about texts' availability for forms of appropriation that may have no relation to the intentions of any author, where their politicization is facilitated by the absence of attachment to any functioning creator-figure who can authorize meaning. By lamenting the intending author's marginalization, *Fury* re-centres the question of Rushdie's own authorship. In doing so, it is akin to a procedure he initiated after the fatwa made it necessary to affirm his authorial intentions, despite having written a novel that questions the idea of origins at every turn. 'In Good Faith,' one passionate defense of *The Satanic Verses*, is packed with statements like 'we must return for a moment to the actually existing book'; 'de-contextualization has created a complete reversal of meaning', and 'the original intentions of *The Satanic Verses* have been so thoroughly scrambled by events as to be lost for ever'.[23]

Fury shows additional signs, though, of the author's more recent conflict with what he constructs as a dominantly South Asian tendency to politicize and critique some Rushdie-figure as the embodiment of IWE's privileged market position. Malik is pursued by Babur, the dictatorial revolutionary, a man descended from those indentured Indian labourers who experienced the authentic migrancy that Rushdie has been accused of mining for his universalizing metaphorics of 'border crossing' and 'mongrel' subjectivity. As the most scorned manipulator of Malik's works for very real political ends, it is Babur who stands in for the more problematic aspects of Rushdie's reception. Rushdie has himself said, in relation to the fatwa, that in attempting to portray an 'objective reality' he 'became its subject',[24] witnessing an alternative self going around as Rushdie but in the image of the devil, and fearing that 'my other may succeed in obliterating me'.[25] Malik has the same fear that Babur might don the mask of one of his characters in order to obliterate the fiction's author. So while it may be the first of Rushdie's major novels to abandon South Asia as subject and setting, it is haunted by 'the East' to which the author is irreparably bound by the mutually-constituted forces of political fiat and industry positioning.

Malik wants to matter as an author of his text's meaning, but not, it seems, as an author-*figure* lionized by the global media and transnational culture industries – the status for which Rushdie has himself received such significant criticism. It is Malik's wilful decision to engage with the political realities of particular locales that has made his works available for certain forms of political appropriation, in a process he might have then predicted. What he seems to want is to separate his biographical self from the real-world impact that his works have had, especially as that impact extends to the violence of public disdain for the writer's self. It is a simultaneous undermining of the author-function and celebrification of the author-figure that permits the writer's demonization – quite literally, in *Fury*, his transmutation into a devilish masked man from which he'd rather remain distinct.

Like Malik's, Rushdie's works have an obvious political relevance that makes them available for contentious debate. His material is controversial and has proven to be offensive to some audiences. In *Fury* he grants this and yet still wonders why it has anything to do with him becoming a celebrated individual. Why must he be lionized in such a way that everything from basic criticism to threats of violence are directed at his person, while opposition to his work routinely has to do with his own ostensible personal venality, or abandonment of South Asia, or deracinated love for the Anglo-American metropoles? It is Rushdie's unrelenting connection to a particular locale – whether he is said to romanticize it, market it, or abandon it – that has been a feature of the most vociferous forms of politicization of his work. What Rushdie opposes in rejecting 'the East' is, thus, the way he feels he has been personally, viscerally, even bodily implicated in a whole series of real world struggles. The problem is his elevation to the status of icon (Rushdie™), and the related privileging of hostile attention to his person, over any consideration of the techniques and concerns that might be associated with a more functional – though less biographically signatured – authorship.

Rushdie's account of a recent trip to India, depicted as an opportunity to heal the rift between himself and his homeland, clarifies a connection between Malik and his author, in this respect. After detailing the various barriers to his acting as an average citizen, such as access restrictions and bodyguards, his emphasis becomes his desire 'to bore India into submission', to be uninteresting to the average person in a way that celebrities rarely are.[26] 'People – journalists, policemen, friends, strangers – all write scripts for me, and I get trapped inside those fantasies', he writes. In his own script, though, 'the problems I've faced are gradually overcome, and I resume the ordinary literary life that is all I've ever wanted'.[27] As Rushdie comes to realize that the country is not so obsessed with his presence as he had been led to believe, and as he begins to think that the burden of *The Satanic Verses* fatwa can finally be cast off, he celebrates. In fact he describes his euphoria about passing into irrelevance as 'an event of immense emotional impact, exceeding in force even the tumultuous reception of *Midnight's Children* almost twenty years ago'.[28] *Fury* shares this same language, depicting a beleaguered writer who wants to stop living in a scenario he did not create for himself, because it causes problems that challenge his right to author the meaning of his own texts and, more importantly, to authorize his own life. In the end it is only in going unnoticed that Rushdie will be reconciled to the place he calls 'the East'.

II. Zulfikar Ghose and exclusion

In marked contrast, attention to Zulfikar Ghose's writing routinely turns on his refusal to make his focus any place identifiable with his own authenticating South Asian background. He has not avoided South Asian settings entirely. *The Murder of Aziz Khan* (1967) is a plainly realist novel set in Pakistan, and Ghose's early poetry and his autobiographical *Confessions of a Native-Alien* (1965) notably deal with his childhood and the perils of incorporation into a new culture. *Confessions of a Native-Alien* even offers South Asian material in a way that accommodates Western readers, teaching them about the geography and culture of both Sialkot and Bombay, and it approaches childhood with a nostalgia tempered only by an understandable wariness about the violence that comes with appeals to a secure national identity. It was with the Incredible Brazilian trilogy, made up of *The Native* (1972), *The Beautiful Empire* (1975), and *A Different World* (1978), that Ghose left the region behind. He shifted his fictional attention to South America, writing novels that fall into the broad category of magic realism, making him literary fiction's only Pakistani-Anglo-American working in South America's most noted mode.

In the only book-length study of Ghose's work, Chelva Kanaganayakam applauds him for being brave enough 'to forsake what could have been a comfortable niche among post-colonial writers'.[29] Feroza Jussawalla and Reed Way Dasenbrock emphasize his outsider status even more, claiming he 'evades most of our accepted ways of talking and the grouping of contemporary literature', while his work has 'steadily moved away from typical concerns and themes of contemporary South Asian writing in English or of Commonwealth writing in general'.[30] He has never won a literary prize, and, as Kanaganayakam notes, he 'continues to remain relatively unknown in academic circles, hardly discussed in literary journals and only tenuously linked to commonwealth, British, and American writing'.[31] There has been little effort, in other words, to incorporate Ghose's work into a canon of literature relevant to post-colonialism. In interview Dasenbrock and Jussawalla thus suggest to Ghose that in terms of the 'degree of awareness' of his work he has suffered from 'the law that everything should fit a nice, neat national category'. Ghose responds: 'my books don't sell, and I receive very little serious critical attention. It is very rare for a reviewer to remark upon the quality of my prose or to reveal a comprehension of the imaginative structure of my work'.[32]

Some critics have insisted that there are in fact significant parallels between Ghose's life and his fiction, given that his experience has been defined by exile and that he has never felt a specific attachment – definable through language, religion, or a clear nationality, for example – to any South Asian location. His work emphasizes the author's biographical deracination, the homelessness that is after all characteristic of his life.[33] He was born in Sialkot, in what was then British India but became Pakistan, and moved to Bombay at a young age, where his father changed their Muslim last name Ghaus to the more Hindu Ghose in order to ensure the family would blend into their new urban environment.[34] His very name embodied one of the early fractures of his identity: his separation from his Muslim origins but also his outsider position within Hindu culture. He has described himself as a 'Native-Alien' both in England and in the Indo-Pakistan of his early life, as an 'Indo-Pakistani born before Pakistan existed, moved to Bombay, then England', and he calls these layers of his early identity the 'schizophrenic theme of much of [his] thinking'.[35]

Still, in interview with Vassanji he berates any suggestion that his origins are a relevant subject for discussion in relation to his fiction.

'Home is in my mind, my imagination', he claims. 'Home is the English language and what I can do with it and what I can read in it.' He evokes his habitation in a language and a world of fictions, and even romanticizes England, claiming it will always be his home, as the place where he began to be a writer, 'or began emerging as a writer and being recognized as a writer'. And he attacks the tendency to 'put a work into a nationalist category because of its content,' calling it 'naïve', and insisting that the 'best works of the second half of the twentieth century have not come from a particular background'.[36] The writing itself is the space in which he develops, so that it is the substantial content of his experience: 'If I spend a year writing a novel and, finishing it, start another one, my only "real experience" has been that I have written a novel'. Appealing to an ostensibly more legitimate Pakistani or South Asian past would be a pose, and evoking an authentic national location would be a sign of the inauthentic in his self-presentation and fictional work. Such an appeal is not an option in part because Ghose was not brought up a religious Muslim and he does not recognize himself as in any way Pakistani: 'I did not have the heritage I am supposed to be guilty of having broken with', he states.[37]

I understand this tendency to focus on an aesthetic or literary impetus as an attempt to separate himself from the postcolonial market that makes the subject of his 'heritage' such an issue. In a similar way, his repeated insistence in his critical non-fiction that writers should espouse no particular 'ism' popular with a current audience,[38] while perhaps too combatively dedicated to a troubled aesthetic ideology, makes sense as an explicit and rather pained reaction to his own racialization at the hands of his critical public. The depth of this reaction is most evident in his 1992 novel, *The Triple Mirror of the Self*. Its first part is made up of the narrative of a man who has taken up residence in a village called Suxavat, a place familiar to readers of Ghose's work accustomed to his South American settings. His name is Urim, and he tells the tale of the village's destruction at the hands of an Interior Ministry in pursuit of gold. He is one of the few survivors. Then, the set of notebooks in which Urim records his tale – the Urim manuscript – passes into the hands of Jonathan Pons, an American academic who is featured in Urim's story, but who insists he was never with Urim in South America and that his presence in Urim's narrative is entirely fictional. Pons' research into the 'origins' of the manuscript moves us backwards in time in pursuit of Urim's past. Pons eventually establishes that before travelling to South America Urim lived a life in exile. He was an American poet and academic called Zinalco Shimomura, after a stint as an immigrant to England, during which time he fell in with a bohemian crowd where he was known as Shimmers. And, before arriving in England, Pons claims, Urim was Roshan Karim, a boy growing up as a Punjabi Muslim in British India during the period just before independence. Roshan's story makes up the novel's third part.

We are left to wonder how much Pons' editorial prerogative controls what we learn about the narrator of the Urim manuscript, and whether or not the entire last section of the novel, detailing Roshan's (Urim's) early life in South Asia, was penned by Pons himself. Presumably assembled after his careful research and editing, the contingent texts that make up the novel's three parts rather carefully map Ghose's own journey, moving from India to England to the USA. They also map his fictional tendencies, present in the Urim manuscript's South American setting and its depiction of the geopolitical violence, encouraged by capitalist accumulation, which leads to Suxavat's destruction. Pons can 'complete' Urim's manuscript because he receives a grant to work on a text left unfinished by the death of its author.[39] Urim's lack of authorial agency is what permits Pons' use of his text, a use then resolutely determined by the question of Urim's authorial identity. Pons' relationship with the Urim manuscript, a manuscript that critiques any geographically-based authenticity, rather carefully mirrors the relationship Ghose's critics have with his works, consistently drawing the author in just as he attempts to leave himself out.

Pons' research is designed to allow him to gloss the obscurities of Urim's text, which is haunted by memories of the life that he left behind, but that creep to the surface of his thoughts at moments of crisis. For example, he hears General Dyer in the gunfire that destroys his village and sees the Hindu Kush in the Andes before his death. These surfacings prompt aspects of Pons' research into the narrator's past and contribute to the story of origins he finally attaches to Urim and his previous British and American incarnations. However, just at the end of the book's second section Pons states:

> I realized that I must concern myself only with that language which would rediscover, oh, not some miserable truth which is but a paltry thing, but the precise detail embedded in the florid, passionate, miraculous and infinitely elusive figures that haunt memory, to reinvent the idea itself or reality after discovering that reality, poor thing, has no existence at all.
>
> (p. 194)

So, after assembling numerous texts collected from a variety of sources, all attesting to Urim's past, the manuscript's 'elusive figures' are no more clear to him than when he began his research, so Pons resolves to 'reinvent' a reality that might provide a fitting gloss for Urim's text. The subsequent narrative is Pons' attempt to find 'precise detail' that could explain the manuscript's obscurities. Because it is thematically consistent with Urim's notebooks we are allowed to imagine that they are of the same authorship, in accord with our expectations about how authored texts relate to one another and to a distinct biography.

Roshan's story also closely mirrors the general narrative of Ghose's autobiographical work, *Confessions of a Native-Alien*. By recasting the material of that book as Pons' own imaginative reconstruction of the early life of the subject of his research, Ghose implicates his earlier writing in the cultural logic of cosmopolitanism that Pons embodies. Here that logic implies a specific understanding of authorship's relation to nationality, and finds the birth of an author's sensibility in a childhood landscape viewed with nostalgia. In this way *The Triple Mirror of the Self* returns to South Asia, but only to suggest that it is less the product of a mind legitimately engaged in a consideration of a specific authenticating past and more the fantastic product of an elite cosmopolitan class. The value attached to biographical authenticity then seems like a prerequisite for Anglo-American cosmopolitanism. Pons is depicted as more committed to the politics of postcolonial identities than he is concerned about the geopolitical violence of late capitalism, as his major interest in the Urim manuscript is a systematic tracing of the origins of its author. The process of tracing those origins entirely ignores the manuscript's own critique of the value attached to authenticity, its positing of a link between national identification and real geopolitical violence, and its overall concern with the incursion of late capitalism into South America's geopolitical landscape.

In sum, one of the primary functions of the book is an interrogation of the status of the cosmopolitan as consumer and interpreter of the local for a global cultural field. Pons is the guarantor of the cultural status of the Urim narrative, a narrative that is a pastiche of Ghose's South American oeuvre. Ghose figures his own narratives as authorized by a cosmopolitan class, and as circulating across continents in a way that privileges that class as the one in the position to sanction cultural texts and make decisions about their importance and relative value. Its primary target is Pons, but also what Pons desires and then constructs: a story of origins for Roshan Karim. It constructs the reception of postcolonial texts as entailing this turn toward an obsession with the authenticity of representation, authenticity as sanctioned by biographical detail, which leads critics to ignore other sources of literary value. This understanding of the market is Ghose's invested response to his own difficulties in achieving significant recognition or acclaim.

III. Conclusion

As a global celebrity and assured member of the cosmopolitan class that Ghose critiques, having in part benefited from the connection between his writings and some authenticating origins, Rushdie's celebrification has made him perilously available for forms of attention that collapse his writing self and his texts with some notion of his 'real' identity. His response to this situation entails an engagement with the question of his own complicity in a marketplace that sanctions and circulates a select group of global texts. For Ghose, alternatively, the question is one of the modes of self-justification necessary to explain his relative lack of access to the global sphere that someone like Rushdie inhabits.

It is interesting to note, in conclusion, that the centrality of questions of biography in reception of postcolonial texts refutes the supposed dominant orthodoxy of anti-authorialism in literary studies. Much though writers might themselves wish otherwise, anti-authorial perspectives simply do not dominate in their experiences of the market for postcolonial literatures, and nor do they much influence the various institutions of postcolonial literary reception and evaluation.

Notes

1. James F. English and John Frow, 'Literary Authorship and Celebrity Culture', in *A Concise Companion to Contemporary British Fiction*, ed. James F. English (Malden, MA: Blackwell, 2006), 45.
2. I explore this argument in greater depth in some of my other published research. See Sarah Brouillette, 'Zulfikar Ghose's *The Triple Mirror of the Self* and Cosmopolitan Authentication', *Modern Fiction Studies* 53.1 (2007) © Purdue Research Foundation. Reprinted with the permission of The Johns Hopkins University Press; and Sarah Brouillette, *Postcolonial Writers in the Global Literary Marketplace* (London: Palgrave Macmillan, 2007). Reproduced with permission of Palgrave Macmillan.
3. Timothy Brennan has done much to identify these characteristics. See *At Home in the World: Cosmopolitanism Now* (Cambridge: Harvard University Press, 1997), and *Salman Rushdie and the Third World: Myths of the Nation* (New York: St Martin's Press, 1989).

4. Aijaz Ahmad, *In Theory: Classes, Nations, Literatures* (London: Verso, 1992), 75.

5. Revathi Krishnaswamy, 'Mythologies of Migrancy: Postcolonialism, Postmodernism, and the Political of (Dis)location', *Ariel* 26 (1995), 129, 139.

6. Leela Gandhi, 'Indo-Anglian Fiction: Writing India, Elite Aesthetics, and the Rise of the "Stephanian" Novel', *Australian Humanities Review* 8 (1997), 12 October 2006, http://www.lib.latrobe.edu.au/AHR/archive/Issue-November-1997/gandhi.html, par. 18.

7. Ahmad, *In Theory*, 44, 80.

8. Ibid., 45.

9. Ibid., 81.

10. Amit Chaudhuri, 'The Construction of the Indian Novel in English', Introduction, *The Picador Book of Modern Indian Literature*, ed. Amit Chaudhuri (London: Picador, 2001), xxiv.

11. Ibid., xxv.

12. Krishnaswamy, 'Mythologies of Migrancy', 128.

13. Ibid., 134.

14. Rob Nixon, 'London Calling: V. S. Naipaul and the License of Exile', *South Atlantic Quarterly* 87 (1988), 7.

15. As early as *Shame*, he wrote: 'I tell myself this will be a novel of leavetaking, my last words on the East from which, many years ago, I began to come loose' (Salman Rushdie, *Shame* [London: Picador, 1984], 28).

16. Salman Rushdie, 'Introduction' in Salman Rushdie, *The Screenplay of Midnight's Children* (London: Vintage, 1999), 10.

17. Ibid., 1, 12.

18. Salman Rushdie, 'Damme, This is the Oriental Scene for You!' *New Yorker* (23 & 30 June 1997), 50.

19. Ibid., 52.

20. Ibid., 54.

21. Pascale Casanova, *The World Republic of Letters* (Harvard University Press, 2004).

22. Salman Rushdie, *Fury* (Toronto: Vintage, 2002).

23. Salman Rushdie, 'In Good Faith', in *Imaginary Homelands: Essays and Criticism 1981–1991* (London: Granta Books, 1991), 395, 402, 403.

24. Ibid., 404.

25. Ibid., 406.

26. Salman Rushdie, 'A Dream of Glorious Return', in *Step Across This Line: Collected Nonfiction 1992–2002* (New York: Random House, 2002), 190.

27. Ibid., 191.

28. Ibid., 206–7.

29. Chelva Kanaganayakam, *Structures of Negation: The Writings of Zulfikar Ghose* (Toronto: University of Toronto Press, 1993), 5.

30. Feroza Jussawalla and Reed Way Dasenbrock, Introduction to *Milan Kundera/Zulfikar Ghose*, spec. issue of *Review of Contemporary Fiction* 9.2 (1989), 108.

31. Chelva Kanaganayakam, 'Zulfikar Ghose: An Interview', *Twentieth Century Literature* 32 (1986), 169.

32. Feroza Jussawalla and Reed Way Dasenbrock, 'Conversation with Zulfikar Ghose', in *Milan Kundera/Zulfikar Ghose*, spec. issue of *Review of Contemporary Fiction* 9.2 (1989), 148.

33. Kanaganayakam, 'Zulfikar Ghose,' 171.

34. Zulfikar Ghose, *Confessions of a Native Alien* (London: Routledge & Kegan Paul, 1965), 2.
35. Ibid., 1–2.
36. Ibid., 17–18.
37. Ibid., 20.
38. See, e.g., Zulfikar Ghose, *Art of Creating Fiction* (London: Macmillan, 1991), 35, 44.
39. Zulfikar Ghose, *The Triple Mirror of the Self* (London: Bloomsbury, 1992), 119. Subsequent page references appear in the body of the text.

Select Bibliography

Acharya, Parames. *Banglar Deshaja Sikshadhara* (Calcutta: Anushtup Prakashani, 1989).

Ahmad, Aijaz. *In Theory: Classes, Nations, Literatures* (Delhi: OUP, 1992).

Altbach, Philip. *Publishing in India: An Analysis* (Delhi: OUP, 1975).

Anderson, Benedict. *Imagined Communities: Reflections on the Origin and Spread of Nationalism*, 2nd ed. (New York: Verso, 1991).

Anand, Mulk Raj. *Untouchable* (London: Wishart, 1935).

——. *Roots and Flowers: Two Lectures on the Metamorphosis of Technique and Content in the Indian-English Novel* (Dharwar: Karnatak University Press, 1972).

——. *Conversations in Bloomsbury* (Delhi: Arnold-Heinemanni, 1981).

——. 'The Making of an Indian-English Novel: *Untouchable*' in Butcher, Maggie (eds), *The Eye of the Beholder* (London: Commonwealth Institute, 1983).

Banerjee, Sumanta. *The Parlour and the Streets: Elite and Popular Culture in Nineteenth-Century Calcutta* (Calcutta: Seagull, 1989).

Barpujari, H. K. *The American Missionaries and North-East India (1836–1900): A Documentary Study.* (Delhi: Spectrum, 1986).

Barrier, Norman G. *Banned: Controversial Literature and Political Control in British India, 1907–1947* (Columbia, MO: University of Missouri Press, 1974).

Barua, Sanjib. *India Against Itself: Assam and the Politics of Nationality* (Delhi: OUP, 1998).

Basu, Aparna. *The Growth of Education and Political Development in India, 1898–1920* (New Delhi: OUP, 1974).

Bayly, C. A. *Empire and Information: Intelligence gathering and social communication in India, 1780–1870* (Cambridge: CUP, 1996).

Bell, Gertrude. *Poems from the Divan of Hafiz* (London: Heinemann, 1897, 1928).

Bhabha, Homi K. (ed.). *Nation and Narration* (London and New York: Routledge, 1990).

——. *The Location of Culture* (London and New York: Routledge, 1994).

Bhattacharya, Jatindranath. *Bangla Mudrita Granthadir Talika, 1743–1852* (Calcutta: A. Mukherjee, 1990).

Blackburn, Stuart and Dalmia Vasudha (eds), *India's Literary History: Essays on the Nineteenth Century* (New Delhi: Permanent Black, 2004).

Bluemel, Kirstin. *George Orwell and the Radical Eccentrics: Intermodernism in Literary London* (Basingstoke: Palgrave Macmillan, 2004).

Brennan, Timothy. *Salman Rushdie and the Third World: Myths of the Nation* (New York: St. Martin's Press, 1989).

——. *At Home in the World: Cosmopolitanism Now* (Cambridge: Harvard University Press, 1997).

Broughton, Thomas Duer. *Selections from the Popular Poetry of the Hindoos* (London: John Martin, 1814).

Brouillette, Sarah. *Postcolonial Writers in the Global Literary Marketplace* (Basingstoke: Palgrave Macmillan, 2007).

Chanda, Mrinal Kanti. *A History of the English Press in Bengal 1780–1857* (Calcutta and New Delhi: K. P. Bagchi, 1987).

Chatterjee, Partha. *The Partha Chatterjee Omnibus* (Delhi: OUP, 2004).

Chatterjee, Rimi B. *Empires of the Mind: A History of the Oxford University Press in India Under the Raj* (Delhi: OUP, 2006).

Chaudhuri, Amit. 'The Construction of the Indian Novel in English,' Introduction, *The Picador Book of Modern Indian Literature* (London: Picador, 2001).

Chaudhuri, Nirad C. *Autobiography of an Unknown Indian* (London: Hogarth, 1987).

——. *Thy Hand, Great Anarch! India 1921–1952* (London: Hogarth, 1990).

Darnton, Robert. 'Literary Surveillance in the British Raj: The Contradictions of Liberal Imperialism', *Book History* 4 (2001), 133–76.

Davison, Peter (ed.). *The Complete Works of George Orwell* (London: Secker and Warburg, 2001).

Davis, Marvin (ed.). *Bengal: Studies in Literature, Society and History*, Occasional Papers on South Asia, no. 27 (Ann Arbor: University of Michigan Asian Studies Centre, 1976).

Deb, Chitra (ed.). *Saralabala Sarkar Racanasangraha* (Calcutta, 1989).

Dutta, Krishna and Robinson, Andrew. *Selected Letters of Rabindranath Tagore*, (Cambridge University Press, 1997).

English, James F. and Frow, John.'Literary Authorship and Celebrity Culture,' in *A Concise Companion to Contemporary British Fiction*, James F. English ed. (Malden, MA: Blackwell, 2006).

Febvre, Lucien and Martin, Henri Jean. *L'apparition du livre* (Paris: Editions Albin Michel, 1958).

Finkelstein, David. *Philip Meadows Taylor (1808–1876)*. Victorian Fiction Research Guides XVIII (Queensland: University of Queensland Press 1990).

Finkelstein, David and Peers, Douglas M. (ed.). *Negotiating India in the Nineteenth-Century Media* (Basingstoke: Palgrave Macmillan, 2000).

Finkelstein, David and McCleery Alistair. *An Introduction to Book History* (London and New York: Routledge, 2005).

Forster, E. M. *A Passage to India* ([1924]; Harmondsworth: Penguin, 1978).

Fraser, Robert and Hammond, Mary (eds). *Books Without Borders, Volume 1: The Cross-National Dimension in Print Culture* (Basingstoke: Palgrave Macmillan, 2008).

Ghose, Zulfikar. *Confessions of a Native-Alien* (London: Routledge, 1965).

——. *The Art of Creating Fiction* (London: Macmillan, 1991).

——. *The Triple Mirror of the Self* (London: Bloomsbury, 1992).

Ghosh, Anindita. *Power in Print: Popular Publishing and the Politics of Language and Culture in A Colonial Society* (Delhi: OUP, 2006).

Greenlees, Duncan. *The Gospel of Guru Granth Sahib* (Madras: The Theosophical Publishing House, 1952).

Grierson,George. *The Modern Vernacular Literature of Hindustan* (Calcutta: The Asiatic Society, 1889).

Griswold, Wendy. *Bearing Witness: Readers, Writers, and the Novel in Nigeria* (Princeton: Princeton UP, 2000).

Hammer[-Purgstall], Joseph. *Der Diwan von Mohammed Schamsed-din Hafis* 2 vols (Stuttgart and Tubingen, 1812, 1813).

Hindley, John Haddon. *Persian Lyrics, or Scattered Poems from the Diwan-i-Hafiz* (London: Oriental Press, 1800).

Jha N. and Rajaram, N. S. *The Deciphered Indus Script: Methodologies, Readings, Interpretations* (Delhi: Aditya Prakashan, 2000).

Johns, Adrian. *The Nature of the Book: Print and Knowledge in the Making* (Chicago and London: University of Chicago Press, 1998).

Jones, William. *The Works of Sir William Jones in Six Volumes* (London, 1799).

Joshi, Svati (ed.). *Rethinking English: Essays in Literature, Languages, History* (Delhi: Trianka, 1991).

Joshi, Priya. *In Another Country: Colonialism, Culture and the English Novel in India* (New York: Columbia University Press, 2002).

Kanaganayakam, Chelva. *Structures of Negation: The Writings of Zulfikar Ghose* (Toronto: University of Toronto Press, 1993).

Kesavan, Belary Shamanna et al. *A History of Printing and Publishing in India: A Story of Cultural Re-awakening* (Delhi: National Book Trust, 1985).

——. *The Book in India* (Delhi: New National Book Trust, 1986).

Kipling, John Lockwood. *Punjab Gazetteer of the Lahore District, 1883–4* (Calcutta: Calcutta Central Press, 1884).

Kipling, Rudyard. *Departmental Ditties and Other Verses* (Lahore: The 'Civil and Military Gazette' Press, 1886).

——. *The Phantom 'Rickshaw, and Other Tales* (Allahabad: A. H. Wheeler & Co., 1888).

——. *In Black and White* (Allahabad: A. H. Wheeler & Co., 1888).

——. *Under the Deodars* (Allahabad: A. H. Wheeler & Co., 1889).

——. *The Story of the Gadsbys: A Tale without a Plot* (Allahabad: A. H. Wheeler & Co., 1890).

Majeed, Javed. *Autobiography, Travel and Postnational Identity: Gandhi, Nehru and Iqbal* (Basingstoke: Palgrave Macmillan, 2007).

Malcolm, John. *Sketches of Persia: From a Journal of a Traveller to the East* (London: John Murray, 1828).

Morgan, Charles. *The House of Macmillan 1843–1943* (London: Macmillan, 1944).

Nasta, Susheila. *Home Truths: Fictions of the South Asian Diaspora in Britain* (Basingstoke: Palgrave Macmillan, 2002).

——. (ed.). *Writing Across Worlds: Contemporary Writers Talk* (Routledge: London, 2004).

Pinney, Thomas and Richards, David Alan (ed.). *Kipling and his first publisher: Correspondence of Rudyard Kipling with Thacker, Spink and Company 1886–1890* (High Wycombe: Rivendale, 2001).

Pollock, Sheldon (ed.). *Literary Cultures in History: Reconstructions from South Asia.* (Berkeley, Los Angeles and London: University of California Press, 2003).

Priolkar, Anant Kakba. *The Printing Press in India* (Bombay: Marathi Samshodhana Mandala, 1958).

Raha, Kironmoy. *Bengali Theatre* (Delhi: National Book Trust, 1978).

Rai, Amrit. *Premchand: His Life and Times*, tr. from Hindi by Harish Trivedi (Delhi: OUP, 1991).

Ranasinha, Ruvani. *South Asian Writers in Twentieth-Century Britain: Culture in Translation* (Oxford: OUP, 2007).

Rose, Jonathon. *The Intellectual Life of the British Working Classes* (New Haven: Yale UP, 2001).

Rushdie, Salman. *Imaginary Homelands: Essays and Criticism 1981–1991* (London: Granta, 1991).

——. *Fury* (Toronto: Vintage, 2002).

——. *Step Across This Line: Collected Non-fiction 1992–2002* (New York: Random House, 2002).

Saenger, Paul. *Space Between Words: The Origins of Silent Reading* (Stanford: Stanford University Press, 1997).

Said, Edward W. *Orientalism* (London: Routledge, 1978).

Saikia, Rajen. *A Social and Economic History of Assam 1853–1921* (Delhi: Manohar, 2000).

St Clair, William. *The Reading Nation in the Romantic Period* (Cambridge: CUP, 2004).

Sandhu, Sukdhev. *London Calling: How Black and Asian Writers Imagined A City* (London: Harper Collins, 2003).

Schwab, Raymond. *The Oriental Renaissance: Europe's Rediscovery of India and the East, 1680–1880* (New York: Columbia University Press, 1984).

Sen, Dinesh Chandra. *History of Bengali Language and Literature* (Calcutta: Calcutta University, 1911).

Sen, Sukumar. *Battalar Chhapa O Chhobi* (Calcutta: Ananda, 1989).

Singh, Brijraj. *The First Protestant Missionary to India: Bartholomeus Ziegenbalg (1683–1719)* (Delhi: OUP, 1999).

Singh, Sahib. *About Compilation of Sri Guru Granth Sahib* (Amritsar: Lok Sahit Prakashan, 1996).

Spivak, Gayatry Chakravorty. *A Critique of Postcolonial Reason: Towards a History of the Vanishing Present* (Cambridge, MA: Harvard University Press, 1999).

Srinivas, M. N. *Village, Caste, Gender and Method: Essays in Indian Social Anthropology* (Delhi: OUP, 1996).

Stark, Ulrike. *Empire of Books: The Naval Kishore Press and the Diffusion of the Printed Word in Colonial India, 1858–1895* (Delhi: Permanent Black, 2008).

Sutcliffe, Peter. *The Oxford University Press: An Informal History* (Oxford: Clarendon, 1978).

Trivedi, Harish. *Colonial Transactions: English Literature and India* (Calcutta: Papyrus, 1993).

Vaidyanathan, K. R. *150 Glorious Years of Indian Railways* (Mumbai, 2004).

Williams, Jane (ed.). *Tambimuttu: Bridge Between Two Worlds* (London: Peter Owen, 1989).

Young, Robert. *Colonial Desire: Hybridity in Theory, Culture and Race* (London: Routledge, 1995).